IN THE NFL, POSSESSION IS SIX POINTS OF THE LAW!

The "in" word during the 1979 campaign was **possession**. The biggest rhubarb of all erupted after the Pittsburgh Steelers won the AFC championship game with Houston, 27–13, on their way to the Super Bowl.

With Pittsburgh leading late in the third quarter, 17–10, Dan Pastorini tossed a six-yard pass to Mike Renfro, who apparently scored a touchdown, making the score 17–16. But no, official Donald Orr ruled that Renfro did not have full possession of the ball before he stepped out of bounds.

Houston had to settle for a field goal, making the score 17–13 with Pittsburgh still in front and victory-bound.

Then came the after-game movies and videotape replays. Postmortems were held in Houston and New York, with the NFL standing by Orr's original decision. But it was admittedly a tough one to call. As such, the call takes its place among those decisions so well known in football and other sports as "judgment calls."

THE POCKET BOOK OF PRO FOOTBALL

1980

Written and Edited by
Herbert M. Furlow

PUBLISHED BY POCKET BOOKS NEW YORK

Cover photo by Mickey Palmer/Focus on Sports

Another *Original* publication of POCKET BOOKS

POCKET BOOKS, a Simon & Schuster division of
GULF & WESTERN CORPORATION
1230 Avenue of the Americas, New York, N.Y. 10020

ISBN: 0-671-41019-9

First Pocket Books printing August, 1980

10 9 8 7 6 5 4 3 2 1

POCKET and colophon are trademarks of Simon & Schuster.

Printed in the U.S.A.

Acknowledgments

As in previous years, upon publication of the *Pocket Book of Pro Football,* full acknowledgment must be given to the NFL's director of public relations, Jim Heffernan, and his staff at the league's New York headquarters. Equally appreciated is the assistance and information provided by each of the NFL's twenty-eight club public relations directors. Special thanks go also to Art McNally, NFL supervisor of officials, and to Don Smith of the Professional Football Hall of Fame in Canton, Ohio.

—Herbert M. Furlow
New York City
1980

Contents

Central Division

Western Division

THE 1980 NFL COLLEGE DRAFT

SUPER FEATURES

NFL 1979 STATISTICS

LET'S LOOK AT THE RECORDS

OFFICIATING IN THE NFL

1980
NATIONAL FOOTBALL LEAGUE
TELEVISION SCHEDULE

REGULAR SEASON

Sept. 8	Dallas at Washington (night)	ABC
Sept. 11	Los Angeles at Tampa Bay (night)	ABC
Sept. 15	Houston at Cleveland (night)	ABC
Sept. 22	New York Giants at Philadelphia (night)	ABC
Sept. 29	Denver at New England (night)	ABC
Oct. 6	Tampa Bay at Chicago (night)	ABC
Oct. 13	Washington at Denver (night)	ABC
Oct. 20	Oakland at Pittsburgh (night)	ABC
Oct. 26	San Diego at Dallas (night)	ABC
Oct. 27	Miami at New York Jets (night)	ABC
Nov. 3	Chicago at Cleveland (night)	ABC
Nov. 10	New England at Houston (night)	ABC
Nov. 17	Oakland at Seattle (night)	ABC
Nov. 20	San Diego at Miami (night)	ABC
Nov. 24	Los Angeles at New Orleans (night)	ABC
Nov. 27	Chicago at Detroit (day)	CBS
Nov. 27	Seattle at Dallas (day)	NBC
Dec. 1	Denver at Oakland (night)	ABC
Dec. 4	Pittsburgh at Houston (night)	ABC
Dec. 8	New England at Miami (night)	ABC
Dec. 13	New York Giants at Washington (day)	CBS
Dec. 13	Seattle at San Diego (day)	NBC
Dec. 15	Dallas at Los Angeles (night)	ABC
Dec. 20	New York Jets at Miami (day)	NBC
Dec. 20	Chicago at Tampa Bay (day)	CBS
Dec. 22	Pittsburgh at San Diego (night)	ABC

TV DOUBLEHEADER GAMES

In addition, weekly CBS/NBC doubleheader games
will be scheduled and seen in many areas.

POSTSEASON CHAMPIONSHIP GAMES

Dec. 28	NFL First Round (Wild Card) Playoffs	CBS & NBC
Jan. 3	AFC and NFC Divisional Playoffs	NBC & CBS
Jan. 4	AFC and NFC Divisional Playoffs	NBC & CBS
Jan. 11	AFC Championship Game	NBC
Jan. 11	NFC Championship Game	CBS
Jan. 25	Super Bowl XV in Superdome, New Orleans	NBC
Feb. 1	AFC-NFC Pro Bowl at Honolulu (day)	ABC

LOOKING TOWARD SUPER BOWL XV

The National Football League is enjoying its greatest popularity in history, with last season's total attendance at 224 regular-season games reaching a record 13,182,039. That tops the 12,771,800 who attended NFL games in 1978—first year of the current 224-game schedule format of sixteen games per club.

The record attendance figure, of course, doesn't include the countless millions of others who viewed the games on television, often having the distinct advantage of closeup views of a controversial call when the instant replay film is rolled. (Is it fair to assume that most officials would like to get their hands on the guy who invented instant replay?)

For a welcome change, the Super Bowl XIV match between Pittsburgh and Los Angeles somehow got through the sixty minutes of playing time without earth-shaking controversy (although the turf surrounding California's Rose Bowl has been known to do a little shaking now and then). Pittsburgh's victory came only after a fourth-quarter letdown by the Rams, with pass defense perhaps the cause of it all. Nevertheless, the Steelers rate tributes of the highest order for winning an unprecedented fourth Super Bowl. Surely, then, Pittsburgh is the "pro football team of the decade," the 1970s decade, that is.

Still, with the arrival of 1980, a new decade begins

and the Steelers, of course, hope that this matter of decade superiority will overlap. But the law of averages may step in here, as if to say, "Enough of a good thing is enough." The Steelers just might have to yield ground to others charging upon the scene, hungry for Super Bowl exposure.

The current Wild Card Playoff format, which keeps a total of ten clubs in the running for playoff spots right up into the closing weeks of the season, somehow makes the Super Bowl tantalizingly attainable for some clubs which normally wouldn't have a chance. That factor alone narrows the preseason predictions to a final showdown between the "contenders." And just who are the contenders?

It's easy enough, perhaps, to pick five, or even six, but choosing the "final ten" who will make the playoffs called for some overtime crystal ball gazing. And that's what produced the predictions you'll see on the next two pages.

NATIONAL FOOTBALL LEAGUE

1980 PREDICTIONS

AMERICAN CONFERENCE

Eastern Division

1. NEW ENGLAND PATRIOTS — Time for the breaks to come their way.
2. MIAMI DOLPHINS — Still to be reckoned with and plenty of Zonk left.
3. NEW YORK JETS — Coming off an 8-8 season, they could flip or flop.
4. BUFFALO BILLS — Even Chuck Knox can't reverse the universe.
5. BALTIMORE COLTS — It should take Mike McCormack at least one year to get acquainted.

Central Division

1. PITTSBURGH STEELERS — How convincing can you get?
2. HOUSTON OILERS — If Bum Phillips could just hold onto that hat of his.
3. CLEVELAND BROWNS — Working from the plus side of things.
4. CINCINNATI BENGALS — Forrest Gregg returns to the NFL wars.

Western Division

1. SAN DIEGO CHARGERS — Don Coryell is living up to promise.
2. OAKLAND RAIDERS — If they'll just sit still long enough.
3. DENVER BRONCOS — Maybe this is their comeback year.
4. SEATTLE SEAHAWKS — Patera has the patience, but do the 'hawks have the consistency?
5. KANSAS CITY CHIEFS — The Chiefs, however, are on the move.

Wild Card Playoff Teams: Miami Dolphins and Houston Oilers
Super Bowl XV: San Diego Chargers

NATIONAL CONFERENCE

Eastern Division

1. DALLAS COWBOYS — Better even than a prime-time soap opera!
2. PHILADELPHIA EAGLES — Could take over the top spot.
3. WASHINGTON REDSKINS — Third part of a three-way shootout.
4. ST. LOUIS CARDINALS — Can Hanifan accomplish what Wilkinson almost did?
5. NEW YORK GIANTS — Everything hinges on Simms's arm.

Central Division

1. CHICAGO BEARS — Beginning to feel at home in the playoffs.
2. TAMPA BAY BUCCANEERS — Ready to terrorize the NFL Central again.
3. GREEN BAY PACKERS — Bart Starr still has his problems.
4. MINNESOTA VIKINGS — A brand new Purple Gang needed?
5. DETROIT LIONS — They'll host Super Bowl in Silverdome in '82, but will they participate?

Western Division

1. LOS ANGELES RAMS — For once, they waited until the Super Bowl to collapse.
2. NEW ORLEANS SAINTS — With lots of luck, the Saints could be Super Bowlers in the Superdome.
3. ATLANTA FALCONS — Their defense ain't what it used to be.
4. SAN FRANCISCO 49ers — And neither is theirs.

Wild Card Playoff Teams: Philadelphia Eagles and Tampa Bay Buccaneers
Super Bowl XV: Dallas Cowboys

AMERICAN
FOOTBALL
CONFERENCE

Pittsburgh's achievement in winning a fourth Super Bowl has sparked anew the claims of those who say American Conference football is clearly superior to that played in the National Conference. The most compelling argument for this, of course, is that the American Conference (and its predecessor, the American Football League) has won ten of the 14 Super Bowls played so far.

Obviously, the National Conference will have to play "catch-up-ball" for some time to come if it is to overtake the American in Super Bowl victories. In the meantime, the pendulum of superiority could swing the other way, toward the National, but on the basis of something else besides Super Bowl triumphs.

For the time being, at least, the "superiority pendulum" seems stuck squarely above the City of Pittsburgh. Among other achievements last season, the Steelers also rang up the second highest total offensive yards in NFL history, averaging 381.1 per game. The actual total of 6,258 yards was second only to Houston's 6,288 in 1961 when the Oilers were members of the American Football League—a loop noted for its wide-open, high-scoring offenses—a "fast track" if there ever was one.

The NFL has three new head football coaches going into the 1980 season and the American Conference has

two of them. Forrest Gregg, who was head coach at
Cleveland for three years until he was let go in 1977,
comes down from the Canadian Football League to
succeed Homer Rice at Cincinnati. And Mike McCormack, a former head coach of the pre-Vermeil Philadelphia Eagles, takes over at Baltimore to succeed Ted
Marchibroda. (The NFL's third new head coach is Jim
Hanifan, a former San Diego assistant, who replaces
Bud Wilkinson at St. Louis.)

The AFC East could develop into a bitter fight for
survival (another term for "playoff spots") with New
England, Miami, the Jets, Buffalo and Baltimore all
capable of either continuing as contenders or coming
to life, whichever applies. Pittsburgh is still the bully
on the block in the AFC Central but Houston doesn't
scare easily, even if Cleveland and Cincinnati are too
busy feuding among themselves.

While the Raiders try to settle down, San Diego bids
to run off-tackle, sidestep Denver, and throw a fast
one over Seattle's head to wind up on top of the AFC
West. But before all that happens, somebody just might
have to ask Kansas City's permission.

NEW ENGLAND PATRIOTS

Head Coach: Ron Erhardt

2nd Year   **Record: 9–7**

1979 RECORD (9-7) (capital letters indicate home games)		1980 SCHEDULE (capital letters indicate home games)	
13	PITTSBURGH	16	CLEVELAND	Sept. 7
56	N.Y. JETS	3	ATLANTA	Sept. 14
20	Cincinnati	14	Seattle	Sept. 21
27	SAN DIEGO	21	DENVER (night, TV)	Sept. 29
14	Green Bay	27	N.Y. Jets	Oct. 5
24	DETROIT	17	MIAMI	Oct. 12
27	Chicago	7	Baltimore	Oct. 19
28	MIAMI	13	Buffalo	Oct. 26
26	Baltimore	31	N.Y. JETS	Nov. 2
26	Buffalo	6	Houston (night, TV)	Nov. 10
10	Denver	45	LOS ANGELES	Nov. 16
50	BALTIMORE	21	BALTIMORE	Nov. 23
13	BUFFALO	16	San Francisco	Nov. 30
24	Miami	39	Miami (night, TV)	Dec. 8
26	N.Y. Jets	27	BUFFALO	Dec. 14
27	MINNESOTA	23	New Orleans	Dec. 21
411		326		

New England, long considered the most conservative region of the nation, has a pro football team that specializes in very radical departures from what might be called normal gridiron behavior. The New England Patriots, it seems, have this hangup about losing games played in the glare of that goldfish bowl known as national television. They also find natural grass a tricky surface upon which to run, pass and tackle—unlike their smoothly negotiable Super Turf playing field in Foxboro, Massachusetts. One way, perhaps, to determine New England's fortunes for the coming season would be to check the 1980 schedule for (a) night games on national TV and (b) games played on natural grass. If the Patriots are going to wind up out of it, those are the kind of games that could possibly do them in.

Steve Grogan continues to be one of the NFL's most unorthodox quarterbacks if only because, for three straight years, he has prevailed as the NFL's No. 1 rushing quarterback. Last season he decided to run 62 times, gained 368 yards for a 5.8 average carry, the longest run being 26. But make no mistake about it, Grogan can pass too. In fact, he is fast becoming, along with Dan Fouts of San Diego, a modern 300-passing-yards-per-game specialist—a field once dominated by Joe Namath.

Patriots' Coach Ron Erhardt sits in the front row of Grogan's admirers. "Steve is such a tough competitor," says Erhardt, "that he'll do anything to win. He'll run the bootlegs, the quarterback draws, the big plays in pressure situations that a lot of guys won't. His intelligence is a big factor, too. Steve knows what's going on out there all the time."

And even more to the point, for the first time Grogan is calling his own plays—not picking them up by signal, or by substitute runners from the sidelines. For that reason, whether the statistics show it or not, he's probably running the ball less and passing it more. In fact, time was when New England's opposition worried about Grogan carrying the ball and picking up yardage with apparent ease. Now all that may be changing because, as Grogan himself admits, he's choosing his own plays. "This way I feel in control of myself, that I understand the offense, and what I'm trying to do."

If the New England offense hinges upon Grogan's arm, the defense certainly lays no claim to any one individual as its basic force. Position for position along the defensive line, among the linebackers and in the secondary, the Patriots can turn back the best of offensive attacks, both on the ground and through the air—if everybody stays healthy. During the season just past, New England ranked no less than third among the 28 NFL clubs in the matter of total defense against both the pass and run.

The figures here are of interest. The top NFL defensive club was Tampa Bay which held the opposition to an average of 246.8 yards per game. Next came Super Bowl champion Pittsburgh with 266.9, and then New England whose yield was 270.2 yards per contest.

Erhardt, known as something of an innovator even before he began coaching with the pros, employed something new and different in pro defenses as the '79 season wore along. Instead of eleven men lining up on defense in the customary manner, the Patriots tried a maneuver that put one player in motion before the ball was snapped. This procedure is a very common one for teams which have the ball, but sending a man in motion behind the *defensive* line is unusual. The idea, according to Erhardt, is to confuse the opposition, especially the carefully planned offensive blocking patterns that go into action just as soon as the ball is snapped. Known as the "rover" or "monster man," this maneuver was conceived at Michigan State by Hank Bullough who, until a few months ago, was defensive coordinator for the Patriots. He resigned to accept the same post with Cincinnati, beginning this season. New England's defensive line coach, Fritz Shurmur, succeeds Bullough.

As head coach of the Patriots, Ron Erhardt has come in for his share of criticism by some who see him as "soft" on discipline. As one observer put it, "The Patriots had better shape up or else George Allen will arrive and the curfew will be on."

At any rate, Erhardt does plan to get a bit tougher this season. Those Patriots who don't live in the Boston or the New England area are due to come back early so, as Erhardt describes it, "I can check them out." Explaining further, the coach says he told each player what he expects his weight to be, and the state of his overall conditioning before the new season gets underway. "We haven't had such a preseason checkup since I've been with the staff," Erhardt admits, "but I feel it'll be the best way to make sure everyone is prepared for the new campaign."

Some day, it might just happen—a team will diet its way to the Super Bowl.

OFFENSE

Quarterbacks	Ht.	Wt.	Age	Exp.	College
Cavanaugh, Matt	6-1	210	24	3	Pittsburgh
Grogan, Steve	6-4	208	27	6	Kansas State
Owen, Tom	6-1	194	28	7	Wichita State

Although he finished no better than 5th among AFC quarterbacks last season, Grogan did set personal season highs of 3,286 yards and 28 TD passes. Owen, of course, didn't see a great deal of action, but he did complete 27 of his 47 throws for a 57.4 percent. That was nearly 10 points better than Grogan's 48.7 percent. Cavanaugh, who once led the University of Pittsburgh's team to the heights, was shelved virtually the entire season with a banged-up knee sustained in preseason practice.

Running Backs	Ht.	Wt.	Age	Exp.	College
Calhoun, Don	6-0	212	28	7	Kansas State
Clark, Allan	5-10	186	23	2	Northern Arizona
Cunningham, Sam	6-3	230	30	8	Southern Cal
Foreman, Chuck	6-2	220	30	8	Miami (Fla.)
Ivory, Horace	6-0	198	26	4	Oklahoma
Johnson, Andy	6-0	204	28	5	Georgia
Tatupu, Mosi	6-0	229	25	3	Southern Cal
Vagas, Ferguson	6-1	194	23	R	Notre Dame

New England's ground attack ranked a respectable 5th in the AFC, and it could have been much better. Cunningham was out of action much of the time with an injured shoulder, ankle and knee, limiting his gains to a mere 140 yards during the season's last half. Ivory

also played hurt, when he did carry the ball. Johnson was out all
season with a bad knee. Rookie Allan Clark carried 19 times and averaged 4.4 per attempt, not bad for openers. There's hope at Foxboro
that some of these walking wounded will start running again this time
around. Foreman comes over from Minnesota for a draft choice and
hopes to get a new start in New England. Ferguson, who is career rushing leader in Notre Dame history, was the 25th player selected in draft's
first round.

Receivers	Ht.	Wt.	Age	Exp.	College
Chandler, Al (T)	6-3	229	30	7	Oklahoma
Francis, Russ (T)	6-6	242	27	6	Oregon
Hasselbeck, Don (T)	6-7	245	25	4	Colorado
Jackson, Harold (W)	5-10	175	34	13	Jackson State
Morgan, Stanley (W)	5-11	180	25	4	Tennessee
Pennywell, Carlos (W)	6-2	180	24	3	Grambling
Westbrook, Don (W)	5-10	184	28	4	Nebraska

W=wide receiver   T=tight end

Jackson and Morgan became the first Patriots ever to attain the 1,000-
yard receiving plateau, Jackson with 45 for 1,013 and seven TDs,
Morgan with 44 for 1,002 and 12 TDs. What's more, Morgan's 22.8-
yard average catch was best in the NFL, followed closely by Jackson
with 22.5. Francis, a New England tower on receptions, missed two
games and caught 39 for the year, including five TDs. Cunningham
came out of the backfield to catch 29.

Interior Linemen	Ht.	Wt.	Age	Exp.	College
Adams, Sam (G)	6-3	260	32	9	Prairie View
Brock, Pete (T-C)	6-5	260	29	5	Colorado
Cryder, Bob (G)	6-4	265	24	3	Alabama
Hannah, John (G)	6-2	265	29	8	Alabama
Jordan, Shelby (T)	6-7	260	28	5	Washington (Mo.)
Lenkaitis, Bill (C)	6-4	255	34	13	Penn State
Puetz, Garry (T)	6-4	265	28	7	Valparaiso
Rosen, Rich (G)	6-3	242	24	1	Syracuse
Wheeler, Dwight (T)	6-3	255	25	3	Tennessee State

T=tackle   G=guard   C=center

The Patriot offense ranked 5th in the AFC, even though it allowed 49
QB sacks, enough to keep Grogan constantly on the move seeking
elbow room. As for Brock, did he set some sort of record by playing
four positions? He moved from guard to tackle to tight end to center,
all within the time span of one game, twice. Puetz, signed as a free
agent released by Philadelphia, went right to work as replacement for
Jordan who was sidelined with a knee injury. That was in the mid-
November Colts game which New England won, 50-21, with the Patriots
rolling up a season-high 248 yards on the ground. Grogan was out-

spoken with his credits: "If any one guy was responsible for that rushing mark, it has to be Puetz."

Kickers	Ht.	Wt.	Age	Exp.	College
Hare, Eddie (P)	6-4	209	23	2	Tulsa
Smith, John (Pk)	6-0	185	31	7	Southampton (Eng.)

Pk=placekicker   P=punter

Suffice it to say that, in the placekicking department, Smith was the '79 NFL scoring champion with 115 points, 26-of-49 points-after and 23-of-33 FGs. He was perfect (6-6) from less than 30 yards out, and drilled 11 of 13 from the 30-39 yard range. Hare's rookie year was something of a disappointment, mainly because he didn't kick the club out of any holes. His 36.6-yard average wasn't exactly in the Ray Guy range either. But punters have been known to improve. . . .

DEFENSE

Front Linemen	Ht.	Wt.	Age	Exp.	College
Adams, Julius (E)	6-4	263	32	9	Texas Southern
Bishop, Richard (NT-E)	6-1	260	30	5	Louisville
Hamilton, Ray (NT)	6-1	245	29	8	Oklahoma
Lunsford, Mel (E)	6-3	260	30	8	Central State (O.)
McDougald, Doug (DE)	6-5	271	23	R	Virginia Tech
McGee, Tony (E)	6-4	250	31	10	Bishop
McMichael, Steve (NT)	6-1	245	23	R	Texas
Price, Ernie (E)	6-4	245	30	7	Texas A&I
Ruben, Marl (NT)	6-3	260	23	1	Tufts
St. Clair, Mike (E)	6-5	245	27	5	Grambling

E=end   NT=nose tackle

The AFC had few defensive lines as good as this one last season. The pass rush was so devastating that it led the NFL with 57 sacks that cost opposing passers a total of 512 yards, another league high. Lunsford, Hamilton and Adams, the starters, add up to a quarter-century of NFL experience, and that's impressive. St. Clair and Price are veterans from Cleveland, traded to New England for draft choices. They'll add depth on both ends. Ruben is big and inexperienced but may muscle in.

Linebackers	Ht.	Wt.	Age	Exp.	College
Costict, Ray (O)	6-0	218	25	4	Mississippi State
Golic, Bob (I)	6-2	240	23	2	Notre Dame
Hawkins, Mike (O)	6-2	232	25	3	Texas A&I
Hunt, Sam (I)	6-1	253	29	7	S.F. Austin
King, Steve (O)	6-4	230	29	8	Tulsa
McGrew, Larry (O)	6-3	231	23	R	Southern Cal
Matthews, Bill (I)	6-2	235	24	2	South Dakota State

Nelson, Steve (I)	6-2	230	29	7	North Dakota State
Petersen, Tim (I)	6-2	232	25	1	Arizona State
Shoate, Rod (O)	6-1	215	27	5	Oklahoma
Zamberlin, John (I)	6-2	232	24	1	Pacific Lutheran

O=outside   I=inside

Hawkins, Nelson, Hunt and Shoate are regulars in the 3-4 defense but Zamberlin and Matthews are coming on. Golic was hurt all year. Shoate was bothered by a throat infection. Petersen is a first-year man from Arizona State. This unit is in good shape, but may need additional depth.

Defensive Backs	Ht.	Wt.	Age	Exp.	College
Beaudoin, Doug (S)	6-1	190	26	5	Minnesota
Clayborn, Ray (CB)	6-1	190	25	4	Texas
Conn, Dick (S)	6-0	180	29	7	Georgia
Flint, Judson (CB)	6-0	201	23	1	Memphis State
Fox, Tim (S)	5-11	190	27	5	Ohio State
Haynes, Mike (CB)	6-2	195	27	5	Arizona State
James, Roland (S)	6-2	189	22	R	Tennessee
McCray, Prentice (S)	6-1	190	29	8	Arizona State
Sanford, Rick (S-CB)	6-1	192	23	2	South Carolina
Jury, Bob (S-CB)	5-11	193	25	3	Pittsburgh

CB=cornerback   S=safety

Sanford is due to start at safety this season, but is an all-around defensive back. When Haynes was out, Sanford was a cornerback—but he's more at home at safety. Clayborn's five interceptions led the club, with Haynes and McCray picking off two each. Generally, the Patriot secondary performed well last season if not in spectacular fashion. A central block in a solid New England defense. James was 14th player selected in first round of draft, and has great credentials as an All-America.

Note: A complete listing of New England's 1980 college draft selections can be found on page 273.

DEFENSIVE UNIT   3-4 DEFENSE

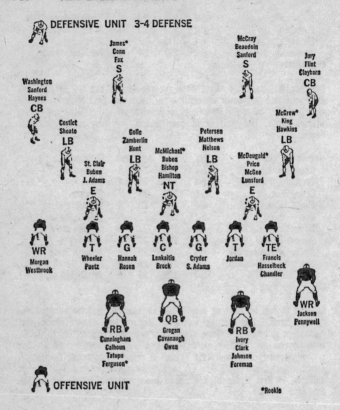

James*
Conn
Fox
S

McCray
Beaudoin
Sanford
S

Jury
Flint
Clayborn
CB

Washington
Sanford
Haynes
CB

Costict
Shoate
LB

Golic
Zamberlin
Hunt
LB

Petersen
Matthews
Nelson
LB

McGrew*
King
Hawkins
LB

St. Clair
Buben
J. Adams
E

McMichael*
Buben
Bishop
Hamilton
NT

McDougald*
Price
McGee
Lunsford
E

WR
Morgan
Westbrook

T
Wheeler
Puetz

G
Hannah
Rosen

C
Lenkaitis
Brock

G
Cryder
S. Adams

T
Jordan

TE
Francis
Hasselbeck
Chandler

WR
Jackson
Pennywell

RB
Cunningham
Calhoun
Tatupu
Ferguson*

QB
Grogan
Cavanaugh
Owen

RB
Ivory
Clark
Johnson
Foreman

OFFENSIVE UNIT

*Rookie

1979 PATRIOTS STATISTICS

	Patriots	Opps.
Total Points Scored	411	326
Total First Downs	318	283
Third Down Efficiency Percentage	44.4	37.7
Yards Rushing—First Downs	2252—132	1781—118
Passes Attempted—Completions	475—237	467—246
Yards Passing—First Downs	3218—159	2553—139
QB Sacked—Yards Lost	49—382	57—512
Interceptions By—Return Average	20—17.6	23—18.1
Punts—Average Yards	84—36.2	94—38.7
Punt Returns—Average Return	37—8.4	28—11.3
Kickoff Returns—Average Return	66—18.8	80—20.3
Fumbles—Ball Lost	28—15	35—22
Penalties—Yards	99—864	103—917

STATISTICAL LEADERS

Scoring	TDs	Rush.	Pass.	Ret.	PATs	FGs	Total
Smith	0	0	0	0	46—49	23—33	115
Morgan	13	0	12	1	0	0	78
Jackson	7	0	7	0	0	0	42
Calhoun	6	5	1	0	0	0	36
Francis	5	0	5	0	0	0	30
Cunningham	5	5	0	0	0	0	30
Ivory	3	1	2	0	0	0	18

Rushing	Atts.	Yds.	Avg.	Longest	TDs
Cunningham	159	563	3.5	27	5
Ivory	143	522	3.7	52	1
Calhoun	137	456	3.3	29	5
Grogan	62	368	5.8	26	2
Johnson	43	132	3.1	15	1
Clark	19	84	4.4	19	2
Tatupu	23	71	3.1	12	0

Passing	Atts.	Com.	Yds.	Pct.	Int.	Longest	TDs
Grogan	423	206	3286	48.7	20	63 (TD)	28
Owen	47	27	248	57.4	3	32	2

Receiving	No.	Yds.	Avg.	Longest	TDs
Jackson	45	1013	22.5	59	7
Morgan	44	1002	22.8	63 (TD)	12
Francis	39	557	14.3	44	5
Cunningham	29	236	8.1	20	0
Ivory	23	216	9.4	24	2
Calhoun	15	66	4.4	14	1
Hasselbeck	13	158	12.2	41	0
Westbrook	9	173	19.2	38	1

Interceptions	No.	Yds.	Avg.	Longest	TDs
Clayborn	5	56	11.2	27	0
Haybes	3	66	22.0	33	0
McCray	3	48	16.0	26	0
Fox	2	38	19.0	25	0
Hawkins	2	35	17.5	35 (TD)	1

Punting	No.	Yds.	Avg.	Longest	Inside 20	Blocked
Hare	83	3038	36.6	58	19	1

Punt Returns	No.	FCs	Yds.	Avg.	Longest	TDs
Morgan	29	21	289	10.0	80 (TD)	1
Haynes	5	1	16	3.2	5	0
Westbrook	2	0	5	2.5	5	0

Kickoff Returns	No.	Yds.	Avg.	Longest	TDs
Clark	37	816	22.1	38	0
Sanford	10	179	17.9	23	0
Westbrook	11	151	13.7	30	0
Tatupu	3	15	5.0	12	0

MIAMI DOLPHINS

Head Coach: Don Shula

11th Year   **Record:** 104–39–1

1979 RECORD (10-6) (capital letters indicate home games)			1980 SCHEDULE (capital letters indicate home games)	
9	Buffalo	7	Buffalo	Sept. 7
19	SEATTLE	10	CINCINNATI	Sept. 14
27	Minnesota	12	Atlanta	Sept. 21
31	CHICAGO	16	NEW ORLEANS	Sept. 28
27	N.Y. Jets	33	BALTIMORE	Oct. 5
3	Oakland	13	New England	Oct. 12
17	BUFFALO	7	BUFFALO	Oct. 19
13	New England	28	N.Y. Jets (night, TV)	Oct. 27
27	GREEN BAY	7	Oakland	Nov. 2
6	HOUSTON	9	Los Angeles	Nov. 9
19	BALTIMORE	0	SAN FRANCISCO	Nov. 16
24	Cleveland	30	SAN DIEGO (night, TV)	Nov. 20
28	Baltimore	24	Pittsburgh	Nov. 30
39	NEW ENGLAND	24	NEW ENGLAND (night, TV)	Dec. 8
28	Detroit	10	Baltimore	Dec. 14
24	N.Y. JETS	27	N.Y. JETS (TV)	Dec. 20
341		257		

Playoffs

| 14 | Pittsburgh | 34 |

Coach Don Shula's contract expires after this season and it's generally agreed that he is seriously thinking about making a change. And if Shula is determined to leave Miami, of all the NFL coaches now active none is in better position to make his own choice of a job. Some Biscayne Bay observers say Shula's decision to leave is already a certainty in all respects except the formalities, that his bags are already packed, and that he just doesn't want to spend any more time with Dolphins' owner Joe Robbie. The Shula-Robbie differences are well known, lending credence to the speculation.

Shula is generally regarded as the most respected coach in the NFL. He came by this distinction during the 'Seventies just gone by, leading the Dolphins into the Super Bowl three times and winning it twice. During the past two seasons, Miami made it into the playoffs both times, but has failed to win a playoff game since 1973. That takes nothing away from a club which came within a whisker of another distinction—that of having the best NFL regular-season record of the 1970s.

The near-miss occurred when the Dolphins lost their final 1979 regular-season game to the New York Jets, 27-24. For all practical purposes, the game was considered meaningless by both clubs, coming as it did after Miami had clinched the AFC East title and with the Jets no longer in contention for a playoff spot. But, in losing, Miami finished the decade with a regular season record of 104-39-1—and that was half-a-game behind the Dallas Cowboys who, in their final game of '79 on the same weekend, defeated Washington to finish the decade with a 105-39-0 record. (And who was the decade's third best team? None other than the Oakland Raiders—100-38-6).

There's still no firm assurance that Shula will depart Miami's shores after 1980 but, if he stays, some hard decisions will have to be made. Some might have to be made even now. There's the quarterback position, for instance. Bob Griese is 35, not exactly the same youthful and gridiron-wise Purdue grad who led Miami to all those great records of the 'Seventies, and his $400,000 annual salary makes him the second highest paid player in the NFL (as of 1979). But even Shula isn't sure Griese is the man to have at the helm as the 1980s begin. Even though his performance improved late last season, critics and admirers alike agree that, overall, Griese's arm isn't what it used to be. And in an era when 300-yard passing games are important, Griese's norm remains somewhere in the 140-yard total or less.

Shula sees something else, too. "The game has changed," he observes, "in that it's opened up to where passing is as important as running. Bob, obviously, operates best when the running game is going good, but he's in trouble when the ball-carriers get only 25 yards, as they did against Pittsburgh."

There's a feeling in Miami that Don Strock, Griese's backup, has an even better throwing arm and Strock definitely wants to spend more time on the field. And the second backup, Guy Benjamin, isn't to be shoved aside. "Of what I've seen," says Shula, "Benjamin's arm strength is somewhere between Griese's and Strock's, and he has the knack of moving the offense."

The Dolphins also have a moment of truth coming up concerning their offensive line. Thirteen-year veteran tackle Mike Current has retired and guard Larry Little may be getting ready to hang it all up after a similar 13 years of gridiron campaigning. Little, along with 11-year-man Bob Kuechenberg and eight-year-vet Ed Newman, form the nucleus of Miami's offensive front line. Center Jim Langer, out with a knee injury last season, was replaced by rookie Mark Dennard—and now Langer vows he'll not play another game unless it's with the Vikings in his longed-for Minnesota home surroundings. Hopefuls for the line include such youngsters as tackle Jon Geisler, and guards Jeff Toews and Eric Laakso. Shula has some spadework to do here.

While the head coach concerns himself with the playing capabilities of Miami's personnel, club owner Joe Robbie finds himself involved in a unique dispute with the Internal Revenue Service over the question: can pro football players be depreciated as a business expense, just like office furniture? Robbie says they can but the IRS disagrees and claims he owes more than $600,000 in back taxes. The case went to the U.S. Tax Court for settlement.

At least one Miami player believes Robbie has a point. Defensive back Tim Foley, who has starred with the Dolphins since 1970, thinks the idea of "depreciating" players is funny, but he doesn't disagree with the theory. "My body depreciated even before I got to Miami," says Foley, "and I think a player reaches a point where the more punishment he takes and the older he gets, he uses up his usefulness. Kind of like a machine. Although they don't treat us that way, that's usually the way it ends up."

OFFENSE

Quarterbacks	Ht.	Wt.	Age	Exp.	College
Benjamin, Guy	6-3½	210	25	3	Stanford
Griese, Bob	6-1	190	35	14	Purdue
Strock, Don	6-5	220	30	7	Virginia Tech

This position is, literally, up in the air. Shula is having second thoughts about keeping Griese in there as the starting QB and Strock may get the call, to open the season at least. Griese may be falling a little behind his backups, his age and limited throwing distance being the retarding factors. Add to that reports that he's becoming a bit isolated from his team members in the personal sense. Both he and Strock did fine last season in pass completions, each averaging 56 percent. And the third Dolphin QB, Benjamin, did even better on much less time. He completed three out of four for 75 percent.

Running Backs	Ht.	Wt.	Age	Exp.	College
Csonka, Larry	6-3	235	34	12	Syracuse
Davis, Gary	5-10	202	26	5	Cal Poly-SLO
Howell, Steve	6-2	222	24	2	Baylor
Nathan, Tony	6-0	201	24	2	Alabama
Torrey, Bob	6-3	232	23	2	Penn State
Williams, Delvin	6-0	197	29	7	Kansas

The fact that Csonka may be nearing the end of his career (wants to play at least one more year), doesn't make him bashful where money is concerned. Simply put, he wants more to go with the raise in his own statistics last season—220 carries for an all-time personal high and 13 TDs which tied a club record. Also, 837 rushing yards was his highest since rambling for 1,003 back in 1973. He earned about $135,000 in '79, wants $200,000 for '80, so they say. Rookie Tony Nathan became first Dolphin ever to lead AFC punt returners, 28 runbacks for a 10.9-yard average. His 86-yard return for a TD against Buffalo may have saved his job, but only Shula knows. All kinds of play at least one more year), doesn't make him bashful where money mishaps befell some Dolphin ball-carriers. Williams damaged some ribs, injuries which stymied his style. Torrey and Howell (4.7 on 13 carries) hope to see more action.

Receivers	Ht.	Wt.	Age	Exp.	College
Bailey, Elmer (W)	6-0	193	22	R	Minnesota
Cefalo, Jimmy (W)	5-11	190	24	3	Penn State
Harris, Duriel (W)	5-11	180	26	5	New Mexico State
Hardy, Bruce (T)	6-4½	235	24	3	Arizona State
Lee, Ronnie (T)	6-3	242	24	2	Baylor
Moore, Nat (W)	5-9	180	29	7	Florida
Tillman, Andre (T)	6-5	230	28	6	Texas Tech

W=wide receiver   T=tight end

Moore led Dolphin pass-catchers for fifth straight season, 48 receptions, six TDs and a career-high 840 yards. Moore, Harris and Cefalo provide Miami with one of league's best receiving trios. Others provide excellent depth, such as Hardy (30 catches in '79) and Lee, now in his second NFL year. One other reminder: Dolphin running backs caught 102 passes among themselves last season, which reveals something about the Miami aerial attack. Starting tight end Andre Tillman was a preseason casualty, out all year.

Interior Linemen	Ht.	Wt.	Age	Exp.	College
Dennard, Mark (C)	6-1	250	25	2	Texas A&M
Giesler, Jon (T)	6-3	265	24	2	Michigan
Green, Cleveland (T)	6-3	265	23	2	Southern U.
Kuechenberg, Bob (T-C)	6-2	255	33	11	Notre Dame
Laakso, Eric (G-T)	6-4	265	24	3	Tulane
Langer, Jim (C)	6-2	257	32	11	South Dakota State
Little, Larry (G)	6-1	265	35	14	Bethune-Cookman
Newman, Ed (G)	6-2	245	29	8	Duke
Stephenson, Dwight (C)	6-3	242	22	R	Alabama
Toews, Jeff (G)	6-3	255	23	2	Washington

T=tackle   G=guard   C=center

Three of Miami's most famous blockers from the "glory years" are still around but, by the time this print sees daylight, they may be gone elsewhere—either retired or retread for further action. They are Kue-

chenberg who's 33, Little 35, and Langer 32. Kuechenberg isn't too rest-
less, but wants to move back to his old position at guard. Langer
wants to play for the Vikings, nearer his home in Minnesota. Little
leans toward retirement. Newman is one of the sound offensive linemen with experience. Dennard received all-rookie team honors for his
first-year work. Giesler is considered a tackle with a future. Toews
needs more work to prove himself. He and Laakso could help by
stepping up their development now, instead of later.

Kickers	Ht.	Wt.	Age	Exp.	College
Roberts, George (P)	6-0	172	25	3	Virginia Tech
Von Schamann, Uwe (Pk)	6-0	200	24	3	Oklahoma

Pk=placekicker   P=punter

Von Schamann had a very shaky start as a Dolphin rookie, but he
finally got on source to become one of league's most consistent field
goal kickers. "In the first three or four games," he explains, "everything you can think of happened to me," like missing four FG attempts
and three extra point kicks. Roberts did OK as a punter in his second
year, averaging 40.2 with one 68-yard boomer.

DEFENSE

Front Linemen	Ht.	Wt.	Age	Exp.	College
Barisich, Carl (NT)	6-4	255	29	8	Princeton
Barnett, Bill (E)	6-5	240	22	R	Nebraska
Baumhower, Bob (NT)	6-5	258	25	4	Alabama
Betters, Doug (E)	6-7	250	24	3	Nevada-Reno
Den Herder, Vern (E)	6-6	252	32	10	Central (Ia.)
Duhe, A. J. (E)	6-4	247	25	4	Louisiana State

E=end   NT=nose tackle

Plenty of opportunity for qualified personnel here. Depth is needed,
to shore up first line of a defense that allowed a meager 257 points
in '79, the AFC's second lowest total. The Dolphins held nine opposing
teams to less than 100 yards, also finished second in AFC average
rushing yards allowed—106.4. Moreover, the Dolphins' defense, while
it was on the field, permitted just 26 TDs, fewest of any NFL defensive unit. At season's close, the front line consisted of Den Herder,
Baumhower and Betters, backed by Barisich (who was out injured at
times) and Duhe (who didn't have as good a year as some others he's
had).

Linebackers	Ht.	Wt.	Age	Exp.	College
Bokamper, Kim (O)	6-6	245	26	4	San Jose State
Chambers, Rusty (I)	6-1	220	27	6	Tulane
Gordon, Larry (O)	6-4	230	26	5	Arizona State

Land, Mel (O)	6-3	243	25	2	Michigan State
Matheson, Bob (O)	6-4	235	36	14	Duke
Ortega, Ralph (I)	6-2	220	27	6	Florida
Rhone, Ernest (I)	6-2	222	27	5	Henderson State
Towle, Steve (I)	6-2	233	27	6	Kansas

O=outside   I=inside

The 3-4 defense lines up with Bokamper, Towle, Chambers and Gordon as the 'backers. Matheson is a powerful backup in experience. Gordon has been having contract problems with the Dolphin front office, but nothing money can't solve. Even though the Miami defense seems superb, Shula isn't entirely satisfied. He says: "When the ball is up in the air, fight for it. Intercept. Cause errors."

Defensive Backs	Ht.	Wt.	Age	Exp.	College
Bessillieu, Don (S)	6-1	199	24	2	Georgia Tech
Blackwood, Glenn (CB)	6-0	183	23	2	Texas
Colzie, Neal (S)	6-2	190	27	6	Ohio State
Foley, Tim (S)	6-2	194	32	10	Purdue
Kozlowski, Mike (S)	6-0	187	24	2	Colorado
McNeal, Don (S)	6-1	187	22	R	Alabama
Small, Gerald (CB)	5-11	187	24	3	San Jose State
Taylor, Ed (CB)	6-0	175	27	6	Memphis State
Thomas, Norris (CB)	5-11	175	26	4	Southern Mississippi

CB=cornerback   S=safety

With the exception of Foley, the Miami secondary has youth and toughness. Colzie and Small together accounted for nearly half of the club's 23 interceptions last season. Blackwood spent most of the season on the injured list.

Note: A complete listing of Miami's 1980 college draft selections can be found on page 272.

DEFENSIVE UNIT 3-4 DEFENSE

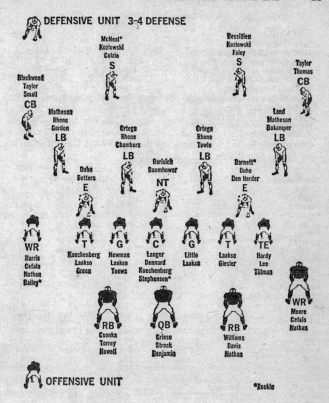

McNeal*
Kozlowski
Colzie
S

Bessillieu
Kozlowski
Foley
S

Blackwood
Taylor
Small
CB

Taylor
Thomas
CB

Matheson
Rhone
Gordon
LB

Ortega
Rhone
Chambers
LB

Ortega
Rhone
Towle
LB

Land
Matheson
Bokamper
LB

Duhe
Betters
E

Barisich
Baumhower
NT

Barnett*
Duhe
Den Herder
E

WR
Harris
Cefalo
Nathan
Bailey*

Kuechenberg
Laakso
Green
T

Newman
Laakso
Toews
G

Langer
Dennard
Kuechenberg
Stephenson*
C

Little
Laakso
G

Laakso
Giesler
T

Hardy
Lee
Tillman
TE

RB
Csonka
Torrey
Howell

QB
Griese
Strock
Benjamin

RB
Williams
Davis
Nathan

WR
Moore
Cefalo
Nathan

OFFENSIVE UNIT

*Rookie

1979 DOLPHINS STATISTICS

	Dolphins	Opps.
Total Points Scored	341	257
Total First Downs	297	238
Third Down Efficiency Percentage	48.3	45.1
Yards Rushing—First Downs	2187—126	1702—87
Passes Attempted—Completions	416—235	418—230
Yards Passing—First Downs	2763—140	2737—135
QB Sacked—Yards Lost	29—255	36—314
Interceptions By—Return Average	23—12.4	22—17.4
Punts—Average Yards	71—39.5	77—37.9
Punt Returns—Average Return	34—9.9	25—5.2
Kickoff Returns—Average Return	51—22.5	69—22.0
Fumbles—Ball Lost	27—15	29—15
Penalties—Yards	79—651	107—834

STATISTICAL LEADERS

Scoring	TDs	Rush.	Pass.	Ret.	PATs	FGs	Total
Von Schamann	0	0	0	0	36—40	21—29	99
Csonka	13	12	1	0	0	0	78
Moore	6	0	6	0	0	0	36
Williams	4	3	1	0	0	0	24
Cefalo	3	0	3	0	0	0	18
Hardy	3	0	3	0	0	0	18
Harris	3	0	3	0	0	0	18
Bulaich	3	2	1	0	0	0	18

Rushing	Atts.	Yds.	Avg.	Longest	TDs
Csonka	220	837	3.8	22	12
Williams	184	703	3.8	39	3
Davis	98	383	3.9	42	1
Nathan	16	68	4.2	18	0
Torrey	13	61	4.7	17	1
Griese	11	30	2.7	18	0

Passing	Atts.	Com.	Yds.	Pct.	Int.	Longest	TDs
Griese	310	176	2160	56.8	16	51	14
Strock	100	56	830	56.0	6	53	6
Benjamin	4	3	28	75.0	0	17	0

Receiving	No.	Yds.	Avg.	Longest	TDs
Moore	48	840	17.5	53	6
Harris	42	798	19.0	51	3
Davis	34	215	6.3	18	0
Hardy	30	386	12.8	28	3
Williams	21	175	8.3	38	1
Nathan	17	213	12.5	35	2
Csonka	16	75	4.7	18	1
Cefalo	12	223	18.6	30	3

Interceptions	No.	Yds.	Avg.	Longest	TDs
Colzie	5	86	17.2	56	0
Small	5	74	14.8	40	0
Gordon	2	33	16.5	33	0
Thomas	2	29	14.5	24	0
Rhone	2	17	8.5	10	0

Punting	No.	Yds.	Avg.	Longest	Inside 20	Blocked
Roberts	69	2772	40.2	68	13	1

Punt Returns	No.	FCs	Yds.	Avg.	Longest	TDs
Nathan	28	14	306	10.9	86 (TD)	1
Kozlowski	3	4	21	7.0	11	0
Cefalo	2	3	10	5.0	10	0

Kickoff Returns	No.	Yds.	Avg.	Longest	TDs
Nathan	45	1016	22.6	43	0
Kozlowski	4	85	21.2	22	0
Davis	2	27	13.5	16	0

NEW YORK JETS

Head Coach: Walt Michaels

4th Year   **Record:** 19–27

1979 RECORD (8-8) (capital letters indicate home games)			1980 SCHEDULE (capital letters indicate home games)	
22	CLEVELAND	25	BALTIMORE	Sept. 7
3	New England	56	Buffalo	Sept. 14
31	DETROIT	10	SAN FRANCISCO	Sept. 21
31	Buffalo	46	Baltimore	Sept. 28
33	MIAMI	27	NEW ENGLAND	Oct. 5
8	Baltimore	10	Atlanta	Oct. 12
14	MINNESOTA	7	SEATTLE	Oct. 19
28	OAKLAND	19	MIAMI (night, TV)	Oct. 27
24	Houston	27	New England	Nov. 2
27	Green Bay	22	BUFFALO	Nov. 9
12	BUFFALO	14	Denver	Nov. 16
13	Chicago	23	HOUSTON	Nov. 23
7	Seattle	30	Los Angeles	Nov. 30
30	BALTIMORE	17	Cleveland	Dec. 7
27	NEW ENGLAND	26	NEW ORLEANS	Dec. 14
27	Miami	24	Miami (TV)	Dec. 20
337		383		

Perhaps the Jets wouldn't have touched off so much speculation about 1980 if they hadn't dealt everybody a surprise by winning the last three games of the '79 season, including upset victories over New England (27-26) and Miami (27-24) after downing Baltimore 30-17. Up until then, their 5-8 record gave no hint that two of the AFC East's top teams were about to bite the dust when both were fighting it out for a playoff spot—a prize the Jets had long since given up for lost. If momentum, that favorite word of the current presidential campaign, means anything in football, the Jets may even yet turn the 1980 AFC race into a finish-line fight involving all five clubs.

In addition to making news at season's end with

their sudden three-game win streak, Walt Michaels' outfit also stirred up a lot of discussion by making the first big trade of the off-season. It sent quarterback Matt Robinson to Denver in exchange for Craig Penrose, a backup QB, and two top draft choices. The importance of this trade, of course, lies in its implications for quarterback Richard Todd's peace of mind.

All last season Michaels was faced with the two-quarterback dilemma, and resolving the question of when to start Robinson and when to start Todd very nearly tore the team apart. As offensive guard Randy Rasmussen, the old pro of the line, describes it, with Robinson gone, Todd may shine through much brighter than before. "This will take a lot of pressure off Todd," says Rasmussen. "At times last season, Todd would get to the ballpark before a game and the first thing he'd see would be a huge sign reading, 'We Want Matt.' Then Todd would start the game, throw one interception and the booing would begin. . . ."

Many of the Jets are sorry to see Robinson go, but most agree Todd will benefit if it stops the booing and general abuse the fans at New York's Shea Stadium heaped upon him with merciless consistency. Linebacker Greg Buttle even sees the reaction of fans as a possible key to a good season. "If the fans are smart and want us to get off on the right foot," says Buttle, "they ought to start cheering Richard from the moment they introduce him at a game. He's our quarterback now, and if the fans really want to see us win, they might as well help us."

The Todd-Robinson dilemma became a problem after Robinson hurt his thumb while playfully wrestling with a teammate only three days before the season's opening game with Cleveland. Michaels, through the exhibition and preseason, had finally decided upon Robinson as the No. 1 quarterback, but the Jets lost to Cleveland in overtime because that injured thumb kept Robinson from throwing long.

Todd took over and, even though New England shell-shocked the Jets 56-3 in the seond game, his quarter-backing progressively improved as the season wore on. Then, in those final three contests against the Colts, Patriots and Dolphins, Todd's passing and leadership ability carried the day, and he finished the season with his best statistics ever—completing 171 of 334 passes for 2,660 yards, 16 TDs and throwing but 22 interceptions. Needless to say, Todd is looking forward to the new season when the quarterback's job will be his from Day One—if those fans will just keep quiet.

And what will happen when a rejuvenated Richard Todd leads a New York Jet offensive that already has the league's best rushing attack? A bunch of hard-running backs, led by Clark Gaines and Scott Dierking to name only two, showed the entire NFL how to carry the ball, averaging 165.4 yards per game. It was the Jets' first team rushing title in the club's 20-year history. Todd and Michaels will be faced with the perennial task of properly balancing that powerful ground attack with the passing game, assuming Todd continues with his recent spectacular demonstration of skill. And the Jet aerial circus will be a good one if wide receiver Wesley Walker returns to form after suffering a knee injury.

Walt Michaels enters his fourth year as the Jets' head coach with a 19-27-0 record. Coming off two consecutive 8-8 seasons, he feels the team has reached what he regards as the "maturity stage." "Yes, they've grown up," says the coach. "They've handled adversity. . . . I feel Richard Todd has learned what it's like to work himself through a problem. He handled the boos, and now he's getting the cheers. No one took us lightly last season. They came after us, and look how our guys went after them! Our weakest point was inexperience on defense."

That inexperience showed up glaringly on defense where rookie starters were the rule rather than the exception. And the figures show that for the second straight year, the Jets had pro football's youngest (and therefore least experienced) team—averaging only 24.5 years of age and 2.0 years of NFL playing time. They might turn out to be the league's youngest again this year, but that doesn't bother Michaels. He's a big booster of the youthful philosophy. "Other teams have tried to go the other way," he reminds us, "and they got castoffs and trouble-makers. I want to go the route by building something solid, something put together brick by brick. Then you know it will last."

OFFENSE

Quarterbacks	Ht.	Wt.	Age	Exp.	College
Merendino, Tony	6-3	212	23	R	Tennessee-Chattanoo
Penrose, Craig	6-3	205	27	5	San Diego State
Ryan, Pat	6-3	205	25	3	Tennessee
Todd, Richard	6-2	203	27	5	Alabama

Now the master of all he surveys among Jet quarterbacks, Todd has a clear track for doing his own thing. Matt Robinson was traded to Denver for Craig Penrose and draft choices. In averaging 51.2 percent completions last season, Todd passed for 2,660 yards—the most aerial yardage by a Jet since Joe Namath led the league with 2,816 in 1972. Penrose didn't throw much for Denver in '79—five times for two completions and one interception. He and Ryan will have to be content to sit and watch until Todd proves himself for once and for all.

Running Backs	Ht.	Wt.	Age	Exp.	College
Bennett, Woody	6-3	217	25	2	Miami (Fla.)
Dierking, Scott	5-10	215	25	4	Purdue
Gaines, Clark	6-1	209	26	5	Wake Forest
Harper, Bruce	5-8	177	25	4	Kutztown State
Long, Kevin	6-1	214	25	4	South Carolina
Newton, Tom	6-0	213	26	4	California

| Paige, Barrett | 6-3 | 218 | 25 | 2 | Central State (O.) |
| Powell, Darnell | 6-0 | 184 | 26 | 4 | Tenn.-Chattanooga |

The Jets led the NFL in rushing yardage last season, averaging 165.4 yards per game with their closest competitor being St. Louis with 161.4. That has to be impressive in considering the Jet offense for 1980. Although none of the RBs cracked the 1,000-yard mark, Gaines rolled for 905 followed by Dierking with 767. Harper rushed for much less but he led the AFC in total offensive yards for the second straight year with 1,980 (1,158 on 55 kickoff returns, 290 on 33 punt returns, 282 rushing yards and 250 on pass receptions). Newton ran for 145 yards but scored six TDs on his way. Gaines is an excellent blocker when he's not carrying. Long adds even more drive to this bunch of overland travelers.

Receivers	Ht.	Wt.	Age	Exp.	College
Barkum, Jerome (T)	6-4	225	30	9	Jackson State
Clayton, Ralph (W)	6-3	216	22	R	Michigan
Darby, Paul (W)	5-10	192	24	2	Southwest Texas
Farmer, Roger (W)	6-3	195	25	2	Baker
Gaffney, Derrick (W)	6-1	180	25	3	Florida
Jones, Bobby (W)	5-11	180	25	3	(None)
Jones, Johnny (W)	5-11	180	22	R	Texas
Paplham, Scott (T)	6-5	230	24	1	Northern Illinois
Raba, Bob (T)	6-1	225	25	4	Maryland
Shuler, Mickey (T)	6-3	229	24	3	Penn State
Walker, Wesley (W)	6-0	175	25	4	California

W=wide receiver   T=tight end

The Jets' passing offense wasn't all that good last season. Walker hurt his knee in midseason, and Jones came on strong as his replacement, catching 19 for 379 yards. There's speculation now that Jones might even challenge Gaffney for a job when Walker returns. Barkum did his usual steady work with 27 receptions and Walker's 569 yards was the club's highest, despite the injury. Gaffney's yardage was second with 534. Johnny (Lam) Jones, the Jets' No. 1 draft choice who was chosen right after Detroit took Billy Sims off the availability board, is widely heralded as the speed burner the club has been seeking. Second round choice Clayton is not only a receiver, but he also plays tight end and running back. Problem is, where to play him.

Interior Linemen	Ht.	Wt.	Age	Exp.	College
Alexander, Dan (G)	6-4	255	25	4	Louisiana State
Cunningham, Eric (G)	6-3	257	23	2	Penn State
Dufek, Bill (G)	6-4	257	24	2	Michigan
Fields, Joe (C)	6-2	253	27	6	Widener
Gibney, John (C)	6-5	225	24	2	Colgate
McGlasson, Ed (C)	6-4	248	24	2	Youngstown State

Powell, Marvin (T)	6-5	268	25	4	Southern Cal
Rasmussen, Randy (G)	6-2	255	35	14	Kearney State
Roman, John (T)	6-4	251	28	5	Idaho State
Waldemore, Stan (G-T-C)	6-4	257	25	3	Nebraska
Ward, Chris (T)	6-3	270	25	3	Ohio State

T=tackle   G=guard   C=center

This is the line that cleared paths for the NFL's leading rushing attack. Although it allowed 32 QB sacks, this unit compensated almost adequately by opening up holes for the runners. Powell led the group and made All-Pro. He coupled with Ward to provide the Jets with a pair of hard-to-move tackle bookends. Guards Alexander and Rasmussen (will he ever run down?) and center Joe Fields were in there with brilliant performances virtually every game. It's fun carrying the ball for the Jets.

Kickers	Ht.	Wt.	Age	Exp.	College
Jacobs, Dave (Pk)	5-7	151	23	2	Syracuse
Leahy, Pat (Pk)	6-0	195	29	7	St. Louis U.
Long, Carson (Pk)	5-11	200	26	3	Pittsburgh
Ramsey, Chuck (P)	6-2	189	28	4	Wake Forest

Pk=placekicker   P=punter

Jacobs came in to replace the injured Leahy, and earned the job—at least for the moment. Jacobs made 10-of-11 extra points, 5-of-9 FGs, all from various distances. Until he strained his knee six games into the season, Leahy was doing fine, with 12-15 points-after and 8 FGs out of 13 kicks. Long, drafted by L.A. in 1977, comes to Jets as a free agent. Jacobs and Leahy bid to fight it out for the regular kicking job. Ramsey is the punter, averaging 40.8 last season, his longest going 64 yards.

DEFENSE

Front Linemen	Ht.	Wt.	Age	Exp.	College
Gastineau, Mark (E)	6-5	257	24	2	East Central
Klecko, Joe (T)	6-3	262	27	4	Temple
Liles, Alva (T)	6-3	255	24	1	Boise State
Lyons, Marty (E)	6-5	245	23	2	Alabama
Pillers, Lawrence (E)	6-3	260	28	5	Alcorn State
Salaam, Abdul (T)	6-3	260	27	5	Kent State
Winkel, Bob (T-E)	6-4	246	25	2	Kentucky

E=end   T=tackle

The Jets ranked 12th in AFC overall defense, and dead last in the NFL in passing defense, allowing a whopping 257.2 yards per game while sacking opposing QBs a mere 22 times. Against the run, however, they did much better and finished third in AFC rushing defense, allowing opposing ball-carriers 106.6 yards per game. Klecko led club in sacks with seven, even though he was moved to a tackle spot when club returned to 4-3 defense lineup. Formerly, he was learning the trade at end and was a great pass rusher, some observers contend. Pillers and Salaam keep the ball-carriers at bay, but pass defense is not their strong point. Lyons and Gastineau showed definite promise as rookies, and have futures. Lyons made at least one all-rookie selection.

Linebackers	Ht.	Wt.	Age	Exp.	College
Beamon, Willie (O)	6-3	240	24	2	Boise State
Blinka, Stan (M)	6-2	230	23	2	Sam Houston State
Buttle, Greg (O)	6-3	232	26	5	Penn State
Crosby, Ron (O)	6-3	225	25	3	Penn State
Hennessy, John (M)	6-3	236	25	4	Michigan
Hennigan, John (M)	6-2	228	29	8	Tennessee Tech
Keller, Larry (O)	6-2	225	27	5	Houston
Kirchbaum, Larry (M)	6-2	240	23	2	Kentucky
McKibben, Mike (O)	6-3	228	24	2	Kent State
Mehl, Lance (O)	6-3	225	22	R	Penn State
Sullivan, John (O)	6-1	221	24	2	Illinois
Zidd, Jim (O)	6-1	232	23	R	Kansas

O=outside   M=middle

Blinka led club in tackles with 27 (122 solo) as a rookie. McKibben, another rookie, made the team, too. Buttle is one of NFL's top 'backers. Hard hitters all, this unit is good at everything except the pass rush and that must improve if the Jets are to move up.

Defensive Backs	Ht.	Wt.	Age	Exp.	College
Dykes, Donald (CB)	5-11	188	25	2	Southeast Louisiana
Jackson, Bobby (CB)	5-9	175	24	3	Florida State
Johnson, Jessee (CB-S)	6-2	185	23	R	Colorado
Lynn, Johnny (CB)	6-0	190	24	2	UCLA
Moresco, Tim (S)	6-0	180	26	4	Syracuse
Ray, Darrol (S)	6-1	206	22	R	Oklahoma
Schroy, Ken (S)	6-2	196	28	4	Maryland
Suggs, Shafer (S)	6-1	204	27	5	Ball State

CB=cornerback   S=safety

Suggs is fast, but the secondary's pass defense still leaves something to be desired. Owens led club interceptions with six. Lynn moved in as a rookie, intercepted two and performed well as a first-year man. Michaels faces the task of upgrading this unit as part of his defensive overhaul.

Note: A complete listing of the New York Jets' 1980 college draft selections can be found on page 274.

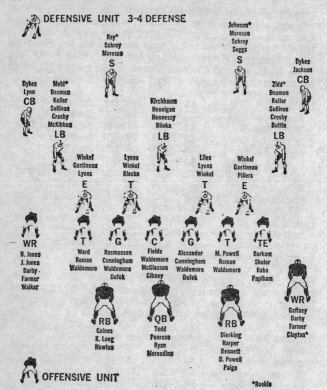

DEFENSIVE UNIT 3-4 DEFENSE

Ray*
Schroy
Moresco
S

Johnson*
Moresco
Schroy
Suggs
S

Dykes
Jackson
CB

Dykes
Lynn
CB

Mehl*
Beamon
Keller
Sullivan
Crosby
McKibben
LB

Kirchbaum
Hennigan
Hennessy
Blinka
LB

Zidd*
Beamon
Keller
Sullivan
Crosby
Buttle
LB

Winkel
Gastineau
Lyons
E

Lyons
Winkel
Klecko
T

Liles
Lyons
Winkel
T

Winkel
Gastineau
Pillers
E

WR
B. Jones
J. Jones
Darby
Farmer
Walker

T
Ward
Roman
Waldemore

G
Rasmussen
Cunningham
Waldemore
Dufek

C
Fields
Waldemore
McGlasson
Gibney

G
Alexander
Cunningham
Waldemore
Dufek

T
M. Powell
Roman
Waldemore

TE
Barkum
Shuler
Raba
Paplham

RB
Gaines
K. Long
Newton

QB
Todd
Penrose
Ryan
Merendino

RB
Dierking
Harper
Bennett
D. Powell
Paige

WR
Gaffney
Darby
Farmer
Clayton*

OFFENSIVE UNIT

*Rookie

1979 JETS STATISTICS

	Jets*	Opps.
Total Points Scored	337*	383
Total First Downs	299	331
Third Down Efficiency Percentage	44.8	48.5
Yards Rushing—First Downs	2646—153	1706—107
Passes Attempted—Completions	369—190	570—339
Yards Passing—First Downs	2598—126	4115—198
QB Sacked—Yards Lost	32—266	22—173
Interceptions By—Return Average	21—11.4	25—16.6
Punts—Average Yards	73—40.8	68—37.1
Punt Returns—Average Return	36—8.7	33—7.9
Kickoff Returns—Average Return	76—20.5	70—21.8
Fumbles—Ball Lost	26—13	34—19
Penalties—Yards	109—876	98—888

* Includes safety

STATISTICAL LEADERS

Scoring	TDs	Rush.	Pass.	Ret.	PATs	FGs	Total
Long	7	7	0	0	0	0	42
Leahy	0	0	0	0	12—15	8—13	36
Newton	6	6	0	0	0	0	36
Todd	5	5	0	0	0	0	30
Walker	5	0	5	0	0	0	30
Jacobs	0	0	0	0	10—11	5—9	25
Barkum	4	0	4	0	0	0	24
Linhart	0	0	0	0	11—14	3—6	20
Dierking	3	3	0	0	0	0	18

Rushing	Atts.	Yds.	Avg.	Longest	TDs
Gaines	186	905	4.9	52	0
Dierking	186	767	4.1	40	3
Long	116	442	3.8	25	7
Harper	65	282	4.3	31	0
Newton	37	145	3.9	51 (TD)	6

Passing	Atts.	Com.	Yds.	Pct.	Int.	Longest	TDs
Todd	334	171	2660	51.2	22	72 (TD)	16
Robinson	31	17	191	54.8	2	33	0

Receiving	No.	Yds.	Avg.	Longest	TDs
Gaffney	32	534	16.7	43	1
Gaines	29	219	7.6	15	0
Barkum	27	401	14.9	40	4
Walker	23	569	24.7	71 (TD)	5
Jones	19	379	19.9	51	1
Harper	17	250	14.7	72 (TD)	2
Shuler	16	225	14.1	46	3

Interceptions	No.	Yds.	Avg.	Longest	TDs
Owens	6	41	6.8	15	0
Jackson	4	63	15.8	58 (TD)	1
Suggs	3	41	13.7	32 (TD)	1
Lynn	2	46	23.0	32	0
Buttle	2	27	13.5	27	0
Blinka	2	12	6.0	8	0

Punting	No.	Yds.	Avg.	Longest	Inside 20	Blocked
Ramsey	73	2979	40.8	64	22	0

Punt Returns	No.	FCs	Yds.	Avg.	Longest	TDs
Harper	33	9	290	8.8	51	0
Schroy	2	0	24	12.0	19	0

Kickoff Returns	No.	Yds.	Avg.	Longest	TDs
Harper	55	1158	21.1	52	0
Jones	7	140	20.0	36	0
Schroy	6	179	29.8	51	0

BUFFALO BILLS

Head Coach: Chuck Knox

3rd Year   **Record:** 12–20

1979 RECORD (7-9) (capital letters indicate home games)		1980 SCHEDULE (capital letters indicate home games)	
7	MIAMI	9	MIAMI	Sept. 7
51	CINCINNATI	24	N.Y. JETS	Sept. 14
19	San Diego	27	New Orleans	Sept. 21
46	N.Y. JETS	31	OAKLAND	Sept. 28
31	Baltimore	13	San Diego	Oct. 5
0	CHICAGO	7	BALTIMORE	Oct. 12
7	Miami	17	Miami	Oct. 19
13	BALTIMORE	14	NEW ENGLAND	Oct. 26
20	Detroit	17	ATLANTA	Nov. 2
6	NEW ENGLAND	26	N.Y. Jets	Nov. 9
14	N.Y. Jets	12	Cincinnati	Nov. 16
19	GREEN BAY	12	PITTSBURGH	Nov. 23
16	New England	13	Baltimore	Nov. 30
16	DENVER	19	LOS ANGELES	Dec. 7
3	Minnesota	10	New England	Dec. 14
0	Pittsburgh	28	San Francisco	Dec. 21
268		279		

Quietly and almost without any sign of fanfare seeping southward from the Niagara Frontier, Chuck Knox is rebuilding the Buffalo Bills from the ground up and, right now at least, the name of the game is defense. After years of emphasis upon an offensive unit that whirled on O. J. Simpson's winged cleats, the Buffalo fans are getting a different football fare—one that glorifies the stonewall, not the run-for-daylight amid a splash of Orange Juice.

During the five seasons he was head coach of the Los Angeles Rams, Knox won five divisional championships. His Rams were noted for two things: their unexciting offense, and their inability to get into the Super Bowl. When he arrived in Buffalo three years ago, Knox was just in time to miss the exciting over-land attack generated by O. J. and the Buffalo offen-sive line which did such a magnificent job of clearing his path. It was the Buffalo defense that was dull and unexciting—and probably the main reason O. J. Simp-son never had a chance to run in the Super Bowl.

Now, the Buffalo fans are witnessing an exchange of sorts. Gone is that flashing offense, gone with O. J. who returned to his West Coast home to finish out his career at San Francisco. There wasn't really anyone to take his place, although quite a case for his successor was made for Terry Miller, the Oklahoma rookie. And Miller did look like a Simpson replacement for one season, his first, when he ran for a thousand yards. But all that faded last season when Miller's yardage total dropped dramatically, or undramatically, accord-ing to one's viewpoint. He managed to run only 484 yards for reasons no one has been able to fathom.

Miller's failure to fill Simpson's shoes, and it *was* a tough act to follow, somehow caused the entire Buffalo offense to roll over and play dead—almost. By the season's end, the Bills ranked exactly last among the 28 NFL clubs in the matter of yards gained rushing. Their average of 101.3 yards per game on the ground was the league's worst—quite a comedown for a team that once had O. J. Simpson in its offensive backfield.

Still, there was another side to this dismal offensive picture—and that was the defensive unit, the "other side of the coin" for any football team. As the 1979 season began, the Buffalo defense was slow to fall into place for at least four weeks. The scores, both for and against, were either strangely low or lopsidedly high. Then, certain decisions affecting the defensive unit began showing through all the turmoil.

For one thing, Knox and the Bills' management had traded for linebacker Isiah Robertson of the Los

Angeles Rams—a player, quite naturally, well known
to Knox. Robertson was unhappy in L.A., and wanted
to join Knox in Buffalo for a new run to the top. The
1979 college draft brought the Bills linebacking sensa-
tion Jim Haslett who had played college football in
the Pennsylvania Conference at Indiana (Pa.). The
same draft produced still another rookie whose play in
the secondary helped turn the Buffalo defense around.
He was Jeff Nixon, out of the University of Richmond
in Virginia.

Knox switched to the 3-4 defense and Haslett teamed
with veteran Shane Nelson in a middle linebacking
operation that put a virtual blockade on opposing
ground-gaining attacks. In 1978, the Bills gave up 201
yards rushing per game. That figure dropped to 155.1
yards in 1979.

The combination of a record-setting passing game
by Joe Ferguson and an improved rushing defense en-
abled the Bills to win more games than they had in
four years. And there were several very narrow defeats.
Five of the nine losses came by a touchdown or less.
And at the finish, the Bills were in fourth place in the
AFC East.

"By winding up fourth in the AFC East, we earned
a 1980 schedule that must rank with the most difficult
the Bills have played in many years." That's Chuck
Knox talking as he examines what's ahead for his club.
"Not only do we get the Pittsburgh Steelers (and everyone knows who they are), we also get their Super
Bowl opposition (and that of course is Knox's old
team, the L.A. Rams). Throw in Oakland, San Diego
and the rest of the AFC East and the task ahead is
obvious."

How will he go about getting the Bills in shape for
these challenges? Knox has some ideas about that, too.
"One of our priorities this fall will be to get that

running game going again while, at the same time, continue improving our pass offense. A number of factors contributed to our inability to move the ball on the ground last season—blocking breakdowns (which are remedial), poor running and key penalties all hurt our running attack."

Knox, however, is making no wide-ranging claims for the 1980 Bills. No doubt he feels there's plenty of time in which to issue announcements like the one John McKay of Tampa Bay made a year ago when he said, "We're no longer pretenders, we're contenders." Still, Knox does have a view of the immediate future, in these words: "I said it last year and it bears repeating: our improvement as a football team next season may not necessarily be reflected in the record. In other words, we could be a better team and not have as good a record."

Yes, even in pro football, things are sometimes not what they seem.

OFFENSE

Quarterbacks	Ht.	Wt.	Age	Exp.	College
Bradley, Gene	6-4	199	23	R	Arkansas State
Ferguson, Joe	6-1	195	30	8	Arkansas
Manucci, Dan	6-2	194	23	2	Kansas State
Munson, Bill	6-2	205	39	17	Utah State

Ferguson set Buffalo club records last season with 238 completions, 458 attempts and 3,572 passing yards. He also became the club's first 3,000-yard passer in a statistical arena long dominated by O. J. Simpson's rushing numbers. Munson, if he continues this season, is 17 years in the NFL. He can still complete three out of seven, as he did last season.

Running Backs	Ht.	Wt.	Age	Exp.	College
Brown, Curtis	5-10	203	26	4	Missouri
Collier, Mike	5-11	200	27	5	Morgan State
Cribbs, Joe	5-11	190	22	R	Auburn

Hooks, Roland	6-0	195	27	5	N.C. State
Johnson, Dennis	6-3	220	24	3	Mississippi State
Miller, Terry	5-10	196	24	3	Oklahoma State
Powell, Steve	5-11	186	24	3	Northeast Missouri

Buffalo ranked last in AFC rushing yardage last season, gaining 101.3 yards per game on the average. Miller hasn't lived up to his all-star promise of two years ago, although he did gain 1,000 yards his first year. That dropped off to 484 in '79. Some claim Miller hasn't had good blocking, and blame Johnson for that. Johnson, however, did have injury problems. Brown led the team in rushing but his 574-yard total was lowest for Buffalo's top ground gainer since 1977. And it was only the second time in past eight years that Buffalo has been without a 1,000-yard rusher. Shades of Orange Juice!

Receivers	Ht.	Wt.	Age	Exp.	College
Brammer, Mark (T)	6-3	238	22	R	Michigan State
Butler, Jerry (W)	6-0	178	23	2	Clemson
Chandler, Bob (W)	6-1	180	31	10	Southern Cal
Fulton, Dan (W)	6-2	180	24	2	Nebraska-Omaha
Gant, Reuben (T)	6-4	225	28	7	Oklahoma State
Howard, Ron (T)	6-4	230	29	6	Seattle U.
Kirtman, Mike (W)	6-1	180	24	1	San Jose State
Lewis, Frank (W)	6-1	196	33	10	Grambling
Piccone, Lou (W)	5-9	175	31	7	West Liberty State
Shipp, Joe (T)	6-4	225	25	2	Southern Cal
Willis, Len (W)	5-11	185	27	5	Ohio State

W=wide receiver   T=tight end

Lewis caught 54 passes for 1,082 yards for his career high, thereby becoming only the third 1,000-yard receiver in club history. Rookie Jerry Butler, fresh out of Clemson, missed three games with a hurt shoulder but still finished with 48 catches for 834 yards and four TDs. He had his best NFL pass-catching game of the year against the Jets with a record 255 yards on 10 receptions. Brown caught 39 for 401 yards as a running back. Chandler was lost for most of '79, but Piccone stepped in and replaced anyone who was hurt—and performed with distinction. Gant played steadily at tight end until the final two games when injury sidelined him. Shipp caught three passes for 43 yards as a rookie replacement. Gant's healthy return would strengthen this unit greatly.

Interior Linemen	Ht.	Wt.	Age	Exp.	College
Borchardt, Jon (T)	6-5	255	23	2	Montana State
DeLamielleure, Joe (G)	6-3	245	29	8	Michigan State
Devlin, Joe (T)	6-5	250	26	5	Iowa
Fulton, Ed (G)	6-3	250	25	3	Maryland
Hardison, Dee (T)	6-4	269	24	3	North Carolina

Grant, Will (C)	6-4	248	26	3	Kentucky
Jones, Ken (T)	6-5	250	28	5	Arkansas State
McKenzie, Reggie (G)	6-5	242	30	9	Michigan
Parker, Willie (C)	6-3	245	32	9	North Texas State
Ritcher, Jim (C)	6-3	251	22	R	North Carolina State
Schmeding, John (G)	6-4	268	25	R	Boston College
Vogler, Tim (C)	6-3	245	24	2	Ohio State
Zelencik, Connie (C)	6-4	245	25	2	Purdue

T=tackle   G=guard   C=center

Coach Chuck Knox has this to say about the offensive line: "It did a good job on pass protection. The fact that our rushing production fell off underlines that we need to do a better job of run blocking. We did have a lot of nagging injuries. Some played hurt. DeLamielleure, Parker and McKenzie all suffered nicks that affected their efficiency. We look for Vogler to challenge for center and Borchardt to make his presence known at tackle. We are thin in backup people at both center and guard." DeLamielleure and McKenzie, with 103 and 117 consecutive starts, are the "iron men." Devlin is becoming more consistent at tackle. Jones was the most improved offensive lineman, say Buffalo insiders. Ritcher, the Bills' No. 1 draftee, won the highly-coveted 1979 Outland Trophy as the outstanding interior lineman in college football. Schmeding is 25 and a rugged blocker. Hardison is being switched from defensive nose guard to offensive tackle.

Kickers	Ht.	Wt.	Age	Exp.	College
Jackson, Rusty (P)	6-2	195	30	4	Louisiana State
Mike-Mayer, Nick (Pk)	5-9	185	30	8	Temple

Pk=placekicker   P=punter

Mike-Mayer enters the 1980 season with a string of 17 consecutive extra points. He led Buffalo scoring last season with 17-18 points-after and 20-29 FGs, even though he didn't join club until fourth game. He's being hailed as best kicker Buffalo has had since Pete Gogolak, 15 years ago in the old AFL. Knox calls the punting "inconsistent, needful of improvement." Jackson got off 96 punts last season, averaging 38.2.

DEFENSE

Front Linemen	Ht.	Wt.	Age	Exp.	College
Dokes, Phil (E)	6-5	255	25	3	Oklahoma State
Hutchinson, Scott (E)	6-4	243	24	3	Florida
Ieremia, Mekeli (E)	6-2	244	26	1	Brigham Young
Johnson, Ken (E)	6-5	253	25	2	Knoxville
Kadish, Mike (NT)	6-5	270	30	8	Notre Dame
Smerlas, Fred (NT)	6-3	270	23	2	Boston College

White, Sherman (E)	6-5	250	32	9	California
Williams, Ben (E)	6-3	245	26	5	Mississippi

E=end   NT=nose tackle

The Buffalo defense showed marked improvement last season, especially against the run. Against the pass, the Bills actually led the AFC by limiting their opponents to 158.1 yards per game through the air. Kadish had one of his best years at nose tackle, and Fred Smerlas gained all-rookie recognition. White blocked five FGs and an extra point from his end position. Williams also had a better than average year, while Hutchinson is proving a good backup. Dokes was out all season with an injured shoulder.

Linebackers	Ht.	Wt.	Age	Exp.	College
Baker, Kevin (I)	6-4	240	25	1	William Penn
Ball, Aaron (O)	6-2	245	25	1	Fullerton State
Ehlers, Tom (O)	6-2	218	28	5	Kentucky
Haslett, Jim (I)	6-3	232	25	2	Indiana (Pa.)
Higgins, Tom (I)	6-2	235	26	2	N.C. State
Jilek, Dan (O)	6-2	225	27	5	Michigan
Keating, Chris (I)	6-2	223	23	2	Maine
Nelson, Shane (I)	6-1	225	25	4	Baylor
Parker, Ervin (I)	6-4	225	22	R	South Carolina State
Robertson, Isiah (O)	6-3	225	31	10	Southern U.
Sanford, Lucius (O)	6-2	216	24	3	Georgia Tech
Villapiano, Phil (I)	6-2	225	31	10	Bowling Green

O=outside   I=inside

Haslett's debut was impressive. The big linebacker, who played high school ball in Pittsburgh and college ball at Indiana (Pa.), proved he could tackle, intercept passes and recover fumbles with the best of them. Nelson led club in solo tackles with 81. Old pro Robertson intercepted two passes and ran one back for a TD. With all that, there is a lack of depth at linebacker.

Defensive Backs	Ht.	Wt.	Age	Exp.	College
Clark, Mario (CB)	6-2	195	26	5	Oregon
Freeman, Steve (S)	5-11	185	27	6	Mississippi State
Greene, Doug (S)	6-2	205	24	3	Texas A&I
Greene, Tony (S)	5-10	175	31	10	Maryland
Kush, Rod (S)	6-0	188	24	1	Nebraska-Omaha
Lee, Keith (CB)	5-11	192	23	R	Colorado State
Moody, Keith (CB)	5-10	170	27	5	Syracuse
Nixon, Jeff (S)	6-3	190	24	2	Richmond
Pyburn, Jeff (CB)	6-1	204	23	R	Georgia
Romes, Charles (CB)	6-1	190	26	4	N.C. Central

CB=cornerback   S=safety

Nixon won the starting free safety post from Tony Greene in last season's final four games. As the Bills' top pass thief, Nixon came on like the furies in his rookie year. He was a fourth-round choice from the University of Richmond whose birthplace is listed as Fursten Feld, Germany. Tony Greene, a one-time Pro Bowler, can play at either safety or cornerback in the "new look" Bills secondary. Moody is a kick-return specialist who holds almost all Buffalo club records. Among other marks, he's only player in Bills' history with 2,000 or more career yards on kickoff returns.

Note: A complete listing of Buffalo's 1980 college draft selections can be found on page 268.

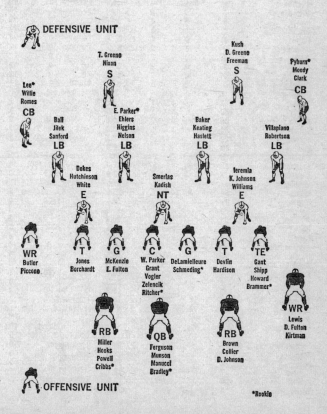

DEFENSIVE UNIT

Kush
D. Greene
Freeman
S

T. Greene
Nixon
S

Pyburn*
Moody
Clark
CB

Lee*
Willie
Romes
CB

Ball
Jilek
Sanford
LB

E. Parker*
Ehlers
Higgins
Nelson
LB

Baker
Keating
Haslett
LB

Villapiano
Robertson
LB

Dokes
Hutchinson
White
E

Smerlas
Kadish
NT

Ieremia
K. Johnson
Williams
E

WR
Butler
Piccone

Jones
Borchardt
T

McKenzie
E. Fulton
G

W. Parker
Grant
Vogler
Zelencik
Ritcher*
C

DeLamielleure
Schmeding*
G

Devlin
Hardison
T

Gant
Shipp
Howard
Brammer*
TE

WR
Lewis
D. Fulton
Kirtman

Miller
Hooks
Powell
Cribbs*
RB

Ferguson
Munson
Manucci
Bradley*
QB

Brown
Collier
D. Johnson
RB

OFFENSIVE UNIT

*Rookie

1979 BILLS STATISTICS

	Bills	Opps.
Total Points Scored	268	279
Total First Downs	252	273
Third Down Efficiency Percentage	34.2	40.3
Yards Rushing—First Downs	1621—83	2481—137
Passes Attempted—Completions	465—241	382—193
Yards Passing—First Downs	3216—147	2530—117
QB Sacked—Yards Lost	43—387	23—183
Interceptions By—Return Average	24—15.4	15—10.7
Punts—Average Yards	96—38.2	92—38.2
Punt Returns—Average Return	38—8.4	61—9.1
Kickoff Returns—Average Return	59—19.2	54—21.1
Fumbles—Ball Lost	32—19	31—17
Penalties—Yards	104—887	106—788

STATISTICAL LEADERS

Scoring	TDs	Rush.	Pass.	Ret.	PATs	FGs	Total
Mike-Mayer	0	0	0	0	17—18	20—29	77
Hooks	6	6	0	0	0	0	36
Brown	4	1	3	0	0	0	24
Butler	4	0	4	0	0	0	24
Collier	2	2	0	0	0	0	12
Gant	2	0	2	0	0	0	12
Lewis	2	0	2	0	0	0	12
Piccone	2	0	2	0	0	0	12
Dempsey	0	0	0	0	8—11	1—4	11

Rushing	Atts.	Yds.	Avg.	Longest	TDs
Brown	172	574	3.3	25	1
Miller	139	484	3.5	75	1
Hooks	89	320	3.6	32 (TD)	6
Collier	34	130	3.8	22	2
Ferguson	22	68	3.1	15	1
Powell	10	29	2.9	9	0

Passing	Atts.	Com.	Yds.	Pct.	Int.	Longest	TDs
Ferguson	458	238	3572	52.0	15	84 (TD)	14
Munson	7	3	31	42.9	0	16	0

Receiving	No.	Yds.	Avg.	Longest	TDs
Lewis	54	1082	20.0	55	2
Butler	48	834	17.4	75 (TD)	4
Brown	39	401	10.3	84 (TD)	3
Piccone	33	556	16.8	49	2
Hooks	26	254	9.8	19	0
Gant	19	245	12.9	22	2

Interceptions	No.	Yds.	Avg.	Longest	TDs
Nixon	6	81	13.5	43	0
Clark	5	95	19.0	36	0
Freeman	3	62	20.7	50 (TD)	1
Sanford	2	44	22.0	25	0
Greene	2	31	15.5	21	0
Robertson	2	29	14.5	23 (TD)	1

Punting	No.	Yds.	Avg.	Longest	Inside 20	Blocked
Jackson	96	3671	38.2	60	14	0

Punt Returns	No.	FCs	Yds.	Avg.	Longest	TDs
Moody	38	10	318	8.4	32	0

Kickoff Returns	No.	Yds.	Avg.	Longest	TDs
Moody	27	556	20.6	35	0
Miller	8	160	20.0	24	0
Collier	7	129	18.4	27	0
Powell	6	97	16.2	22	0
Willis	4	92	23.0	33	0

BALTIMORE COLTS

Head Coach: Mike McCormack
(1st Year)

1979 RECORD (5-11) (capital letters indicate home games)			1980 SCHEDULE (capital letters indicate home games)	
0	Kansas City	14	N.Y. Jets	Sept. 7
26	TAMPA BAY	29	PITTSBURGH	Sept. 14
10	Cleveland	13	Houston	Sept. 21
13	Pittsburgh	17	N.Y. JETS	Sept. 28
13	BUFFALO	31	Miami	Oct. 5
10	N.Y. JETS	8	Buffalo	Oct. 12
16	HOUSTON	28	NEW ENGLAND	Oct. 19
14	Buffalo	13	ST. LOUIS	Oct. 26
31	NEW ENGLAND	26	Kansas City	Nov. 2
38	CINCINNATI	28	CLEVELAND	Nov. 9
0	Miami	19	Detroit	Nov. 16
21	New England	50	New England	Nov. 23
24	MIAMI	28	BUFFALO	Nov. 30
17	N.Y. Jets	30	Cincinnati	Dec. 7
7	KANSAS CITY	10	MIAMI	Dec. 14
31	N.Y. Giants	7	KANSAS CITY	Dec. 21
271		351		

The only certain thing about the Colts this year is that they will remain in Baltimore. Beyond that, much depends on whether Bert Jones's now famous shoulder will heal, for once and for all, and withstand any additional pounding it could receive after taking the field again. In the meantime, that Jones shoulder has produced still another casualty—head coach Ted Marchibroda who has departed Baltimore, clearly the victim of Jones's inability to play.

Moving in as Marchibroda's replacement is Mike McCormack, one of the better known, and liked, NFL coaches whose career includes a three-year head coaching assignment with the Philadelphia Eagles from 1973 to 1975, his overall record being 16-25-1. Until accepting the Baltimore post, McCormack was an assistant with Cincinnati. Among his other distinctions, he can say that, before coming to Philadelphia in '73, he worked under no less than four former Washington Redskin coaches—Otto Graham, Vince Lombardi, Bill Austin and George Allen.

Marchibroda, as was said earlier, was clearly a casualty of circumstances beyond his control. During his five years with the Colts, they won three AFC East titles while compiling a 41-36-0 record. But it was the 5-11 records in each of the past two seasons that put Marchibroda out in the Maryland cold, ending a stormy relationship with club owner Robert Irsay. Still, in firing Marchibroda, Irsay was gracious enough to say: "This is one decision I hoped I would never have to make, a decision I agonized over for the past two weeks." Three years remain on Marchibroda's contract and he'll receive $100,000 in salary and $50,000 in deferred benefits for each of those years.

Irsay's decision climaxed a season of discontent in Baltimore. Even the fans, or at least a great many of them, felt that Marchibroda was "too conservative" with an unimaginative and usually dull offense. He also caught the blame for failure of draft picks to produce, and for trading away offensive stars like Lydell Mitchell and Raymond Chester. Things got so unexciting that Baltimore's home games attendance dropped to the NFL's lowest, averaging fewer than 37,00 per game, or about 60 percent of Memorial Stadium's capacity. And those who did turn out booed Marchibroda, the Colts generally and one announcement in particular—a suggestion that 1980 season tickets would make splendid Christmas gifts.

Irsay himself didn't help matters much when he began flying from city to city, checking out the possibilities of moving the franchise elsewhere. Amid great fanfare and publicity, even welcoming parades, he flew to such possible franchise locations as Jacksonville, Memphis and Los Angeles where he was looking over the Coliseum even before Al Davis began moving in from Oakland. As one observer put it, Irsay's travels around the country produced more press than the Colts did all season long. Even so, the motion to move the Colts did result in some favorable results. Irsay's biggest gripe was the need for improved local stadium facilities and Maryland's governor, along with Baltimore's mayor, have given tacit approval to a 21-million-dollar stadium improvement bill, assuming it passes the state legislature.

McCormack, however, may be inheriting a situation that will be difficult to resolve—unless Bert Jones returns to form. The past two seasons have fashioned a Baltimore axiom—"The Colts can win with Jones; they can't win without him." It's as simple as that. Over the past five years, with Jones at quarterback, the Colts have won 36 games and lost 13. Without him, the record is five wins against 20 defeats. No wonder, then, they call him "Mr. Franchise."

Jones's shoulder first became injured in the final exhibition game of 1978 when he was tackled on artificial turf by Al (Bubba) Baker and Ernest Price, then of the Detroit Lions. After missing six regular season games, he came back against the New York Jets and reinjured the same shoulder, sidelining him for two more games. When he did return, a third injury against the Seahawks finished him for the 1978 campaign.

He seemed in fine shape for 1979, but in the opening regular season game against Kansas City, he was dropped again and back he went to the training room for treatment. Greg Landry took over at quarterback, and six games later Jones returned to lead the Colts to victories over Buffalo and New England, clicking them off like clockwork. Then, the following Sunday, it happened again. The shoulder became disjointed anew and Landry had to take over for the remainder of the season.

Along with his recognized ability, there is also a Bert Jones mystique that players and coaches alike are conscious of whenever the game is played in Baltimore. Running back Joe Washington (who may be switched to wide receiver this season) senses it: "Bert has that extra ingredient, that fire, that desire to excel. It's like electricity flowing to a light bulb. You never see it, but you know it's there."

Yes, there is a "Jones Mystique."

OFFENSE

Quarterbacks	Ht.	Wt.	Age	Exp.	College
Golsteyn, Jerry	6-4	210	26	4	Northern Illinois
Jones, Bert	6-3	199	29	8	Louisiana State
Landry, Greg	6-4	207	34	13	Massachusetts

Just as has been the case for two seasons now, Baltimore's fortunes are riding on Jones's injured shoulder. Will it stand up and function properly once he takes the field again? Landry started 12 games last season, basically as a replacement for Jones. Fill-in or not, Landry proceeded to set new club records with 270 completions in 457 attempts. Former Giants' QB Golsteyn is available to back up Landry, if he needs one.

Running Backs	Ht.	Wt.	Age	Exp.	College
Bailey, Mark	6-3	237	25	3	Long Beach State
Dickey, Curtis	6-2	205	22	R	Texas A&M
Franklin, Cleveland	6-2	216	25	4	Baylor
Garry, Ben	6-0	203	24	2	Southern Mississippi
Leaks, Roosevelt	5-10	219	27	6	Texas
Lee, Ron	6-4	234	27	4	West Virginia
McCauley, Don	6-1	208	31	10	North Carolina
Washington, Joe	5-10	179	27	5	Oklahoma
White, Charlie	6-0	220	27	3	Bethune-Cookman

Washington was only AFC player to rank among conference's top ten in both rushing and receiving. Leaks is the fullback but that position continues to be a problem. White comes to Baltimore via the free-agent route after stints with the Chargers and Buccaneers. McCauley doesn't run up the yardage he once did. It's a very slow offensive unit.

Receivers	Ht.	Wt.	Age	Exp.	College
Alston, Mack (T)	6-3	237	33	11	U. Md.-Eastern Shore
Burke, Randy (W)	6-2	190	25	3	Kentucky
Butler, Raymond (W)	6-3	200	22	R	Southern Cal
Carr, Roger (W)	6-2	193	28	7	Louisiana Tech
DeRoo, Brian (W)	6-3	190	24	2	Redlands
Doughty, Glenn (W)	6-1	202	29	9	Michigan
McCall, Reese (T)	6-6	230	24	3	Auburn
Siani, Mike (W)	6-2	199	30	9	Villanova

W=wide receiver   T=tight end

The name of Baltimore's top receiver doesn't appear above. Rather it's with the running backs. Joe Washington's 82 receptions last season was tops in the NFL, marking the second time in the past three years that a Colt has been the league's leading pass-catcher. Along with that, the Colts had four receivers (Washington, RB McCauley, McCall and Doughty) who each gained more than 500 yards in receptions. No other AFC team could lay a similar claim. The Colts have plenty of able catchers around for anyone able to throw. Carr continues to be unavailable on and off because of injuries and training-room visits.

Interior Linemen	Ht.	Wt.	Age	Exp.	College
Baker, Ron (G)	6-4	245	26	3	Oklahoma State
Donaldson, Ray (C)	6-3	253	22	R	Georgia
Foley, Tim (T)	6-5	265	22	R	Notre Dame
Griffin, Wade (T)	6-5	253	26	4	Mississippi
Gross, Lee (C)	6-3	232	27	5	Auburn
Hart, Jeff (T)	6-5	258	27	4	Oregon State
Huff, Ken (G)	6-4	250	27	6	North Carolina
Kunz, George (T)	6-5	265	33	11	Notre Dame
Mendenhall, Ken (C)	6-3	241	32	10	Oklahoma
Pratt, Robert (G)	6-4	249	29	7	North Carolina
Van Duyne, Bob (G-C)	6-4	247	28	7	Idaho

T=tackle   G=guard   C=center

Baltimore's rushing offense ranked 12th in the AFC last season, which makes this unit questionable in its efficiency. Also, the opposing defense sacked Baltimore's QB 52 times, one of the league's highest totals. Griffin, Pratt, Mendenhall, Huff and Hart comprised the front line at season's end. McCormack may do some shaking up here. Kunz is coming out of retirement now that his back problem has healed. He has expressed admiration for McCormack as the new coach.

Kickers	Ht.	Wt.	Age	Exp.	College
Dilts, Bucky (P)	5-9	183	27	4	Georgia
Mike-Mayer, Steve (Pk)	6-0	180	33	6	Maryland
Clabo, Neil (P)	6-0	205	28	4	Tennessee

Pk=placekicker   P=punter

Mike-Mayer led club in scoring with an unimpressive 61 points. Still, he made good 28-29 points-after and 11-of-20 FGs when the Colts' offense put him in proper position to kick for the money. Dilts punted 99 times but his average was not all that high, being 36.2. The kicking game lacks overall punch.

DEFENSE

Front Linemen	Ht.	Wt.	Age	Exp.	College
Barnes, Mike (T)	6-6	255	30	8	Miami (Fla.)
Cook, Fred (E)	6-4	252	28	7	Southern Mississippi
Ehrmann, Joe (T)	6-4	262	31	8	Syracuse
Fernandes, Ron (E)	6-4	255	29	6	Eastern Michigan
Fields, Greg (E)	6-7	254	25	2	Grambling
Krahl, Jim (T)	6-5	252	25	3	Texas Tech
Orvis, Herb (T)	6-4	249	34	9	Colorado
Ozdowski, Mike (E)	6-5	243	25	3	Virginia
Schaum, Greg (E)	6-4	260	26	3	Michigan State

E=end   T=tackle

Ehrmann's injury problems have left a big void in the defensive line. More depth is needed to either replace or shore up a defensive unit which showed little to commend itself last season. Cook led club in QB sacks with 11. Schaum comes to his hometown of Baltimore after three seasons with the Cowboys and two with Patriots. He could help local folks. When they aren't playing, tackles Ehrmann and Barnes are catering—not to opposing quarterbacks, but to people who want to serve food to groups and parties. They have trucks rolling through the Baltimore area, their sides painted with two football helmets, a knife and a fork.

Linebackers	Ht.	Wt.	Age	Exp.	College
Heimkreiter, Steve (O)	6-2	228	23	1	Notre Dame
Krauss, Barry (M)	6-3	233	23	2	Alabama
Priestner, John (O)	6-2	230	22	1	Western Ontario
Shiver, Sanders (O)	6-2	226	25	5	Carson-Newman
Simonini, Ed (M)	6-0	215	26	5	Texas A&M
Smith, Ed (O)	6-1	220	23	R	Vanderbilt
Woods, Mike (O)	6-2	228	26	2	Cincinnati

O=outside   M=middle

Simonini reclaimed his regular middle linebacking job from rookie Barry Krauss at midseason. After playing against Miami's Csonka twice and Houston's Campbell once, Simonini made a statement that may surprise some. "I'd much rather go against Campbell," he reveals. "Csonka ran into me once and let me tell you, if he's lost anything I don't know about it." But don't short-sell Krauss. He's in the league to stay with the future stretching out brightly ahead. Simonini led club with 158 tackles, 13 assists. Shiver was second with 114 and 16, and he also intercepted four passes.

Defensive Backs	Ht.	Wt.	Age	Exp.	College
Anderson, Kim (CB-S)	5-11	172	23	1	Arizona State
Blackwood, Lyle (S)	6-1	187	29	8	Texas Christian
Braziel, Larry (CB)	6-0	191	26	2	Southern Cal
Brown, Keith (S)	5-11	200	23	R	Minnesota
Cale, Bobby (CB)	6-1	191	23	1	North Carolina
Dunn, Mike (CB)	6-4	185	23	1	Duke
Glasgow, Nesby (S-CB)	5-10	176	23	2	Washington
Hatchett, Derrick (CB)	5-11	182	22	R	Texas
Laird, Bruce (S)	6-1	194	30	9	American Intern'tl
Nettles, Doug (CB)	5-11	180	29	6	Vanderbilt
Pinkney, Reggie (S)	5-11	181	25	4	East Carolina
Perry, Harold (S)	6-2	190	24	R	Southern Methodist

CB=cornerback   S=safety

Braziel and Glasgow, as rookies, started in the secondary, but further hard knocks will determine their future. Glasgow is also the club's very good punt and kickoff returner. Anderson, of whom great things were expected, spent the year on injured reserve. He could displace somebody if healthy. Braziel made at least one all-rookie team at season's end. Brown, Cale and Dunn have some training camp or actual experience in the NFL, but not much. Still, they're looking for work in the right place.

Note: A complete listing of Baltimore's 1980 college draft selections can be found on page 268.

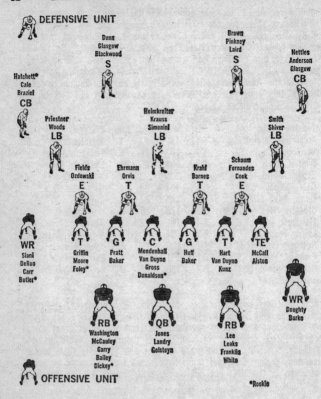

DEFENSIVE UNIT

Dunn
Glasgow
Blackwood
S

Brown
Pinkney
Laird
S

Nettles
Anderson
Glasgow
CB

Hatchett*
Cale
Braziel
CB

Priestner
Woods
LB

Heimkreiter
Krauss
Simonini
LB

Smith
Shiver
LB

Fields
Ozdowski
E

Ehrmann
Orvis
T

Krahl
Barnes
T

Schaum
Fernandes
Cook
E

WR
Siani
DeRoo
Carr
Butler*

Griffin
Moore
Foley*
T

Pratt
Baker
G

Mendenhall
Van Duyne
Gross
Donaldson*
C

Huff
Baker
G

Hart
Van Duyne
Kunz
T

McCall
Alston
TE

WR
Doughty
Burke

RB
Washington
McCauley
Garry
Bailey
Dickey*

QB
Jones
Landry
Golsteyn

RB
Lee
Leaks
Franklin
White

OFFENSIVE UNIT

*Rookie

1979 COLTS STATISTICS

	Colts	Opps.
Total Points Scored	271	351
Total First Downs	291	265
Third Down Efficiency Percentage	41.2	38.7
Yards Rushing—First Downs	1674—97	2306—106
Passes Attempted—Completions	550—313	411—203
Yards Passing—First Downs	3172—158	2768—130
QB Sacked—Yards Lost	52—403	39—312
Interceptions By—Return Average	23—16.6	19—16.9
Punts—Average Yards	101—36.2	95—40.0
Punt Returns—Average Return	49—8.0	43—6.9
Kickoff Returns—Average Return	70—20.0	57—18.7
Fumbles—Ball Lost	36—21	25—16
Penalties—Yards	137—1239	112—1014

STATISTICAL LEADERS

Scoring	TDs	Rush.	Pass.	Ret.	PATs	FGs	Total
Mike-Mayer	0	0	0	0	28—29	11—20	61
Washington	7	4	3	0	0	0	42
McCauley	6	3	3	0	0	0	36
Hardeman	4	3	1	0	0	0	24
McCall	4	0	4	0	0	0	24
Braziel	2	0	0	2	0	0	12
Doughty	2	0	2	0	0	0	12
Linhart	0	0	0	0	3—4	3—8	12

Rushing	Atts.	Yds.	Avg.	Longest	TDs
Washington	242	884	3.7	26	4
Hardeman	109	292	2.7	16	3
McCauley	59	168	2.8	13	3
Leaks	49	145	3.0	17	1
Landry	31	115	3.7	17	0
Garry	13	41	3.2	14	0

Passing	Atts.	Com.	Yds.	Pct.	Int.	Longest	TDs
Landry	457	270	2932	59.1	15	67 (TD)	15
Jones	92	43	643	46.7	3	59	3

Receiving	No.	Yds.	Avg.	Longest	TDs
Washington	82	750	9.1	43 (TD)	3
McCauley	55	575	10.5	35	3
McCall	37	536	14.5	36	4
Doughty	35	510	14.6	54	2
Carr	27	400	14.8	37	1
Hardeman	25	115	4.6	14	1
Siani	15	214	14.3	31 (TD)	2
Leaks	14	119	8.5	15	0

Interceptions	No.	Yds.	Avg.	Longest	TDs
Shiver	4	85	21.3	52	0
Blackwood	4	63	15.8	27	0
Braziel	4	49	12.3	31 (TD)	1
Laird	3	101	33.7	68	0
Thompson	2	38	19.0	26	0
Nettles	2	30	15.0	30	0

Punting	No.	Yds.	Avg.	Longest	Inside 20	Blocked
Dilts	99	3657	36.9	53	21	2

Punt Returns	No.	FCs	Yds.	Avg.	Longest	TDs
Glasgow	44	11	352	8.0	75 (TD)	1

Kickoff Returns	No.	Yds.	Avg.	Longest	TDs
Glasgow	50	1126	22.5	58	0
Garry	8	135	16.9	24	0
Laird	3	34	11.3	16	0
Blackwood	3	41	13.7	19	0
McCauley	2	29	14.5	17	0

PITTSBURGH STEELERS

Head Coach: Chuck Noll

12th Year   **Record:** 100–57–1

1979 RECORD (12-4) (capital letters indicate home games)		1980 SCHEDULE (capital letters indicate home games)	
16 New England	13	HOUSTON	Sept. 7
38 HOUSTON	7	Baltimore	Sept. 14
24 St. Louis	21	Cincinnati	Sept. 21
17 BALTIMORE	13	CHICAGO	Sept. 28
14 Philadelphia	17	Minnesota	Oct. 5
51 Cleveland	35	CINCINNATI	Oct. 12
10 Cincinnati	34	OAKLAND (night, TV)	Oct. 20
42 DENVER	7	Cleveland	Oct. 26
14 DALLAS	3	GREEN BAY	Nov. 2
38 WASHINGTON	7	Tampa Bay	Nov. 9
30 Kansas City	3	CLEVELAND	Nov. 16
7 San Diego	35	Buffalo	Nov. 23
33 CLEVELAND	30	MIAMI	Nov. 30
37 CINCINNATI	17	Houston (night, TV)	Dec. 4
17 Houston	20	KANSAS CITY	Dec. 14
28 BUFFALO	0	San Diego (night, TV)	Dec. 22
416	262		
Playoffs			
34 MIAMI	14		
27 HOUSTON	13		
31 LOS ANGELES	19		

If the Pittsburgh Steelers have any weaknesses, they certainly know how to hide them. And with four Super Bowl titles on their record book and in their trophy room, all they have to shoot for now is a bid to surpass the legendary Green Bay Packers as perhaps the greatest team in NFL history. It's something like trying to become greater than the Yankees in baseball lore. (The Babe Ruth–Lou Gehrig Yankees, that is—not the current edition.)

Still, the Steelers have work that must be done. They must shore up their personnel against the day when they can no longer call on the services of 34-year-old

Jon Kolb, 30-year-old Franco Harris, or 34-year-old
L. C. Greenwood. Around these aging, if but slowly
aging, players the Pittsburgh offense and defense find
their true balance between gung-ho youth and veteran
experience. It's understandably unusual for rookies to
break into the Pittsburgh starting lineup, and the abilities of Steeler draft picks remain a mystery for at least
a year or two. It's that kind of a club. After all, how do
you improve upon a four-time Super Bowl winner? It's
hard to believe there's at least one pro football team
that doesn't have to worry about improvement.

Heading all this No. 1 effort is head coach Chuck
Noll and 1980 presents a goal no different from his
eleven other seasons at Pittsburgh: stay ahead of the
AFC Central pack who've been chasing the Steelers
for years. Commenting at a news conference at the
Los Angeles Marriott just before Super Bowl XIV, Noll
gave an insight into his thinking about the game and
the team. Moving from subject to subject, he answered
questions and offered opinions: "I think this is my
best team. Football is progress and we've progressed.
Our players and training methods are more efficient.
In our viewpoint, this Super Bowl game is no different
than any other big game. Our players respond to big
games. They really get excited about them. This Pittsburgh team has more depth. Early in the season we had
problems in the defensive line, but Gary Dunn and
Tom Beasley came forward and played well. When
we lost linebackers Robin Cole and Loren Toews,
Dennis Winston came in and did very well. And I think
good defense is a thing of beauty."

And it's defense where the Steelers have the greatest
depth. It isn't called the Steel Curtain for nothing.
What used to be the Pittsburgh "front four" is now
the front seven—meaning there's plenty more where
the first four came from. Behind ends L. C. Greenwood

and John Banaszak, tackles Joe Greene and Gary Dunn, there's Dwight White, and beyond them are the proven reserves such as Tom Beasley, Steve Furness and newcomer Willie Fry. The linebacking corps has the same kind of depth, as Noll so aptly pointed out during the Super Bowl news conference.

At the heart of the Pittsburgh offense, of course, is Terry Bradshaw, who received his second straight Most Valuable Player Award at Super Bowl XIV. Even though he threw more touchdown passes last season than most quarterbacks, he still didn't rate among the first five in the AFC. Houston linebacker Greg Bingham sees the Steeler quarterback through the competitor's eyes: "With Bradshaw, the Steelers are much tougher. He's an excellent physical specimen. He has excellent eyesight. He has excellent receivers. He knows what he's doing. When he throws the ball seven feet, two inches in the air and Lynn Swann leaps up to get it, how you gonna stop them?"

As for the future, Bradshaw says he'll play football for two more years and then retire. In a recent moment of reflective philosophy, he surveyed his personal scene: "I've given football everything I've had and football has given me everything I have. I never dreamed of having this success. I've won every award there is and there aren't that many. All I can do is give it all I've got, and maybe win another Super Bowl."

So, there we have it. The die is cast. The Steelers are out to win their fifth Super Bowl. Which teams will they have to overrun in 1980 in order to earn the right to play in Super Bowl XV in New Orleans on January 25, 1981? In addition to the customary AFC Central opponents—Cincinnati, Houston and Cleveland—the Steelers take on the following other NFL teams with the all-time series records shown in parentheses:

HOME: Miami (2-3), Oakland (5-6), Kansas City (6-2), Chicago (3-16-1) and Green Bay (8-19). AWAY: Buffalo (5-1), Baltimore (7-3), San Diego (6-1), Minnesota (3-4) and Tampa Bay (1-0). (Series record with Cincinnati is 14-6, Cleveland 24-36 and Houston 16-6.)

One pertinent footnote to the schedule's home-and-away aspect. The Steelers rarely lose a game on their home field at Three Rivers Stadium. They were 10-0 there last season, but could do no better than break even at 4-4 on the opposition's home fields. Probably no team in the NFL derives a greater advantage from playing in its own backyard. Even in Super Bowl XIV in the Rose Bowl at Pasadena, was Los Angeles the home team? Of course not. The designated "home team" was Pittsburgh!

OFFENSE

Quarterbacks	Ht.	Wt.	Age	Exp.	College
Bradshaw, Terry	6-3	215	32	11	Louisiana Tech
Hurley, Bill	5-11	195	22	R	Syracuse
Kruczek, Mike	6-1	205	27	5	Boston College
Malone, Mark	6-4	223	21	R	Arizona State
Stoudt, Cliff	6-4	218	25	4	Youngstown State

Bradshaw set club records by completing 259 passes out of 472 attempts for 3,724 yards, thereby becoming also the Steelers' first 3,000-yard passer. Kruczek didn't play much, but when he did his passing was excellent—13 completions of 20 throws for a 65 percent average. Bradshaw couldn't hope for a better backup. Stoudt doesn't see much action these days. And what's this! Pittsburgh chose two quarterbacks in the draft, both of them top round picks. Highly regarded Mark Malone was tapped in the first round as the 28th and last choice. Hurley was chosen in the fourth. Perhaps Chuck Noll is taking seriously Bradshaw's talk about calling it quits and strumming a guitar with his throwing hand.

Running Backs	Ht.	Wt.	Age	Exp.	College
Anderson, Anthony	6-0	197	24	2	Temple
Bleier, Rocky	5-11	210	34	12	Notre Dame
Davis, Russell	6-1	215	24	2	Michigan
Harris, Franco	6-2	225	30	9	Penn State
Hawthorne, Greg	6-2½	225	24	2	Baylor
Moser, Rick	6-0	210	24	3	Rhode Island
Thornton, Sidney	5-11	230	26	4	NW Louisiana

Harris finished the season as the NFL's No. 4 all-time runner. By traveling 1,000 yards or more for seven seasons, Harris also tied Jim Brown's NFL record. Bleier and Thornton together rushed for a thousand yards. Hawthorne, a rookie in such fast company, had a chance to both play and sit and watch. He carried 28 times for 123 yards and a 4.4 average. Anderson did even better, averaging 6.6 in 18 carries. The ground offense stays strong.

Receivers	Ht.	Wt.	Age	Exp.	College
Bell, Theo (W)	5-11	180	27	4	Arizona
Cunningham, Bennie (T)	6-5	247	26	5	Clemson
Douglas, Larry (W)	6-1	187	23	2	Southern U.
Grossman, Randy (T)	6-1	215	28	7	Temple
Smith, Jim (W)	6-2	205	25	4	Michigan
Stallworth, John (W)	6-2	183	28	7	Alabama A&M
Swann, Lynn (W)	6-0	180	28	7	Southern Cal
Sweeney, Calvin (W)	6-0	180	25	2	Southern Cal
Sydnor, Ray (T)	6-8	225	22	R	Wisconsin

W=wide receiver   T=tight end

Stallworth's 1,183 yards receiving are second most in Steeler history, behind Buddy Dial's 1,295 in 1963. Stallworth and Swann comprise the greatest pass receiving duo this side of basketball. Both are gifted acrobats and their hands are superb. Cunningham is fast and goes deep if the defenses come in close. And who's surprised to learn that Swann is now a trustee of the Pittsburgh Ballet Theatre? After all, he did study dance for 14 years including two years of ballet, and attributes his agility on the field to that training. Tickets to Swann Lake, anyone? At 6-foot-8 and 225 pounds, rookie Ray Sydnor just has to be the biggest tight end in the business.

Interior Linemen	Ht.	Wt.	Age	Exp.	College
Brown, Larry (T)	6-4	245	31	10	Kansas
Courson, Steve (G)	6-1	260	25	3	South Carolina
Davis, Sam (G)	6-1	255	36	14	Allen University
Dornbrook, Thom (C-G)	6-2	240	24	2	Kentucky
Kolb, Jon (T)	6-2	262	33	12	Oklahoma State
Mullins, Gary (G)	6-3	244	31	10	Southern Cal
Petersen, Ted (T)	6-5	244	25	4	Eastern Illinois

Pinney, Ray (T)	6-4	240	26	5	Washington
Webster, Mike (C)	6-1½	250	28	7	Wisconsin
Wolfley, Craig (G)	6-1	267	21	R	Syracuse

T=tackle   G=guard   C=center

Best clue to the Steeler offensive line is the fact that Pittsburgh led all 28 NFL teams in total offense. The total rushing-passing yardage of 6,258 was second highest in league history. (Only Houston's 6,288 yards in 1961 was higher, but that total was run up in the old American Football League which often featured more offensive fireworks than a three-ring circus.) All hail, then, to the Super Bowl offensive line—Kolb and Petersen, Davis, Webster, Mullins and Brown.

Kickers	Ht.	Wt.	Age	Exp.	College
Bahr, Matt (Pk)	5-10	165	24	2	Penn State
Colquitt, Craig (P)	6-1½	182	26	3	Tennessee

Pk=placekicker   P=punter

Bahr convinced even Gerela's Gorillas in his rookie year out of Penn State. He nailed 50 of 52 points-after, and 18 of 30 FGs, six of them coming from 40-to-49 yards out. He was perfect at 6-6 between the 20-29 yard lines. Colquitt, in his second year out of Tennessee, averaged 40.8 which keeps him in place. His longest boot was 61 yards.

DEFENSE

Front Linemen	Ht.	Wt.	Age	Exp.	College
Anderson, Fred (E)	6-4½	250	26	3	Prairie View
Banaszak, John (E)	6-3	244	30	6	Eastern Michigan
Beasley, Tom (T)	6-5	253	26	3	Virginia Tech
Dunn, Gary (T)	6-3	247	27	4	Notre Dame
Furness, Steve (T)	6-4	255	30	9	Rhode Island
Goodman, John (E)	6-6	245	21	R	Oklahoma
Greene, Joe (T)	6-4	260	34	12	North Texas State
Greenwood, L. C. (E)	6-6½	250	34	12	Arkansas AM&N
White, Dwight (E)	6-4	255	31	10	East Texas State

E=end   T=tackle

The Steelers held opponents to less than 100 yards on the ground during nine regular season games. The Super Bowl defensive line was Greenwood, Greene, Dunn and Banaszak. It was an historic line. Regarding that soft drink TV commercial starring Joe Greene during the off-season, the advertising agency says, "Joe was a real trooper. We started at seven in the morning and finished up with Joe drinking from a 16-ounce bottle—16 of them in a row at three o'clock in the morning." The kid who got Joe's jersey apparently had his price, in that highly popular and well-received commercial.

Linebackers	Ht.	Wt.	Age	Exp.	College
Cole, Robin (O)	6-2	220	25	4	New Mexico
Graves, Tom (O)	6-3	228	25	2	Michigan State
Ham, Jack (O)	6-1	225	32	10	Penn State
Kohrs, Bob (O)	6-3	224	21	R	Arizona State
Lambert, Jack (M)	6-4	220	28	7	Kent State
Toews, Loren (O)	6-3	222	29	8	California
Valentine, Zack (O)	6-2	220	23	2	East Carolina
Winston, Dennis (M)	6-0	228	25	4	Arkansas

O=outside   M=middle

Lambert has been Pittsburgh's leading tackler for each of his six seasons with the team, having 119 tackles and 46 assists in 1979. He also intercepted six passes, a league high for linebackers. Jim Murray, writing in the Los Angeles Times on Super Bowl weekend, described Lambert this way: "He plays football the way Attila the Hun sacked villages. Seeing a man with a football drives him into a towering rage, and the resultant reaction looks like a reformer busting up a saloon, or a cop jumping through a skylight into a crap game." Ham hurt his ankle and missed the playoffs, but he'll be back. Winston started several games and impressed everybody, including the coaches. They shall not pass. . . .

Defensive Backs	Ht.	Wt.	Age	Exp.	College
Anderson, Larry (CB)	5-11	177	24	3	Louisiana Tech
Blount, Mel (CB)	6-3	205	32	11	Southern U.
Johnson, Ron (CB)	5-10	200	24	3	Eastern Michigan
Shell, Donnie (S)	5-11	190	28	7	South Carolina State
Thomas, J. T. (S)	6-2	196	29	7	Florida State
Wagner, Mike (S)	6-1½	200	31	10	Western Illinois
Woodruff, Dwayne (CB-S)	5-11	189	23	2	Louisville

CB=cornerback   S=safety

When Wagner is hurt, Thomas goes in and everything stays right on track. Two of these defensive backs played in the Pro Bowl last season and two others have been there before. All these secondary players are hard tacklers. Blount is powerful on single coverage. Shell intercepted five passes, Wagner four. The team stole 27 passes during season. Perhaps former Oakland Coach John Madden sized it up best by saying, "The Pittsburgh secondary tackles like linebackers. . . . It's the equivalent of seven linebackers."

Note: A complete listing of Pittsburgh's 1980 college draft selections can be found on page 276.

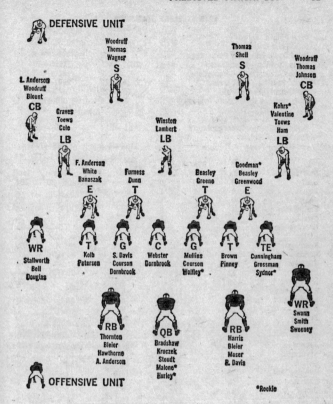

DEFENSIVE UNIT

Woodruff
Thomas
Wagner
S

Thomas
Shell
S

Woodruff
Thomas
Johnson
CB

L. Anderson
Woodruff
Blount
CB

Graves
Toews
Cole
LB

Winston
Lambert
LB

Kohrs*
Valentine
Toews
Ham
LB

F. Anderson
White
Banaszak
E

Furness
Dunn
T

Beasley
Greene
T

Goodman*
Beasley
Greenwood
E

WR
Stallworth
Bell
Douglas

T
Kolb
Petersen

G
S. Davis
Courson
Dornbrook

C
Webster
Dornbrook

G
Mullins
Courson
Wolfley*

T
Brown
Pinney

TE
Cunningham
Grossman
Sydnor*

RB
Thornton
Bleier
Hawthorne
A. Anderson

QB
Bradshaw
Kruczek
Stoudt
Malone*
Hurley*

RB
Harris
Bleier
Moser
R. Davis

WR
Swann
Smith
Sweeney

OFFENSIVE UNIT

*Rookie

1979 STEELERS STATISTICS

	Steelers	Opps.
Total Points Scored	416	262
Total First Downs	337	260
Third Down Efficiency Percentage	43.2	30.8
Yards Rushing—First Downs	2603—141	1709—95
Passes Attempted—Completions	492—272	480—226
Yards Passing—First Downs	3655—179	2561—135
QB Sacked—Yards Lost	27—222	49—351
Interceptions By—Return Average	27—7.4	26—15.4
Punts—Average Yards	68—40.8	100—40.0
Punt Returns—Average Return	63—8.3	31—8.9
Kickoff Returns—Average Return	51—19.4	81—20.6
Fumbles—Ball Lost	47—26	32—15
Penalties—Yards	108—866	95—744

STATISTICAL LEADERS

Scoring	TDs	Rush.	Pass.	Ret.	PATs	FGs	Total
Bahr	0	0	0	0	50—52	18—30	104
Harris	12	11	1	0	0	0	72
Thornton	10	6	4	0	0	0	60
Stallworth	8	0	8	0	0	0	48
Swann	6	1	5	0	0	0	36
Cunningham	4	0	4	0	0	0	24
Bleier	4	4	0	0	0	0	24

Rushing	Atts.	Yds.	Avg.	Longest	TDs
Harris	267	1186	4.4	71 (TD)	11
Thornton	118	585	5.0	75	6
Bleier	92	434	4.7	70 (TD)	4
Hawthorne	28	123	4.4	19	1
A. Anderson	18	118	6.6	31	1
Bradshaw	21	83	4.0	28	0
Moser	11	33	3.0	8	1

Passing	Atts.	Com.	Yds.	Pct.	Int.	Longest	TDs
Bradshaw	472	259	3724	54.9	25	65 (TD)	26
Kruczek	20	13	153	65.0	1	31	0

Receiving	No.	Yds.	Avg.	Longest	TDs
Stallworth	70	1183	16.9	65 (TD)	8
Swann	41	808	19.7	65	5
Cunningham	36	512	14.2	41	4
Harris	36	291	8.1	21	1
Bleier	31	277	8.9	28	0
Smith	17	243	14.3	25	2
Thornton	16	231	14.4	32	4
Grossman	12	217	18.1	54	1
Hawthorne	8	47	5.9	17	0

Interceptions	No.	Yds.	Avg.	Longest	TDs
Lambert	6	29	4.8	23	0
Shell	5	10	2.0	8	0
Wagner	4	31	7.8	19	0
Winston	3	48	16.0	41 (TD)	1
Blount	3	1	0.3	1	0
Ham	2	8	4.0	6	0

Punting	No.	Yds.	Avg.	Longest	Inside 20	Blocked
Colquitt	68	2773	40.8	61	19	0

Punt Returns	No.	FCs	Yds.	Avg.	Longest	TDs
Smith	16	1	146	9.1	38	0
Bell	45	7	378	8.4	27	0

Kickoff Returns	No.	Yds.	Avg.	Longest	TDs
L. Anderson	34	732	21.5	44	0
A. Anderson	13	200	15.4	26	0
Hawthorne	2	46	23.0	23	0

HOUSTON OILERS

Head Coach: O. A. (Bum) Phillips

6th Year   **Record: 44–30**

1979 RECORD (11-5) (capital letters indicate home games)			1980 SCHEDULE (capital letters indicate home games)	
29	Washington	27	Pittsburgh	Sept. 7
7	Pittsburgh	38	Cleveland (night, TV)	Sept. 15
20	KANSAS CITY	6	BALTIMORE	Sept. 21
30	Cincinnati	27	Cincinnati	Sept. 28
31	CLEVELAND	10	SEATTLE	Oct. 5
17	ST. LOUIS	24	Kansas City	Oct. 12
28	Baltimore	16	TAMPA BAY	Oct. 19
14	Seattle	34	CINCINNATI	Oct. 26
27	N.Y. JETS	24	Denver	Nov. 2
9	Miami	6	NEW ENGLAND (night, TV)	Nov. 10
31	OAKLAND	17	Chicago	Nov. 16
42	CINCINNATI	21	N.Y. Jets	Nov. 23
30	Dallas	24	CLEVELAND	Nov. 30
7	Cleveland	14	PITTSBURGH (night, TV)	Dec. 4
20	PITTSBURGH	17	Green Bay	Dec. 14
20	PHILADELPHIA	26	MINNESOTA	Dec. 21
362		331		
Playoffs				
13	DENVER	7		
17	San Diego	14		
13	Pittsburgh	27		

It was a highly charged, extremely emotional moment in Houston, a city where football competes with oil as a prime topic of conversation. Coach Bum Phillips and his Oilers, "fallen heroes" as they were called in the Texas press releases, had just returned `home to the Astrodome, there to receive a thunderous welcome from some 70,000 assembled fans. They were gathered there to assure the Oilers that losing the AFC championship and a spot in the Super Bowl to Pittsburgh didn't necessarily mean the world was coming to an end—at least, not right away. Only hours before in Pittsburgh, the Steelers had triumphed in the title game,

27-13, and were already packing their bags for the trip to Pasadena.

As the massed fans alternately cheered, applauded or remained silent, the Oilers arose one by one to express thanks for the loyal support they had received all season long. Some spoke in very emotional terms, choking up and speaking slowly, with feeling. It was that kind of a homecoming for a team which had beaten four NFL divisional championship teams, including the Steelers, and still fell 15 points short of the Super Bowl.

Then came Bum Phillips's time to say a few words, and the applause rose to a crescendo as he moved to a hastily improvised microphone on the platform overlooking the huge crowd. Words came hard for Bum too, very hard. In fact, he was moved to tears. Loyalty in the face of adversity will do that for a man.

"I'd like to tell you why I don't want to talk, because I'm crying," he finally managed to say. "There's not any way, I'm not smart enough, not eloquent enough. But let me say this. [and here his voice began to rise] Last year, we knocked on the door. This year we beat on it, and next year we're going to kick it in!"

In referring to "next year" of course, Bum meant 1980, and he looks forward to the new campaign confident the Oilers have no major weaknesses to fill. True, the team must accommodate the style of a new, left-handed quarterback in Ken Stabler who came to Houston from Oakland in a much-heralded, off-season trade for Dan Pastorini. If Stabler can make his eleventh NFL season a productive one, it could be the spark that not only puts the Oilers in the playoffs again, but could even take them beyond that. Still, there's something else that bothers Bum in considering his team's future. Strangely, the Oilers seem to play much better and win against the NFL's strong clubs, and then fold up and lose when playing the weaker clubs. "We've got to develop a killer instinct," says the kindly Phillips. "If we're ever going to get the home-field advantage for the playoffs, we've got to learn to hammer the teams we're supposed to merely jump on. We need to bury them, put them away in the first half like Pittsburgh does. We play good against the good teams, but not against the weaker ones."

All that talk about getting tough with the weaker teams may have been what Bum had in mind when he traded running back Kenny King for Oakland safety Jack Tatum, otherwise known as an author who wrote a biography entitled, "They Call Me Assassin." Tatum, now in his 10th NFL year, isn't noted for exercising physical restraint on the field, especially when defending against pass-receivers who venture into his territory.

Phillips makes a good point there. Early in the season, the Oilers lost to underdog St. Louis, 17-24, in the Astrodome and the defeat eventually could have meant playing at home in the playoffs against a team like, say, Pittsburgh. More and more, playoff-bound teams are including a bid for home-field advantage in their overall season-long strategy. And Phillips would like nothing better than playing at home for no other reason perhaps than saving his hat. For the second straight year, somebody stole his cowboy hat during or after the game in Pittsburgh, although this year it was returned by the snatcher.

The Stabler–Pastorini trade has touched off much speculation concerning the overall effect it will have on both the Oilers and the Raiders once the new campaign gets underway. Some NFL observers believe both teams will benefit from the exchange, but at least one qualified person sees it in an entirely different light. Bud Carson, the Los Angeles Rams' defensive coordinator, believes marked differences in the offensive styles of the two clubs will necessitate tremendous adjustments for both quarterbacks. "I don't think either team will be as good as it would have been had it kept their quarterbacks," Carson explains. "For one thing, the Oakland and Houston passing games are very different. Oakland's receivers, for instance, run much deeper routes than other teams—18 to 22 yards—then they whirl around and come back to meet the pass. Pastorini will have to make that adjustment and, of course, the Oakland offensive line will have to protect him that extra second. As for Stabler and the Oilers, while at Oakland he was used to dropping back, holding the football and looking around for one of those turn-around targets. Now he's gonna have to throw quicker. Obviously, I'd rather play either team early, before all that adjustment takes place. . . ."

Earl Campbell, who seems to have already replaced O. J. Simpson as the NFL's premier running back, is reported to have signed a $3-million contract, covering six years with the Oilers. This supposedly also substantially improves the five-year pact for $1.3-million he negotiated originally when he joined the Oilers in '78. And that's quite a financial plum for the lad from Tyler, Texas, who is known affectionately to the Houston fans as the "Tyler Rose."

OFFENSE

Quarterbacks	Ht.	Wt.	Age	Exp.	College
Bradshaw, Craig	6-5	215	22	R	Utah State
Merkens, Guido	6-1	200	25	3	Sam Houston State
Nielsen, Gifford	6-4	205	26	3	Brigham Young
Stabler, Ken	6-3	210	35	11	Alabama

Dan Pastorini has gone home to California (that's where he's from), and will be pitching for Oakland while Ken Stabler throws 'em for Bum Phillips and the Oilers. The debate rages on. Did both teams gain by the swap? Or did they suffer, at least temporarily? Stabler was rated second among AFC passers last season, throwing for 3,615 yards, 26 TDs and a 61 percent completion average. He just might give the Oilers a championship boost. Nielsen continues to show good form whenever the opportunity arises. As a backup to Pastorini, he completed 32 of 61 passes last season for 52.5 percent. Merkens is also a backup wide receiver. Houston received a seventh round draft pick from Oakland as part of the trade which brought safety Jack Tatum to the Oil Capital. And that selection turned out to be none other than Craig Bradshaw, younger brother of Pittsburgh's Terry. If he makes the team, Craig won't find his role as a backup QB an unfamiliar one. That's what he was at Utah State last season, second-string QB to Eric Hipple who was drafted in the fourth round by Detroit.

Running Backs	Ht.	Wt.	Age	Exp.	College
Campbell, Earl	5-11	224	25	3	Texas
Carpenter, Rob	6-1	214	25	4	Miami (O.)
Clark, Boobie	6-2	245	30	8	Bethune-Cookman
Coleman, Ronnie	5-11	198	29	7	Alabama A&M
Wilson, Tim	6-3	220	26	4	Maryland

Campbell became only the third player in NFL history to capture the league rushing title in each of his first two seasons. Gaining 1,450 yards in '78 and 1,697 in '79, he also became the first NFL runner ever to surpass 3,000 yards in his first two seasons. Campbell also enters the 1980 campaign with a string of seven consecutive 100-yard games. If he reaches the 100 mark in the first game of '80, he'll break a tie he holds with O. J. Simpson who ran for 100 yards or more in seven straight games during 1972-73 schedules. Carpenter and Wilson were the main alternate ball-carriers. Together they ran for more than 600 yards while giving Campbell chances to catch his breath.

Receivers	Ht.	Wt.	Age	Exp.	College
Barber, Mike (T)	6-3	235	27	4	Louisiana Tech
Burrough, Ken (W)	6-3	210	32	11	Texas Southern
Caster, Rich (W)	6-5	230	32	11	Jackson State
Combs, Chris (T)	6-3	242	22	R	New Mexico
Ellender, Richard (W)	5-11	171	23	2	McNeese State
Groth, Jeff (W)	5-10	172	23	2	Bowling Green
Johnson, Billy (W)	5-9	170	28	7	Widener
Renfro, Mike (W)	6-0	184	25	3	Texas Christian
Rucker, Conrad (T)	6-3	260	26	3	Southern U.
Smith, Tim (W)	6-3	194	22	R	Nebraska

W=wide receiver   T=tight end

For the sixth consecutive year, Ken Burrough (No. 00 to TV fans) is Houston's leading receiver. Last season it was 40 for 752 yards and six TDs. Running back Tim Wilson caught 29, while Barber pulled in 27. Stabler will find plenty of targets here. Johnson is still trying to recover from what one doctor calls "the worst knee injury I've ever seen." "Johnny White Shoes" was injured in the season's second game against Pittsburgh, but vows he'll be back this year.

Interior Linemen	Ht.	Wt.	Age	Exp.	College
Carter, David (G-C)	6-2	225	27	4	Western Kentucky
Fields, Angelo (T)	6-6	295	22	R	Michigan State
Fisher, Ed (G)	6-3	250	31	6	Arizona State
Gray, Leon (T)	6-3	260	29	8	Jackson State
Hayman, Conway (T)	6-3	270	31	7	Delaware
Mauck, Carl (C)	6-4	250	33	11	Southern Illinois
Randall, Tom (G)	6-5	245	24	3	Iowa State
Reihner, George (G)	6-4½	263	25	4	Penn State
Schuhmacher, John (G)	6-3½	275	25	3	Southern Cal
Towns, Morris (T)	6-4	275	29	3	Missouri
Young, Randall (G)	6-4	252	26	2	Iowa State

T=tackle   G=guard   C=center

Early last season, the offensive line lost tackle Greg Sampson who has since retired. Also, Reihner had to undergo knee surgery. Only the acquisition of All-Pro tackle Leon Gray from New England kept the line that paves the way for Campbell in business. The left side of the line had been, somehow, patched up. At season's end, the starting line consisted of Gray, Carter, Mauck, Fisher and Hayman. Unless personnel pictures change, they will protect Stabler against the pass rush. Gray believes there'll be added pressure on his position because Stabler, a left-handed passer, is vulnerable to blind-side hits. "It'll be a challenge," Gray predicts, "but I want to give Snake every chance to do well."

Kickers	Ht.	Wt.	Age	Exp.	College
Fritsch, Toni (Pk)	5-7	195	35	9	(None)
Parsley, Cliff (P)	6-1	211	26	4	Oklahoma State

Pk=placekicker   P=punter

Again in '79, Fritsch captured AFC honors as the leading FG percentage kicker (second time in three years) by making good 21 of 25 attempts. Since joining the Oilers as a free agent in 1977, he has converted 47 of 59 FG attempts to become the AFC's all-time most accurate field goal kicker. He played for Dallas and San Diego before signing with Houston. Parsley hit the 40.6 average mark with his 93 punts.

DEFENSE

Front Linemen	Ht.	Wt.	Age	Exp.	College
Baker, Jessee (E)	6-5	265	23	2	Jacksonville State
Bethea, Elvin (E)	6-2	255	34	13	North Carolina A&T
Culp, Curley (MG)	6-1	265	34	13	Arizona State
Dorris, Andy (E)	6-4	240	29	8	New Mexico State
Kennard, Ken (MG)	6-2	245	26	4	Angelo State
Skaugstad, Daryle (T)	6-4	250	22	R	California
Stensrud, Mike (E)	6-5	280	24	2	Iowa State

E=end   MG=middle guard

Culp and Bethea continue to be the backbone of Houston's defense now going into their 13th year. Rookie Jessee Baker showed great talent in the matter of sacking QBs, leading the club with 15 while being used mostly when the opposition seemed ready to pass. Dorris is the third starter in the 3-4 defense.

Linebackers	Ht.	Wt.	Age	Exp.	College
Baumgartner, Steve (O)	6-7	245	29	8	Purdue
Bingham, Greg (I)	6-1	230	29	8	Purdue
Brazile, Robert (O)	6-4	238	27	6	Jackson State
Corker, John (O)	6-5	220	22	R	Oklahoma State
Green, Sammy (O)	6-2	230	26	5	Ohio State
Hunt, Daryl (I)	6-3	220	24	2	Oklahoma
Murphy, Mike (I)	6-2	222	23	2	Southwest Missouri
Stringer, Art (I)	6-2	223	26	4	Ball State
Thompson, Ted (I)	6-1	220	27	6	Southern Methodist
Towns, Tony (O)	6-0	230	24	2	Western Kentucky
Washington, Ted (O)	6-2	245	32	8	Mississippi Valley

O=outside   I=inside

The main trio here is Brazile, Bingham and Washington. Brazile again made All-Pro. He's known as "Mr. Doom" of Houston's fierce 3-4 defense. Bingham led in total tackles, seconded by Brazile. A solid unit for the 1980s.

Defensive Backs	Ht.	Wt.	Age	Exp.	College
Currier, Bill (S)	6-0	195	25	4	South Carolina
Hartwig, Carter (S-CB)	6-0	205	24	2	Southern Cal
Jefferson, Charles (CB)	6-0	178	23	2	McNeese State
Perry, Vernon (S)	6-2	211	27	2	Jackson State
Reinfeldt, Mike (S)	6-2	195	27	3	U. Wis.-Milwaukee
Stemrick, Greg (CB)	5-11	185	29	6	Colorado State
Tatum, Jack (S)	5-11	205	32	10	Florida

Whittington, C. L. (S)	6-1	200	28	7	Prairie View
Wilson, J. C. (CB)	6-0	177	24	3	Pittsburgh

CB=cornerback   S=safety

Reinfeldt's 12 interceptions topped the NFL, as did Houston's 34 pass thefts. Wilson came in with six, while just about everybody else in the secondary got in on the act. Perry received post-season all-rookie honors on at least one team selection. He won a safety position over Bill Currier while Wilson took over a cornerback post.

Note: A complete listing of Houston's 1980 college draft selections can be found on page 271.

DEFENSIVE UNIT 3-4 DEFENSE

Hartwig
Tatum
Reinfeldt
S

Whittington
Currier
Perry
S

Jefferson
J. Wilson
CB

Hartwig
Stemrick
CB

Corker*
Green
Baumgartner
Brazile
LB

Murphy
Hunt
Stringer
LB

Thompson
Bingham
LB

T. Towns
Baumgartner
Washington
LB

Baker
Bethea
E

Skaugstad*
Kennard
Culp
MG

Stensrud
Dorris
E

WR
Burrough
Ellender
Johnson
Groth

T
Gray
Hayman
Fields*

G
Carter
Reihner
Schuhmacher
Young

C
Mauck
Carter

G
Fisher
Carter
Randall

T
Hayman
M. Towns

TE
Barber
Rucker
Combs*

WR
Caster
Renfro
Merkens
Smith*

RB
Campbell
Coleman

QB
Stabler
Nielsen
Merkens

RB
T. Wilson
Carpenter
Clark

OFFENSIVE UNIT

*Rookie

1979 OILERS STATISTICS

	Oilers	Opps.
Total Points Scored	362	331
Total First Downs	268	304
Third Down Efficiency Percentage	41.9	42.9
Yards Rushing—First Downs	2571—149	2225—125
Passes Attempted—Completions	386—195	465—242
Yards Passing—First Downs	2256—100	2765—158
QB Sacked—Yards Lost	32—238	51—422
Interceptions By—Return Average	34—18.2	21—13.8
Punts—Average Yards	93—40.6	73—40.9
Punt Returns—Average Return	38—5.8	64—11.7
Kickoff Returns—Average Return	67—18.4	69—18.9
Fumbles—Ball Lost	31—11	29—16
Penalties—Yards	109—947	103—894

STATISTICAL LEADERS

Scoring	TDs	Rush.	Pass.	Ret.	PATs	FGs	Total
Campbell	19	19	0	0	0	0	114
Fritsch	0	0	0	0	41—43	21—25	104
Burrough	6	0	6	0	0	0	36
Carpenter	4	3	1	0	0	0	24
Barber	3	0	3	0	0	0	18
T. Wilson	3	2	1	0	0	0	18
Renfro	2	0	2	0	0	0	12

Rushing	Atts.	Yds.	Avg.	Longest	TDs
Campbell	368	1697	4.6	61 (TD)	19
Carpenter	92	355	3.9	13	3
T. Wilson	84	319	3.8	19	2
Clark	25	74	2.9	10	0
Coleman	18	58	3.2	9	0
Pastorini	13	23	1.8	14	0

Passing	Atts.	Com.	Yds.	Pct.	Int.	Longest	TDs
Pastorini	324	163	2090	50.3	18	55 (TD)	14
Nielson	61	32	404	52.5	3	41	3

Receiving	No.	Yds.	Avg.	Longest	TDs
Burrough	40	752	18.8	55 (TD)	6
T. Wilson	29	208	7.2	24 (TD)	1
Barber	27	377	13.9	37 (TD)	3
Caster	18	260	14.4	36	1
Renfro	16	323	20.2	49	2
Carpenter	16	116	7.3	22	1
Campbell	16	94	5.9	46	0
Coleman	12	114	9.5	17	1

Interceptions	No.	Yds.	Avg.	Longest	TDs
Reinfeldt	12	205	17.1	39	0
J. Wilson	6	135	22.5	66	1
Bingham	3	78	26.0	54	0
Perry	3	35	11.7	24	0
Stemrick	2	50	25.0	50	0
Brazile	2	45	22.5	26	0
Hartwig	2	24	12.0	24	0
Stringer	2	21	10.5	21	0

Punting	No.	Yds.	Avg.	Longest	Inside 20	Blocked
Parsley	93	3777	40.6	57	14	0

Punt Returns	No.	FCs	Yds.	Avg.	Longest	TDs
Ellender	31	2	203	6.5	36	0
Merkens	2	5	6	3.0	6	0

Kickoff Returns	No.	Yds.	Avg.	Longest	TDs
Ellender	25	541	21.6	35	0
Coleman	16	321	20.1	27	0
Hartwig	10	181	18.1	36	0

CLEVELAND BROWNS

Head Coach: Sam Rutigliano

3rd Year   **Record: 17–15**

1979 RECORD (9-7) (capital letters indicate home games)			1980 SCHEDULE (capital letters indicate home games)	
25	N.Y. Jets	22	New England	Sept. 7
27	Kansas City	24	HOUSTON (night, TV) *	Sept. 15
13	BALTIMORE	10	KANSAS CITY	Sept. 21
26	DALLAS	7	Tampa Bay	Sept. 28
10	Houston	31	DENVER	Oct. 5
35	PITTSBURGH	51	Seattle	Oct. 12
9	WASHINGTON	13	GREEN BAY	Oct. 19
28	CINCINNATI	27	PITTSBURGH	Oct. 26
38	St. Louis	20	CHICAGO (night, TV)	Nov. 3
24	Philadelphia	19	Baltimore	Nov. 9
24	SEATTLE	29	Pittsburgh	Nov. 16
30	MIAMI	24	CINCINNATI	Nov. 23
30	Pittsburgh	33	Houston	Nov. 30
14	HOUSTON	7	N.Y. JETS	Dec. 7
14	Oakland	19	Minnesota	Dec. 14
12	Cincinnati	16	Cincinnati	Dec. 21
359		352		

If the Browns can do as well this year, with all their talent healthy and on the field, as they did last year with some of their best players injured, then a playoff berth come December should be a cinch. Even with so many things working against them last season, they still fell barely short of the playoffs, after close losses to Oakland and Cincinnati in the final weeks of their season.

It was the Cleveland offensive unit that kept the team on the move, and bids fair to do it again, especially with the return of Greg Pruitt and his mended knee. The Browns ranked no less than third offensively in the NFL with an average of 360.8 yards per game, passing and rushing. And it was the aerial game that sparked most of those offensive fireworks—a game that returns intact but may not remain so if quarterback Brian Sipe gets hurt. In that event, the passing offense might come apart at the seams unless a capable reserve quarterback is available. Baltimore and Cincinnati are prime examples of teams which lost their way when the club's one and only quarterback became immobilized.

A unit that started out as perhaps one of the league's best defenses received severe setbacks with injuries to key personnel such as end Lyle Alzado and tackle Jerry Sherk. Alzado, who had arrived from Denver in a trade, wound up the season as Cleveland's only defensive end. Mike St. Clair and Ernie Price have gone elsewhere, also via the trade route, while Jack Gregory was given his release.

And now, the outlook for defense remains bleak with Sherk's chances of playing this season quoted as about 50-50. At least, he's not being counted on. At season's end, he suffered a staph infection that makes his immediate availability doubtful. Regarded as one of the league's finest lineman, Sherk was showing his former All-Pro form when he was sidelined.

In fact, Sherk's injury may have been the primary reason for Cleveland's loss of four games during the stretch run to the playoffs—games lost by a margin of five points or less. In each of these contests, a stronger defense might have saved the day. Add the loss of Sherk's talents to the melancholy fact that the top offensive player, Greg Pruitt, appeared in only five games while premier kickoff returner Keith Wright was likewise sidelined for eleven contests. Rutigliano, obviously, had bad breaks aplenty to contend with all season long.

Just the same, the Cleveland coach believes something positive for the future resulted from all the reversals. He says, "I think we proved a lot of things to ourselves. After being labeled in recent years as a team that couldn't win against contenders, the 1979 season disproved that. We played five playoff teams and defeated four of them, including Dallas, Philadelphia, Miami and Houston. Also, we lost a very close overtime contest to Pittsburgh. I believe we came of age, and belong in the upper echelon of the NFL."

It's worthy of comment that Cleveland played Pittsburgh twice last season and lost both games, the first 51-35 and the second, 33-30. But one admirer of the Cleveland offensive capability cited these two games as an example of the Browns' scoring power: "What kind of an offense does Cleveland have? The Browns scored 65 points in two games against Pittsburgh . . . that's the kind of offense they have!" The comment has a point.

As he faces the new problems that are bound to beset the Browns in the upcoming campaign, Rutigliano is designating his priorities. "There's no question," he admits, "we must make gains in our defense. But that doesn't call for drastic means. We have a number of injured players returning to action. These, along with help we hope for from the college draft, should solidify our defensive line, which is the questionable part of the defensive unit."

One outstanding candidate for a defensive end position is Kent Perkov who came to the Browns as an eighth round choice from San Diego State in the 1979 college draft. Perkov made his presence known forcefully during summer camp while participating in only a few practice sessions—then came down with an injured knee. The Cleveland coaches, however, saw enough to be convinced and Perkov will be welcomed back with some to spare when he comes off knee surgery.

The AFC Central is one of the NFL's most formidable divisions. It not only harbors the four-time Super Bowl champion Pittsburgh Steelers, it's also home port for the Houston Oilers and Cincinnati Bengals—two clubs which usually give the opposition more than a fair share of trouble. The Browns, of course, play each of these clubs twice, and list among their other 1980 opponents such strong teams as Chicago, New York Jets, Denver, Tampa Bay, Minnesota, New England and Seattle. It's going to be a hard row to hoe all the way.

Of interest is the signing of placekicker Berj Yepremian, younger brother of Garo Yepremian who was formerly of the Miami Dolphins and is now with the New Orleans Saints. Berj, a native of Cyprus, set Southeastern Conference placekicking records at the University of Florida. These include 16 field goals in one season and a string of eleven srtaight. He isn't expected to take Don Cockroft's job away just like that—but Don is 35 which makes him almost a senior citizen in the calendar-conscious world of pro football.

OFFENSE

Quarterbacks	Ht.	Wt.	Age	Exp.	College
Evans, Johnny	6-1	197	24	3	North Carolina State
McDonald, Paul	6-2	180	22	R	Southern Cal
Miller, Mark	6-2	176	24	3	Bowling Green
Sipe, Brian	6-1	195	31	7	San Diego State

Sipe was the spark for one of the NFL's best passing attacks, as shown by his new club records for attempts, completions and yards (535-286-3, 793). His 28 passing TDs tied with Grogan of New England as NFL leader. Miller is Sipe's backup, if that test should ever come. Evans is also a quarterback but his main job is punting.

Running Backs	Ht.	Wt.	Age	Exp.	College
Anderson, Rickey	6-1	211	27	2	South Carolina State
Boykin, Greg	6-0	224	27	3	Northwestern

Collins, Larry	5-11	189	25	2	Texas A&I
Hall, Dino	5-7	165	25	2	Glassboro State
Hill, Calvin	6-4	227	33	11	Yale
Miller, Cleo	5-11	214	28	7	Arkansas-Pine Bluff
Moriarty, Pat	6-0	195	25	2	Georgia Tech
Pruitt, Greg	5-10	190	29	8	Oklahoma
Pruitt, Mike	6-0	225	26	5	Purdue
White, Charles	6-0	185	22	R	Southern Cal

Mike Pruitt's career-high 1,294 yards were most by a Brown since Jim Brown's 1,544 in '65. Greg Pruitt went down with a knee injury in early season. If he returns in good shape, the running game will definitely improve. Hill and Miller shared running assignments with Mike Pruitt. Miller is slated to see more action this year. Moriarty and Hall are waiting for game experience, if they can get it. With Billy Sims gone to Detroit as the No. 1 NFL draft pick, the Browns took another Heisman Trophy winner, Charles White, the Southern Cal running back, in the first round as the 27th choice of the day. Which of these Heisman honorees is the most likely to succeed?

Receivers	Ht.	Wt.	Age	Exp.	College
Adams, Willis (W)	6-2	194	24	2	Houston
Feacher, Rickey (W)	5-10	174	26	5	Mississippi Valley
Logan, Dave (W)	6-4	216	26	5	Colorado
Newsome, Ozzie (T)	6-2	232	24	3	Alabama
Rucker, Reggie (W)	6-2	190	33	11	Boston University
Smith, John (W)	6-0	175	24	2	Tennessee State
Weathers, Curtis (T)	6-5	220	24	2	Mississippi
Wright, Keith (W)	5-9½	175	24	3	Memphis State

W=wide receiver   T=tight end

Logan, Rucker and Newsome provide the Browns with one of league's best receiving trios. Logan and Newsome each caught more than 50 passes, first time ever for two Cleveland receivers in the same season. If the reception corps lacks anything, it's outside speed. Rucker caught 43, and Mike Pruitt 41 as a receiving running back. This is Cleveland's strongest offensive unit.

Interior Linemen	Ht.	Wt.	Age	Exp.	College
Brzoza, Tom (C)	6-3	245	24	1	Pittsburgh
Claphan, Sam (T)	6-6	271	24	1	Oklahoma
DeLeone, Tom (C)	6-2	248	30	9	Ohio State
Dieken, Doug (T)	6-5	252	31	10	Illinois
Evans, Gary (G)	6-3	250	24	1	Grand Valley State
Jackson, R. E. (G)	6-5	260	27	6	Duke
Miller, Matt (T)	6-6	270	24	2	Colorado
Risien, Cody (G)	6-7	255	23	2	Texas A&M

Sheppard, Henry (T)	6-6	263	28	5	Southern Mississippi
Sullivan, Gerry (C-T)	6-4	250	28	7	Illinois

T=tackle   G=guard   C=center

Sheppard was moved from guard to tackle, affording better pass protection. Even so, the line permitted 43 QB sacks, a fairly high figure. DeLeone was a Pro Bowler for first time. Claphan was on injured reserve all year. Miller was used to advantage on special teams. Risien showed rapid rookie progress and started final ten games last season. Best reference for offensive line is this: Cleveland third in the entire NFL in total offensive yards gained with average of 360.8 per game.

Kickers	Ht.	Wt.	Age	Exp.	College
Cockroft, Don (Pk)	6-1	195	35	13	Adams State
Evans, Johnny (P)	6-1	197	24	3	North Carolina State

Pk=placekicker   P=punter

Cockroft still kicks well but age may be cutting him back, especially from beyond the 40, even though he nailed one 50-yarder last season. Rutigliano still has confidence in Cockroft's ability to do the job, perhaps for several seasons yet. Evans punted at 41.2 clip, sixth best in NFL, but coaches want him to improve hang time (keep ball in air longer).

DEFENSE

Front Linemen	Ht.	Wt.	Age	Exp.	College
Alzado, Lyle (E)	6-3	250	31	10	Yankton
Bradley, Henry (T)	6-2	260	27	2	Alcorn State
Crews, Ron (E)	6-3	251	22	R	Nevada-Las Vegas
Crosby, Cleveland (E)	6-5	250	22	R	Arizona
Dimler, Rich (T)	6-6	260	24	2	Southern Cal
Harris, Marshall (E)	6-6	261	25	1	Texas Christian
Perkov, Kent (E)	6-6	262	27	1	San Diego State
Ronan, Jim (T)	6-5	255	24	1	Minnesota
Sherk, Jerry (T)	6-4½	250	32	11	Oklahoma State
Sims, Mickey (T)	6-5	270	25	4	South Carolina State

E=end   T=tackle

Dimler took over for the injured Sherk, then Dimler went down and out of action himself. The Browns are hopeful, but Sherk may not be able to play this season. Defensively, Cleveland ranked low in the AFC last season, especially against the run. Alzado, in from Denver, played several different positions on the line, but an injured knee hampered his style. Sims continues to show improvement, starting every game in his third season. Perkov impressed everybody, then came down with a hurt knee.

Linebackers	Ht.	Wt.	Age	Exp.	College
Ambrose, Dick (M)	6-0	235	27	6	Virginia
Cowher, Bill (O)	6-2	225	23	1	North Carolina State
Graf, Dave (O)	6-2½	221	27	6	Penn State
Hall, Charlie (O)	6-3½	235	32	10	Houston
Irons, Gerald (O)	6-2	230	33	11	Md-Eastern Shore
Jackson, R. L. (M)	6-1	230	26	3	Texas A&M
Jones, Ricky (O)	6-1	215	25	4	Tuskegee
Matthews, Clay (O)	6-2	230	24	3	Southern Cal
Odom, Cliff (O)	6-3	219	22	R	Texas-Arlington

O=outside   M=middle

Main crew here is Ambrose in middle, Hall and Matthews on the outside. The same trio led the Browns in tackles last season, Ambrose being first with 103 solos and 34 assists. The linebacking corps has depth, and Cleveland may turn to a 3-4 defense, a formation used at times last season when injuries decimated the line.

Defensive Backs	Ht.	Wt.	Age	Exp.	College
Bolton, Ron (CB)	6-2	170	30	9	Norfolk State
Burrell, Clinton (CB)	6-1½	192	24	2	Louisiana State
Cesare, Billy (CB)	5-11	190	25	3	Miami (Fla.)
Darden, Thom (S)	6-2	193	30	8	Michigan
Davis, Oliver (CB)	6-1½	205	26	4	Tennessee State
Johnson, Lawrence (CB)	5-11½	204	23	2	Wisconsin
McCoy, Steve (CB)	6-1	195	23	1	Cheyney State
Rich, Randy (S)	5-10	181	27	4	New Mexico
Scott, Clarence (S)	6-0	190	31	10	Kansas State

CB=cornerback   S=safety

Darden returned as one of the best safeties in league. He intercepted five passes to lead club. Rookies Burrell and Johnson passed their tests and face more action this season. Burrell was used whenever the Browns went to the "nickel defense," i.e., when five defensive backs were used. In addition to Darden, the starters are Bolton and Davis at the corners, Scott at the strong safety.

Note: A complete listing of Cleveland's 1980 college draft selections can be found on page 269.

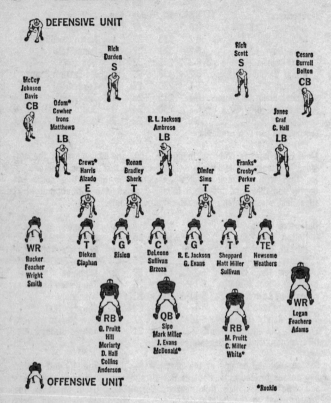

DEFENSIVE UNIT

Rich
Darden
S

Rich
Scott
S

Cesare
Burrell
Bolton
CB

McCoy
Johnson
Davis
CB

Odom*
Cowher
Irons
Matthews
LB

R. L. Jackson
Ambrose
LB

Jones
Graf
C. Hall
LB

Crews*
Harris
Alzado
E

Ronan
Bradley
Sherk
T

Dimler
Sims
T

Franks*
Crosby*
Perkov
E

WR
Rucker
Feacher
Wright
Smith

Dieken
Claphan
T

Risien
G

DeLeone
Sullivan
Brzoza
C

R. E. Jackson
G. Evans
G

Sheppard
Matt Miller
Sullivan
T

Newsome
Weathers
TE

WR
Logan
Feachers
Adams

RB
G. Pruitt
Hill
Moriarty
D. Hall
Collins
Anderson

QB
Sipe
Mark Miller
J. Evans
McDonald*

RB
M. Pruitt
C. Miller
White*

OFFENSIVE UNIT

*Rookie

1979 BROWNS STATISTICS

	Browns	Opps.
Total Points Scored	359	352
Total First Downs	350	307
Third Down Efficiency Percentage	44.6	42.5
Yards Rushing—First Downs	2281—125	2604—136
Passes Attempted—Completions	545—289	468—271
Yards Passing—First Downs	3491—189	3046—158
QB Sacked—Yards Lost	43—347	31—243
Interceptions By—Return Average	16—17.4	27—11.7
Punts—Average Yards	71—40.1	80—41.4
Punt Returns—Average Return	41—8.4	45—8.3
Kickoff Returns—Average Return	75—20.4	70—18.9
Fumbles—Ball Lost	29—17	39—16
Penalties—Yards	83—709	118—1019

STATISTICAL LEADERS

Scoring	TDs	Rush.	Pass.	Ret.	PATs	FGs	Total
Cockroft	0	0	0	0	38—44	17—29	89
M. Pruitt	11	9	2	0	0	0	66
Newsome	9	0	9	0	0	0	54
Logan	7	0	7	0	0	0	42
Rucker	6	0	6	0	0	0	36
Hill	3	1	2	0	0	0	18
Moriarty	2	2	0	0	0	0	12
Sipe	2	2	0	0	0	0	12

Rushing	Atts.	Yds.	Avg.	Longest	TDs
M. Pruitt	264	1294	4.9	77 (TD)	9
G. Pruitt	62	233	3.8	27	0
C. Miller	39	213	5.5	39 (TD)	1
Hill	53	193	3.6	33	1
Sipe	45	178	4.0	34	2
D. Hall	22	152	6.9	52 (TD)	1
Moriarty	14	11	0.8	8	2

Passing	Atts.	Com.	Yds.	Pct.	Int.	Longest	TDs
Sipe	535	286	3793	53.5	26	74	28

Receiving	No.	Yds.	Avg.	Longest	TDs
Logan	59	982	16.6	46	7
Newsome	55	781	14.2	74	9
Rucker	43	749	17.4	54	6
M. Pruitt	41	372	9.0	50 (TD)	2
Hill	38	381	10.0	31	2
C. Miller	26	251	9.7	15	0
G. Pruitt	14	155	11.1	27	1
Feacher	7	103	14.7	25	1

Interceptions	No.	Yds.	Avg.	Longest	TDs
Darden	5	125	25.0	39 (TD)	1
Scott	3	56	18.7	29	0
Bolton	3	20	6.7	13	0
C. Hall	2	14	7.0	11	0

Punting	No.	Yds.	Avg.	Longest	Inside 20	Blocked
Evans	69	2844	41.2	59	7	0

Punt Returns	No.	FCs	Yds.	Avg.	Longest	TDs
D. Hall	29	5	295	10.2	47	0
Wright	12	6	50	4.2	13	0

Kickoff Returns	No.	Yds.	Avg.	Longest	TDs
D. Hall	50	1014	20.3	33	0
Wright	15	402	26.8	45	0
Feacher	2	51	25.5	27	0
Rich	2	10	5.0	6	0

CINCINNATI BENGALS

Head Coach: Forrest Gregg
(1st Year)

1979 RECORD (4-12) (capital letters indicate home games)		1980 SCHEDULE (capital letters indicate home games)	
0 Denver	10	TAMPA BAY	Sept. 7
24 Buffalo	51	Miami	Sept. 14
14 NEW ENGLAND	20	PITTSBURGH	Sept. 21
27 HOUSTON	30	HOUSTON	Sept. 28
13 Dallas	38	Green Bay	Oct. 5
7 KANSAS CITY	10	Pittsburgh	Oct. 12
34 PITTSBURGH	10	MINNESOTA	Oct. 19
27 Cleveland	28	Houston	Oct. 26
37 PHILADELPHIA	13	SAN DIEGO	Nov. 2
28 Baltimore	38	Oakland	Nov. 9
24 SAN DIEGO	26	BUFFALO	Nov. 16
21 Houston	42	Cleveland	Nov. 23
34 ST. LOUIS	28	Kansas City	Nov. 30
17 Pittsburgh	37	BALTIMORE	Dec. 7
14 Washington	28	Chicago	Dec. 14
16 CLEVELAND	12	CLEVELAND	Dec. 21
337	421		

What's wrong with the Bengals? That's the question uppermost with sports-minded Cincinnati fans these days as their local favorites prepare for the new NFL campaign against a backdrop of two consecutive 4-12 seasons. In many ways, the question is a good one, for the Bengals have been behaving in mystifying fashion. For instance, during one period of seven straight weeks, Cincinnati scored a total of 205 points and, normally, that would be enough points to win five or six games. But not so with the Bengals—they managed to win only three.

Even psychologists are taking an interest in what makes the Bengals tick, or not tick. Dr. Joel Warm of the University of Cincinnati was quoted in a local newspaper as saying: "The Bengals may be learning how to lose. Some players may be losing confidence in their ability to do the task required of them. And others may be losing confidence in their teammates' abilities. They may get to the point where they believe that, no matter what they do, the result is always a loss. That's when they become depressed and their level of activity goes down, maybe even imperceptibly to them, but enough to take the cutting edge off their performance."

To that, a pro football coach might reply, "What does a psychologist know about sacking a quarterback?" Still, discipline, or the lack of it, seems to be one of Cincinnati's playing personnel problems. Marty Williams, for instance, writing in *Pro Football Weekly,* was especially critical:

"Some of the Bengals," he writes, "were guilty of gross neglect of duty last year, particularly toward the season's end. They were fat and out of shape, mentally and physically. When you can smuggle beer on the team plane after a 42-21 loss (at Houston) and then laugh and sing all the way home, there's something basically wrong with your competitive nature."

Whether it's in a bar or on a plane, it's not the beer-drinking that annoys others—it's the laughing and singing. No sooner had the Bengals finished their second dismal season last December than they found themselves with a new coach. And he is none other than Forrest Gregg, the NFL Hall of Famer and offensive lineman who played on two of Vince Lombardi's Green Bay Super Bowl teams. He replaces Homer Rice who took over in midseason two years ago and wound up his coaching efforts with an 8-19 record. Gregg comes to Cincinnati after one year as head coach of the Toronto Argonauts of the Canadian League. Cincinnati is not his first NFL head coaching assignment.

In 1975, he was named head coach of the Cleveland Browns, a post he held until the 1977 season was almost over. On leaving Cleveland, his overall record there was 18-23.

Cincinnati players had mixed reactions on learning of Gregg's appointment. His reputation as a tough disciplinarian goes before Gregg and there's probably one thing he won't tolerate for sure, and that's singing and laughing on the plane after losing a game. In fact, in commenting on his newest assignment, he told a news conference in Cincinnati that he didn't care whether certain players disliked him because, as he put it, "I'm in the business to win football games. There have been football players who don't like me, but I'm not in the business to be loved. There is talent here to win. What we want to do is put that talent together and step forward from this day on. Discipline means a lot of things. Every football team has rules and regulations and we'll be no different."

Gregg faces numerous problems as he seeks to turn the Bengals around, and perhaps his biggest lies in the offensive line. When going back to pass last season, quarterback Ken Anderson hardly knew a moment when he didn't look up to see an unfriendly player rushing up to do him in. The Cincinnati total of 63 QB muggings allowed was the league's highest. Anderson was sacked for a total of 46 of the 63 sacks, which was more than team totals permitted by 21 NFL clubs.

The Cincinnati defense is another critical area of concern for the coaching staff Gregg brings with him, since all of Rice's assistants were fired in the turnover. In leading the league in total offensive yards allowed, the Bengals won the dubious distinction of setting a new "yards-permitted" record—5, 911. That's supposed to be the highest one-season total ever permitted in the history of pro football.

Gregg has an aversion to being compared with his famous coach of the Green Bay playing days, the late Vince Lombardi. "I think everyone assumes that since I played for Lombardi, I automatically try to be like Vince. To try to be someone else comes across as false. I just try to coach my own philosophy and be Forrest Gregg."

An independent attitude probably comes naturally for a man who was born 46 years ago in a forthright town called Birthright, Texas.

OFFENSE

Quarterbacks	Ht.	Wt.	Age	Exp.	College
Anderson, Ken	6-3	208	31	10	Augustana (Ill.)
Thompson, Jack	6-3	217	24	2	Washington State

Anderson was intercepted only 10 times last season as he returned to something resembling his old form, ranking third among AFC QBs. His completion average was 55.8. Thompson, a scrambler in the Tarkenton tradition, saw quite a bit of action last season, completing 44.8 percent of 87 passes and running the ball for 235 yards to average 5.5 yards per gain. He personally carried the ball in for five TDs.

Running Backs	Ht.	Wt.	Age	Exp.	College
Alexander, Charles	6-1	221	23	2	Louisiana State
Griffin, Archie	5-8	184	26	4	Ohio State
Johnson, Pete	6-0	259	26	4	Ohio State
Poole, Nathan	5-8	210	24	2	Louisville
Turner, Deacon	5-11	210	25	3	San Diego State

Highly regarded LSU rookie Alexander played enough games, but didn't impress all that much. Pete Johnson set club records with 14 TDs rushing and 15 TDs in a season. Griffin began living up to his Heisman Trophy promise, rushing for 688 yards and a 4.9-yard average, and catching 43 passes—something he seldom did while at Ohio State. Turner did most of his ball-carrying as a kickoff returner, tying an NFL record with 55 KO runbacks and setting a new club mark with 1,149 yards. Poole was used effectively on special teams.

Receivers	Ht.	Wt.	Age	Exp.	College
Bass, Don (T)	6-2	218	24	3	Houston
Brooks, Billy (W)	6-3	203	27	5	Oklahoma
Corbert, Jim (T)	6-4	217	25	4	Pittsburgh
Curtis, Isaac (W)	6-1	192	30	8	San Diego State
Kreider, Steve (W)	6-3	192	22	2	Lehigh
Levenseller, Mike (W)	6-1	180	24	3	Washington State
Ross, Dan (T)	6-4	238	23	2	Northeastern
Walker, Rick (T)	6-4	235	25	4	UCLA

W=wide receiver   T=tight end

This unit should be solid for some time to come. Bass set a new club record with 58 receptions for the season. Curtis caught eight TD passes among his 32. Brooks was doing fine until injury stopped him. Ross was one of the more talked-about rookie tight ends in the NFL. He caught 41 passes and proved himself to be a fine blocker. Veterans Corbert and Walker shared playing time with Ross. Punter Pat McInally is a backup wide receiver. So is Kreider who caught three last season. Levenseller returns kicks as well.

Interior Linemen	Ht.	Wt.	Age	Exp.	College
Bujnoch, Glenn (G)	6-6	255	27	5	Texas A&M
Bush, Blair (C)	6-3	252	24	3	Washington
Cotton, Barney (G)	6-6	261	24	2	Nebraska
Donahue, Mark (G)	6-3	251	24	3	Michigan
Fairchild, Greg (G)	6-4	265	26	3	Tulsa
Glass, Bill (G)	6-4	264	21	R	Baylor
Holland, Vern (T)	6-5	267	32	10	Tennessee State
Lapham, Dave (G)	6-4	258	28	7	Syracuse
Montoya, Max (T)	6-5	278	24	2	UCLA
Munoz, Anthony (T)	6-5	287	21	R	Southern Cal
Wilson, Mike (T)	6-5	280	25	3	Georgia

T=tackle   G=guard   C=center

This unit is very thin and could use some shoring up, both in quality and quantity. Cincinnati ranked far down the list of 28 NFL clubs in toal offense last season, averaging a mere 289.9 yards a game. The rushing attack didn't do too badly, but Bengal QBs were sacked a league-high 63 times. Ken Anderson, obviously, had a difficult time staying on his feet. Still, Bujnoch and Wilson showed some development on line's right side. Lapham, Donahue and 10-year man Holland were on the left. Fairchild is a former Bengal who played in Canada for Toronto under coach, that's right, Forrest Gregg. Bush was out with a knee injury in midseason and underwent surgery. No sooner had the Lions chosen Billy Sims No. 1 in the draft, and the Jets had taken Johnny (Lam) Jones No. 2, than the Bengals latched on to Anthony Munoz, the Southern Cal tackle, as No. 3 and for good reason. Except for a few knee problems, this consensus All-America is known as the "complete defensive lineman."

Kickers	Ht.	Wt.	Age	Exp.	College
Bahr, Chris (Pk)	5-10	172	27	5	Penn State
McInally, Pat (P)	6-6	209	27	5	Harvard

Pk=placekicker   P=punter

Bahr kicked two of NFL's longest goals in '79—55 and 52 yards, both in the same game against Houston. McInally was AFC's No. 3 punter with a 41.3 average, and he's one of more accurate booters in placing the ball inside the 20.

DEFENSE

Front Linemen	Ht.	Wt.	Age	Exp.	College
Browner, Ross (E)	6-3	261	26	3	Notre Dame
Burley, Gary (E)	6-3	269	28	5	Pittsburgh
Edwards, Eddie (E-NT)	6-5	256	26	4	Miami (Fla.)
Horn, Rod (NT)	6-4	268	22	R	Nebraska
Mitchell, Mack (E)	6-7	253	28	6	Houston
White, Mike (E-NT)	6-5	266	23	2	Albany State (Ga.)
Whitley, Wilson (NT)	6-3	265	25	4	Houston

E=end   NT=nose tackle

Cincinnati ranked No. 28, dead last, among NFL clubs in total defense against the pass and run, permitting 369.4 yards per game. The pass rush was especially inadequate. Gregg has his work cut out for him here, turning this group of youthful linemen into an effective unit for Cincinnati's 3-4 defense. Some give Whitley the nod as the most effective lineman here.

Linebackers	Ht.	Wt.	Age	Exp.	College
Cameron, Glenn (I)	6-2	230	27	6	Florida
Criswell, Kirby (O)	6-5	232	22	R	Kansas
Dinkel, Tom (I)	6-3	246	24	3	Kansas
Harris, Bo (O)	6-3	226	27	6	Louisiana State
Kurnick, Howie (O)	6-2	219	23	2	Cincinnati
LeClair, Jim (I)	6-3	234	30	9	North Dakota
Barrett, Oliver (O)	6-1	240	24	1	Texas Southern
Ruud, Tom (O)	6-3	226	27	6	Nebraska
Williams, Reggie (O)	6-0	228	26	5	Dartmouth
Ebeling, Ken (O)	6-5	215	23	1	Colgate

O=outside   I=inside

Cameron can play both inside and outside. LeClair is a true-blue veteran of great talent, and led club in tackles with 92 solos and 46 assists.

But LeClair is thinking about coaching high school and retiring to his Minnesota farm, or playing out his final season with his neighbors, the Vikings. Harris rates high with the Bengal coaches. Williams does too, but missed much of last season with a hurt knee. The backups are Kurnick, Dinkel and Rudd. Ebeling is a free agent who gets a tryout. Kurnick, however, is sidelined for the 1980 season because of surgery after a water skiing accident.

Defensive Backs	Ht.	Wt.	Age	Exp.	College
Breeden, Louis (CB)	5-11	187	27	3	N.C. Central
Browner, Jim (S)	6-1	209	25	2	Notre Dame
Burk, Scott (S)	6-2	193	24	2	Oklahoma State
Cobb, Marvin (S)	6-0	188	27	6	Southern Cal
Griffin, Ray (CB)	5-10	183	24	3	Ohio State
Hicks, Bryan (CB)	6-0	194	23	R	McNeese State
Jauron, Dick (S)	6-0	184	30	8	Yale
Lusby, Vaughn (CB)	5-10	178	24	2	Arkansas
Riley, Ken (CB)	6-0	183	33	12	Florida A&M

CB=cornerback   S=safety

This is a critical area for Gregg's attention. Breeden and Riley were hampered considerably by injuries last season and much depends on their healthy return. Jauron, an eight-year veteran, led club in interceptions with six. Cobb is a starter who'll be challenged by Browner. Griffin (Archie's brother) wants a regular spot and underlined his bid by intercepting four passes and returning one for 96 yards and a TD against San Diego. Lusby is the club's punt returner, but also seeks a secondary job.

Note: A complete listing of Cincinnati's 1980 college draft selections can be found on page 269.

DEFENSIVE UNIT

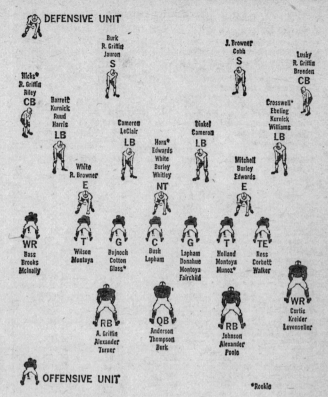

Burk
R. Griffin
Jauron
S

J. Browner
Cobb
S

Lusby
R. Griffin
Breeden
CB

Hicks*
R. Griffin
Riley
CB

Barrett
Kurnick
Ruud
Harris
LB

Cameron
LeClair
LB

Horn*
Edwards
White
Burley
Whitley
NT

Dinkel
Cameron
LB

Mitchell
Burley
Edwards
E

Crosswell*
Ebeling
Kurnick
Williams
LB

White
R. Browner
E

WR
Bass
Brooks
McInally

Wilson
Montoya
T

Bujnoch
Cotton
Glass*
G

Bush
Lapham
C

Lapham
Donahue
Montoya
Fairchild
G

Holland
Montoya
Munoz*
T

Ross
Corbett
Walker
TE

WR
Curtis
Kreider
Levenseller

RB
A. Griffin
Alexander
Turner

QB
Anderson
Thompson
Burk

RB
Johnson
Alexander
Poole

OFFENSIVE UNIT

*Rookie

1979 BENGALS STATISTICS

	Bengals	Opps.
Total Points Scored	337	421
Total First Downs	289	334
Third Down Efficiency Percentage	35.4	48.8
Yards Rushing—First Downs	2329—138	2219—133
Passes Attempted—Completions	426—228	492—275
Yards Passing—First Downs	2310—131	3692—175
QB Sacked—Yards Lost	63—505	32—216
Interceptions By—Return Average	20—13.0	15—20.3
Punts—Average Yards	91—40.4	71—39.6
Punt Returns—Average Return	42—7.5	48—6.8
Kickoff Returns—Average Return	81—19.4	63—19.9
Fumbles—Ball Lost	24—14	39—24
Penalties—Yards	88—844	98—858

STATISTICAL LEADERS

Scoring	TDs	Rush.	Pass.	Ret.	PATs	FGs	Total
P. Johnson	15	14	1	0	0	0	90
Bahr	0	0	0	0	40—42	13—23	79
Curtis	8	0	8	0	0	0	48
Thompson	5	5	0	0	0	0	30
Bass	3	0	3	0	0	0	18
Anderson	2	2	0	0	0	0	12
A. Griffin	2	0	2	0	0	0	12

Rushing	Atts.	Yds.	Avg.	Longest	TDs
P. Johnson	243	865	3.6	35 (TD)	14
A. Griffin	140	688	4.9	63	0
Alexander	88	286	3.3	17	1
Anderson	28	235	8.4	20	2
Thompson	21	116	5.5	21	5
Turner	28	86	3.1	10	1

Passing	Atts.	Com.	Yds.	Pct.	Int.	Longest	TDs
Anderson	339	189	2340	55.7	10	73 (TD)	16
Thompson	87	39	481	44.8	5	50	1

Receiving	No.	Yds.	Avg.	Longest	TDs
Bass	58	724	12.5	50	3
A. Griffin	43	417	9.7	52 (TD)	2
Ross	41	516	12.6	30	1
Curtis	32	605	19.0	67 (TD)	8
P. Johnson	24	154	6.4	15 (TD)	1
Alexander	11	91	8.3	13	0

Interceptions	No.	Yds.	Avg.	Longest	TDs
Jauron	6	41	6.8	12	0
R. Griffin	4	167	41.8	96 (TD)	1
Cobb	3	19	6.3	14	0
Williams	2	5	2.5	3	0

Punting	No.	Yds.	Avg.	Longest	Inside 20	Blocked
McInally	89	3678	41.3	61	19	2

Punt Returns	No.	FCs	Yds.	Avg.	Longest	TDs
Lusby	32	4	260	8.1	40	0
Levenseller	8	1	46	5.8	21	0

Kickoff Returns	No.	Yds.	Avg.	Longest	TDs
Turner	55	1149	20.9	36	0
J. Browner	8	116	14.5	26	0
Poole	7	128	18.3	24	0
Lusby	6	92	15.3	28	0

SAN DIEGO CHARGERS

Head Coach: Don Coryell

3rd Year   **Record:** 20–8

1979 RECORD (12-4) (capital letters indicate home games)		
33	Seattle	16
30	OAKLAND	10
27	BUFFALO	19
21	New England	27
31	SAN FRANCISCO	9
0	Denver	7
20	SEATTLE	10
40	Los Angeles	16
22	Oakland	45
20	Kansas City	14
26	Cincinnati	24
35	PITTSBURGH	7
28	KANSAS CITY	7
26	ATLANTA	28
35	New Orleans	0
17	DENVER	7
411		246
Playoffs		
14	HOUSTON	17

1980 SCHEDULE (capital letters indicate home games)	
Seattle	Sept. 7
OAKLAND	Sept. 14
Denver	Sept. 21
Kansas City	Sept. 28
BUFFALO	Oct. 5
Oakland	Oct. 12
N.Y. GIANTS	Oct. 19
Dallas (night, TV)	Oct. 26
Cincinnati	Nov. 2
DENVER	Nov. 9
KANSAS CITY	Nov. 16
Miami (night, TV)	Nov. 20
PHILADELPHIA	Nov. 30
Washington	Dec. 7
SEATTLE (TV)	Dec. 13
PITTSBURGH (night, TV)	Dec. 22

Someone, finally, has drawn a parallel between the game action in the AFC West and a demolition derby. The keen observer in this instance is Dave Newhouse and he pictured the scene in a column written for *The Sporting News:*

"In the blue car with the lighting bolts, it's Don (The Destroyer) Coryell. In the orange car, it's Rammin' Red Miller. There in the black beauty, we have Tom (Four to the Floor) Flores. Driving the red car, it's Malevolent Marv Levy. Finally, in the blue-green special, let's hear it for Jarrin'

Jack Patera! Okay, gentlemen, start your engines,
begin colliding, and may the best . . ."

That would seem to set the stage for playoff pursuit
in the AFC West where, last season, the cellar team did
no worse than 7-9, which was the best last-place
record in the league. The Chargers were division champions, but Denver, Seattle, and Oakland were breath-
ing down their necks right up to the finish. There's
probably no division in the NFL where pro football
is played in such a wide variety of crowd-pleasing
forms.

The Chargers have all the attributes of a team that
has finally found themselves. This sense of discovery
can be credited to two individuals—quarterback Dan
Fouts and head coach Don Coryell, who are listed here
without reference to their order of importance. They're
both important, as San Diego's opponents have learned
and are sure to rediscover as the new season proceeds.

San Diego won the AFC West last season relying
almost solely on the pass, with Fouts of course doing
the tossing. The 12-4 record was the Chargers' best
since the pre-Super Bowl days of 1963 when they won
the American Football League championship. Fouts,
who incidentally is the son of a former San Francisco
sports announcer, also became the first Charger since
John Hadl (1965) to capture an individual passing
title by completing 332 of 530 for a league record
4,082 yards. Only Pittsburgh scored more points (416)
than San Diego's club record 411—and only Tampa
Bay allowed the opposition fewer points (237) than
San Diego's 246. With statistics such as these to chart
their progress, little wonder the Chargers looked as
good on the field as they did on paper.

Don Coryell is one of those coaches whose emotions
are completely attuned to whatever is happening on the

field. He lives every excruciating moment. He walks
up and down the sidelines, nervously running his hands
through his hair, sitting, standing, kneeling on one
knee, then the other, all the while wearing an un-
smiling, almost painful, expression on his face. In fact,
once the season begins, Coryell is like a man walking
and talking in another world—one that bears no resem-
blance to workaday everyday reality.

How does all this come across with his players? Defensive tackle Gary Johnson has an opinion. He says,
"Coryell has a great influence on a team. When his
vibes hit you, you want to go out and win." Guard Ed
White speaks out too: "Coryell's a lovable, down-to-
earth kind of guy. A lot of head coaches aren't like
that. He's someone you can really talk to, so he has
an emotional tie with his players. And he'll laugh at
himself along with everyone else if something goes
wrong."

Still, in the midst of San Diego's new-found success,
some credit should be given to former Charger coach
Tommy Prothro, the man Coryell replaced. It
was Prothro who used the college draft, particularly
the 1975 selections, to build today's San Diego team.
No one ever questioned Prothro's ability to recognize
talent, whether he was dealing with draft choices or
trades, and his personnel decisions will provide the
Chargers with basic strength for some time to come.

There is, however, one position that could use some
help, and it's the running back. If the Chargers had a
hard-driving, bowl-you-over type of ball-carrier in the
style of, say, Earl Campbell or Ottis Anderson to go
with that fantastic aerial game, conquering the world
of pro football might just become a cinch. In an obvious move to improve that running game, they have
traded a future draft choice for John Cappelletti who
was Los Angeles's best ground-gainer in 1978 but since

then has been pretty much on the sidelines with an injury. Says Coryell: "John is a valuable addition as a strong runner, outstanding blocker and a very good receiver." But he's no Campbell or Anderson.

The Chargers will defend their first AFC West title (since 1965) with games against all four divisional opponents in the 1980 schedule's first quarter. The opening four games take them to Seattle on September 7th, then back home against Oakland, followed by on-the-road games in Denver and Kansas City. It might just happen—the AFC West championship could be decided before the September Song ends.

OFFENSE

Quarterbacks	Ht.	Wt.	Age	Exp.	College
Fouts, Dan	6-3	210	29	8	Oregon
Harris, James	6-3½	221	33	11	Grambling
Kirkland, Mike	6-1½	190	26	4	Arkansas
Luther, Ed	6-3	215	22	R	San Jose State
Olander, Cliff	6-5	187	25	4	New Mexico State

Fouts was Mr. Everything in San Diego last season, setting an NFL record with 4,082 yards passing, surpassing Joe Namath's 1967 mark of 4,007. At the height of San Diego's aerial attack, Fouts threw four consecutive 300-yard passing games, setting still another league standard. Harris tossed nine as the backup, completing five. Olander sat and watched all this.

Running Backs	Ht.	Wt.	Age	Exp.	College
Bauer, Hank	5-11	200	26	4	Cal Lutheran
Cappelletti, John	6-1	220	28	6	Penn State
Matthews, Bo	6-3½	222	29	7	Colorado
Mitchell, Lydell	5-11	198	31	9	Penn State
Owens, Artie	5-11½	182	27	5	West Virginia
Thomas, Mike	5-11	190	27	4	Nevada-Las Vegas
Williams, Clarence	5-10	195	25	4	South Carolina
Woods, Don	6-2	208	29	7	New Mexico

Williams set a club record with 12 rushing TDs. His 752 yards overland led Charger runners. Other backs were comparatively idle on an aerial-minded team, Thomas leading the "also-rans" with 353 yards. Cappelletti comes to San Diego in a draft choice swap after leading the Rams in rushing in 1978, and then sitting out the '79 season with an injured groin.

Receivers	Ht.	Wt.	Age	Exp.	College
Burton, Larry (W)	6-1	195	29	5	Purdue
Floyd, John (W)	6-1	195	24	2	Northeast Louisiana
Jefferson, John (W)	6-1	198	24	3	Arizona State
Joiner, Charlie (W)	5-11	183	33	12	Grambling
Klein, Bob (T)	6-5	237	33	12	Southern Cal
McCrary, Gregg (T)	6-2	235	28	5	Clark
Winslow, Kellen (T)	6-5½	252	23	2	Missouri

W=wide receiver   T=tight end

This is premier San Diego offensive unit, coupled with Fouts's throwing arm. Joiner and Jefferson each had 1,000-yard seasons. Jefferson tied Tony Hill of Dallas for NFL third place in TD receptions, 10 (Morgan of Patriots 12, Carmichael of Eagles 11). Winslow played both WR and TE long enough to catch 25 passes and otherwise distinguish himself—then he broke his leg. Floyd filled in during the late season drive and may become Joiner's eventual successor. Clarence Williams led running back receivers with 51 catches. As long as the passes fly, this crowd will drag them in.

Interior Linemen	Ht.	Wt.	Age	Exp.	College
Audick, Dan (G)	6-3	253	26	3	Hawaii
Hardaway, Milton (T)	6-9	305	26	2	Oklahoma State
Macek, Don (C-G)	6-2½	253	26	5	Boston College
Perretta, Ralph (C)	6-1½	251	27	6	Purdue
Rush, Bob (C)	6-5	264	25	4	Memphis State
Shields, Billy (T)	6-8	275	27	6	Georgia Tech
Washington, Russ (T)	6-7	288	34	13	Missouri
White, Ed (G)	6-2½	271	33	12	California
Wilkerson, Doug (G)	6-3	262	33	11	N. C. Central

T=tackle   G=guard   C=center

The Charger offensive line defended Fouts as he led the NFL's most effective passing attack in '79. Even though it allowed 31 QB sacks, there's reason to be complimented. Shields, Wilkerson, White, Washington and Rush are the front five. White played in the Pro Bowl, hurt his knee, and underwent surgery four days later. He hopes to be in good shape for the opener. This unit didn't have to do too much on running plays. San Diego finished next to last among NFL's 28 clubs in rushing offense, averaging a mere 104.3 yards per game.

Kickers	Ht.	Wt.	Age	Exp.	College
Benirschke, Rolf (Pk)	6-1	165	25	4	California-Davis
Cummins, Scott (P)	6-3	200	24	R	Hawaii

Kirkland, Mike (P)	6-1½	190	26	4	Arkansas
West, Jeff (P)	6-2	210	27	6	Cincinnati
Wood, Mike (Pk)	5-11	199	26	3	Southeast Missouri

Pk=placekicker   P=punter

Wood did most of the placekicking last season, with Benirschke out after four games due to illness and surgery. Latest word is that Benirschke's weight went up from 128 to 163 pounds, but he remained agile enough to gain finals of NFL Players Association tennis tournament where he lost to RB Andy Johnson of the Patriots. Wood connected for 28-31 PATs and 11-14 FGs. Before going out, Benirschke had 12-13 PATs and 4-4 FGs. West punted for 36.5 average, and Coryell may ask him for better distance.

DEFENSE

Front Linemen	Ht.	Wt.	Age	Exp.	College
Bell, Richard (E)	6-4	255	25	1	Rhode Island
Dean, Fred (E)	6-2½	230	28	6	Louisiana Tech
DeJurnett, Charles (T)	6-4	260	28	5	San Jose State
Johnson, Gary (T)	6-3	252	27	6	Grambling
Jones, Leroy (E)	6-8	260	30	5	Norfolk State
Kelcher, Louie (T)	6-4½	282	27	6	Southern Methodist
Lee, John (E)	6-2	259	27	5	Nebraska
Young, Wilbur (E)	6-6	290	31	10	William Penn

E=end   T=tackle

Though not quite as spectacular as San Diego's offense, the Charger defensive unit ranked fourth in the AFC in defense against both pass and run. Best performance was against the pass, allowing 159.3 yards per game and sacking the opposing QB 42 times. Young, normally an end, moved into the tackle spot opened up by Kelcher's injury followed by DeJurnett's. Among his other achievements at tackle, the ten-year veteran somehow harassed quarterbacks into throwing prematurely. Jones, Young, Johnson and Dean were the starting front four at season's end.

Linebackers	Ht.	Wt.	Age	Exp.	College
Goode, Don (O)	6-2	231	29	7	Kansas
Horn, Bob (M)	6-4	230	26	5	Oregon State
King, Keith (O)	6-4	230	25	3	Colorado State
Laslavic, Jim (M)	6-2½	236	29	7	Penn State
Lowe, Woodrow (O)	6-0	227	26	5	Alabama
McGee, Carl (O)	6-3	228	24	1	Duke
Preston, Ray (O)	6-0	218	26	5	Syracuse
Thrift, Cliff (M)	6-2	232	24	2	East Central U.

O=outside   M=middle

Lowe tied Preston for club interceptions, each with five. Linebacking unit, like the Charger defense itself, is solid if not flashy. Goode is top man here, and came through after early season injury. Thrift spent year backing up Horn at middle 'backer, and showed some noteworthy form. He could rate higher this year. Preston, Horn and Lowe are the starting trio.

Defensive Backs	Ht.	Wt.	Age	Exp.	College
Buchanon, Willie (CB)	6-0½	195	30	9	San Diego State
Carter, Keith (CB)	5-11½	190	24	1	Delaware State
Dove, Jerome (CB)	6-2½	193	27	4	Colorado State
Duncan, Frank (S)	6-1	188	24	2	San Francisco State
Edwards, Glen (S)	6-0	183	33	10	Florida A&M
Fuller, Mike (S)	5-9½	182	27	6	Auburn
Gregor, Bob (S)	6-2	190	22	R	Washington State
Shaw, Pete (S)	5-10½	178	26	4	Northwestern
Stringert, Hal (CB)	5-11	187	28	6	Hawaii
Williams, Mike (CB)	5-10	179	27	6	Louisiana State

CB=cornerback   S=safety

Buchanon gave a good account of himself, helping cut down the TD pass totals of previous years. Edwards, Williams and Fuller had four interceptions to their credits in '79; Shaw had three. Pass defense is a strong suit with the Chargers. Coryell can't do much here but gauge the depth properly.

Note: A complete listing of San Diego's 1980 college draft selections can be found on page 277.

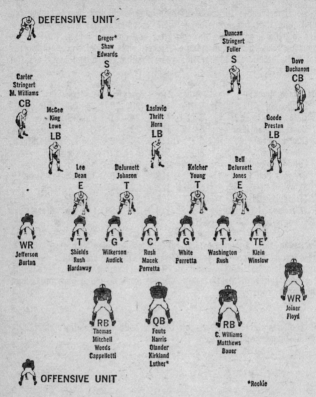

DEFENSIVE UNIT

Gregor*
Shaw
Edwards
S

Duncan
Stringert
Fuller
S

Carter
Stringert
M. Williams
CB

Dove
Buchanon
CB

McGee
King
Lowe
LB

Laslavic
Thrift
Horn
LB

Goode
Preston
LB

Lee
Dean
E

DeJurnett
Johnson
T

Kelcher
Young
T

Bell
DeJurnett
Jones
E

WR
Jefferson
Burton

T
Shields
Rush
Hardaway

G
Wilkerson
Audick

C
Rush
Macek
Perretta

G
White
Perretta

T
Washington
Rush

TE
Klein
Winslow

WR
Joiner
Floyd

RB
Thomas
Mitchell
Woods
Cappelletti

QB
Fouts
Harris
Olander
Kirkland
Luther*

RB
C. Williams
Matthews
Bauer

OFFENSIVE UNIT

*Rookie

1979 CHARGERS STATISTICS

	Chargers	Opps.
Total Points Scored	411*	246
Total First Downs	330	268
Third Down Efficiency Percentage	42.4	35.1
Yards Rushing—First Downs	1668—114	1907—117
Passes Attempted—Completions	541—338	472—261
Yards Passing—First Downs	3915—192	2549—132
QB Sacked—Yards Lost	31—223	42—332
Interceptions By—Return Average	28—20.1	25—11.2
Punts—Average Yards	75—36.5	82—40.8
Punt Returns—Average Return	52—9.4	34—6.0
Kickoff Returns—Average Return	50—21.3	72—21.3
Fumbles—Ball Lost	31—11	31—19
Penalties—Yards	108—908	101—922

*Includes 2 safeties

STATISTICAL LEADERS

Scoring	TDs	Rush.	Pass.	Ret.	PATs	FGs	Total
C. Williams	12	12	0	0	0	0	72
Wood	0	0	0	0	28—31	11—14	61
Jefferson	10	0	10	0	0	0	60
Bauer	8	8	0	0	0	0	48
Klein	5	0	5	0	0	0	30
Benirschke	0	0	0	0	12—13	4—4	24
Joiner	4	0	4	0	0	0	24
Winslow	2	0	2	0	0	0	12
Lowe	2	0	0	2	0	0	12
Owens	2	1	1	0	0	0	12

Rushing	Atts.	Yds.	Avg.	Longest	TDs
C. Williams	200	752	3.8	55 (TD)	12
Thomas	91	353	3.9	21	1
Mitchell	63	211	3.3	15	0
Owens	40	151	3.8	23	1
Matthews	30	112	3.7	22	1

Passing	Atts.	Com.	Yds.	Pct.	Int.	Longest	TDs
Fouts	530	332	4082	62.6	24	65 (TD)	24
Harris	9	5	38	55.6	1	10	0

Receiving	No.	Yds.	Avg.	Longest	TDs
Joiner	72	1008	14.0	39	4
Jefferson	61	1090	17.9	65 (TD)	10
C. Williams	51	352	6.9	14	0
Klein	37	424	11.5	54 (TD)	5
Thomas	32	388	12.1	32	0
Winslow	25	255	10.2	30	2
Mitchell	19	159	8.4	24	1

Interceptions	No.	Yds.	Avg.	Longest	TDs
Lowe	5	150	30.0	77 (TD)	2
Preston	5	121	24.2	35	0
Edwards	4	99	24.8	53	0
M. Williams	4	55	13.8	50	0
Fuller	4	39	9.8	23	0
Shaw	3	54	18.0	30	0

Punting	No.	Yds.	Avg.	Longest	Inside 20	Blocked
West	75	2736	36.5	62	22	0

Punt Returns	No.	FCs	Yds.	Avg.	Longest	TDs
Fuller	46	7	448	9.7	27	0
M. Williams	3	0	19	6.3	10	0

Kickoff Returns	No.	Yds.	Avg.	Longest	TDs
Owens	35	791	22.6	40	0
Fuller	6	115	19.2	41	0
Bauer	4	92	23.0	31	0

OAKLAND RAIDERS

Head Coach: Tom Flores

2nd Year   **Record: 9–7**

1979 RECORD (9-7)			1980 SCHEDULE	
(capital letters indicate home games)			(capital letters indicate home games)	
24	Los Angeles	17	Kansas City	Sept. 7
10	San Diego	30	San Diego	Sept. 14
10	Seattle	27	WASHINGTON	Sept. 21
7	Kansas Ciy	35	Buffalo	Sept. 28
27	DENVER	3	KANSAS CITY	Oct. 5
13	MIAMI	3	SAN DIEGO	Oct. 12
50	ATLANTA	19	Pittsburgh (night, TV)	Oct. 20
19	N.Y. Jets	28	SEATTLE	Oct. 26
45	SAN DIEGO	22	MIAMI	Nov. 2
23	SAN FRANCISCO	10	CINCINNATI	Nov. 9
17	Houston	31	Seattle (night, TV)	Nov. 17
21	KANSAS CITY	24	Philadelphia	Nov. 23
14	Denver	10	DENVER (night, TV)	Dec. 1
42	New Orleans	35	DALLAS	Dec. 7
19	CLEVELAND	14	Denver	Dec. 14
24	SEATTLE	29	N.Y. Giants	Dec. 21
365		337		

As the 28 NFL clubs unlimber their big guns in preparation for the 1980 campaign, about the only thing that could conceivably jar Al Davis and his Raiders out of Oakland would be a California earthquake—but it would have to be a legal earthquake.

For the moment, at least, the Raiders are foregoing Los Angeles and staying put in their Oakland surroundings where they have been since becoming a member of the American Football League in 1960, the year the AFL was organized. And since September 18, 1966, they have played their home games in the 30-million-dollar Oakland Coliseum which was built by the city and Alameda County in a joint financial venture. Over the subsequent years the Raiders have succeeded, to a marked degree, in living up to their own designation as "Pro Football's Most Dynamic Organization." They went to the Super Bowl twice and won it once. Their trophy room also proclaims an AFL championship, an AFC title and nine divisional flags. And through all those years, Oakland fans have been both responsive and appreciative as the club's record sale of 51,825 season tickets in 1979 would indicate.

When former Raider star quarterback Tom Flores became head coach at the start of last season, he already stood in the long shadow of Al Davis, the club's managing general partner and, as most knowledgeable people would agree, its moving spirit. His credits include a stint as the team's head coach. He also served as Commissioner of the American Football League for two hectic months in the spring of 1966 when the six-year war between the AFL and NFL reached its roaring climax and a merger was accomplished. Still, merger or not, the feud that quite naturally arose between NFL Commissioner Pete Rozelle and his AFL counterpart, Al Davis, has persisted through the years, even down to this day. There's little doubt that each will say of the other, "He's not my type of guy."

So when Tom Flores, a mild, easy-going kind of guy, took over the coaching reins, he not only stood in Davis's long shadow, he also had a very sensational act to follow. John Madden had retired as head coach after 12 years and an astonishing 103-32-7 record of achievement. And by the time the '79 season came to a close, with the Raiders on the winning side of a 9-7 record, it seemed altogether miraculous that Flores had been able to accomplish even that, considering the ordeal he had gone through all season long. For instance . . .

(1) Quarterback Ken Stabler continued his feud

with Al Davis, culminating in a trade which sent Stabler to Houston in exhange for Dan Pastorini. Said Stabler: "I haven't even spoken to Al Davis in more than a year."

(2) At height of the '79 season, Davis insisted on going to a 4-3 defensive lineup, instead of the 3-4 alignment then in use. (The difference here is 4 down linemen and 3 linebackers, or 3 down linemen and 4 linebackers.) Oakland defensive coordinator Myrel Moore differed with Davis on the change, but the Raiders did seem to win more games with the 4-3 in place. As a result of all this, Moore was fired.

The defensive lineup fuss reached its final stage, perhaps, while the Raiders were losing to the New Orleans Saints with the score 35-14 even before halftime had arrived. The Oakland defense was in 3-4 alignment and already the three-man line had yielded 212 yards and 14 first downs to the New Orleans attack. At halftime, Davis personally ordered a switch to the four-man line and, in the second half, the Saints could move only 68 yards, scoring no points at all. And, as if the Davis magic had worked its wonders, the Raiders won the game, 42-35. But in the season's final game against the Seattle Seahawks, guess which way the Oakland defense lined up? That's right, the 3-4!

As the Raiders enter the new season, much will depend on whether former Houston quarterback Dan Pastorini can adjust to his new job. As one observer sees it, "It's hard to imagine the Raiders without Stabler at quarterback." And there are the concerned persons, like San Diego head coach Don Coryell whose Chargers must battle the Raiders twice in the AFC West. How does he feel about the trade, and its effect upon both the Oilers and Raiders? For one thing, Coryell believes both teams will benefit because "personal issues have been diffused by the trade." Also, says Coryell, "Pastorini can throw the ball long and has Cliff Branch to throw to. On the other hand, Stabler is good at play action, faking. In Houston with Earl Campbell, that will be quite a combination. I have the utmost respect for both Pastorini and Stabler as complete quarterbacks."

Just as Dallas has its glamorous Cheerleaders and Los Angeles its Embraceable Ewes, Oakland has its Raiderettes swinging, dancing and cavorting up and down the sidelines. The Raiderettes even flew to Tokyo recently where they received the all-time high rating for any show ever aired on Japanese Educational TV. If the move to Los Angeles falls through, maybe the Raiders will wind up in Tokyo. The Tokyo Raiders . . . but does that sound right?

OFFENSE

Quarterbacks	Ht.	Wt.	Age	Exp.	College
Humm, David	6-2	190	28	6	Nebraska
Pastorini, Dan	6-3	205	31	10	Santa Clara
Plunkett, Jim	6-2	205	33	10	Stanford
Wilson, Marc	6-5	204	22	R	Brigham Young

Now that he's gone, let it be said that in his final season as a Raider, Ken Stabler completed 304 passes in 498 attempts for 3,615 yards, all new club records. That's going out with a flourish. Plunkett only saw action enough to throw 15 and completed seven. Pastorini's stats at Houston ranked him 13th among AFC passers—163 completions in 324 attempts, average 50.3. He was intercepted 18 times. Humm, it would seem, is no longer heir-apparent to the starting QB post. The Raiders found Brigham Young's All-American Marc Wilson still available after 14 choices in the draft's first round and chose him No. 15. Wilson could become one of the good ones.

Running Backs	Ht.	Wt.	Age	Exp.	College
Christensen, Todd	6-3	230	24	2	Brigham Young
Gordon, Fred	6-1	230	23	1	North Texas State
Hawkins, Clarence	6-0	205	24	2	Florida A&M

Jensen, Derrick	6-1	225	24	2	Texas-Arlington
King, Kenny	5-11	203	23	2	Oklahoma
Matthews, Ira	5-8	175	23	2	Wisconsin
Robiskie, Terry	6-1	205	26	4	Louisiana State
Russell, Booker	6-2	230	24	3	Southwest Texas
van Eeghen, Mark	6-2	225	28	7	Colgate
Whittington, Arthur	5-11	180	25	3	Southern Methodist

Van Eeghen led rushers with 818 yards, falling somewhat short of the thousand-yard goal-line. But that was because of knee and hamstring problems. Rookie Ira Matthews (along with Raider wide receiver Larry Brunson) led the AFC in kickoff returning with 24.9-yard average. Brunson's was a 25.9 average. Matthews returned one kickoff 104 yards against the Chargers after hesitating four yards deep in the end zone. The saying goes, "He who hesitates is lost," but not in this case. Whittington was club's second leading rusher with 397 yards. The Oakland ground game wasn't all that exciting.

Receivers	Ht.	Wt.	Age	Exp.	College
Bradshaw, Morris (W)	6-1	195	28	7	Ohio State
Branch, Cliff (W)	5-11	170	32	9	Colorado
Brunson, Larry (W)	5-11	180	31	6	Colorado
Casper, Dave (T)	6-4	230	28	7	Notre Dame
Chandler, Bob (W)	6-1	180	31	10	Southern Cal
Chester, Raymond (T)	6-4	235	32	11	Morgan State
Martini, Rich (W)	6-2	185	25	2	California-Davis
Pough, Ernest (W)	6-1	175	28	4	Texas Southern
Ramsey, Derrick (T)	6-4	220	24	3	Kentucky
Stewart, Joe (W)	5-11	180	25	3	Missouri

W=wide receiver   T=tight end

Oakland's two Pro Bowl tight ends each caught more than 50 passes last season—Chester 58 for 712 yards, 8 TDs, Casper for 57-771-3. Branch, too, caught 59 for 844 yards and 6 TDs. Not to be outdone in this department, Mark van Eeghen emerged from the backfield to catch 51 for 474 yards and 2 TDs. Stabler, of course, was the fountainhead for all those aerials. Martini did just fine his rookie year, playing in all 16 games and pulling in 24 passes for 10.8 average. Back in his college days at Notre Dame, Casper was a tackle and often yearns to play that position again before retiring from football. He remembers that "playing tackle was nice. . . . Pass receiving makes me nervous. . . . There's lots of pressure and anybody who says they enjoy pressure is either crazy or lying. . . . Nobody ever booed me for dropping a pass when I played tackle!"

Interior Linemen	Ht.	Wt.	Age	Exp.	College
Dalby, Dave (C)	6-3	250	30	9	UCLA
Davis, Bruce (T)	6-6	280	24	2	UCLA

Lawrence, Henry (T)	6-4	270	29	7	Florida A&M
Marvin, Mickey (G)	6-4	270	25	4	Tennessee
Mason, Lindsey (T)	6-5	260	25	2	Kansas
Medlin, Dan (G)	6-4	250	31	7	N. C. State
Meseroll, Mark (T)	6-5	275	25	2	Florida State
Moritz, Brett (G)	6-4	240	25	2	Nebraska
Shell, Art (T)	6-5	275	34	13	Md.-Eastern Shore
Sylvester, Steve (T)	6-4	260	27	6	Notre Dame
Upshaw, Gene (G)	6-5	255	35	14	Texas A&I
Vella, John (T)	6-4	260	30	9	Southern Cal
Winans, Jeff (G)	6-4	260	29	5	Southern Cal

T=tackle   G=guard   C=center

Shell, Upshaw, Dalby, Sylvester and Lawrence were the front five at season's end. The offensive line didn't contribute much to a ground game that lagged, but pass protection for Stabler was good. He bit the dust 36 times (or the Oakland QB did) and that wasn't bad, considering the difficulty many NFL quarterbacks have staying on their feet. Sylvester is a tackle, most of the time. But when Dalby was sidelined at center, Sylvester snapped the ball, and when Marvin went on injured reserve, Sylvester was his replacement. A man for all seasons and positions.

Kickers	Ht.	Wt.	Age	Exp.	College
Breech, Jim (Pk)	5-6	155	24	2	California
Guy, Ray (P)	6-3	190	31	8	Southern Mississippi

Pk=placekicker   P=punter

Guy was Oakland's No. 1 draft choice back in 1973. The 31-year-old punter has more than justified that early rating. In last season's 45-22 win over San Diego, he averaged an incredible 49.6 yards on five punts to keep the Chargers deep in their own territory early in the game. Two of those kicks traveled 56 and 71 yards. Punting the ball is a fine art with Guy. Breech did well as a rookie placekicker, nailing 41-45 PATs and 18-of-27 FGs, 10 of them from the beyond-30 range.

DEFENSE

Front Linemen	Ht.	Wt.	Age	Exp.	College
Browning, Dave (E)	6-5	245	24	3	Washington
Jones, Willie (E)	6-4	240	23	2	Florida State
Kinlaw, Reggie (MG)	6-1	240	23	2	Oklahoma
Matuszak, John (E)	6-8	275	30	8	Tampa
Pear, Dave (MG)	6-2	250	27	6	Washington
Philyaw, Charles (E)	6-9	280	26	5	Texas Southern

Sistrunk, Otis (MG)	6-4	270	33	8	(None)
Toomay, Pat (E)	6-6	245	32	11	Vanderbilt

E=end   MG=middle guard

Coach Flores will have to man his defenses if the Raiders are to rise again. Last season, an inner-club controversy raged over whether they would play a 3-4 or a 4-3 defense. In the 3-4, the front three are Browning, Pear- and Toomay, a blend of youth, middle-age and age. Jones distinguished himself at times as a pass rusher. Kinlaw's rookie season was impressive, and he stays.

Linebackers	Ht.	Wt.	Age	Exp.	College
Adams, John (O)	6-3	233	22	R	Louisiana State
Barnes, Jeff (O)	6-2	215	25	4	California
Bowens, William (O)	6-3	225	22	R	North Alabama
Hendricks, Ted (O)	6-7	220	33	12	Miami (Fla.)
Huddleston, John (I)	6-3	230	26	3	Utah
Hudgens, Dave (I)	6-5	230	25	1	Oklahoma
Johnson, Monte (I)	6-5	240	29	8	Nebraska
Lewis, Kenny (O)	6-0	194	22	R	Virginia Tech
Martin, Rod (O)	6-2	210	26	4	Southern Cal
Massey, Mike (O)	6-2	225	22	R	Arkansas
Millen, Matt (O)	6-1	256	22	R	Penn State

O=outside   I=inside

Hendricks has a long playing record—and that's not a reference to his music library. He's getting a little old as football players go, especially the linebacking species. Johnson is beginning to slow down a bit himself, according to some observers who use slide rules to gauge the Raiders. Martin had a great season, showing speed along with an instinctive knack of getting to the ball. In the draft, the Raiders really loaded up on linebackers in the first five rounds, picking four—and then took Mike Massey of Arkansas in the 11th for good measure.

Defensive Backs	Ht.	Wt.	Age	Exp.	College
Bess, Rufus (CB)	5-9	180	24	2	South Carolina State
Davis, Mike (S)	6-2	200	24	3	Colorado
Harrison, Dwight (CB)	6-2	185	32	9	Texas A&I
Hayes, Lester (CB)	6-0	195	25	4	Texas A&M
Jackson, Monte (CB)	5-11	190	27	6	San Diego State
McKinney, Odis (S)	6-2	187	23	3	Colorado
Owens, Burgess (S)	6-2	200	29	8	Miami (Fla.)
Parker, Kerry (CB)	6-1	180	25	1	Grambling
Phillips, Charles (S)	6-2	215	28	6	Southern Cal
Williams, Henry (CB)	5-10	180	24	2	San Diego State

CB=cornerback   S=safety

Williams showed talent his rookie year, intercepting three passes and otherwise making himself useful. Hayes intercepted seven, good enough for second place in AFC. Williams and Hayes open at the corners. Opposition quarterbacks threw 21 TD passes against the Oakland secondary last season, and that was a fair-to-middling number.

Note: A complete listing of Oakland's 1980 college draft selections can be found on page 275.

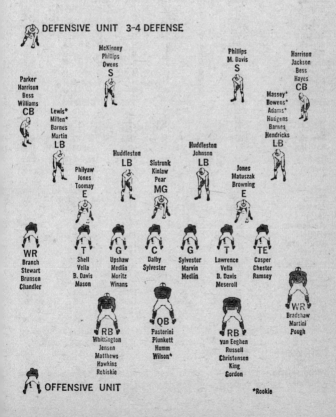

DEFENSIVE UNIT 3-4 DEFENSE

McKinney / Phillips / Owens — S
Phillips / M. Davis — S
Harrison / Jackson / Bess / Hayes — CB
Parker / Harrison / Bess / Williams — CB
Massey* / Bowens* / Adams* / Hudgens / Barnes / Hendricks — LB
Lewis* / Millen* / Barnes / Martin — LB
Huddleston — LB
Sistrunk / Kinlaw / Pear — MG
Huddleston / Johnson — LB
Philyaw / Jones / Toomay — E
Jones / Matuszak / Browning — E

OFFENSIVE UNIT

WR — Branch / Stewart / Brunson / Chandler
T — Shell / Vella / B. Davis / Mason
G — Upshaw / Medlin / Moritz / Winans
C — Dalby / Sylvester
G — Sylvester / Marvin / Medlin
T — Lawrence / Vella / B. Davis / Meseroll
TE — Casper / Chester / Ramsey
WR — Bradshaw / Martini / Pough
QB — Pastorini / Plunkett / Humm / Wilson*
RB — Whittington / Jensen / Matthews / Hawkins / Robiskie
RB — van Eeghen / Russell / Christensen / King / Gordon

*Rookie

1979 RAIDERS STATISTICS

	Raiders	Opps.
Total Points Scored	365	337
Total First Downs	321	335
Third Down Efficiency Percentage	43.7	42.3
Yards Rushing—First Downs	1763—102	2374—145
Passes Attempted—Completions	513—311	471—247
Yards Passing—First Downs	3411—191	3112—154
QB Sacked—Yards Lost	36—293	33—254
Interceptions By—Return Average	24—13.0	23—20.6
Punts—Average Yards	70—42.0	63—37.7
Punt Returns—Average Return	35—5.1	40—10.4
Kickoff Returns—Average Return	65—22.7	66—19.5
Fumbles—Ball Lost	34—14	35—22
Penalties—Yards	119—1029	106—1018

STATISTICAL LEADERS

Scoring	TDs	Rush.	Pass.	Ret.	PATs	FGs	Total
Breech	0	0	0	0	41—45	18—27	95
van Eeghen	9	7	2	0	0	0	54
Chester	8	0	8	0	0	0	48
Branch	6	0	6	0	0	0	36
Russell	4	4	0	0	0	0	24
Casper	3	0	3	0	0	0	18
Ramsey	3	0	3	0	0	0	18
Hayes	2	0	0	2	0	0	12
Martini	2	0	2	0	0	0	12
Whittington	2	2	0	0	0	0	12

Rushing	Atts.	Yds.	Avg.	Longest	TDs
van Eeghen	223	818	3.7	19	7
Whittington	109	397	3.6	22	2
Jensen	73	251	3.4	15	0
Russell	33	190	5.8	72	4
Hawkins	21	72	3.4	34	0

Passing	Atts.	Com.	Yds.	Pct.	Int.	Longest	TDs
Stabler	498	304	3615	61.0	22	66 (TD)	26
Plunkett	15	7	89	46.7	1	39	1

Receiving	No.	Yds.	Avg.	Longest	TDs
Branch	59	844	14.3	66 (TD)	6
Chester	58	712	12.3	39	8
Casper	57	771	13.5	42	3
van Eeghen	51	474	9.3	36	2
Martini	24	259	10.8	22 (TD)	2
Whittington	19	240	12.6	39	0
Ramsey	13	161	12.4	40	3

Interceptions	No.	Yds.	Avg.	Longest	TDs
Hayes	7	100	14.3	52 (TD)	2
Phillips	4	92	23.0	30	0
Williams	3	37	12.3	33	0
Tatum	2	26	13.0	13	0
M. Davis	2	22	11.0	11	0
Jackson	2	5	2.5	5	0

Punting	No.	Yds.	Avg.	Longest	Inside 20	Blocked
Guy	69	2939	42.6	71	16	0

Punt Returns	No.	FCs	Yds.	Avg.	Longest	TDs
Matthews	32	7	165	5.2	20	0

Kickoff Returns	No.	Yds.	Avg.	Longest	TDs
Matthews	35	873	24.9	104 (TD)	1
Brunson	17	441	25.9	89	0

DENVER BRONCOS

Head Coach: Red Miller

4th Year   **Record:** 32–14

1979 RECORD (10-6) (capital letters indicate home games)		1980 SCHEDULE (capital letters indicate home games)	
10	CINCINNATI	0	Philadelphia	Sept. 7
9	LOS ANGELES	13	DALLAS	Sept. 14
20	Atlanta	17	SAN DIEGO	Sept. 21
37	SEATTLE	34	New England (night, TV)	Sept. 29
3	Oakland	27	Cleveland	Oct. 5
7	SAN DIEGO	0	WASHINGTON (night, TV)	Oct. 13
24	Kansas City	10	KANSAS CITY	Oct. 19
7	Pittsburgh	42	N.Y. Giants	Oct. 26
20	KANSAS CITY	3	HOUSTON	Nov. 2
10	NEW ORLEANS	3	San Diego	Nov. 9
45	NEW ENGLAND	10	N.Y. JETS	Nov. 16
38	San Francisco	28	SEATTLE	Nov. 23
10	OAKLAND	14	Oakland (night, TV)	Dec. 1
19	Buffalo	16	Kansas City	Dec. 7
23	Seattle	28	OAKLAND	Dec. 14
7	San Diego	17	Seattle	Dec. 21
289		262		

Playoffs

7	Houston	13

Before Red Miller took over the head coaching duties at Denver three years ago, the Broncos had never won a spot in the playoffs. By the time the 1979 season came to a close, they were in the playoffs for the third time which is an impressive reminder of what Miller's presence in Denver means to the AFC West. And that meaning is abundantly clear—the Broncos must be reckoned with, defensively for sure and offensively, well maybe.

Late last April, just before the NFL college draft, Miller expressed himself as being generally satisfied with his team. "We don't feel we have to make any wholesale changes," he ventured, "but we need help like all teams do, even Pittsburgh as strong as they are. But we're an established team and I don't see us doing anything except getting better."

Even so, Miller is plotting changes, some of which may well alter the club's conservative stance, especially on offense. The biggest alterations are due in the offensive unit where an off-season trade with the Jets brought quarterback Matt Robinson to Denver in exchange for QB Craig Penrose, plus first and second round choices in the '79 college draft. It was a high price to pay for Robinson who sat out most of last season with a sore thumb, sustained while wrestling with a teammate. Miller's decision to go for Robinson had been based on certain developments in the quarterback situation.

First, early this past January, Craig Morton decided to return for the 1980 season, even though he had talked retirement only a few weeks before. That did nothing, however, to deter a decision that Miller, along with general manager Fred Gehrke and personnel chief Carroll Hardy, had made regarding Denver's quarterback position. They had decided that, first and foremost and without any more fooling around, Denver must acquire a first-class, bona fide, NFL-type quarterback in the mold of Bradshaw, Tarkenton, Griese, or you name it. This was given the highest priority.

Several candidates were considered, such as Marc Wilson of Brigham Young and Mark Malone of Arizona State, and NFL quarterbacks such as Robinson of the Jets, Danielson of Detroit and Owen of New England, all of whom were in various stages of availability. When decision time came, it was Robinson's previous showing with the Jets, especially during the 1978 season, that swung the balance in his favor. And the decision came after the hiring of former Stanford head coach Rod

Dowhower who is a noted developer of quarterback talent. He is now Denver's offensive coordinator.

Dowhower is acting under orders to install a more effective offensive game, a more potent attack to go with one of the league's premier defensive units. Does that mean that Matt Robinson automatically gets the quarterback's job? "No," says Red Miller, "this doesn't necessarily mean he's the No. 1 choice. He will have to compete with Craig Morton, Norris Weese and Pete Woods as we go to work and we'll see what happens."

During all three of his years at Denver, Miller has often been criticized for having too conservative an offense, with the 1979 season giving those critics plenty to complain about. Denver's offensive unit ranked 25th in third-down efficiency (conversion to a first down on the third, thereby avoiding a punt and keeping the ball). The 289 points scored by the Broncos was only the league's 20th best. The running game ranked 19th in average gain per carry. Certainly not the kind of statistics that are identified with high-scoring football operations.

Obviously, Denver made the playoffs last season for the third consecutive year on the basis of another strong defensive performance. The Broncos allowed the opposition just 262 points, the AFC's third lowest figure behind Pittsburgh and Kansas City, and they yielded a stingy average of 303.3 yards a game, including an NFL-low 105.8 yards rushing. A strong defense, then, has been the hallmark of Miller's Denver teams, even though he had personally served as the club's offensive coordinator until the recent appointment of Dowhower to that post.

Shortly after the final whistle in the Astrodome last December, while Houston fans were still whooping it up over the Oilers' 13-7 playoff victory over Denver, Miller set the pattern for future strategy. "No alibis, excuses," he said in the almost tomb-like silence of the Broncos' locker room: "Congratulations to the Houston Oilers. We just can't score seven points and expect to win games. We must analyze and do something about our offense next year."

"Next year" begins at Philadelphia on September 7th as the Broncos begin their regular season against one of the NFC East's strongest teams—one that ranks high in NFC defensive ratings. It should be a fine test flight for that new Denver passing game.

OFFENSE

Quarterbacks	Ht.	Wt.	Age	Exp.	College
Morton, Craig	6-4	211	37	16	California
Robinson, Matt	6-2	196	25	4	Georgia
Weese, Norris	6-1	200	29	5	Mississippi
Woods, Pete	6-4	215	24	1	Missouri

What complicates the Denver quarterback picture is the fact that Morton did a grand job last season, posting career passing highs in several categories: attempts 370, completions 204, yardage 2,626 and completion percentage 55.1. But the Denver offense didn't set any new records, far from it. Hence the arrival of Matt Robinson at Mile High Stadium (and the departure of Craig Penrose) in a trade with the Jets. Robinson did not play much for the Jets last season after injuring his passing thumb, but he did throw 31 times and completed 17 for a 54.8 percentage. Weese passed 97 times for a 54.6 completion percentage and Woods is a free agent who hasn't really had a chance to show his throwing stuff. Still, Miller must like the idea of open QB competition.

Running Backs	Ht.	Wt.	Age	Exp.	College
Armstrong, Otis	5-10	196	30	8	Purdue
Canada, Larry	6-2	220	26	3	Wisconsin
Hardeman, Don	6-1	240	28	6	Texas A&I
Jensen, Jim	6-3	230	27	4	Iowa
Keyworth, Jon	6-3	230	30	7	Colorado
Lytle, Rob	6-1	195	26	4	Michigan
McCutcheon, Lawrence	6-1	205	30	8	Colorado State
Parros, Rick	6-0	200	22	R	Utah State
Preston, Dave	5-11	195	25	3	Bowling Green

No one was outstanding in this unit last season, Armstrong's 453 yards being the club high. Miller kept rotating six backs game-in and game-out and yardage production was fairly evenly divided among all, depending upon the amount of playing time accorded each. Canada was used mostly in short yardage situations. Preston missed five games with injury. McCutcheon wasn't happy at Los Angeles after Wendell Tyler replaced him as a starter. Can he be a born again thousand-yarder in Denver? Miller would like to know.

Receivers	Ht.	Wt.	Age	Exp.	College
Dolbin, Jack (W)	5-10	180	32	6	Wake Forest
Egloff, Ron (T)	6-5	227	25	4	Wisconsin
Kinney, Vince (W)	6-2	190	24	3	Maryland
Larson, Bill (T)	6-4	230	26	4	Colorado State
Moorehead, Emery (W)	6-2	210	26	4	Colorado
Moses, Haven (W)	6-2	201	34	13	San Diego State
Odoms, Riley (T)	6-4	244	30	9	Houston
Richards, Golden (W)	6-0	180	29	8	Hawaii
Upchurch, Rick (W)	5-10	176	28	6	Minnesota
Watson, Steve (W)	6-4	192	23	2	Temple

W=wide receiver   T=tight end

Upchurch's 64 catches (for 937 yards and 7 TDs) were most receptions for a Bronco receiver since Lionel Taylor caught 85 back in the AFL days of 1965. Moses reached new personal career highs with 54 catches for 943 yards. Odoms, third member of Denver's first-line receiving corps, caught 40 for 638 yards. Still, the question persists: Would Denver be better off with another WR and TE to add depth? Dolbin had a knee injury last season, and Moses is getting along in years. Larson has played with 49ers, Lions and Eagles, and comes to Denver as a free agent. A 1981 draft choice was traded to the Giants in exchange for Moorehead, probably because of worries about Dolbin's knee and Moses's age.

Interior Linemen	Ht.	Wt.	Age	Exp.	College
Brown, Ken (C)	6-1	245	26	2	New Mexico
Bryan, Bill (C)	6-2	244	25	4	Duke
Clark, Kelvin (T)	6-3	245	24	2	Nebraska
Glassic, Tom (G)	6-4	250	26	5	Virginia
Howard, Paul (G)	6-3	260	30	7	Brigham Young
Hyde, Glenn (G)	6-3	252	29	5	Pittsburgh
Keys, Richard (C-G)	6-3	256	24	1	Mississippi State
Minor, Claudie (T)	6-4	275	29	7	San Diego State
Studdard, Dave (T)	6-4	255	25	2	Texas
Uperesa, Keith (G)	6-3	275	24	1	Brigham Young

T=tackle   G=guard   C=center

Miller feels that his offensive line showed improvement last season, but there's still room for more. Studdard became a starting tackle in his rookie year, and sticks to his guns again this season. Minor is the other starter at tackle along with Howard and Glassic at guards, Bryan at center. Of significance is the fact that offensive linemen have made up three of Denver's last four draft choices. Says Miller: "We think we've finally got the people we want and the more they play, the better they're going to be."

Kickers	Ht.	Wt.	Age	Exp.	College
Prestridge, Luke (P)	6-4	235	24	2	Baylor
Steinfort, Fred (Pk)	5-11	180	28	5	Boston College
Turner, Jim (Pk)	6-2	212	39	17	Utah State

Pk=placekicker   P=punter

Turner became the second NFL player ever to kick more than 300 career FGs with 304 in 16 seasons. Only George Blanda has more, 355. Turner's career point total stands at 1,439, again second to Blanda's 2,002. And there's something else—Turner goes into the 1980 season with a string of 228 consecutive games played as a pro. Prestridge had what the Denver press release calls "a satisfactory first year," averaging 39.9 with his punts and dropping 17 of them inside the opposing 20-yard line. He also kicked the Broncos out of bad field position on several occasions, and that's very good. Steinfort, a placekicker who formerly handled kickoff chores for San Diego, was signed in last season and will bid for work with the Broncos.

DEFENSE

Front Linemen	Ht.	Wt.	Age	Exp.	College
Boyd, Greg (E)	6-6	280	26	4	San Diego State
Carter, Rubin (NT)	6-0	253	28	6	Miami (Fla.)
Chavous, Barney (E)	6-3	245	29	8	South Carolina State
Grant, John (E-NT)	6-3	240	30	8	Southern Cal
Jones, Rulon (E)	6-7	265	22	R	Utah State
Latimer, Don (NT)	6-2	253	25	3	Miami (Fla.)
Manor, Brison (E)	6-4	248	28	4	Arkansas
Radford, Bruce (E)	6-4	252	25	2	Grambling
Short, Laval (NT)	6-3	255	22	R	Colorado

E=end   NT=nose tackle

The defensive unit returns all starters. That's good news for Miller whose defense is one of the league's finest—if not the finest. It led the league in depriving the opposition of overland yardage last season, permitting just 3.37 yards per rush. But the defensive line could manage only 19 sacks of opposing quarterbacks in what must have been a hesitating pass rush. Carter is one of NFL's best nose tackles. Latimer showed much improvement in '79. Chavous was consistently good with 82 tackles and 40 assists. Manor became a starter and did OK with 72 tackles, 30 assists and a club high 6½ QB sacks. Free agent Boyd is a former Patriot. Still, Miller said: "I do think we need some help on the defensive line."

Linebackers	Ht.	Wt.	Age	Exp.	College
Evans, Larry (O)	6-2	220	27	5	Mississippi College
Gradishar, Randy (I)	6-3	231	28	7	Ohio State
Jackson, Tom (O)	5-11	228	29	8	Louisville
Narine, Rob (O)	6-4	220	26	4	Oregon State
Nichols, Mark (O)	6-3	225	23	1	Colorado State
Rizzo, Joe (I)	6-1	220	30	7	Merchant Marine
Ryan, Jim (O)	6-1	212	23	2	William & Mary
Swenson, Bob (O)	6-3	222	27	6	California
Smith, Arthur (O)	6-1	225	23	1	Hawaii

O=outside   I=inside

Gradishar and Rizzo are the insiders, Jackson and Swenson the out-siders. Gradishar led club in tackles with 146 solos, 89 assists, despite playing half the season with a surgical cast on his finger. Swenson led in turnovers, stealing three passes and recovering four fumbles, two of which led directly to Denver TDs. Gradishar and Jackson were Pro Bowlers for the third straight year. There's precious little room for complaint here.

Defensive Backs	Ht.	Wt.	Age	Exp.	College
Atkinson, George (S)	6-0	185	33	12	Morris Brown
Carter, Larry (S)	5-11	179	22	R	Kentucky
Foley, Steve (CB)	6-2	190	27	5	Tulane
Harden, Mike (CB)	6-0	183	22	R	Michigan
Harvey, Maurice (S)	5-10	190	24	2	Ball State
Holloway, Jerry (S)	6-4	235	23	1	Western Illinois
Jackson, Bernard (S)	6-0	180	30	9	Washington State
Johnson, Dickie (CB)	5-10	170	23	1	Southern Colorado
Pane, Chris (CB)	5-11	188	27	5	Chico State
Smith, Perry (CB)	6-0	190	29	8	Colorado State
Thompson, Bill (S)	6-1	197	34	12	Md.-Eastern Shore
West, Charlie (S)	6-1	195	34	13	Texas-El Paso
Wright, Louis (CB)	6-2	200	27	6	San Jose State

CB=cornerback   S=safety

Both the age factor and depth weigh here as factors for the future of Denver's secondary. Thompson, Atkinson, Jackson and West have 46 accumulated NFL years behind them, although their abilities stand up well against time. Still, the depth is thin. Harvey looked good but banged up a knee. Jackson was sidelined for four games with a sprained ankle. Foley led club in pass thefts for second straight year with six. Holloway and Johnson were signed on as free agents. Thompson is the team's defensive captain. . . .

Note: A complete listing of Denver's 1980 college draft selections can be found on page 270.

DEFENSIVE UNIT 3-4 DEFENSE

Harvey
Atkinson
West
B. Jackson
S

L. Carter
Holloway
West
Thompson
S

P. Smith
Pane
Wright
CB

Harden*
Pane
Foley
CB

A. Smith
Ryan
Evans
T. Jackson
LB

A. Smith
Nichols
Evans
Gradishar
LB

Evans
Nairne
Rizzo
LB

Nichols
Ryan
Nairne
Swenson
LB

Boyd
Radford
Manor
E

Short*
Grant
Latimer
R. Carter
NT

Jones*
Grant
Chavous
E

WR
Upchurch
Watson
Dolbin
Richards

T
Studdard
Clark
Hyde

G
Glassic
Hyde
Keys

C
Bryan
Brown
Keys

G
Howard
Hyde
Uperesa

T
Minor
Clark

TE
Odoms
Egloff
Larson

WR
Moses
Kinney
Watson
Moorehead

RB
Armstrong
Preston
McCutcheon
Parros*

QB
Morton
Weese
Robinson
Woods

RB
Keyworth
Jensen
Canada
Lytle
Hardeman

OFFENSIVE UNIT

*Rookie

1979 BRONCOS STATISTICS

	Broncos	Opps.
Total Points Scored	289	262
Total First Downs	306	273
Third Down Efficiency Percentage	35.0	38.0
Yards Rshing—First Downs	2040—130	1693—100
Passes Attempted—Completions	476—260	512—296
Yards Passing—First Downs	3102—149	3159—146
QB Sacked—Yards Lost	44—331	19—162
Interceptions By—Return Average	19—9.9	23—12.7
Punts—Average Yards	89—39.9	88—42.1
Punt Returns—Average Return	43—9.3	52—9.2
Kickoff Returns—Average Return	50—19.3	57—20.6
Fumbles—Ball Lost	35—18	30—19
Penalties—Yards	116—1006	118—1033

STATISTICAL LEADERS

Scoring	TDs	Rush.	Pass.	Ret.	PATs	FGs	Total
Turner	0	0	0	0	32—34	13—21	71
Upchurch	7	0	7	0	0	0	42
Moses	6	0	6	0	0	0	36
Lytle	4	4	0	0	0	0	24
Weese	3	3	0	0	0	0	18
Armstrong	3	2	1	0	0	0	18
Preston	2	1	1	0	0	0	12
Jensen	2	1	1	0	0	0	12

Rushing	Atts.	Yds.	Avg.	Longest	TDs
Armstrong	108	453	4.2	26	2
Jensen	106	400	3.8	30	1
Lytle	102	371	3.6	19	4
Keyworth	81	323	4.0	17	1
Preston	43	169	3.9	18	1
Canada	36	143	4.0	17	0
Weese	18	116	6.4	20	3
Morton	22	17	0.8	7	1

Passing	Atts.	Com.	Yds.	Pct.	Int.	Longest	TDs
Morton	370	204	2626	55.1	19	64 (TD)	16
Weese	97	53	731	54.6	3	50	1

Receiving	No.	Yds.	Avg.	Longest	TDs
Upchurch	64	937	14.6	47	7
Moses	54	943	17.5	64 (TD)	6
Odoms	40	638	16.0	45	1
Jensen	19	144	7.6	25 (TD)	1
Preston	19	137	7.2	19	1
Keyworth	18	132	7.3	18	0
Armstrong	14	138	9.9	17	1
Lytle	13	93	7.2	12	0

Interceptions	No.	Yds.	Avg.	Longest	TDs
Foley	6	14	2.3	7	0
Thompson	4	57	14.3	28	0
Swenson	3	0	—	—	0
Rizzo	2	25	12.5	25	0
Wright	2	20	10.0	15	0

Punting	No.	Yds.	Avg.	Longest	Inside 20	Blocked
Prestridge	89	3555	39.9	63	17	0

Punt Returns	No.	FCs	Yds.	Avg.	Longest	TDs
Upchurch	30	5	304	10.1	44	0
Preston	7	1	78	11.1	22	0

Kickoff Returns	No.	Yds.	Avg.	Longest	TDs
Pane	18	354	19.7	30	0
Preston	13	336	25.8	37	0
Upchurch	5	79	15.8	26	0

SEATTLE SEAHAWKS

Head Coach: Jack Patera

5th Year   **Record:** 25–35

1979 RECORD (9-7) (capital letters indicate home games)		
16	SAN DIEGO	33
10	Miami	19
27	OAKLAND	10
34	Denver	37
6	KANSAS CITY	24
35	San Francisco	24
10	San Diego	20
34	HOUSTON	14
31	Atlanta	28
0	LOS ANGELES	24
29	Cleveland	24
38	NEW ORLEANS	24
30	N.Y. JETS	7
21	Kansas City	37
28	DENVER	23
29	Oakland	24
378		372

1980 SCHEDULE (capital letters indicate home games)	
SAN DIEGO	Sept. 7
Kansas City	Sept. 14
NEW ENGLAND	Sept. 21
Washington	Sept. 28
Houston	Oct. 5
CLEVELAND	Oct. 12
N.Y. Jets	Oct. 19
Oakland	Oct. 26
PHILADELPHIA	Nov. 2
KANSAS CITY	Nov. 9
OAKLAND (night, TV)	Nov. 17
Denver	Nov. 23
Dallas (TV)	Nov. 27
N.Y. GIANTS	Dec. 7
San Diego (TV)	Dec. 13
DENVER	Dec. 21

If Ringling Brothers, Barnum and Bailey ever decided to give up the circus and buy a pro football team, the Seattle Seahawks would be their first choice as a likely acquisition. When Gamblin' Jack Patera's offensive unit takes the field, it usually removes the lid from a whole series of plays, featuring show-business gimmicks that keep opposing players wondering just when the elephants will start parading across the field.

The Seahawks, by deliberate design, are dedicated to the idea of entertaining the fans and if, by chance, their performance is good enough to get them into the Super Bowl, well that's just fine. Patera, himself, is aware of his club's approach to a game that a lot of other people take seriously, very seriously, perhaps too seriously. "I think the image is good," he confides, "and we searched for three years to find ways to win and have fun, too. This helps, but consistency is still the key to winning."

Right now, the most consistent thing about the Seahawks is their flair for the unorthodox. They do things on fourth down, for instance, that would be against the law in the NFC Central, or the AFC East for that matter. Most football teams, if not all, regard the fourth down as a lost cause—either you punt the ball or run the risk of a goal-line stand, if you're on your side of the 50-yard line. Let it be said for posterity that the Seattle Seahawks don't see it exactly that way. Why give up the ball without a fight when six points are waiting within shouting distance? Why try for a three-point field goal when a touchdown gets you six and probably seven?

On four different occasions last season, Herman Weaver, whose kicks sail an average of 40 yards, dropped back to punt on fourth down situations, but elected to pass the ball intsead. What's even more intriguing is the fact he completed three of those tosses, one of them going 39 yards while picking up the first down as well. Weaver was appropriately modest about his 75 percent completion average, saying, "I had three in a row, but the fourth one kinda got caught up in the wind and sailed high."

And there's placekicker Efren Herrera, one of the NFL's best—except that nobody, not even Herrera, knows what he'll really do when the Seahawks send out their special team for a fourth down placekick. Sometimes what does happen brings a laugh, like the night Seattle played Atlanta on Monday TV. Herrera stood in position for a field goal attempt, but it was a fake. Instead of kicking the ball, Herrera casually trotted through the vaunted Atlanta defense and caught a 20-yard pass from Zorn. But when the same gimmick was tried in another game against Denver in the King-dome, Herrera dropped the pass, and the Seattle fans cheered! In still another contest against New Orleans, the placekicker ran a pass pattern down the sidelines, only to look up and see Zorn rolling out in the opposite direction for a first down. Asked why Zorn hadn't thrown him the ball, Herrera had an ego-fulfilling reply: "I guess I was double-covered."

The fake-placekick routine was only one of several razzle-dazzle type of plays the Seahawks sprang on the opposition, much to the delight of Seattle fans who seemed resigned to the idea of laughing while losing. Even so, the Seahawks narrowly missed getting into the playoffs with their 9-7 record (same as in '78). Let it be noted that the Los Angeles Rams also had a 9-7 record, and wound up in the Super Bowl. But Seattle's won-lost record followed a strange pattern in '79. The season began with everything in reverse, and after seven games the record was 2-5. Then came a scintillating turnaround, and for the next nine games the Seahawk whirlwind swept through seven victories against two defeats. This kind of record points up what Patera has to say about consistency, i.e., "it's the key to winning."

Seattle was hardly consistent in '79. They ran the Saints and Jets off the field on two successive weekends with winning scores of 38-24 and 30-7, then pro-ceeded to fall flat on their faces before the Chiefs, 37-21. The Seahawks were held to minus-seven yards by the Rams who won 24-0, then they traveled to Cleve-land and outscored the Browns, 29-24. They were 24 points ahead against Denver, and wound up three points behind, losing 37-34. It was that kind of a ball game whenever the Seahawks were involved.

Regardless of whether they continue to play a wide

open, spectacular type of football, or whether they decide to become somewhat more conformist in their style, the Seahawks do need some new faces in both their offensive and defensive units. On offense they could use a power-driving running back, plus a tight end and a wide receiver to provide more depth for Zorn's receivers, along with better blocking for the runners. The offensive line could use a guard and a tackle as backups for the regulars. On defense, the line badly needs a tackle and an end for a better pass rush; the secondary hurts for a cornerback and a safety to shore up a sieve-like pass defense.

And maybe, just maybe, the Seahawks will also need a new bag—something new and fancy in which to carry all those old tricks as well as some new ones.

OFFENSE

Quarterbacks	Ht.	Wt.	Age	Exp.	College
Adkins, Sam	6-2	214	25	4	Wichita State
Myer, Steve	6-2	200	26	5	New Mexico
Zorn, Jim	6-2	200	27	5	Cal Poly-Pomona

Zorn broke his own club records (set in '78) by completing 285 passes of 505 for 3,661 yards in 1979. His 20 TD passes are also a new Seahawk mark. As for Myer and Adkins, strange thing is that Myer threw eight times completing two for 25 percent completion average; Adkins threw three times completing none while Herman Weaver, the Seahawk punter, threw four passes and completed three for a 75 percent completion figure! Tricky types, those Seahawks.

Running Backs	Ht.	Wt.	Age	Exp.	College
Benjamin, Tony	6-3	225	25	4	Duke
Doornink, Dan	6-3	210	24	3	Washington State
Green, Tony	5-9	185	24	3	Florida
Hunter, Al	5-11	195	25	4	Notre Dame
Moore, Jeff	6-0	195	24	2	Jackson State
Smith, Sherman	6-4	225	26	5	Miami (O.)
Steele, Joe	6-4	210	22	R	Washington
Tate, Ezra	5-10	195	25	1	Mississippi College

This is a unit which needs help. Ever since David Sims was forced to retire two years ago after a neck injury, running back has been a Seahawk problem. Smith still gains good yardage (775, 4.0-yard average in '79) and Doornink is steady, but the ground attack lacks a flair. Hunter and Moore both saw some action last season, but they're hardly answers to depth requirements.

Receivers	Ht.	Wt.	Age	Exp.	College
Allen, Mike (W)	6-3	190	24	1	Washington State
Bell, Mark (T)	6-4	235	23	2	Colorado State
Carter, Terry (W)	6-1	195	25	R	Kent State
Dorsey, Larry (W)	6-0	190	27	4	Tennessee State
Green, Jessie (W)	6-3	194	26	2	Tulsa
Largent, Steve (W)	5-11	184	26	5	Tulsa
McCullum, Sam (W)	6-2	190	28	7	Montana State
Peets, Brian (T)	6-4	225	24	3	Pacific (Calif.)
Raible, Steve (W)	6-2	195	26	5	Georgia Tech
Sawyer, John (T)	6-2	230	27	5	Southern Mississippi

W=wide receiver   T=tight end

Largent was the fireworks here. He caught 66 passes for 1,237 yards, thus becoming the only NFL receiver to exceed 1,200 reception yards in the 1970s decade. (Warren Wells of Oakland had 1,260 yards in 1969.) After those achievements, Largent missed the season finale against Oakland because of a broken wrist. He wore a cast for four months afterward. McCullum caught 46 passes for 739 yards, adding fuel to the Seahawk aerial game. Running backs Smith and Doornink together went out for passes that gained 931 yards, and that added even more fire-power to Zorn's overhead circus. Tight end Bell didn't develop quite as fast as some coaches had hoped. Peets gains experience, and gives signs of getting there. Zorn needs short-pass tight end targets to go with his long bombs.

Interior Linemen	Ht.	Wt.	Age	Exp.	College
August, Steve (T)	6-5	254	26	4	Tulsa
Bebout, Nick (T)	6-5	260	29	8	Wyoming
Bullard, Louis (T)	6-6	265	24	3	Jackson State
Coder, Ron (G)	6-4	250	26	4	Penn State
Fifer, Bill (T)	6-4	250	25	3	West Texas State
Hines, Andre (T)	6-6	250	22	R	Stanford
Kuehn, Art (C)	6-3	255	27	5	UCLA
Lynch, Tom (G)	6-5	260	25	4	Boston College
Newton, Bob (G)	6-5	260	31	10	Nebraska
Salzano, Mike (T)	6-4	250	23	1	North Carolina
Sevy, Jeff (T)	6-5	260	28	6	California
Yarno, John (C)	6-5	251	26	4	Idaho

T=tackle   G=guard   C=center

Bebout, Lynch, Yarno, Coder and August are the starters, or were at season's end. They led the charge for one of NFL's most spectacular offenses, one that provides plenty of shooting stars for the TV audience. This unit is young but game-wise. Bebout and Newton are the only two who qualify as "vets." Coder recovered from injury and relieved Newton. Bullard was pushing for a starting job when injury stopped him. He'll resume pushing this year. Only 11 offensive holding penalties were called against the Seahawks last season. Still, the Seattle quarterback was sacked only 23 times, the AFC's lowest figure.

Kickers	Ht.	Wt.	Age	Exp.	College
Herrera, Efren (Pk)	5-9	190	29	6	UCLA
Strecker, Hartmut (Pk)	6-1	180	24	1	Dayton
Weaver, Herman (P)	6-4	210	32	11	Tennessee

Pk=placekicker   P=punter

As he enters the 1980 season, Herrera has going a string of 12 consecutive successful field goals. He nailed 19-of-23 last season, six from 40 or more yards out. The high-scoring Seahawks gave him the opportunity to make good 43-of-46 PATs to score an even 100 points for the season. Weaver averaged 40.2 with his punts, when he wasn't passing the ball.

DEFENSE

Front Linemen	Ht.	Wt.	Age	Exp.	College
Boyd, Dennis (E)	6-6	255	25	4	Oregon State
Cooke, Bill (T)	6-5	250	29	6	Massachusetts
Dion, Terry (E)	6-5	246	22	R	Oregon
Eller, Carl (E)	6-6	247	38	17	Minnesota
Green, Jacob (E)	6-3	247	22	R	Texas A&M
Gregory, Bill (E)	6-5	260	31	10	Wisconsin
Hardy, Robert (T)	6-2	250	24	2	Jackson State
Jacobs, Daniel (E)	6-6	273	22	R	Winston-Salem
McNeal, Mark (E)	6-7	225	22	R	Idaho
Sandifer, Bill (T)	6-6	260	28	6	UCLA
Tuiasosopo, Manu (T)	6-3	252	23	2	UCLA

E=end   T=tackle

Patera has high praise for Tuiasosopo and Hardy as "the best rookie tackles" he's seen. Eller and Gregory are getting to the point where their replacement is mandatory—like mandatory retirement. Still, Gregory is the only really experienced hand on the line. Cooke was a pleasant surprise at tackle, not for the opposition though. He sacked the enemy QB seven times. Boyd was hampered by a broken ankle and a fractured thumb, both. If Seattle is ever to have an effective defense, it starts here. And it looks as though it's already started at defensive end. The Seahawks drafted no less than five DEs in the first six rounds, including their No. 1 choice Jacob Green of Texas A&M.

Linebackers	Ht.	Wt.	Age	Exp.	College
Beeson, Terry (M)	6-3	240	25	4	Kansas
Butler, Keith (O)	6-4	225	24	3	Memphis State
Cronan, Peter (M)	6-2	238	25	4	Boston College
Jackson, Michael (O)	6-1	220	23	2	Washington
Norman, Joe (O)	6-1	220	24	2	Indiana
Polowski, Larry (O)	6-3	235	23	2	Boise State

O=outside   M=middle

Long-time starter Sammy Green lost his job in mid-season to Jackson. Then Jackson underwent postseason surgery for a damaged knee cartilage. Beeson has led Seahawks in tackles for past three years (114 in '79). Patera sees Norman as a "real competitor" and Polowski as a "smart player." Cronan is a good gap-plugger when called upon.

Defensive Backs	Ht.	Wt.	Age	Exp.	College
Beamon, Autry (S)	6-1	190	27	6	East Texas State
Brown, Dave (CB)	6-2	190	27	6	Michigan
Dufek, Don (S)	6-0	195	26	4	Michigan
Harris, John (S)	6-2	200	24	3	Arizona State
Justin, Kerry (CB)	5-11	175	25	3	Oregon State
Simpson, Keith (S)	6-1	195	24	3	Memphis State
Webster, Cornell (CB)	6-0	180	26	4	Tulsa
Young, Anthony (S)	6-3	173	24	1	Jackson State

CB=cornerback   S=safety

Brown led club interceptors with five pass thefts. Simpson is definitely Seattle's quality defensive back. Webster lost his job to Justin, then went AWOL for final game against Oakland. He may want to be traded. This unit could use some help, too.

Note: A complete listing of Seattle's 1980 college draft selections can be found on page 278.

DEFENSIVE UNIT

Young
Harris
Beamon
S

Dufek
O'Brien
Simpson
S

Webster
Justin
CB

Justin
Brown
CB

Norman
Butler
LB

Cronan
Beeson
LB

Polowski
Jackson
LB

McNeal*
Dion*
Boyd
Gregory
E

Cooke
Tuiasosopo
T

Sandifer
Cooke
Hardy
T

Jacobs*
Jacob Green*
Boyd
Eller
E

WR
McCullum
Jessie Green
Carter

Bebout
Sevy
Bullard
T

Lynch
Fifer
G

Varno
Kuehn
C

Coder
Fifer
Newton
Hines*
G

August
Sevy
Salzano
T

Peets
Bell
Sawyer
TE

RB
Doornink
Hunter
T. Green
Tate

QB
Zorn
Myer
Adkins

RB
Smith
Moore
Benjamin
Steele*

WR
Largent
Raible
Allen
Dorsey

OFFENSIVE UNIT

*Rookie

1979 SEAHAWKS STATISTICS

	Seahawks	Opps.
Total Points Scored	378	372
Total First Downs	315	350
Third Down Efficiency Percentage	42.8	39.3
Yards Rushing—First Downs	1967—121	2375—146
Passes Attempted—Completions	523—292	508—317
Yards Passing—First Downs	3590—171	3459—171
QB Sacked—Yards Lost	23—201	37—280
Interceptions By—Return Average	17—16.7	18—10.3
Punts—Average Yards	70—38.4	69—37.9
Punt Returns—Average Return	34—8.3	42—6.8
Kickoff Returns—Average Return	69—20.9	70—17.7
Fumbles—Ball Lost	31—18	36—13
Penalties—Yards	104—903	113—990

STATISTICAL LEADERS

Scoring	TDs	Rush.	Pass.	Ret.	PATs	FGs	Total
Herrera	0	0	0	0	43—46	19—23	100
Smith	15	11	4	0	0	0	90
Doornink	9	8	1	0	0	0	54
Largent	9	0	9	0	0	0	54
McCullum	4	0	4	0	0	0	24
Moore	2	2	0	0	0	0	12
Zorn	2	2	0	0	0	0	12

Rushing	Atts.	Yds.	Avg.	Longest	TDs
Smith	194	775	4.0	31	11
Doornink	152	500	3.3	26 (TD)	8
Zorn	46	279	6.1	41	2
Hunter	34	174	5.1	67	1
Moore	44	168	3.8	18	2
Sims	20	53	2.7	8	0

Passing	Atts.	Com.	Yds.	Pct.	Int.	Longest	TDs
Zorn	505	285	3661	56.4	18	65 (TD)	20
Weaver	4	3	73	75.0	0	39	0

Receiving	No.	Yds.	Avg.	Longest	TDs
Largent	66	1237	18.7	55 (TD)	9
Doornink	54	432	8.0	42	1
Smith	48	499	10.4	35	4
McCullum	46	739	16.1	65 (TD)	4
Peets	25	293	11.7	28	1
Raible	20	252	12.6	41	1
Moore	14	128	9.1	24	0

Interceptions	No.	Yds.	Avg.	Longest	TDs
Brown	5	46	9.2	23	0
Simpson	4	72	18.0	41	0
Harris	2	30	15.0	25	0

Punting	No.	Yds.	Avg.	Longest	Inside 20	Blocked
Weaver	66	2651	40.2	60	11	3

Punt Returns	No.	FCs	Yds.	Avg.	Longest	TDs
T. Green	16	3	121	7.6	30	0
Moore	10	1	90	9.0	29	0
Harris	8	2	70	8.8	19	0

Kickoff Returns	No.	Yds.	Avg.	Longest	TDs
T. Green	20	437	21.9	31	0
Moore	30	641	21.4	39	0
Hunter	15	299	19.9	30	0

KANSAS CITY CHIEFS

Head Coach: Marv Levy

3rd Year   **Record:** 11–21

1979 RECORD (7-9) (capital letters indicate home games)			1980 SCHEDULE (capital letters indicate home games)	
14	BALTIMORE	0	OAKLAND	Sept. 7
24	CLEVELAND	27	SEATTLE	Sept. 14
6	Houston	20	Cleveland	Sept. 21
35	OAKLAND	7	SAN DIEGO	Sept. 28
24	Seattle	6	Oakland	Oct. 5
10	Cincinnati	7	HOUSTON	Oct. 12
10	DENVER	24	Denver	Oct. 19
17	N.Y. GIANTS	21	DETROIT	Oct. 26
3	Denver	20	BALTIMORE	Nov. 2
14	SAN DIEGO	20	Seattle	Nov. 9
3	PITTSBURGH	30	San Diego	Nov. 16
24	Oakland	21	St. Louis	Nov. 23
7	San Diego	28	CINCINNATI	Nov. 30
37	SEATTLE	21	DENVER	Dec. 7
10	Baltimore	7	Pittsburgh	Dec. 14
0	Tampa Bay	3	Baltimore	Dec. 21
238		262		

"We've got a young team with lots of promise," head coach Marv Levy says with obvious assurance, "and I've got a promising young quarterback who can grow with it. So to establish some direction, I named Steve Fuller the regular quarterback over Mike Livingston. Steve has already completed over 50 percent of his passes, something a lot of fine quarterbacks fail to accomplish as rookies. Even Terry Bradshaw struggled for a number of years . . . now he's a great quarterback surrounded by a great team. I'm hoping we can anticipate the same thing happening in Kansas City."

When Levy took over the head coaching assignment two seasons ago, he listed as his first priority the building of a strong defense. That priority has been well

attended to, as current defensive ratings would show.
The Chiefs ranked sixth in the AFC last season in
total defense against both pass and rush, allowing 310.7
yards per game. This also graphed out to sixth place
in ground defense, the Chiefs allowing opposing runners 115.4 yards per game. If anything was weak, it
was pass defense in which they could rate no better
than tenth, although they did sack the enemy quarterback 38 times. Best sign of the times defensively, however, was in the total points yielded to the other side—
which was 262. And that was the fewest points the
Chiefs had permitted since 1973 when the figure was
192. And how did Levy account for this improvement
in defensive capability?

"If I had to put my finger on a single element," he
says, "it would be the play of young veterans like Art
Still, Gary Spani, Gary Green and Gary Barbaro.
They're vastly improved over a year ago when they
were good, but raw." Carrying his opinions further,
Levy also considers Bob Grupp's NFL punting leadership another big factor in keeping the opposing offensive units at bay. And thereby hangs an NFL success
tale.

It took Grupp, a Duke University graduate, a three-
time effort to make it into the National Football League
but when he did, it was with a flourish. His 43.6 yard
average last season as a rookie was the league's best
punting mark, better than Dave Jenning's 42.7 with the
New York Giants, and better even than Ray Guy's
42.6 for the Oakland Raiders. And it's no consolation
to the New York Jets that Grupp failed to impress them
as a punter after they had drafted him in 1977.

"I reported to the Jets' summer camp as a defensive
back and at that time didn't really kick that much,"
Grupp remembers. When the Jets released him, Grupp
played briefly with Calgary in the Canadian League.

Then, in 1978, he went back to the Jets, strictly as a punter. "Chuck Ramsey was their regular punter then, and in preseason games my average was only 33 yards. But I brought off five coffin-corner kicks. It was just a case of New York sticking with its veteran punter." When the Jets released him the second time, Grupp went briefly into the real estate business until, to his surprise, the Chiefs called him last summer and invited him to camp. There's this thing about the NFL— you never know when a football player is going to come into his own.

During each of his two seasons at Kansas City, Levy brought in 17 new players, with some of the second group replacing some of the first as the personnel elimination process continued. But it's the revolving door that characterizes any team-building operation in pro football. Still, it's a wearisome business, and Levy looks forward to the day when he can add only five or six new players a year, tops.

Where are the Chiefs most vulnerable as they enter the new campaign? Assuming Fuller continues to shine at quarterback, he'll need a capable backup. And there's plenty of room for another running back in a ground game that has a tendency to bog down. Levy could also use another receiver and a tight end or two. The defensive unit, despite its achievements, could use a tackle, a cornerback and a couple of linebackers. That's quite a shopping list, and there aren't that many days left before Christmas—and the playoffs.

And speaking of playoffs, and the Big Playoff otherwise known as the Super Bowl, Kansas City is the backdrop for the answer to an interesting question: how did the Super Bowl get its name? Texas E. (Tex) Schramm, president and general manager of the Dallas Cowboys, has the answer. Just after the American Football and National Football Leagues officially

merged in 1966, Lamar Hunt, who is the Kansas City
Chiefs' sole owner, the AFL's founder and current
president of the AFC, noticed that his sons were
playing with rubber-type balls that bounced sky high.
They were called "Super Balls." Hunt apparently had
this on his mind when he went to New York to attend
a meeting of representatives from the two leagues.
When the conversation focused on the projected championship game between the winners of the AFC and
NFC, Hunt began referring to it as the "Super Bowl,"
just as a conversation piece, so to speak. But the name
caught on almost immediately and, although the contest was officially designated as the World Championship Game, the media and everybody else started referring to it as the Super Bowl. And ever since then
the attendance, just like those rubber balls, has gone
sky high.

OFFENSE

Quarterbacks	Ht.	Wt.	Age	Exp.	College
Clements, Tom	5-10	185	26	R	Notre Dame
Fuller, Steve	6-4	198	23	2	Clemson
Kenney, Bill	6-4	210	25	2	Northern Colorado
Livingston, Mike	6-4	210	35	13	Southern Methodist

Rookie Steve Fuller took over starting role from Livingston and proceeded to win six games (of 12 starts). A scrambler, he also gained
264 yards on 50 scrambles, averaging 5.3 per run, one of which was
for a TD. The Chiefs aren't even sure they need Livingston any longer,
and he may go the waiver route if no trade can be made. Kenney didn't
get a chance to throw in a regular game, but this is another season
coming up. Clements, a former Notre Dame passer, was one of the
Canadian League's most successful quarterbacks. The Chiefs signed him
to a series of five one-year contracts to play here for a change.

Running Backs	Ht.	Wt.	Age	Exp.	College
Morgado, Arnold	5-11	204	28	4	Hawaii
McKnight, Ted	6-1	216	26	4	Minnesota-Duluth
Gant, Earl	6-0	207	23	2	Missouri
Reed, Tony	5-10	197	25	4	Colorado

Haslip, Wilbert	5-11	212	24	2	Hawaii
Belton, Horace	5-8	200	25	3	SE Louisiana
Williams, Mike	6-3	222	22	2	New Mexico
Blackwell, Alois	5-10	190	26	2	Houston
Cowins, Ben	6-0	192	24	1	Arkansas
Hadnot, James	6-2	230	22	R	Texas Tech

McKnight led club with a career-high 755 yards (4.9-yard average) but the KC ground game needs even more yardage if it's to compete in the NFL. Reed was providing much of that yardage when he went down with an injured knee. Williams started several games as a rookie, and averaged 3.8 yards on 69 carries. He replaced the injured Morgado. Belton returns kickoffs at a 21.0-yard clip. Gant could develop into something more valuable than a backup. If this unit improves its yardage output, and Fuller's passing game really catches fire, then Kansas City is on its way to the playoffs.

Receivers	Ht.	Wt.	Age	Exp.	College
Dirden, Johnny (W)	6-0	190	28	3	Sam Houston State
Samuels, Tony (T)	6-4	233	25	4	Bethune-Cookman
Kellar, Bill (W)	5-11	194	24	3	Stanford
Gaunty, Steve (W)	5-10	175	23	2	Northern Colorado
Dixon, Al (T)	6-5	220	26	4	Iowa State
Beckman, Ed (T)	6-4	226	25	4	Florida State
Smith, J. T. (W)	6-2	185	24	3	North Texas State
Rome, Stan (W)	6-5	205	24	2	Clemson
Carson, Carlos (W)	5-10	173	22	R	Louisiana State
Marshall, Henry (W)	6-2	214	26	5	Missouri
Gaines, Robert (W)	6-2	187	23	R	Washington
Taylor, Charlie (W)	6-3	196	24	1	Rice
Youngblood, Cecil (T)	6-2	230	24	1	Augustana (Ill.)
Iwanowski, Mark (T)	6-5	247	24	1	Pennsylvania

W=wide receiver   T=tight end

Among the receivers, Smith led with 33 catches for 444 yards. But most receptions were made by running backs McKnight (38 for 226 yards) and Reed (34 for 352 yards). RBs Williams and Gant caught their share, too. In fact, none of the receivers (except Smith) seemed to be usual targets for Fuller's or Livingston's passes. It was that kind of a passing offense, one oriented to running backs coming out of the backfield—a procedure which no doubt tipped the opposing defenses time and again. In addition to his receiving chores, Smith was the one and only KC punt returner, averaging 10.6 on 58 returns, good enough for second place in the AFC.

Interior Linemen	Ht.	Wt.	Age	Exp.	College
Ane, Charlie (C)	6-1	237	28	6	Michigan State
Rudnay, Jack (C)	6-2	242	32	11	Northwestern

Herkenhoff, Matt (T)	6-4	270	29	5	Minnesota
Condon, Tom (G)	6-3	254	28	7	Boston College
Choma, John (G-T)	6-6	259	25	1	Virginia
Nicholson, Jim (T)	6-6	275	30	7	Michigan State
Simmons, Bob (G)	6-4	260	26	4	Texas
Walters, Rod (G)	6-3	258	26	4	Iowa
Getty, Charles (T)	6-4	269	28	7	Penn State
Brown, Larry (T)	6-5	264	25	3	Miami (Fla.)
Robinson, Joe (T)	6-4	255	24	R	Ohio State
Rourke, Jim (G-T)	6-4	257	24	1	Boston College
Smith, Frank (T)	6-6	278	24	1	Alabama A&M
Kirchner, Bruce (C)	6-2	245	24	1	Colorado
Jonker, Kurtis (T)	6-4	250	24	1	Augustana (Ill.)
Tearry, Larry (C)	6-3	260	24	2	Wake Forest
Budde, Brad (G)	6-5	253	22	R	Southern Cal

T=tackle   G=guard   C=center

Looking over this lengthy roster, it's hard to believe the offensive line needs help, but it does. Levy wasn't as satisfied with its performance in '79, as compared with the year before. Big factor in any decline, of course, was the loss of best blocker Herkenhoff after only five games. Rudnay has a string of 144 consecutive games at center. Condon and Simmons are the guards, Getty and Herkenhoff the tackles, if Herkenhoff is ready and able. Ane is deep-snap man as Rudnay's center backup. Walters still has to be reckoned with in competition at guard.

Kickers	Ht.	Wt.	Age	Exp.	College
Grupp, Bob (P)	5-11	192	25	2	Duke
Stenerud, Jan (Pk)	6-2	187	37	14	Montana State
Guzman, Jose (Pk)	6-0	187	24	1	US International
Lowery, Nick (Pk)	6-4	190	24	1	Dartmouth

Pk=placekicker   P=punter

Grupp led the NFL in punting with a 43.6-yard average as a rookie, and became the first Chief to go to the Pro Bowl in three years. Stenerud, now in his 14th NFL year, hit 28-29 PATs and 12-22 FGs, adding to an already distinguished set of career statistics. Seven of his missed FGs came from 40 yards or beyond. Free agents Lowery and Guzman will seek recognition as Stenerud's possible replacement whenever the veteran kicker decides to call it a day.

DEFENSE

Front Linemen	Ht.	Wt.	Age	Exp.	College
Parrish, Don (NT)	6-2	249	25	3	Pittsburgh
Still, Art (E)	6-7	252	24	3	Kentucky

Lindstrom, Dave (E)	6-6	257	25	3	Boston University
Hicks, Sylvester (E)	6-4	252	25	3	Tennessee State
Anderson, Curtis (E)	6-6	250	23	2	Central State (O.)
Kremer, Ken (NT-E)	6-4	250	23	2	Ball State
Bell, Mike (E)	6-4	255	23	2	Colorado State
Pensick, Dan (NT)	6-5	250	22	R	Nebraska

E=end   NT=nose tackle

Against Pittsburgh, Still made 15 tackles, 11 of them unassisted, and he's only just beginning. There's more to come from Still who hardly lives up to his name when on the field. Parrish is the starting nose tackle but Kremer surprised with his fine play as a rookie backup. Bell, another rookie, turns out to be a great pass rusher and teams with Still to give the Chiefs one of the league's best pair of defensive ends. Only a glance at the above age column provides a clue to the future of this crowd. They're going to be just fine . . . if not impregnable.

Linebackers	Ht.	Wt.	Age	Exp.	College
Peterson, Cal (O)	6-4	220	27	5	UCLA
Jackson, Charles (I)	6-2	220	25	3	Washington
Howard, Thomas (O)	6-2	208	25	4	Texas Tech
Whitney, Paul (O)	6-3	220	26	5	Colorado
Manumaleuga, Frank (I)	6-2	245	24	2	San Jose State
Rozumek, Dave (I)	6-1	222	25	5	New Hampshire
Blanton, Jerry (O)	6-1	225	23	2	Kentucky
Spani, Gary (I)	6-2	230	24	3	Kansas State
Dupree, Michael (O)	6-2	221	24	R	Florida
Smith, Kelvin (O)	6-0	247	24	1	Angelo State
Klug, Dave (O)	6-4	228	22	R	Concordia (Moorhead)

O=outside   I=inside

The 3-4 defense lines up with Whitney and Howard on the outside, Spani and Manumaleuga on the inside. Spani was very active last season, leading the club in tackles with 157, 115 unassisted. Manumaleuga won a regular job as a rookie, and was fourth in tackle totals. Levy said the San Jose State product "got better as he went along, despite some rookie mistakes." Howard faces competition as a starter from Jackson and Peterson. Whitney has made transition from down lineman to linebacker. Rozumek, a starter in '77, missed part of '79 with injury. Blanton performed well on the kicking teams.

Defensive Backs	Ht.	Wt.	Age	Exp.	College
Perkins, Horace (CB)	5-11	180	26	2	Colorado
Green, Gary (CB)	5-11	184	24	4	Baylor
Barbaro, Gary (S)	6-4	204	26	5	Nicholls State
Powers, Clyde (S)	6-1	195	28	6	Oklahoma
Reese, Jerry (S)	6-3	192	25	2	Oklahoma

Christopher, Herb (S)	5-10	190	26	2	Morris Brown
Carter, M. L. (CB)	5-9	173	24	2	Fullerton State
Jackson, Gerald (S)	6-1	195	24	2	Mississippi State
Williams, Raye (CB)	6-2	200	24	1	Arizona State
Harris, Eric (CB)	6-3	187	25	R	Memphis State

CB=cornerback   S=safety

Barbaro led KC pass interceptors for second year, this time with seven which was second best in AFC. He carried one for a 70-yard TD against Oakland. Barbaro and Green (five interceptions) are rapidly approaching All-Pro status at their present rate of development. Reese won a starting job at strong safety a year ago until a knee injury forced him out. He'll be back to challenge. Powers will also attempt a comeback after injury. Harris spent three years in the Canadian League and now has a million-dollar contract with the Chiefs. Carter earned a starting job after an injury sidelined Tim Collier. The result: Collier was traded to St. Louis. Cruel world.

Note: A complete listing of Kansas City's 1980 college draft selections can be found on page 271.

DEFENSIVE UNIT 3-4 DEFENSE

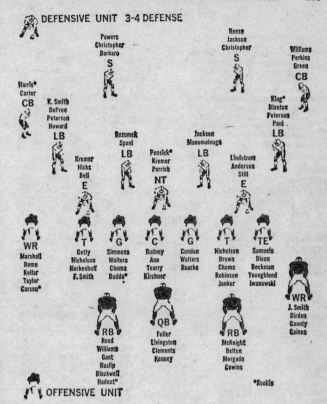

Powers
Christopher
Barbaro
S

Reese
Jackson
Christopher
S

Williams
Perkins
Green
CB

Harris*
Carter
CB

K. Smith
DuPree
Peterson
Howard
LB

Rozumek
Spani
LB

Jackson
Manumaleuga
LB

Klug*
Blanton
Peterson
Paul
LB

Kremer
Hicks
Bell
E

Pensick*
Kremer
Parrish
NT

Lindstrom
Anderson
Still
E

WR
Marshall
Rome
Kellar
Taylor
Carson*

Getty
Nicholson
Herkenhoff
F. Smith
T

Simmons
Walters
Choma
Budde*
G

Rudnay
Ane
Yearry
Kirchner
C

Condon
Walters
Rourke
G

Nicholson
Brown
Choma
Robinson
Jonker
T

Samuels
Dixon
Beckman
Youngblood
Iwanowski
TE

WR
J. Smith
Dirden
Gaunty
Gaines

RB
Reed
Williams
Gant
Haslip
Blackwell
Hadnot*

QB
Fuller
Livingston
Clements
Kenney

RB
McKnight
Belton
Morgado
Cowins

OFFENSIVE UNIT

*Rookie

1979 CHIEFS STATISTICS

	Chiefs	Opps.
Total Points Scored	238	262
Total First Downs	241	297
Third Down Efficiency Percentage	32.0	42.0
Yards Rushing—First Downs	2316—122	1847—102
Passes Attempted—Completions	361—190	528—296
Yards Passing—First Downs	1660—91	3124—169
QB Sacked—Yards Lost	42—293	38—280
Interceptions By—Return Average	23—19.0	18—11.6
Punts—Average Yards	90—43.1	88—38.8
Punt Returns—Average Return	58—10.6	49—6.4
Kickoff Returns—Average Return	51—19.7	51—19.9
Fumbles—Ball Lost	31—18	34—14
Penalties—Yards	108—971	127—1012

STATISTICAL LEADERS

Scoring	TDs	Rush.	Pass.	Ret.	PATs	FGs	Total
Stenerud	0	0	0	0	28—29	12—22	64
McKnight	8	8	0	0	0	0	48
Smith	5	0	3	2	0	0	30
Morgado	4	4	0	0	0	0	24
Williams	3	1	2	0	0	0	18
Marshall	2	1	1	0	0	0	12

Rushing	Atts.	Yds.	Avg.	Longest	TDs
McKnight	153	755	4.9	84 (TD)	8
Reed	113	446	4.0	23	1
Fuller	50	264	5.3	49	1
Williams	69	261	3.8	22	1
Morgado	75	231	3.1	19	4
Gant	56	196	3.5	16	1
Belton	44	134	3.0	12	1

Passing	Atts.	Com.	Yds.	Pct.	Int.	Longest	TDs
Fuller	270	146	1484	54.1	14	40	6
Livingston	90	44	469	48.9	4	38 (TD)	1

Receiving	No.	Yds.	Avg.	Longest	TDs
McKnight	38	226	6.0	24	0
Reed	34	352	10.4	40	0
Smith	33	444	13.5	34	3
Marshall	21	332	15.8	38 (TD)	1
Williams	16	129	8.1	25	2
Gant	15	101	6.7	26	0
Samuels	14	147	10.5	30	0

Interceptions	No.	Yds.	Avg.	Longest	TDs
Barbaro	7	142	20.3	70 (TD)	1
Green	5	148	29.6	57	0
Carter	3	33	11.0	20	0
Collier	2	45	22.5	40	0
Christopher	2	1	0.5	1	0

Punting	No.	Yds.	Avg.	Longest	Inside 20	Blocked
Grupp	89	3883	43.6	74	23	1

Punt Returns	No.	FCs	Yds.	Avg.	Longest	TDs
Smith	58	10	612	10.6	88 (TD)	2

Kickoff Returns	No.	Yds.	Avg.	Longest	TDs
Belton	22	463	21.0	52	0
Gaunty	12	271	22.6	50	0
Dirden	7	154	22.0	32	0
Gant	4	75	19.3	20	0

NATIONAL FOOTBALL CONFERENCE

The scene at Dallas can best be described as comparatively chaotic. With the retirement of Roger Staubach following up a similar "call it quits" decision by All-Pro safety Cliff Harris, the calm and collected Tom Landry finds whirls of uncertainty around him. Decisions must be made to keep the Cowboys from declining, not gradually over a period of years, but all at once. It's a challenge, straightening it all out, but Landry is capable of accomplishing things others would find impossible. As a pro football coach, he's the difference between a good team and a mediocre one.

The Cowboys will have a tough time staying on top in the NFC East but still have the talent and, more importantly, the morale to prevail over the Philadelphia Eagles and Washington Redskins, the two clubs most likely to push them off the pinnacle. Dick Vermeil's Eagles won everybody's trophy as the "NFC's most improved team of 1979." They outscored the opposition by some 57 points which says something about both their offense and defense. Washington did the same, by 53 points, and quarterback Joe Theismann is becoming more effective as each season progresses. He just might be the NFC's quarterback of the future with Staubach, like some of those battleships he used to sail, now in moth balls.

The St. Louis Cardinals may have to settle for a

troublemaker's role, now that they've changed coaches again. As for the New York Giants, it all depends on how Phil Simms performs in his debut as a first-string, no-reservations-about-it quarterback.

The Chicago Bears and Tampa Bay Buccaneers are ready to battle it out for the NFC Central title, with Green Bay, Minnesota and Detroit offering resistance tempered by rebuilding problems.

The Los Angeles Rams seem to hold sway again in the NFC West, although the New Orleans Saints could become the "surprise team" of the NFL—just as the Denver Broncos were some four seasons ago. The Atlanta Falcons are struggling to get that once formidable defensive unit into some semblance of its former glory again. The San Francisco 49ers are likewise trying to regroup, both their defense and offense.

DALLAS COWBOYS

Head Coach: Tom Landry

21st Year   **Record:** 172–104–6

1979 RECORD (11-5) (capital letters indicate home games)		1980 SCHEDULE (capital letters indicate home games)	
22	St. Louis 21	Washington (night, TV)	Sept. 8
21	San Francisco 13	Denver	Sept. 14
24	CHICAGO 20	TAMPA BAY	Sept. 21
7	Cleveland 26	Green Bay at Milwaukee	Sept. 28
38	CINCINNATI 13	N.Y. GIANTS	Oct. 5
36	Minnesota 20	SAN FRANCISCO	Oct. 12
30	LOS ANGELES 6	Philadelphia	Oct. 19
22	ST. LOUIS 13	SAN DIEGO (night, TV)	Oct. 26
3	Pittsburgh 14	St. Louis	Nov. 2
16	N.Y. Giants 14	N.Y. Giants	Nov. 9
21	PHILADELPHIA 31	ST. LOUIS	Nov. 16
20	Washington 34	WASHINGTON	Nov. 23
24	HOUSTON 30	SEATTLE (TV)	Nov. 27
28	N.Y. GIANTS 7	Oakland	Dec. 7
24	Philadelphia 17	Los Angeles (night, TV)	Dec. 15
35	WASHINGTON 34	PHILADELPHIA	Dec. 21
371	313		

Playoffs

19	LOS ANGELES 21

The best measure of Tom Landry's success as an NFL coach is the type of questions people ask about the Cowboys whenever, for one reason or another, they don't play in the Super Bowl. If they have a shortfall season, merely making it to the playoffs, then there's something drastically wrong. So looking back on 1979 while peering forward into 1980, the Dallas faithful all across the land are asking the question, right on schedule: "What's the matter with the Cowboys?"

This time, maybe Tom Landry is asking himself the very same thing, though already he may have the answer. What he doesn't know, perhaps, is just how to go about setting things right with that once impregnable Dallas defense and the soon-to-be-altered offense, now that Roger Staubach has lifted anchors and sailed off into retirement. Landry very definitely has a point when he says: "We know that without Roger it's going to take time to re-establish the kind of offense we've been used to. Our problems are twofold—for the offensive team to regain confidence in a quarterback, and for the defense to perform at a higher level overall."

Dallas led the NFC in total offense last season, running and passing some 5,968 yards for an average of 373 per game. The defense wasn't quite that good, but it wasn't all that bad either. In standings with other NFC clubs, the Cowboys ranked fourth in total defense, fourth against the run and third against the pass. Overall, it was an offensive and defensive performance quite becoming to a team that won the NFC East even while falling by the wayside on the way to Super Bowl XIV.

Still, there *was* something wrong with the Cowboys last season, and it wasn't just one thing. It was a lot of things which added up to a total just short of everything. Perhaps it all began when Ed (Too Tall) Jones decided he was bored with football and wanted to enter the boxing ring. That little career change took away one of the best defensive ends ever to play the game. Now, as would be expected, Too Tall is bored with boxing, and has made himself available to pro football.

Tony Dorsett kept Landry guessing about his availability on and off all season long, and you should never keep Landry guessing. After dropping a mirror, a gift from an admiring fan at the Hall of Fame game in Canton, O., on his foot, Dorsett missed the entire preseason and first regular season game, not to mention the last contest because of an injured shoulder. Still, he managed to run more than a thousand yards.

When All-Pro Charlie Waters hurt his knee in the

Seattle game and was laid up for the season, Randy Hughes replaced him. Then in an accident that could have been borrowed from Dorsett, a lamp fell on Hughes's head in the middle of the night and nearly sidelined him for the preseason's last game.

Not even the once-and-future quarterback, Danny White, was able to avoid the zany things that were happening to the Cowboys. Just before summer camp was over, he banged up his passing thumb against a teammate's helmet during a passing drill. That immobilized White's passing arm for an entire month.

And there was the Thomas (Hollywood) Henderson Affair. Landry is by no means a straitlaced type of coach, but he can get impatient with players who tend to go a little "far out" in their relations with the media, or their attitude toward the fans, the team, or the game of football itself. He has been known to be extremely patient in dealing with such personnel matters, but once that patience is stretched beyond its natural limits, there's usually no recall. If the reports were accurate, Landry lowered the boom on Henderson because he was "clowning" for the television cameras while standing on the sidelines. That, however, was the culmination of a lot of things; and even though Henderson expressed a desire to return to Dallas, he was traded to San Francisco for a draft choice.

As for sideline "clowning," the TV cameramen should share some of the blame. In recent broadcasts of NFL games, they have been zooming in on various players on the sidelines who usually feel compelled to respond by making silly gestures with their hands, or by "hamming it up" in some other fashion while impressing no one among the millions who are watching the game. If TV cameramen really want to do the NFL a big favor, they should start zooming in on pretty girls among the cheerleaders and spectators as they once did, and let the players grimace and gesticulate to themselves.

Roger Staubach's decision to retire at age 38 may have its merits. But there's a feeling in Dallas that he may get back into uniform if and when the Cowboys need him. Staubach is just that kind of a person. He even left the door open when asked if he would return should something happen to, say, Danny White or his backup, Glenn Carano. "That would be a real problem," Staubach agreed, "and I'm not adverse to helping . . . it would depend on the circumstances."

Perhaps veteran tackle Norm Evans said it best when he retired after more than a decade of playing in the NFL. "I'm so darned healthy," Evans exulted, "that I'm going to quit while I'm still able . . . I'm the only guy I know who has been around the NFL for 14 years and doesn't have zippers on his knees."

OFFENSE

Quarterbacks	Ht.	Wt.	Age	Exp.	College
Carano, Glenn	6-3	202	24	4	Nevada-Las Vegas
Hogeboom, Gary	6-4	195	22	R	Central Michigan
White, Danny	6-2	192	28	5	Arizona State

Roger Staubach announced his retirement at what might be called "the peak" of his career (if his age of 38 is disregarded). During 1979, he led the NFL in passing for the fourth time, and the second year in a row. White now moves up to full status as the Cowboy quarterback, after being told many times that he's probably the best backup QB in the NFL. Now, he must shake the "backup QB image." White also has also been the Dallas punter and a good one. If he continues in a dual role, it'll be interesting to see how often he can avoid the necessity of punting with his field generalship. Carano remains mostly an untested reserve quarterback and Landry may look around for another one.

Running Backs	Ht.	Wt.	Age	Exp.	College
Brinson, Larry	6-0	214	26	4	Florida
Dorsett, Tony	5-11	190	26	4	Pittsburgh

Jones, James	5-10	200	22	R	Mississippi State
Laidlaw, Scott	6-0	205	27	6	Stanford
Newhouse, Robert	5-10	215	30	9	Houston
Pearson, Preston	6-1	206	35	14	Illinois
Springs, Ron	6-1	200	24	2	Ohio State
Russell, Wayne	6-1	221	26	1	Cheyney State

Dorsett cracked the thousand-yard mark again with 1,107, but most other Dallas running backs came up with only average gains. But that's par for the course in a pass-oriented offense (or at least it was pass-oriented up through last season). Springs may be asked to play fullback next to Dorsett. Newhouse was bothered with an injured leg. Both he and Laidlaw were slowed by their injuries. Brinson is being groomed for a halfback post after looking "pretty good," as Landry puts it, while running from a tailback position in practice. Accidents seem to follow Dorsett around, waiting to happen. After being hit by a falling mirror on a bus, he returned to practice one afternoon last October with an injured knee from falling off a horse during a dove hunt.

Receivers	Ht.	Wt.	Age	Exp.	College
Cosbie, Doug (T)	6-6	230	24	2	Santa Clara
DuPree, Billy Joe (T)	6-4	229	30	8	Michigan State
Hill, Tony (W)	6-2	198	24	4	Stanford
Johnson, Butch (W)	6-1	192	26	5	Calif.-Riverside
Pearson, Drew (W)	6-0	183	29	8	Tulsa
Saldi, Jay (T)	6-3	227	26	5	South Carolina
Wilson, Steve (W)	5-10	192	23	2	Howard

W=wide receiver   T=tight end

The Dallas passing game ranked second to, surprisingly, the 49ers in the NFC. Hill led the pass receptionists with 60 followed by Drew Pearson with 55. Each surpassed a thousand yards for the season and, taken together with Tony Dorsett's similar figure rushing, Dallas became the first NFL team with three 1,000-yard players. Cosbie did O.K. his rookie year at tight end. Wilson's main forte is returning punts. Johnson wants to play first-string, even if it means going elsewhere. Saldi is versatile at either TE or WR. DuPree goes on and on as a starter who does his job, and well.

Interior Linemen	Ht.	Wt.	Age	Exp.	College
Cooper, Jim (C-T)	6-5	260	25	4	Temple
Donovan, Pat (T)	6-4	250	27	6	Stanford
Fitzgerald, John (C)	6-5	260	32	10	Boston College
Frederick, Andy (T)	6-6	255	26	4	New Mexico
Lawless, Burton (G)	6-4	255	27	6	Florida
Rafferty, Tom (G)	6-3	250	26	5	Penn State
Scott, Herbert (G)	6-2	252	27	6	Virginia Union

	Ht.	Wt.	Age	Exp.	College
Shaw, Robert (C-G)	6-4	245	24	2	Tennessee
Grimmett, Richard (T)	6-6	265	25	1	Illinois

T=tackle   G=guard   C=center

Cooper is considered a young, and only possible, replacement for the departed Rayfield Wright (now with Philadelphia). Grimmett, an injured first-year man, and Frederick will also compete. Fitzgerald, Rafferty and Scott give the mid-line a solid front. Shaw has done everything expected of a Dallas No. 1 draft choice. Lawless is good at backing up, and that doesn't mean driving in reverse. The Dallas overall offensive game ranked second only to Pittsburgh's in the entire NFL last season, advancing an average of 373 yards per game. So the line must be doing something right.

Kickers	Ht.	Wt.	Age	Exp.	College
Septien, Rafael (Pk)	5-9	171	27	4	Southwest Louisiana
White, Danny (P)	6-2	192	28	5	Arizona State

Pk=placekicker   P=punter

Septien performed admirably last season, making good 40-44 PATs and 19-29 FGs. Two of the FGs came from 50 yards or more out, and three from the 40-49-yard range. He was perfect (7-7) from the 20-29-yard sector. Danny White averaged 41.7 with his punts and again drew praise from Landry who says the newly crowned first-string QB will continue to do the punting until another one becomes available. (That raises an interesting question: Does a first-string quarterback who also does the punting get paid for two jobs?)

DEFENSE

Front Linemen	Ht.	Wt.	Age	Exp.	College
Bethea, Larry (T)	6-5	254	24	3	Michigan State
Cole, Cally (T)	6-5	252	32	13	Hawaii
Dutton, John (E)	6-7	265	29	7	Nebraska
Martin, Harvey (E)	6-5	250	30	8	East Texas State
Petersen, Kurt (E)	6-5	255	23	R	Missouri
Stalls, Dave (T)	6-4	245	25	4	Northern Colorado
Thornton, Bruce (E-T)	6-5	265	22	2	Illinois
White, Randy (T)	6-4	250	27	6	Maryland

E=end   T=tackle

Landry wasn't too happy with the pass rush last season, but Martin continues to be the best the Cowboys have in that department. White has gone to three Pro Bowls, led Cowboy tacklers last season despite a hurt foot. Donovan made his first Pro Bowl appearance, the first Dallas offensive lineman to represent the Cowboys since the '77 Pro Bowl. Thornton showed good form as a rookie end and says he's developing his own "pass rush style." Thornton explains: "Harvey Martin, for instance, just runs by people. Randy White uses his strength. Dave Stalls is quick and can spin out of blocks. I've got a style of my own, something that'll work best for me." Dutton came to the Cowboys from Baltimore last October in exchange for two top draft picks. His job was to replace Too Tall Jones who, at the time, was pursuing an unimpressive boxing career. Even though Jones won six heavyweight fights in ten months, he has decided to quit boxing and return to football, preferably with the Cowboys. But he and his agent did a little shopping around.

Linebackers	Ht.	Wt.	Age	Exp.	College
Breunig, Bob (M)	6-2	225	27	6	Arizona State
Brown, Guy (O)	6-4	228	25	4	Houston
Hegman, Mike (O)	6-1	225	27	5	Tennessee State
Huther, Bruce (M)	6-1	220	26	4	New Hampshire
Lewis, D. D. (O)	6-1	215	35	12	Mississippi State
Roe, Bill (O)	6-5	234	22	R	Colorado

O=outside   M=middle

The depth here is alarmingly thin, even for a crew as youthful as these. Lewis is the only bona fide veteran-type here. Breunig led the club in tackles with 81 solos and 86 assists. He underwent post-season surgery on a shoulder. Brown has the makings of a starter on the outside to succeed the released Thomas (Hollywood) Henderson who became a good example of what can happen if you rub Tom Landry the wrong way. Huther is considered best in the middle rather than on the perimeter, at least that's Landry's thinking. There's a "help wanted" sign in this unit's future. The Cowboys didn't have a choice until the 1980 draft's third round (having traded their first and second round choices to Baltimore for Dutton). Then they selected linebacker Bill Roe of Colorado, the Big Eight Conference's leading tackler last season.

Defensive Backs	Ht.	Wt.	Age	Exp.	College
Barnes, Benny (CB)	6-1	195	29	9	Stanford
Hughes, Randy (S)	6-4	207	27	6	Oklahoma
Kyle, Aaron (CB)	5-11	185	26	5	Wyoming
Manning, Wade (CB)	5-11	190	25	2	Ohio State
Mitchell, Aaron (CB)	6-1	196	24	2	Nevada-Las Vegas
Thurman, Dennis (CB)	5-11	170	24	3	Southern Cal
Waters, Charlie (S)	6-2	200	32	10	Clemson

CB=cornerback   S=safety

No one in this secondary intercepted more than two passes last season. In fact, Dallas led the entire NFL in NOT intercepting passes by stealing only 13. But strangely enough, the Cowboys also led the NFL in keeping passes within the family. Only 13 of Dallas's passes were intercepted (likewise, only 13 of Philadelphia's). Mitchell will stick it out at cornerback with experience. Waters missed '79 with a bad knee, but aims for '80. Barnes recently had foot surgery, will take it easy for a while. Kyle may miss preseason games because of surgery to remove calcium deposits on his knee.

Note: A complete listing of Dallas's 1980 college draft selections can be found on page 270.

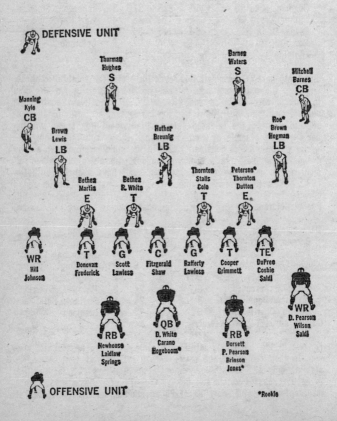

DEFENSIVE UNIT

Thurman
Hughes
S

Barnes
Waters
S

Mitchell
Barnes
CB

Manning
Kyle
CB

Brown
Lewis
LB

Huther
Breunig
LB

Roe*
Brown
Hegman
LB

Bethea
Martin
E

Bethea
R. White
T

Thornton
Stalls
Cole
T

Peterson*
Thornton
Dutton
E

WR
Hill
Johnson

T
Donovan
Frederick

G
Scott
Lawless

C
Fitzgerald
Shaw

G
Rafferty
Lawless

T
Cooper
Grimmett

TE
DuPree
Cosbie
Saldi

RB
Newhouse
Laidlaw
Springs

QB
D. White
Carano
Hogeboom*

RB
Dorsett
P. Pearson
Brinson
Jones*

WR
D. Pearson
Wilson
Saldi

OFFENSIVE UNIT

*Rookie

1979 COWBOYS STATISTICS

	Cowboys	Opps.
Total Points Scored	371*	313
Total First Downs	339	259
Third Down Efficiency Percentage	49.7	35.0
Yards Rushing—First Downs	2375—122	2115—105
Passes Attempted—Completions	503—287	435—207
Yards Passing—First Downs	3593—195	2471—135
QB Sacked—Yards Lost	41—290	43—362
Interceptions By—Return Average	13—14.8	13—8.8
Punts—Average Yards	76—41.7	96—40.8
Punt Returns—Average Return	51—6.5	43—7.4
Kickoff Returns—Average Return	68—19.4	68—23.2
Fumbles—Ball Lost	33—21	20—10
Penalties—Yards	100—845	70—704

* Includes safety

STATISTICAL LEADERS

Scoring	TDs	Rush.	Pass.	Ret.	PATs	FGs	Total
Septien	0	0	0	0	40—44	19—29	97
Hill	10	0	10	0	0	0	60
D. Pearson	8	0	8	0	0	0	48
Dorsett	7	6	1	0	0	0	42
DuPree	5	0	5	0	0	0	30
Newhouse	4	3	1	0	0	0	24
Laidlaw	3	3	0	0	0	0	18
Springs	3	2	1	0	0	0	18

Rushing	Atts.	Yds.	Avg.	Longest	TDs
Dorsett	250	1107	4.4	41	6
Newhouse	124	449	3.6	21	3
Springs	67	248	3.7	15	2
Laidlaw	69	236	3.4	15	3
Staubach	37	172	4.5	20	0
Brinson	14	48	3.6	10	0

Passing	Atts.	Com.	Yds.	Pct.	Int.	Longest	TDs
Staubach	461	267	3586	57.9	11	75 (TD)	27
White	39	19	267	48.7	2	45	1

Receiving	No.	Yds.	Avg.	Longest	TDs
Hill	60	1062	17.7	75 (TD)	10
D. Pearson	55	1026	18.7	56 (TD)	8
Dorsett	45	375	8.3	32	1
DuPree	29	324	11.2	33	5
P. Pearson	26	333	12.8	26 (TD)	1
Springs	25	251	10.0	27	1
Saldi	14	181	12.9	23 (TD)	1
Laidlaw	12	59	4.9	12	0

Interceptions	No.	Yds.	Avg.	Longest	TDs
Hughes	2	91	45.5	68	0
Harris	2	35	17.5	20	0
Barnes	2	20	10.0	11	0
Lewis	2	8	4.0	5	0
Kyle	2	0	—	—	0

Punting	No.	Yds.	Avg.	Longest	Inside 20	Blocked
D. White	76	3168	41.7	73	21	0

Punt Returns	No.	FCs	Yds.	Avg.	Longest	TDs
Wilson	35	12	236	6.8	13	0
Manning	10	2	55	5.5	17	0
Hill	6	1	43	7.2	12	0

Kickoff Returns	No.	Yds.	Avg.	Longest	TDs
Springs	38	780	20.5	70	0
Wilson	19	328	17.2	26	0
Manning	7	145	20.7	47	0

PHILADELPHIA EAGLES

Head Coach: Dick Vermeil

5th Year   **Record:** 29–31

1979 RECORD (11-5) (capital letters indicate home games)			1980 SCHEDULE (capital letters indicate home games)	
23	N.Y. GIANTS	17	DENVER	Sept. 7
10	ATLANTA	14	Minnesota	Sept. 14
26	New Orleans	14	N.Y. GIANTS (night, TV)	Sept. 22
17	N.Y. Giants	13	St. Louis	Sept. 28
17	PITTSBURGH	14	WASHINGTON	Oct. 5
28	WASHINGTON	17	N.Y. Giants	Oct. 12
24	St. Louis	20	DALLAS	Oct. 19
7	Washington	17	CHICAGO	Oct. 26
13	Cincinnati	37	Seattle	Nov. 2
19	CLEVELAND	24	New Orleans	Nov. 9
31	Dallas	21	Washington	Nov. 16
16	ST. LOUIS	13	OAKLAND	Nov. 23
21	Green Bay	10	San Diego	Nov. 30
44	DETROIT	7	ATLANTA	Dec. 7
17	DALLAS	24	ST. LOUIS	Dec. 14
26	Houston	20	Dallas	Dec. 21
339		282		

Playoffs

| 27 | CHICAGO | 17 |
| 17 | Tampa Bay | 24 |

The story of the Philadelphia Eagles' return to higher ground in the National Football League is largely the story of Dick Vermeil and how he galvanized a floundering team into action in only a year or two. From the NFL's viewpoint, it's a pro football Philadelphia Story with Vermeil leading the cast, and only he could make a comment such as this one after losing the NFC East title to the Dallas Cowboys by the narrowest of margins:

"I had hoped to give the game ball to the people of Philadelphia," he confessed, "but I wasn't able to do that this year; still it won't be long before I can." That can be taken as a double-edged promise and threat—one to the long-suffering Eagle fans, the other to the rest of the NFC East.

At the close of last season, Vermeil received the highest honor possible for an NFL head coach when his league counterparts named him NFL Coach of the Year. Coming from his peers, it was a fitting tribute for a man who had led his team to an 11-5 record, and into the NFC playoffs for the second straight year. The '79 record represented the largest regular season winning total for the Eagles since 1961, ending a very long victory drought. Even though his record stands at 29-31 for four years, 20 of those wins came during the past two seasons. It's a record of notable achievement for a man who served as an assistant coach with the Rams under both George Allen and Tommy Prothro, and who was also the winning head coach at UCLA at the time he took charge of the Eagles five years ago.

Vermeil, it seems, is a bit inhibited by his comparative lack of pro football coaching experience. "One weakness of mine," he confesses, "is a lack of depth in pro football background. People who've been in the game for years have a depth of thinking I can't yet have, until there's more years of experience. Adding a Sid Gillman to my staff provides depth in offensive thinking. I surround myself with strong assistants like Gillman and Marion Campbell, but I've had trouble delegating responsibility. I'm getting better at it; though I do too much because I've always felt, if you want to do a job right, do it yourself."

The Eagles might have distinguished themselves even more last season if Bill Bergey hadn't been forced off the field with an injured knee. In his eleven NFL seasons, the big linebacker had started 141 games (of a possible 142), including the last 75 since becoming an Eagle. The string came to an end in the season's third game against New Orleans in the Superdome, and Bergey blames the artificial turf for it all. "I'd beaten the odds for eleven years," Bergey said, "and the good Man above had been very good to me. I believe I've got a knack to roll with a play. I can almost act like a drunk and go limp. Instead of fighting a hit, I roll with it. But this time I had my feet planted in the turf. Conrad Dobler hit me high with a clean shot, but I couldn't pick my foot up off the turf. It was locked there . . ."

Bergey has been undergoing a rehabilitation program for the knee and, if he's ready, the Philadelphia defense will be ready too. As for the offense, Ron Jaworski is the key man at quarterback and he must be doing something right. He was ranked third among NFC quarterbacks last season, right behind Roger Staubach and Joe Theismann. It would seem that Jaworski has certainly clinched the No. 1 spot. Still, the question persists. Who's the No. 2 quarterback? Five-year back-up QB John Walton has decided to become a college coach at Elizabeth City (N.C.) State, and the No. 2 "we try harder" field is left to the competitive efforts of two free agents, Rob Hertel and Mark Manges, and erstwhile New York Giant quarterback Joe Pisarcik who comes to Philadelphia looking for work after being bartered for a draft choice next year. Is Philadelphia's signing of Pisarcik an act of gratitude? It will be remembered that Pisarcik was the quarterback who fumbled that famous handoff in the Meadowlands in 1978, giving the Eagles a key victory and a ticket to the play-offs. The Giants called it "The Fumble." The Eagles called it "Miracle in the Meadowlands."

Dick Vermeil is one Philadelphia success story, Tony Franklin is another. It would be an even greater success story if Franklin's first name were Ben, instead of Tony. The story begins back in Texas where Tony

Franklin, a high school student, decided he would kick a football barefooted instead of with shoes attached to his lower extremities. The kick sailed 50 yards and Franklin immediately had visions of a fabulous career, without shoes. At Texas A&M, that career began to shape up when he established no less than 18 NCAA field goal records, becoming also the only person (with or without shoes) ever to kick two field goals for more than 60 yards in one game.

The rest is Eagles' history. Franklin became the first placekicker ever drafted by Philadelphia as high as the third round. He went on to finish his rookie season as the NFL's third leading scorer among kickers. Vermeil, however, is finding that Franklin has a tendency to do some things the opposite of what he's told, like kicking off to the right instead of the left, or kicking shallow when he's supposed to kick deep. And the inevitable just had to happen, and it did. Early in November, Franklin stepped on a piece of glass on the Philadelphia Navy Base practice field and cut the big toe on his kicking right foot. But it was only a minor injury and soon righted itself. "I don't want to get athlete's foot," says Franklin. "That's about the only thing to worry about, that and getting the foot stepped on. I can tell if someone is coming for my foot and I jump in the air or something. They're not going to get my foot, I can tell you that right now."

OFFENSE

Quarterbacks	Ht.	Wt.	Age	Exp.	College
Hertel, Rob	6-2	195	25	2	Southern Cal
Jaworski, Ron	6-2	195	29	6	Youngstown State
Manges, Mark	6-2	210	24	2	Maryland
Pisarcik, Joe	6-4	220	28	4	New Mexico State

Jaworski is still trying to prove himself to be a top-rated NFL quarterback. He completed 50% of his passes in '79, and his league QB rating jumped from a 68 to 76.9—a healthy rise. Still, the Eagles don't have a high-flying aerial attack, at least not yet. Pisarcik comes down from New York (Giants) after alternately bench-sitting and playing in the Meadowlands for three seasons. His stats in '79 weren't too impressive—a 39.8 completion percentage being the least of these. Hertel and Manges are free agents who would like to be reserves, if nothing else. And there's definitely a job opening for a backup QB in Philadelphia.

Running Backs	Ht.	Wt.	Age	Exp.	College
Barnes, Larry	5-11	220	26	4	Tennessee State
Betterson, James	6-0	210	26	4	North Carolina
Campfield, Billy	5-11	185	24	3	Kansas
Culbreath, Jim	6-0	210	28	4	Oklahoma
Giammona, Louie	5-9	180	27	4	Utah State
Harrington, Perry	5-11	208	22	R	Jackson State
Harris, Leroy	5-9	230	26	4	Arkansas State
Montgomery, Wilbert	5-10	195	26	4	Abilene Christian

Montgomery broke his own club rushing record with 1,512 yards on 338 carries and 14 TDs. His average gain was 4.5 yards. Harris carried 107 times for 504 yards and a 4.7 average. Giammona is an excellent blocker and runs back kicks on the special teams. Harris, according to Vermeil, "is just learning what it is to be an Eagle." This ground attack ranked sixth among NFC clubs in '79, and could be better if the heights are to be scaled.

Receivers	Ht.	Wt.	Age	Exp.	College
Carmichael, Harold (W)	6-8	225	31	10	Southern University
Fitzkee, Scott (W)	6-0	187	23	2	Penn State
Henry, Wally (W)	5-8	170	26	4	UCLA
Krepfle, Keith (T)	6-3	225	28	6	Iowa State
McRae, Jerrold (W)	6-0	187	25	3	Tennessee State
Rivers, Nate (W)	6-1	210	22	R	South Carolina State
Smith, Charles (W)	6-1	185	30	7	Grambling
Spagnola, John (T)	6-4	240	23	2	Yale

W=wide receiver   T=tight end

Carmichael goes into the '80 season with an NFL record string of 112 games in which he's caught at least one pass. In '79, he had 52 receptions for 872 yards. Henry is a special teams man, and ranks high among NFC kick returners, averaging 23.9 yards on KO runbacks and better than nine yards on punts. Krepfle and RB Montgomery caught 41 passes each in what could become a potent passing game this season. The Eagles need another good wide receiver to go with Carmichael. That would pressure the opposing secondaries no end.

Interior Linemen	Ht.	Wt.	Age	Exp.	College
Biederman, Leo (T)	6-7	275	25	2	California
Key, Wade (G)	6-5	245	34	11	Southwest Texas
Morriss, Guy (C)	6-4	255	29	8	Texas Christian
Peoples, Woody (G)	6-2	252	37	11	Grambling
Perot, Petey (G)	6-2	261	23	2	Northwest Louisiana
Sisemore, Jerry (T)	6-4	260	29	8	Texas
Slater, Mark (C)	6-1	257	25	3	Minnesota
Walters, Stan (T)	6-6	270	32	9	Syracuse
Wright, Rayfield (T)	6-6	260	35	14	Fort Valley State

T=tackle   G=guard   C=center

Starters are Walters, Key, Morriss, Peoples and Sisemore. Perot may push for a first-string guard job this season. Peoples and Key are getting a little aged, giving Perot ideas, no doubt. The Philadelphia offensive line was highly honored by sending both tackles, Walters and Sisemore, to the 1980 Pro Bowl. Wright, lately of the Dallas Cowboys, may get his second wind in Philadelphia and do a fine job for Vermeil. The Cowboys felt that time had caught up with the rugged tackle.

Kickers	Ht.	Wt.	Age	Exp.	College
Franklin, Tony (Pk)	5-8	182	24	2	Texas A&M
Runager, Max (P)	6-1	189	24	2	South Carolina

Pk=placekicker   P=punter

Franklin's 59-yard FG at Dallas last season was second longest in NFL annals. Ten of his 23 FGs came from 40 yards or more out. Runager, a rookie punter, didn't quite average 40 yards but the Eagles wanted him to hang the ball high which he generally did. Only 34 of his 74 punts were returned for a 5.9-yard average.

DEFENSE

Front Linemen	Ht.	Wt.	Age	Exp.	College
Burnham, Lem (E)	6-4	240	33	4	US International
Clarke, Ken (MG)	6-2	255	24	3	Syracuse
Hairston, Carl (E)	6-3	245	28	5	Md.-Eastern Shore
Harrison, Dennis (E)	6-8	275	24	3	Vanderbilt
Humphrey, Claude (E)	6-5	265	36	13	Tennessee State
Johnson, Charlie (MG)	6-3	262	28	3	Colorado
Johnson, Stan (T)	6-4	275	25	2	Tennessee State
McCray, Willie (E)	6-5	255	27	2	Troy State
Sistrunk, Manny (E)	6-5	275	33	11	Arkansas-Pine Bluff

E=end   MG=middle guard

Johnson was a starting defensive tackle in the Pro Bowl. Humphrey and Hairston led a pass rush that sacked the QB 45 times, one of the

NFC's most effective aerial defensives. In fact, Hairston's 15 sacks led the NFC. Humphrey has convinced the doubters by becoming the club's No. 1 lineman in total, pass and rush defense, his age notwithstanding. This unit is one of club's main assets.

Linebackers	Ht.	Wt.	Age	Exp.	College
Bergey, Bill (I)	6-3	245	35	12	Arkansas State
Bunting, John (O)	6-1	220	30	9	North Carolina
Chesley, Al (I)	6-3	240	23	2	Pittsburgh
LeMaster, Frank (I)	6-2	231	28	7	Kentucky
Phillips, Ray (O)	6-4	217	26	4	Nebraska
Robinson, Jerry (I)	6-2	216	24	2	UCLA
Tautolo, Terry (I)	6-2	235	26	5	UCLA
Wilkes, Reggie (O)	6-4	230	24	3	Georgia Tech
Young, Roynell (CB)	6-1	181	22	R	Alcorn State

O=outside   I=inside

LeMaster led the club in tackles with 79 solos, 49 assists. Bergey played only three games last season, because of a knee injury. His return will put him and LeMaster on the inside, Robinson and either Bunting or Wilkes on the outside. That prospect makes Vermeil smile. The Eagle 'backers have both youth and, with Bergey around, powerful experience.

Defensive Backs	Ht.	Wt.	Age	Exp.	College
Blackmore, Richard (CB)	5-10	174	24	2	Mississippi State
Edwards, Herman (CB)	6-0	190	26	4	San Diego State
Howard, Bobby (CB)	6-1	175	36	14	San Diego State
Latimer, Al (CB)	5-11	172	23	2	Clemson
Logan, Randy (S)	6-1	195	29	8	Michigan
Monroe, Henry (CB)	5-11	180	24	2	Mississippi State
Sciarra, John (S)	5-11	185	26	3	UCLA
Wilson, Brenard (S)	6-0	170	25	2	Vanderbilt
Young, Roynell (CB)	6-1	181	22	R	Alcorn State

CB=cornerback   S=safety

Howard is 36, getting along in years for an effective cornerback, but he sticks in there. Wilson won a starting job at safety, then led club in interceptions with four. Edwards had his best season in '79, Logan has had better, Sciarra can do anything, including lead the NFC in punt returns with an 11.4-yard average. He can also play either safety position, quarterback or wide receiver if the occasion demands.

Note: A complete listing of Philadelphia's 1980 college draft selections can be found on page 275.

DEFENSIVE UNIT 3-4 DEFENSE

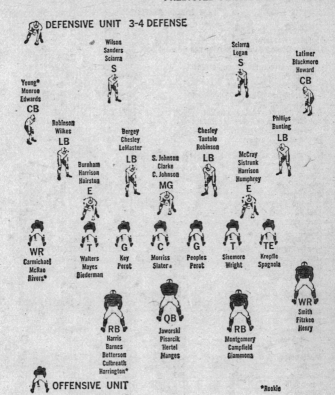

Wilson
Sanders
Sciarra
S

Sciarra
Logan
S

Latimer
Blackmore
Howard
CB

Young*
Monroe
Edwards
CB

Robinson
Wilkes
LB

Bergey
Chesley
LeMaster
LB

Chesley
Tautolo
Robinson
LB

Phillips
Bunting
LB

Burnham
Harrison
Hairston
E

S. Johnson
Clarke
C. Johnson
MG

McCray
Sistrunk
Harrison
Humphrey
E

WR
Carmichael
McRae
Rivers*

T
Walters
Mayes
Biederman

G
Key
Perot

C
Morriss
Slater*

G
Peoples
Perot

T
Sisemore
Wright

TE
Krepfle
Spagnola

RB
Harris
Barnes
Betterson
Culbreath
Harrington*

QB
Jaworski
Pisarcik
Hertel
Manges

RB
Montgomery
Campfield
Giammona

WR
Smith
Fitzkee
Henry

OFFENSIVE UNIT

*Rookie

1979 EAGLES STATISTICS

	Eagles	Opps.
Total Points Scored	339	282
Total First Downs	292	273
Third Down Efficiency Percentage	40.4	43.5
Yards Rushing—First Downs	2421—122	2271—128
Passes Attempted—Completions	410—209	459—243
Yards Passing—First Downs	2610—150	2474—125
QB Sacked—Yards Lost	43—272	45—324
Interceptions By—Return Average	22—12.0	13—10.2
Punts—Average Yards	76—38.9	85—39.9
Punt Returns—Average Return	57—9.5	34—5.9
Kickoff Returns—Average Return	56—22.5	69—18.4
Fumbles—Ball Lost	37—16	20—11
Penalties—Yards	90—689	86—641

STATISTICAL LEADERS

Scoring	TDs	Rush.	Pass.	Ret.	PATs	FGs	Total
Franklin	0	0	0	0	36—39	23—31	105
Montgomery	14	9	5	0	0	0	84
Carmichael	11	0	11	0	0	0	66
Campfield	4	3	0	1	0	0	24
Krepfle	3	0	3	0	0	0	18
Jaworski	2	2	0	0	0	0	12
Harris	2	2	0	0	0	0	12

Rushing	Atts.	Yds.	Avg.	Longest	TDs
Montgomery	338	1512	4.5	62 (TD)	9
Harris	107	504	4.5	80	2
Campfield	30	165	5.5	40	3
Jaworski	43	119	2.8	21	2
Barnes	25	74	3.0	21	1
Giammona	15	38	2.5	9	0

Passing	Atts.	Com.	Yds.	Pct.	Int.	Longest	TDs
Jaworski	374	190	2669	50.8	12	53 (TD)	18
Walton	36	19	213	52.8	1	31	3

Receiving	No.	Yds.	Avg.	Longest	TDs
Carmichael	52	872	16.8	50	11
Krepfle	41	760	18.5	45	3
Montgomery	41	494	12.0	53 (TD)	5
Smith	24	399	16.6	39	1
Harris	22	107	4.9	15	0
Campfield	16	115	7.2	17	0
Fitzkee	8	105	13.1	19	1

Interceptions	No.	Yds.	Avg.	Longest	TDs
Wilson	4	70	17.5	50	0
Logan	3	57	19.0	35	0
Howard	3	34	11.3	34	0
Edwards	3	6	2.0	6	0
Sciarra	2	45	22.5	34	0
Chesley	2	39	19.5	25	0
Bunting	2	13	6.5	13	0
Wilkes	2	0	—	—	0

Punting	No.	Yds.	Avg.	Longest	Inside 20	Blocked
Runager	74	2927	39.6	57	14	0

Punt Returns	No.	FCs	Yds.	Avg.	Longest	TDs
Henry	35	7	320	9.14	34	0
Sciarra	16	0	182	11.4	38	0
Giammona	5	0	42	8.4	14	0

Kickoff Returns	No.	Yds.	Avg.	Longest	TDs
Henry	28	668	23.9	53	0
Giammona	15	294	19.6	31	0
Campfield	7	251	35.9	92 (TD)	1

WASHINGTON REDSKINS

Head Coach: Jack Pardee

3rd Year

Record: 18–14

1979 RECORD (10-6) (capital letters indicate home games)			1980 SCHEDULE (capital letters indicate home games)	
27	HOUSTON	29	DALLAS (night, TV)	Sept. 8
27	Detroit	24	N.Y. Giants	Sept. 14
27	N.Y. GIANTS	0	Oakland	Sept. 21
17	St. Louis	7	SEATTLE	Sept. 28
16	Atlanta	7	Philadelphia	Oct. 5
17	Philadelphia	28	Denver (night, TV)	Oct. 13
13	Cleveland	9	ST. LOUIS	Oct. 19
17	PHILADELPHIA	7	NEW ORLEANS	Oct. 26
10	NEW ORLEANS	14	MINNESOTA	Nov. 2
7	Pittsburgh	38	Chicago	Nov. 9
30	ST. LOUIS	28	PHILADELPHIA	Nov. 16
34	DALLAS	20	Dallas	Nov. 23
6	N.Y. Giants	14	Atlanta	Nov. 30
38	GREEN BAY	21	SAN DIEGO	Dec. 7
28	CINCINNATI	14	N.Y. GIANTS (TV)	Dec. 13
34	Dallas	35	St. Louis	Dec. 21
348		295		

It came as no real surprise when it was disclosed recently that Jack Pardee has three more years remaining on his coaching contract with the Washington Redskins instead of only one, as most observers had thought. When Pardee signed the pact in '78, reports were that it covered only three years. Now it turns out the figure is five—and it's just as well, for the club came within a whisker of winning the NFC East title with its 10-6 record. In fact, many knowledgeable NFL observers believe Pardee's 1979 Redskins were better than some of the teams that made it to the playoffs. They were denied that privilege in the final eight seconds of a Roger Staubach, come-from-behind drive in Dallas which Washington lost 34-35. It was a bitter turn of events for a team that might have crashed its way into the Super Bowl, had it stayed alive for the playoffs.

Looking back on that 10-6 season, Pardee now believes it was the "transition" year the Redskins have needed all along. "We made great strides at being physically stronger," he says, "and should be much stronger this season in view of our priority of maintaining a tough off-season conditioning program. What I like about it all is that we're in a position now of not depending on a draft choice to turn us around. That's risky. Instead, we can work with our new people without pressuring them."

There's little doubt about it—Washington projects the image of a club on its way up. For nine consecutive seasons, the Redskins have finished with a .500 record or better, a success streak currently matched by only two other clubs—Oakland (15 straight) and Dallas (14 straight). And significantly, the Redskins continue to be very tough on their home turf—RFK Stadium. They won six of eight there last season, and since 1972 have defeated visiting teams 47 times out of 60 games. And that's not all. The Redskins have a perfect record at home on Monday Night television. By shutting out the New York Giants 27-0, their mark now stands as 8-0 on the first-of-the-week TV broadcasts from RFK Stadium since the ABC programs began ten years ago.

Pardee's phasing out of what used to be called George Allen's "Over-the-Hill Gang" is now virtually completed. It all began with the 1978 season and, since then, ten of the 22 starters have been replaced. Caught up and dropped in the mass exodus were such longtime Redskin stalwarts as Billy Kilmer, Ron McDole, Chris Hanburger, Len Hauss, Mike Curtis and others, not to mention George Allen himself. The aging statistics are now different—much different. The average

Redskin is 27 years old, and has only five years of NFL experience.

With Joe Theismann gaining more self-confidence at quarterback now that the starting role is his alone, and with John Riggins sparking a personal running game (that needs support), the 'Skins are truly accomplishing some outstanding feats, both offensively and defensively as this check-list would show:

● With 21 opposing fumbles recovered and 26 passes intercepted for a total of 47 takeaways, and giving away only 25 fumbles and passes of their own, the Redskins had a plus-22 on last season's takeaway-giveaway table—best in the NFL. They finished five points ahead of Houston in this regard, the Oilers sporting a plus-17.

● Washington's special teams are known as "The Wild Bunch," and this colorful crowd once again led the entire league in coverage. The punt return team gave up an average of only 4.7 yards on opposing runbacks. And the kickoff coverage unit surrendered only 16.8 yards per return, more than a full point ahead of Seattle's second place average of 17.7.

● Ironically, Washington was the only NFL club to convert all of its extra point attempts last season, 39-for-39, and then lost a chance to compete in the playoffs when Dallas kicked an extra point to win, 35-34, even though the Cowboys had missed four of their PATs during the regular 16-game schedule!

The excellent takeaway-giveaway record didn't just happen, as the club's defensive coordinator, Doc Urich, tells us. "We emphasized it in training camp," Urich recalls. "We had to get more turnovers and made the point of having our defense swarming around the ball. By driving this home, we're getting people around the football and it makes things happen." (This, it would seem, is a variation of a famous strategy once employed with

great success in college football by Major Bob Neyland, coach of the University of Tennessee Volunteers.
Neyland's strategy: "Keep a tight defense, and play for
the breaks.")

The Washington offensive unit could use new talent
at several positions, including running back, tight end,
wide receiver and along the line. The defense seems
fairly well set, but would welcome at least one more
game-wise pass rusher at end. One position, however,
where help isn't needed is placekicker. There, Mark
Moseley is busy redeeming the lost art of conventional,
straight-away field goal kicking—a style all but replaced by soccer-type, sidewinder kickers who whip
the ball with the side of their foot. "There's only five
of us left," says Moseley in naming the other NFL
straight-away kickers, "and they're Jim Turner of
Denver, Don Cockroft of Cleveland, Rick Danmeier of
Minnesota and Russell Erxleben of New Orleans."

OFFENSE

Quarterbacks	Ht.	Wt.	Age	Exp.	College
McQuilken, Kim	6-3	203	29	7	Lehigh
Mortensen, Fred	6-2	195	26	2	Arizona State
Theismann, Joe	6-0	195	31	7	Notre Dame

Theismann finished the '79 season having performed statistically best
as a Redskin QB of the 'Seventies with 233 for 2,297 yards. His 84.0
QB rating was second best in the NFL (with Roger Staubach rated first).
Theismann gives all signs of rapidly coming into his own as a first-
class NFL quarterback.

Running Backs	Ht.	Wt.	Age	Exp.	College
Forte, Ike	6-0	211	26	5	Arkansas
Hammond, Bobby	5-10	170	28	5	Morgan State
Hardeman, Buddy	6-0	189	26	2	Iowa State
Harmon, Clarence	5-11	211	25	4	Mississippi State
Malone, Benny	5-10	193	28	7	Arizona State
Riggins, John	6-2	230	31	10	Kansas
Testerman, Don	6-2	230	28	4	Clemson

Riggins had his third 1,000-yard season, his 1,153 yards being the second highest ever by a Redskin (Larry Brown had 1,216 in '72). Harmon's five receiving TDs was club's best (he scored none rushing). As a rookie, Hardeman displayed a running and pass receiving ability that indicates future greatness. Malone is a splendid blocker but his rushing gain average left lots to be desired last season (2.7). The Redskin ground game needs something else to go with Riggins who always seems to be the workhorse, wherever he plays.

Receivers	Ht.	Wt.	Age	Exp.	College
Alexander, John (T)	6-2½	250	25	4	Rutgers
Boyd, Elmo (W)	6-0	188	26	2	Eastern Kentucky
DuBois, Phil (T)	6-2	220	24	2	San Diego State
McDaniel, John (W)	6-1	197	29	7	Lincoln U.
Monk, Art (W)	6-2	209	22	R	Syracuse
Owens, Morris (W)	6-0	200	27	6	Arizona State
Richardson, Gary (T)	6-4	225	28	2	Fullerton State
Thompson, Ricky (W)	6-0	174	26	5	Baylor
Warren, Don (T)	6-4	255	25	3	Rhode Island
Henry, Lloyd (W)	6-3	208	25	1	Northeast Missouri
Dixon, Vollon (W)	6-2	205	26	1	San Diego State

W=wide receiver   T=tight end

Thompson and McDaniel started slowly, but came on as season progressed, working with a group of running backs and receivers that gave Theismann a wide variety of targets. Seven Redskins caught 20 or more of his passes. Yet, the Washington aerial attack rated a lowly 11th within the NFC. This unit may undergo a lot of juggling before Pardee chooses the starters.

Interior Linemen	Ht.	Wt.	Age	Exp.	College
Anderson, Gary (G)	6-3	250	25	2	Stanford
Carlton, Darryl (T)	6-5	285	27	6	Tampa
Dean, Fred (G)	6-3	253	25	4	Texas Southern
Dubintez, Greg (G)	6-4	260	26	2	Yale
Fritsch, Ted (C-G)	6-2	247	30	9	St. Norbert
Gibbons, Mike (T-G)	6-4	262	29	3	SW Oklahoma
Hermeling, Terry (T)	6-5	255	34	11	Nevada-Reno
Kuziel, Bob (C)	6-5	255	30	6	Pittsburgh
Nugent, Dan (G)	6-3	250	27	4	Auburn
Saul, Ron (G)	6-3	254	32	11	Michigan State
Starke, George (T)	6-5	250	32	8	Columbia
Williams, Jeff (G)	6-4	255	25	3	Rhode Island

T=tackle   G=guard   C=center

At season's end, Hermeling, Saul, Kuziel, Williams and Starke were the starters. It took an off-season weight-control program to whip this unit into shape. Opposing pass rushers got through this line for

34 QB sacks last season, not bad but not good either. Pardee will no doubt give this group a long look before lining 'em up.

Kickers	Ht.	Wt.	Age	Exp.	College
Bragg, Mike (P)	5-11	186	34	13	Richmond
Moseley, Mark (Pk)	6-0	205	32	9	S. F. Austin

Pk=placekicker   P=punter

Moseley's 1979 season was his career best, leading the NFC with 114 points. He has a consecutive string of 69 PATs going into 1980. Nine of his 25 FGs came from the 40-49-yard range. Bragg punted for a 38.4 average, his longest being 74 yards. Do those distances satisfy Pardee?

DEFENSE

Front Linemen	Ht.	Wt.	Age	Exp.	College
Bacon, Coy (E)	6-4	265	37	13	Jackson State
Brooks, Perry (T)	6-3	260	25	3	Southern U.
Butz, Dave (T)	6-7	285	30	8	Purdue
Jones, Joe (E)	6-6	250	32	10	Tennessee State
Lorch, Karl (E)	6-3	258	30	5	Southern Cal
Mendenhall, Mat (E)	6-6	237	22	R	Brigham Young
Smith, Paul (E)	6-3	255	35	13	New Mexico
Talbert, Diron (T)	6-5	255	36	14	Texas
Milanovich, Tom (E)	6-4	245	27	1	Wis.-Superior

E=end   T=tackle

Bacon, Smith and Talbert may need replacements soon as retirement looms. Bacon, however, shows no signs of slowing down. He had two QB sacks and two fumble recoveries against Dallas and led club with 15 sacks for season. Always a great pass rusher, Bacon has improved against the run. When the last whistle blew in '79, the defensive line was Lorch, Butz, Talbert and Bacon. That could change. The Redskins defense didn't rank very high in '79.

Linebackers	Ht.	Wt.	Age	Exp.	College
Coleman, Monte (O)	6-2	220	23	2	Central Arkansas
Dusek, Brad (O)	6-2	227	30	7	Texas A&M
Hickman, Dallas (O)	6-6	235	28	5	California
Hover, Don (M)	6-3	227	26	3	Washington State
Milot, Rich (O)	6-4	225	23	2	Penn State
Olkewicz, Neal (M)	6-0	218	23	2	Maryland
Wysocki, Pete (O)	6-1	224	32	6	Western Michigan

O=outside   M=middle

This unit is solid with youth and fire. Olkewicz was a free agent who led the club in tackles last season (84 solos) while starting on half the time. Coleman and Milot, both coming off their rookie seasons, will challenge Wysocki for jobs. Dusek seems set at his outside post. Hover can't be dismissed, either. This crowd means business.

Defensive Backs	Ht.	Wt.	Age	Exp.	College
Harris, Don (S)	6-2	185	26	3	Rutgers
Houston, Ken (S)	6-3	198	36	14	Prairie View
Lavender, Joe (CB)	6-4	190	31	8	San Diego State
Murphy, Mark (S)	6-4	210	25	4	Colgate
Parrish, Lemar (CB)	5-10	180	33	11	Lincoln U.
Peters, Tony (S)	6-1	185	27	6	Oklahoma
Waddy, Ray (CB)	5-11	175	24	2	Texas A&I
White, Jeris (CB)	5-11	185	28	7	Hawaii

CB=cornerback   S=safety

Pardee can be assured of good work here. Parrish and Lavender had fine seasons in '79, both going to the Pro Bowl. Peters filled in for the injured Houston and did a great job. Murphy started for first time and looked good. Parrish led NFC in pass thefts with nine. Lavender did O.K. too, stealing five. Eleven different Redskins intercepted at least one pass last season for a total of 26. White comes to Washington in a draft-choice trade (4th round) with Tampa Bay, where he reportedly had contract problems. John McKay was probably unhappy over White's departure, for it meant tinkering with that very fine Buccaneer defense.

Note: A complete listing of Washington's 1980 college draft selections can be found on page 278.

DEFENSIVE UNIT

Houston
Harris
Murphy
S

Harris
Peters
S

White
Waddy
Parrish
CB

Waddy
Lavender
CB

Milot
Coleman
Wysocki
LB

Hover
Olkewicz
LB

Coleman
Hickman
Dusek
LB

Milanovich
Jones
Bacon
E

Brooks
Smith
Talbert
T

Brooks
Smith
Butz
T

Mendenhall*
Smith
Jones
Lorch
E

WR
Buggs
McDaniel
Boyd
Dixon
Monk*

T
Hermeling
Dubinetz
Carlton

G
Saul
Dean
Anderson

C
Kuziel
Fritsch

G
Williams
Dean
Nugent

T
Starke
Dubinetz
Gibbons

TE
Warren
Fugett
DuBois
Alexander
Richardson

WR
Thompson
Harris
Owens
Henry

RB
Malone
Forte
Hammond

QB
Theismann
McQuilken
Mortensen

RB
Riggins
Harmon
Testerman

OFFENSIVE UNIT

*Rookie

1979 REDSKINS STATISTICS

	Redskins	Opps.
Total Points Scored	348	295
Total First Downs	297	320
Third Down Efficiency Percentage	46.9	43.0
Yards Rushing—First Downs	2328—126	2150—126
Passes Attempted—Completions	401—235	470—234
Yards Passing—First Downs	2576—144	2992—165
QB Sacked—Yards Lost	34—263	47—347
Interceptions By—Return Average	26—9.6	15—5.5
Punts—Average Yards	78—38.4	70—38.4
Punt Returns—Average Return	33—8.2	29—4.7
Kickoff Returns—Average Return	55—20.8	76—16.8
Fumbles—Ball Lost	21—10	34—21
Penalties—Yards	86—749	77—619

STATISTICAL LEADERS

Scoring	TDs	Rush.	Pass.	Ret.	PATs	FGs	Total
Moseley	0	0	0	0	39—39	25—33	114
Riggins	12	9	3	0	0	0	72
Harmon	5	0	5	0	0	0	30
Thompson	4	0	4	0	0	0	24
Malone	4	3	1	0	0	0	24
Theismann	4	4	0	0	0	0	24
Fugett	3	0	3	0	0	0	18
McDaniel	2	0	2	0	0	0	12

Rushing	Atts.	Yds.	Avg.	Longest	TDs
Riggins	260	1153	4.4	66 (TD)	9
Malone	176	472	2.7	14	3
Harmon	65	267	4.1	18	0
Theismann	46	181	3.9	22	4
Forte	25	125	5.0	20 (TD)	1
Hardeman	31	124	4.0	22	0

Passing	Atts.	Com.	Yds.	Pct.	Int.	Longest	TDs
Theismann	395	233	2797	59.0	13	62	20

Receiving	No.	Yds.	Avg.	Longest	TDs
Buggs	46	631	13.7	45	1
Harmon	32	434	13.6	40	5
Riggins	28	163	5.8	23	3
Warren	26	303	11.7	23	0
McDaniel	25	357	14.3	62	2
Thompson	22	366	16.6	35	4
Hardeman	21	197	9.4	41 (TD)	1
Malone	13	137	10.5	55 (TD)	1
Fugett	10	128	12.8	30 (TD)	3
Forte	10	105	10.5	22	0

Interceptions	No.	Yds.	Avg.	Longest	TDs
Parrish	9	65	7.2	23	0
Lavender	6	77	12.8	27	0
Murphy	3	29	9.7	16	0

Punting	No.	Yds.	Avg.	Longest	Inside 20	Blocked
Bragg	78	2998	38.4	74	12	0

Punt Returns	No.	FCs	Yds.	Avg.	Longest	TDs
Hardeman	24	6	207	8.6	52	0
Hammond	7	7	54	7.7	16	0

Kickoff Returns	No.	Yds.	Avg.	Longest	TDs
Hardeman	19	404	21.3	33	0
Hammond	14	314	22.4	33	0
Forte	8	211	26.4	38	0
Harris	6	80	13.3	23	0
Harmon	5	63	12.6	19	0

ST. LOUIS CARDINALS

Head Coach: Jim Hanifan
(1st Year)

1979 RECORD (5-11) (capital letters indicate home games)			1980 SCHEDULE (capital letters indicate home games)	
21	DALLAS	22	N.Y. GIANTS	Sept. 7
27	N.Y. Giants	14	San Francisco	Sept. 14
21	PITTSBURGH	24	Detroit	Sept. 21
7	WASHINGTON	17	PHILADELPHIA	Sept. 28
0	Los Angeles	21	New Orleans	Oct. 5
24	Houston	17	LOS ANGELES	Oct. 12
20	PHILADELPHIA	24	Washington	Oct. 19
13	Dallas	22	Baltimore	Oct. 26
20	CLEVELAND	38	DALLAS	Nov. 2
37	MINNESOTA	7	ATLANTA	Nov. 9
28	Washington	30	Dallas	Nov. 16
13	Philadelphia	16	KANSAS CITY	Nov. 23
28	Cincinnati	34	N.Y. Giants	Nov. 30
13	SAN FRANCISCO	10	DETROIT	Dec. 7
29	N.Y. GIANTS	20	Philadelphia	Dec. 14
6	Chicago	42	WASHINGTON	Dec. 21
307		358		

Three new head coaches will be at the helm of NFL teams this season—and the St. Louis Cardinals have the dubious honor of choosing theirs earlier than anyone else. The 1979 season had just passed its 13th weekend when club owner Bill Bidwell called a news conference to announce he was letting Bud Wilkinson go as head coach because, Bidwell said painfully, of a difference of opinion over who should play quarterback in the season's final three games.

Jim Hart, admittedly, was having problems as the Cardinals' regular quarterback. Now 36 years old, the strong-armed Hart is beginning to show signs of decline from his glory days. Either that, or his supporting cast isn't what it used to be—one can pick and choose between theories.

At any rate, Bidwell, who wasn't too happy with the way things were going on the field, wanted backup Steve Pisarkiewicz to see some playing time in the final three games against the 49ers, Giants and Bears. The St. Louis record stood 3-10 at that point, and maybe asking Wilkinson to send Pisarkiewicz into action wasn't unreasonable. But Wilkinson didn't like the idea, or the principle of the thing, and refused. So out he went, although Bidwell said this wasn't the "only" reason. Rather, it was the "catalyst." And there were other reasons, plenty of them, much too numerous to detail here. Suffice it to say that Wilkinson's 9-20 record in less than two years didn't help matters.

With the former Oklahoma coach's departure, the interim job was assigned the club's personnel director, Larry Wilson, who proceeded to coach the Cardinals to two victories in those last three games. Wilson even had hopes that Bidwell would give him the contract, but it wasn't to be—Jim Hanifan, lately of the Cardinals as an assistant and more recently a member of Don Coryell's San Diego staff, was to receive Bidwell's nod as Wilkinson's successor. And Hanifan wasn't backwards about accepting. "Sometimes," he mused, "I hear NFL assistant coaches saying that they wouldn't take this job or that, but there are only 28 of these jobs in the entire world."

Hanifan served as offensive line coach at St. Louis from 1973 to '78 when he joined Coryell in San Diego (not long after Coryell himself had been dismissed by Bidwell). Among his more notable achievements was directing a Cardinal line that, for three straight seasons, allowed the fewest quarterback sacks in the league. If he can do the same for Hart, maybe there's a future for Hanifan there on the Mississippi.

"Jim Hart is one of the NFL's top quarterbacks," says the new coach, "so we'll be throwing the ball a lot. You'll also probably see part of San Diego's passing offense in action here. On the other hand, Ottis Anderson is a player we're lucky to have, so we'll give him the ball and let him carry us at times."

If "at times" means merely now and then, Hanifan may be setting himself up for some suggestions from Bidwell who is all too aware that Anderson's rookie season was one of the most sensational witnessed by the NFL in a long time. It was not only that he set new league records for rookie rushing. Anderson—whose first name is spelled with two "t's" because the doctor misspelled "Otis" on the birth certificate—has also been timed at 4.65 seconds in the 40-yard dash. And that's fast moving, especially for a 6-1, 210-pounder. St. Louis led the NFC in rushing yardage last season with a total of 2,582—and more than half those yards were personally traveled by Anderson (1,605).

The 1979 season and Wilkinson's eventual fate hung at times on the very thin margin of four points or less, the margins by which the Cardinals lost five of their games. These cliff-hangers that went the wrong way included two close losses to Super Bowl champion Pittsburgh, 22-21 and 24-21; two defeats by Philadelphia, 24-20 and 16-13; and a close decision to Washington, 30-28. Switch those five games into the win column of a 5-11 record and you have a 10-6, and perhaps a play-off berth. It's one of the mathematical games losing teams play.

Even so, there's good reason to believe that some of those scores could have come out the other way but for the walking wounded on the club's injured reserve. Offensive tackle Dan Dierdorf was lost with a knee injury in the second game. Then followed hospital visits by linebacker Tim Kearney, defensive end John Zook,

running backs Willard Harrell, Rod Phillips and
Thomas Lott, tight end Gary Parris and wide receivers
Mark Bell and Jeff Lee. Much depends on whether this
group will be ready when the new season opens against
the New York Giants in Busch Memorial Stadium on
September 7th.

Hanifan says he never likes being labeled "an offensive-minded coach," but appreciates the importance
of the Cardinal offensive line. "O. J. Anderson gained
1,605 yards and the team set a record for total yards
behind a good, but hurt, line. You put Dan Dierdorf
back in there with a healthy Bob Young, Tom Banks,
Keith Wortman and Terry Stieve and you've got something going."

OFFENSE

Quarterbacks	Ht.	Wt.	Age	Exp.	College
Hart, Jim	6-1	210	36	15	Southern Illinois
Lisch, Rusty	6-4	210	22	R	Notre Dame
Loyd, Mike	6-2	216	24	2	Missouri Southern
Pisarkiewicz, Steve	6-2	205	27	4	Missouri

Hart didn't have as good a season as usual, although his completion
average was 51.4%. For whatever reason, perhaps injuries in the
offensive line, perhaps other factors, the Cardinals didn't gain through
the air with consistency as they did in Hart's better seasons. Pisarkiewicz (Zark, as he is called) was the club's No. 1 draft choice in '77,
but he's failed to live up to that rating, at least so far. He threw
109 times last season, completed 52 for a 47.7%. Even so, his NFL
quarterback rating of 59.5 was better than Hart's 55.8. Loyd, a rookie
last season, waits and hopes.

Running Backs	Ht.	Wt.	Age	Exp.	College
Anderson, Ottis	6-2	210	23	2	Miami (Fla.)
Brown, Theotis	6-2	225	23	2	UCLA
Harrell, Willard	5-8	182	28	6	Pacific (Calif.)
Lott, Thomas	5-10	205	23	2	Oklahoma
Love, Randy	6-1	205	24	2	Houston
Morris, Wayne	6-0	208	26	5	Southern Methodist
Phillips, Rod	6-0	221	28	6	Jackson State

Harrell, Lott and Phillips were hampered by injuries, but Anderson made up ground for everybody. This latter-day "O. J." (those are Anderson's actual initials) had the best rookie debut of any running back in NFL history, and that says a lot. His total of 1,605 yards was league's third best, exceeding Earl Campbell's rookie record by 155 yards. Anderson was also the only rookie on the 1980 Pro Bowl squads, NFC or AFC. Brown showed promise, averaging 4.4 yards on 72 carries. He could give Morris a strong challenge at starting fullback. Harrell, when he played, averaged 5.3 yards per carry.

Receivers	Ht.	Wt.	Age	Exp.	College
Bell, Mark (W)	5-9	175	23	2	Colorado State
Childs, Jim (W)	6-2	194	24	3	CP-San Luis Obispo
Gray, Mel (W)	5-9	173	32	10	Missouri
Lee, Jeff (W)	6-2	185	25	2	Nebraska
Marsh, Doug (T)	6-3	233	22	R	Michigan
Murrell, Bill (T)	6-3	220	24	2	Winston-Salem
Parris, Gary (T)	6-2	226	30	8	Florida State
Stief, Dave (W)	6-3	195	24	3	Portland State
Tilley, Pat (W)	5-10	171	27	5	Louisiana Tech

W=wide receiver   T=tight end

Gray has a pass-catching string going at 89 consecutive games, but the Cardinals perhaps should groom his heir-apparent. With leg injuries, he's 32 and counting. Tilley was this unit's only first-rate receiver in '79 with 57 catches for 938 yards and a 16.4-yard average. Ottis Anderson can catch too, with 41 for 308 yards as a rookie out of the backfield. Stief is club's tallest wide receiver at 6-3, but he's used at tight end occasionally along with Murrell. Bell and Lee are speed-burners who bowed out with injuries in preseason games. If they return in good shape, the receiving personnel picture could change, drastically.

Interior Linemen	Ht.	Wt.	Age	Exp.	College
Banks, Tom (C)	6-2	245	32	9	Auburn
Bostic, Joe (T)	6-2	265	23	2	Clemson
Brahaney, Tom (C)	6-2	246	29	8	Oklahoma
Brown, Chuck (C-G)	6-1	235	23	2	Houston
Collins, George (G)	6-2	248	25	3	Georgia
Dierdorf, Dan (T)	6-3	288	31	10	Michigan
Oates, Brad (T)	6-6	275	27	5	Brigham Young
Sinnott, John (T)	6-5	270	22	R	Brown
Stieve, Terry (G)	6-2	263	26	5	Wisconsin
Wortman, Keith (T)	6-2	275	30	9	Nebraska
Young, Bob (G)	6-1	279	38	15	Howard Payne

T=tackle   G=guard   C=center

Bostic impressed the coaches when called in to replace the injured Dierdorf at tackle. He also gained recognition by at least one all-rookie team. Young, the 38-year-old, went to the Pro Bowl. The '79 windup found Oates, Young, Banks, Stieve and Bostic as the front five. Despite all else, the Cardinal ground game ranked first in the NFC, averaging 161.4 yards per game. That says a great deal for the offensive line that cleared the way for Ottis Anderson.

Kickers	Ht.	Wt.	Age	Exp.	College
Gerela, Roy (Pk)	5-10	185	32	12	New Mexico State
Little, Steve (P-Pk)	6-0	180	24	3	Arkansas

Pk=placekicker   P=punter

Little was Mr. Everything here, doing both punting and placekicking. But not as well as the coaches would like it. His extra point conversions were only 24 out of 32 tries, and FGs numbered 10 successful boots out of 19, but one of those (out of one attempt) came from the 50-yard-plus range. Little was a star kicker at Arkansas, and may be trying to adjust his talent to the pros before really making his mark. Another placekicker added recently is none other than Roy Gerela of Pittsburgh fame (remember Gerela's Gorillas?). Released by the Steelers in '79, he was with San Diego last season, appearing in only two games. Gerela has made good on 63% of his career FG attempts inside the 50-yard line and ranks 13th among the NFL's all-time high scorers with 903 points.

DEFENSE

Front Linemen	Ht.	Wt.	Age	Exp.	College
Davis, Charlie (NT)	6-2	275	29	6	Texas Christian
Dawson, Mike (E)	6-4	275	27	5	Arizona
Greer, Curtis (E)	6-5	245	22	R	Michigan
Pollard, Bob (E)	6-3	252	32	10	Weber State
Ramey, Jim (E)	6-4	247	23	2	Kentucky
Simons, Keith (NT)	6-3	254	26	5	Minnesota
Yankowski, Ron (E)	6-5	258	24	10	Kansas State
Zook, John (E)	6-5	254	33	12	Kansas

E=end   NT=nose tackle

Pollard, Davis and Dawson are the front men in the 3-4 defense. Pollard led club in QB sacks with nine. Zook is being slowed down by a knee injury. This outfit ranked 26th in the NFL in rushing the passer last season, although it did do a good job of stopping the opposition's ground game. But Hanifan has his work cut out for him here.

Linebackers	Ht.	Wt.	Age	Exp.	College
Allerman, Kurt (I)	6-3	222	25	4	Penn State
Arneson, Mark (O)	6-2	224	31	9	Arizona
Baker, Charles (O)	6-2	218	22	R	New Mexico

Barefield, John (O)	6-2	224	25	3	Texas A&I
Clancy, Sean (O)	6-4	218	24	3	Amherst
Favron, Calvin (O)	6-1	225	23	2	SE Louisiana
Kearney, Tim (I)	6-2	221	30	9	Northern Michigan
Neils, Steve (O)	6-2	218	29	7	Minnesota
Williams, Eric (I)	6-2	225	25	4	Southern Cal

O=outside   I=inside

The four linebackers who started the '79 season didn't stay together
at all. Three were out at least five weeks of the campaign with injuries. The team's chief tackler, Kearney, went out after the fifth game.
Arneson missed five games but returned in good form. Neils missed
seven contests because of a broken bone in his leg, but he too returned to action. Allerman did well filling in for Kearney. Barefield and
Favron are getting experience in midst of the injuries. Barefield,
Allerman, Williams and Arneson were the LBs at season's end.

Defensive Backs	Ht.	Wt.	Age	Exp.	College
Allen, Carl (CB)	6-0	186	25	4	Southern Mississippi
Collier, Tim (CB)	6-0	174	26	5	East Texas State
Green, Roy (S)	5-11	190	23	2	Henderson State
Greene, Ken (S)	6-3	203	24	3	Washington State
Henry, Steve (S)	6-2	190	23	2	Emporia State
Nelson, Lee (CB)	5-10	185	25	5	Florida State
Stone, Ken (S)	6-1	180	30	8	Vanderbilt
Wehrli, Roger (CB)	6-0	194	33	12	Missouri

CB=cornerback   S=safety

Stone and Allen led the pass interceptors with six and five. Greene
(the one with the "e" on the end) led the team in forcing fumbles (5),
total tackles (114) and solo tackles (81). Wehrli is still the main man
in the Cardinal secondary, earning his seventh Pro Bowl bid for his
play in '79. Green (the one without the "e" on the end) returned kickoffs for a thousand yards and a 24.6-yard average, including a 106-yard
runback against Dallas which tied an NFL record.

Note: A complete listing of St. Louis's 1980 college draft selections
can be found on page 276.

DEFENSIVE UNIT 3-4 DEFENSE

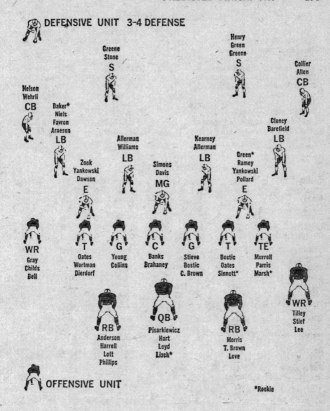

Greene
Stone
S

Henry
Green
Greene
S

Collier
Allen
CB

Nelson
Wehrli
CB

Baker*
Niels
Favron
Arneson
LB

Allerman
Williams
LB

Kearney
Allerman
LB

Clancy
Barefield
LB

Zook
Yankowski
Dawson
E

Simons
Davis
MG

Green*
Ramey
Yankowski
Pollard
E

WR
Gray
Childs
Bell

Oates
Wortman
Dierdorf
T

Young
Collins
G

Banks
Brahaney
C

Stieve
Bostic
C. Brown
G

Bostic
Oates
Sinnott*
T

Murrell
Parris
Marsh*
TE

RB
Anderson
Harrell
Lott
Phillips

QB
Pisarkiewicz
Hart
Loyd
Lisch*

RB
Morris
T. Brown
Love

WR
Tilley
Stief
Lee

OFFENSIVE UNIT

*Rookie

1979 CARDINALS STATISTICS

	Cardinals	Opps.
Total Points Scored	307	358
Total First Downs	305	302
Third Down Efficiency Percentage	39.0	38.0
Yards Rushing—First Downs	2582—145	2204—125
Passes Attempted—Completions	492—249	478—258
Yards Passing—First Downs	2602—136	2870—149
QB Sacked—Yards Lost	39—268	28—194
Interceptions By—Return Average	18—16.0	24—12.5
Punts—Average Yards	80—38.2	90—39.2
Punt Returns—Average Return	48—7.7	49—7.7
Kickoff Returns—Average Return	71—22.7	57—23.4
Fumbles—Ball Lost	42—21	40—19
Penalties—Yards	104—941	94—758

STATISTICAL LEADERS

Scoring	TDs	Rush.	Pass.	Ret.	PATs	FGs	Total
Anderson	10	8	2	0	0	0	60
Morris	9	8	1	0	0	0	54
Little	0	0	0	0	24—32	10—19	54
Brown	7	7	0	0	0	0	42
Tilley	6	0	6	0	0	0	36
Chandler	2	0	2	0	0	0	12

Rushing	Atts.	Yds.	Avg.	Longest	TDs
Anderson	331	1605	4.8	76 (TD)	8
Morris	106	387	3.6	16	8
Brown	72	318	4.4	30 (TD)	7
Harrell	19	100	5.3	19	0
Lott	11	50	4.5	13	0
Pisarklewlcz	11	20	1.8	12	0

Passing	Atts.	Com.	Yds.	Pct.	Int.	Longest	TDs
Hart	379	195	2218	51.4	20	51 (TD)	9
Pisarkiewicz	109	52	621	47.7	4	78 (TD)	3

Receiving	No.	Yds.	Avg.	Longest	TDs
Tilley	57	938	16.4	37	6
Anderson	41	308	7.5	28	2
Morris	35	237	6.7	20	1
Gray	25	447	17.8	78	1
Brown	25	191	7.6	22	0
Stief	22	324	14.7	32	0
Parris	14	174	12.4	39	0

Interceptions	No.	Yds.	Avg.	Longest	TDs
Stone	6	70	11.6	30	0
Allen	5	126	25.2	78	0
Greene	3	37	12.3	21	0
Wehrli	2	8	4.0	9 (TD)	1

Punting	No.	Yds.	Avg.	Longest	Inside 20	Blocked
Little	80	3060	38.2	56	17	2

Punt Returns	No.	FCs	Yds.	Avg.	Longest	TDs
Harrell	32	12	205	6.4	68	0
Green	8	3	42	5.3	14	0
Nelson	4	0	88	22.0	77	0
Lott	4	3	33	8.2	13	0

Kickoff Returns	No.	Yds.	Avg.	Longest	TDs
Green	41	1007	24.5	106 (TD)	1
Harrell	22	497	22.6	53	0

NEW YORK GIANTS

Head Coach: Ray Perkins

2nd Year   **Record:** 6–10

1979 RECORD (6-10) (capital letters indicate home games)		1980 SCHEDULE (capital letters indicate home games)	
17	Philadelphia 23	St. Louis	Sept. 7
14	ST. LOUIS 27	WASHINGTON	Sept. 14
0	Washington 27	Philadelphia (night, TV)	Sept. 22
13	PHILADELPHIA 17	LOS ANGELES	Sept. 28
14	New Orleans 24	Dallas	Oct. 5
17	TAMPA BAY 14	PHILADELPHIA	Oct. 12
32	SAN FRANCISCO 16	San Diego	Oct. 19
21	Kansas City 17	DENVER	Oct. 26
20	Los Angeles 14	Tampa Bay	Nov. 2
14	DALLAS 16	DALLAS	Nov. 9
24	ATLANTA 3	GREEN BAY	Nov. 16
3	Tampa Bay 31	San Francisco	Nov. 23
14	WASHINGTON 6	ST. LOUIS	Nov. 30
7	Dallas 28	Seattle	Dec. 7
20	St. Louis 29	Washington (TV)	Dec. 13
7	BALTIMORE 31	OAKLAND	Dec. 21
237	323		

Will the New York Giants finally, and at long last, find it possible to lift themselves from the 6-10 record they've been floundering in for the past two seasons? That question, in itself, is literally loaded with all kinds of controversial answers and probably could never be resolved until the season has run its course, and the Christmas calm has fallen over Giants Stadium in the Jersey Meadowlands. On second thought, it won't be so calm out in those flatlands if the Giants make it to the playoffs.

Is that really possible? Stranger things have happened in the NFL where almost every franchise can come up with either a rags-to-riches story, or a skeleton-in-the-closet wearing a football helmet. The Giants do have talent and if they get off on the right foot and the foot isn't injured, then the other NFC East clubs will be in for trouble.

Second-year head coach Ray Perkins is partial to an offensive-minded football team. He likes to see points flashing on the scoreboard, particularly New York Giants points. He prefers to see the air filled with forward passes, mainly Giants passes. The reason for this is his own background as a wide receiver at the University of Alabama where he caught passes thrown by both Joe Namath and Ken Stabler. Also with the Baltimore Colts where he received aerials from Johnny Unitas, and his experience as an assistant with offensive-minded NFL coaches like Chuck Fairbanks and Don Coryell. Only problem is, right now the Giants don't have much of an offense, but Perkins intends to work on that. After all, the 1979 Giants' offensive machine, if it can be called that, finished at the very bottom of the NFL's 28-team rankings, with low ratings on total offense, rushing and passing.

In all fairness, it should be pointed out that the offensive line was hit by a whole barrage of crippling injuries at the onset of the '79 season. This not only deprived the ground game of a rushing attack, it also exposed starting quarterback Joe Pisarcik to the onslaught of defensive pass rushers who sacked him 17 times in the first three games. That all added up to five straight defeats, with mid-season already staring the Giants in the face.

Things began to happen when rookie quarterback Phil Simms took over and the Giants sailed through four consecutive victories over undefeated Tampa Bay, San Francisco, Kansas City and Los Angeles. And when they played the Dallas Cowboys the following week, the Giants led 14-6 going into the final three minutes, only to fall victim to a Cowboy rally and lose, 16-14. Still, they bounced back, defeating Atlanta and Washington although losing to Tampa Bay in a return engagement. It was that kind of a see-saw all season long until the final three games which were dismally dropped to Dallas, St. Louis and Baltimore. And it was those three losses that seemed to demoralize the Giants most, causing the season to end in an atmosphere of gloom about the future.

But now that the future has arrived in the guise of a new season, things are expected to brighten considerably, one reason being that Phil Simms probably won't have to undergo surgery on his throwing thumb, after all. He had played the last month of the '79 schedule with a strained thumb on his throwing hand, with surgery a prospect. Now it appears the operation won't be necessary.

If Simms can repeat his passing performance of last season, the running game may be improved enough to provide him with a better offensive balance—something a quarterback has to have if he doesn't throw all the time. An off-season trade brought running back Mike Hogan to the Giants from San Francisco where he had spent '79 on injured reserve. Hogan, a 6-2, 215-pounder, was a ninth round draft selection of the Eagles two years ago and, according to one knowledgeable NFL scout, "he's a punishing blocker who loves to hit." After arriving in San Francisco, Hogan incurred a shoulder separation after two games and went on the injury list. During those two games, he carried nine times for 31 yards and a 3.4 average. The Giants also received a former Pittsburgh safety, Tony Dungy, in the trade with the 49ers, sending along cornerback Ray Rhodes and wide receiver Jimmy Robinson in exchange.

Dave Jennings continues to be the outstanding punter of the NFC, breaking his own club records almost each succeeding season. His 104 punts in '79 broke his own all-time club mark of 100 set in '77. He also has a couple of unusual streaks going. He hasn't had a punt blocked since 1976, and when he completed two forward passes (on fake plays) out of two attempts for 48 yards last season, he lifted his career passing totals to three-for-three for a 100% average.

Phil Simms . . . look out!

OFFENSE

Quarterbacks	Ht.	Wt.	Age	Exp.	College
Brunner, Scott	6-5	200	23	R	Delaware
Dean, Randy	6-3	194	25	4	Northwestern
Rader, Dave	6-3	215	23	2	Tulsa
Simms, Phil	6-3	216	25	2	Morehead State

Simms didn't get into action until the fifth game, then went on to complete 134 passes in 265 attempts for a 50.6%. As the 1980 campaign approaches, the fortunes of both New York teams—the Giants and Jets—are very much tied to their quarterbacks, Phil Simms and Richard Todd. Can they, and will they? Those are the questions. Dean is still around as a backup but Joe Pisarcik has gone to Philadelphia, there hopefully to back up Ron Jaworski. Rader is a future on the Giant QB reserve list.

Running Backs	Ht.	Wt.	Age	Exp.	College
Best, Art	6-1	206	27	3	Kent State
Dixon, Zachary	6-0	200	24	2	Temple
Franklin, George	6-3	225	26	3	Texas A&I
Hicks, Eddie	6-2	210	25	2	East Carolina
Hogan, Mike	6-2	215	26	5	Tenn.-Chattanooga
Johnson, Ken	6-2	220	24	2	Miami (Fla.)
Kotar, Doug	5-11	205	29	7	Kentucky
Taylor, Billy	6-0	215	24	3	Texas Tech

Taylor had a fine season in only his second year, rushing 700 yards on 198 carries. Counting pass receptions (28), his TDs totaled 11 which made him the Giants' top point-getter. Kotar ran for 616 yards on 160 carries. Simms showed scrambling ability by averaging 5.7 yards on 29 carries, including one TD. But make no mistake about it—the Giants ranked 28th in the league in total offense with an average of 235.9 per game, rushing and passing. They ranked 12th in the NFC in rushing alone. Perhaps Mike Hogan, the former Eagle who once rushed for 607 yards before being traded to San Francisco, can help change that. He also distinguished himself as a blocker for Eagle running back Wilbert Montgomery. Hogan could be the missing pin in the Giants' ground game.

Receivers	Ht.	Wt.	Age	Exp.	College
Gray, Earnest (W)	6-3	195	23	2	Memphis State
Jackson, Cleveland (T)	6-4	230	24	2	Nevada-Las Vegas
McCreary, Loaird (T)	6-5	227	27	5	Tennessee State
Mullady, Tom (T)	6-3	232	23	2	Southwestern (Tenn.)
Odom, Steve (W)	5-8	175	28	7	Utah
Perkins, Johnny (W)	6-2	205	27	4	Abilene Christian
Pittman, Dan (W)	6-2	205	22	R	Wyoming
Scales, Dwight (W)	6-2	182	27	5	Grambling
Shirk, Gary (T)	6-1	220	30	5	Morehead State

W=wide receiver   T=tight end

Gray showed good form as a starter his rookie year, catching 28 passes for a 19.2-yard average per reception. Shirk led the club in receptions with 31 for 471 yards and a 15.2 average. And look where he played his college football—Morehead State in Kentucky, where Phil Simms sprang from. Little wonder he became one of Simms's favorite receivers.

Interior Linemen	Ht.	Wt.	Age	Exp.	College
Benson, Brad (T)	6-3	258	25	3	Penn State
Clack, Jim (C)	6-3	250	33	10	Wake Forest
Coppens, Gus (T)	6-5	270	25	2	UCLA
Eck, Keith (C)	6-5	255	25	2	UCLA
King, Gordon (T)	6-6	275	24	3	Stanford
Mikolajczyk, Ron (T)	6-3	275	30	5	Tampa
Simmons, Roy (G)	6-3	264	24	2	Georgia Tech
Turner, J. T. (G)	6-3	250	27	4	Duke
Van Horn, Doug (G)	6-3	245	36	14	Ohio State
Weston, Jeff (G)	6-5	250	24	2	Notre Dame
Falcon, Terry (T)	6-3	260	25	3	Montana

T=tackle   G=guard   C=center

Van Horn plays hard but age has its limits. Turner and Clack remained consistent, but the line's play was spotty overall. Consistency gets lost in the overall performance. Benson is coming around and will stay, filling a much needed tackle post. Mikolajczyk is recovering from knee problems, and his availability remains uncertain. Perkins will have to whip this outfit into a ground-clearing machine.

Kickers	Ht.	Wt.	Age	Exp.	College
Danelo, Joe (Pk)	5-9	166	27	6	Washington State
Jennings, Dave (P)	6-4	205	28	7	St. Lawrence
Jones, Craig (Pk)	5-11	160	22	R	VMI
Lansford, Mike (Pk)	6-1	187	22	R	Washington

Pk=placekicker   P=punter

Jennings led NFC punters with a 42.7 average, his longest being 72 yards. Danelo didn't do as well with his placekicking last season as in '78 when he hit 21-of-29. If he gets back on track with FGs, the kicking game will be more than adequate. The Giants chose placekicker Mike Lansford of Washington in the draft's 12th round and later signed Craig Jones as a free agent. The draft had passed Jones by, even though he had kicked 55 field goals at Virginia Military—one short of the NCAA record held by Tony Franklin (formerly of Texas A&M, now of Philadelphia).

DEFENSE

Front Linemen	Ht.	Wt.	Age	Exp.	College
Jeter, Gary (E)	6-4	260	25	4	Southern Cal
Lapka, Myron (T)	6-4	255	22	R	Southern Cal
Martin, George (E)	6-4	245	27	6	Oregon
McCoy, Mike (T)	6-5	275	32	11	Notre Dame
Mendenhall, John (T)	6-1	255	32	9	Grambling
Miller, Calvin (T)	6-2	270	27	2	Oklahoma State
Tabor, Phil (T)	6-4	255	24	2	Oklahoma

E=end   T=tackle

The front line consisted of Jeter and Martin, Mendenhall at nose tackle in the 3-4 defense alignment. Martin led club with 11 QB sacks. Jeter wasn't exactly consistent and Mendenhall may already be on his career downside. This is a priority area for Perkins's attention. Tabor appears to be a good fourth round draft selection. Latest word is that the Giants will revert to the 4-3 (four down linemen) defense when the 1980 season begins, and if it works, of course, it'll stay that way.

Linebackers	Ht.	Wt.	Age	Exp.	College
Carson, Harry (I)	6-2	235	27	5	S.C. State
Coffield, Randy (I)	6-3	215	27	5	Florida State
Kelley, Brian (O)	6-3	222	29	8	Cal Lutheran
Lloyd, Dan (I)	6-2	225	27	5	Washington
Marion, Frank (O)	6-3	228	29	4	Florida A&M
Skorupan, John (I)	6-3	225	29	8	Penn State
Van Pelt, Brad (O)	6-5	235	29	8	Michigan State

O=outside   I=inside

If the defense had a highlight, the LB unit was it. Carson and Van Pelt made the Pro Bowl for the second straight year. Kelley and Lloyd played like they expected to be invited, too. Lloyd, though, came down with a knee injury and his status medically is uncertain for the new season. Carson still dreams of playing fullback sometime, someday— if he doesn't retire. He led the Giants in tackles in '79 with 185, 117 solos and 68 assists.

Defensive Backs	Ht.	Wt.	Age	Exp.	College
Blount, Tony (S)	6-1	193	22	R	Virginia
Caldwell, Alan (CB)	6-0	176	24	2	North Carolina
Dungy, Tony (S)	6-0	190	25	4	Minnesota
Haynes, Mark (CB)	5-11	185	22	R	Colorado
Jackson, Terry (CB)	5-10	197	25	3	San Diego State
Jones, Ernie (S)	6-3	180	27	5	Miami (Fla.)
Oldham, Ray (S)	5-11	192	29	8	Middle Tennessee
Reece, Beasley (S)	6-1	195	26	5	North Texas State

CB=cornerback   S=safety

Reece had a good season, finishing fourth among team tacklers with 117. He also played more than any other squad member. Jackson shared the club lead in interceptions with three—LBs Carson and Kelley also having three. Dungy comes from San Francisco as part of the Hogan trade. A former Steeler, Dungy led Pittsburgh in interceptions with six a couple of years back. Jones was on injured reserve with a knee problem. Oldham showed flashes of form at safety. The Giants are counting on great things from Haynes, their No. 1 draftee who was chosen eighth in the first round. He was consensus All-America at Colorado.

Note: A complete listing of the New York Giants' 1980 college draft selections can be found on page 274.

DEFENSIVE UNIT

Blount*
Dungy
Oldham
Reece
S

Jones
Oldham
S

Caldwell
T. Jackson
CB

Jury
McKinney
Haynes*
CB

Skorupan
Kelley
LB

Lloyd
Coffield
Carson
LB

Marion
Van Pelt
LB

Weston
Jeter
E

McCoy
Lapka*
T

Tabor
Miller
Mendenhall
T

Tabor
Martin
E

WR
Perkins
Scales

T
Benson
Coppens
Falcon

G
Van Horn
Simmons
Weston

C
Clack
Eck

G
Turner
Simmons

T
King
Mikolaczyk

TE
Shirk
McCreary
Mullady
C. Jackson

RB
Kotar
Dixon
Best
Hogan
Moorehead

QB
Simms
Dean
Rader

RB
Taylor
Hicks
Franklin
Johnson

WR
Gray
Scales
Odom
Pittman*

OFFENSIVE UNIT

*Rookie

AFC ALL-STARS

KIM BOKAMPER
Linebacker
Miami Dolphins

TIM FOLEY
Cornerback
Miami Dolphins

AFC ALL-STARS

LARRY CSONKA
Running Back
Miami Dolphins

TONY FRITSCH
Placekicker
Houston Oilers

ROBERT BRAZILE
Linebacker
Houston Oilers

JIMMY CEFALO
Wide Receiver
Miami Dolphins

AFC ALL-STARS

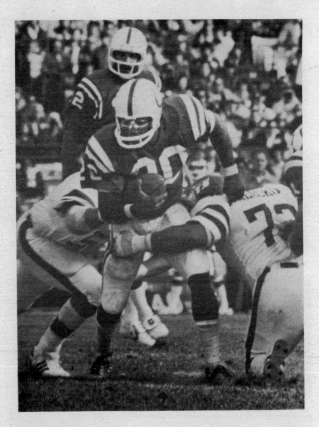

JOE WASHINGTON
Running Back
Baltimore Colts

RUSS WASHINGTON
Tackle
San Diego Chargers

EARL CAMPBELL
Running Back
Houston Oilers

MIKE PRUITT
Running Back
Cleveland Browns

MARVIN POWELL
Tackle
New York Jets

KEN BURROUGH
Wide Receiver
Houston Oilers

STANLEY MORGAN
Wide Receiver
New England Patriots

JACK LAMBERT
Linebacker
Pittsburgh Steelers

AFC ALL-STARS

JOE GREENE
Defensive Tackle
Pittsburgh Steelers

VERN DEN HERDER
Defensive End
Miami Dolphins

JOE FERGUSON
Quarterback
Buffalo Bills

SAM (BAM) CUNNINGHAM
Running Back
New England Patriots

DON COCKROFT
Placekicker
Cleveland Browns

NFC ALL-STARS

RON JAWORSKI
Quarterback
Philadelphia Eagles

HENRY CHILDS
Tight End
New Orleans Saints

NFC ALL-STARS

PAT DONOVAN
Tackle
Dallas Cowboys

BOB BREUNIG
Linebacker
Dallas Cowboys

ROGER WEHRLI
Cornerback
St. Louis Cardinals

MEL GRAY
Wide Receiver
St. Louis Cardinals

NFC ALL-STARS

FRED DRYER
Defensive End
Los Angeles Rams

JACK YOUNGBLOOD
Defensive End
Los Angeles Rams

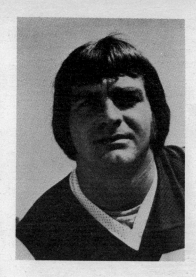

JIM YOUNGBLOOD
Linebacker
Los Angeles Rams

FRANK CORRAL
Placekicker
Los Angeles Rams

NFC ALL-STARS

TOM SKLADANY
Punter
Detroit Lions

GARY DANIELSON
Quarterback
Detroit Lions

LEMAR PARRISH
Cornerback
Washington Redskins

MARK MOSELEY
Placekicker
Washington Redskins

AHMAD RASHAD
Wide Receiver
Minnesota Vikings

BRAD VAN PELT
Linebacker
New York Giants

NFC ALL-STARS

STEVE DE BERG
Quarterback
San Francisco 49ers

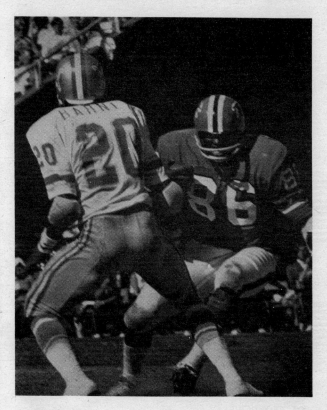

JIM MITCHELL
Tight End
Atlanta Falcons

JOE FEDERSPIEL
Linebacker
New Orleans Saints

JAMES LOFTON
Wide Receiver (80)
Green Bay Packers

NFC ALL-STARS

TERDELL MIDDLETON
Running Back (34)
Green Bay Packers

1979 GIANTS STATISTICS

	Giants	Opps.
Total Points Scored	237*	323
Total First Downs	223	322
Third Down Efficiency Percentage	32.8	37.2
Yards Rushing—First Downs	1820—82	2452—130
Passes Attempted—Completions	401—190	463—253
Yards Passing—First Downs	1954—111	2926—159
QB Sacked—Yards Lost	59—465	32—228
Interceptions By—Return Average	21—7.9	22—20.4
Punts—Average Yards	104—42.7	80—36.7
Punt Returns—Average Return	28—3.9	60—7.5
Kickoff Returns—Average Return	67—18.7	44—20.5
Fumbles—Ball Lost	34—18	36—17
Penalties—Yards	122—1047	105—800

* Includes safety

STATISTICAL LEADERS

Scoring	TDs	Rush.	Pass.	Ret.	PATs	FGs	Total
Taylor	11	7	4	0	0	0	66
Danelo	0	0	0	0	28—29	9—20	55
Gray	4	0	4	0	0	0	24
Perkins	4	0	4	0	0	0	24
Kotar	3	3	0	0	0	0	18
Shirk	2	0	2	0	0	0	12

Rushing	Atts.	Yds.	Avg.	Longest	TDs
Taylor	198	700	3.5	27	7
Kotar	160	616	3.9	32	3
Johnson	62	168	2.7	12	0
Simms	29	166	5.7	27	1
Moorehead	36	95	2.6	8	0

Passing	Atts.	Com.	Yds.	Pct.	Int.	Longest	TDs
Simms	265	134	1743	50.6	14	61	13
Pisarcik	108	43	537	39.8	6	48	2
Dean	26	11	91	42.3	2	20	0

Receiving	No.	Yds.	Avg.	Longest	TDs
Shirk	31	471	15.2	61	2
Gray	28	537	19.2	32	4
Taylor	28	253	9.0	43	4
Kotar	25	230	9.2	37	0
Perkins	20	337	16.9	38 (TD)	4
Johnson	16	108	6.8	15	1
Scales	14	222	15.9	55	0

Interceptions	No.	Yds.	Avg.	Longest	TDs
Kelley	3	41	13.7	16	0
Carson	3	28	9.3	14	0
Jackson	3	10	3.3	10	0
Jones	2	42	21.0	31 (TD)	1
Lloyd	2	10	5.0	7	0
Oldham	2	4	2.0	4	0
Caldwell	2	2	1.0	2	0

Punting	No.	Yds.	Avg.	Longest	Inside 20	Blocked
Jennings	104	4445	42.7	72	19	0

Punt Returns	No.	FCs	Yds.	Avg.	Longest	TDs
Green	3	6	17	5.7	8	0
Robinson	6	4	29	4.8	13	0
Hammond	6	3	21	3.5	8	0
Odom	9	3	26	2.9	10	0

Kickoff Returns	No.	Yds.	Avg.	Longest	TDs
Odom	15	327	21.8	75	0
Hammond	11	230	20.9	39	0
Green	12	214	17.8	24	0

CHICAGO BEARS

Head Coach: Neill Armstrong

3rd Year   **Record:** 17–15

1979 RECORD (10-6) (capital letters indicate home games)		1980 SCHEDULE (capital letters indicate home games)	
6	GREEN BAY	3	Green Bay	Sept. 7
26	MINNESOTA	7	NEW ORLEANS	Sept. 14
20	Dallas	24	MINNESOTA	Sept. 21
16	Miami	31	Pittsburgh	Sept. 28
13	TAMPA BAY	17	TAMPA BAY (night, TV)	Oct. 6
7	Buffalo	0	Minnesota	Oct. 12
7	NEW ENGLAND	27	DETROIT	Oct. 19
27	Minnesota	30	Philadelphia	Oct. 26
28	San Francisco	27	Cleveland (night, TV)	Nov. 3
35	DETROIT	7	WASHINGTON	Nov. 9
27	LOS ANGELES	23	HOUSTON	Nov. 16
23	N.Y. JETS	13	Atlanta	Nov. 23
0	Detroit	20	Detroit (TV)	Nov. 27
14	Tampa Bay	0	GREEN BAY	Dec. 7
15	Green Bay	14	CINCINNATI	Dec. 14
42	ST. LOUIS	6	Tampa Bay (TV)	Dec. 20
306		249		
Playoffs				
17	Philadelphia	27		

In more ways than one, the story of Chicago's dramatic turnaround in the NFC Central is the story of Mike Phipps, the eleven-year pro quarterback whose career has experienced more highs and lows than the elevator at 55 East Jackson Boulevard where the Bears maintain their administrative offices. The 33-year-old quarterback who, during his college playing days at Purdue, had the distinction of directing the Boilermakers to three successive victories over arch-rival Notre Dame may finally have found himself in the NFL, and that's no mean trick in itself. Many players, talented and otherwise, somehow never do.

Phipps's almost sudden ability to take command of

the Bears and move them was noted in midseason after they had lost five of their first eight games in the '79 schedule. With Phipps rallying the club, three successive victories were posted over the 49ers, Lions and Rams, placing the Bears squarely in the middle of the playoff picture (where the camera eventually caught them losing to Philadelphia). Head Coach Neill Armstrong was outspoken with his appraisal of Phipps's performance:

"Mike is doing an excellent job," he said. "Although under a lot of pressure, he still comes up with big plays . . . that's something we have going for us."

And by season's end, Armstrong's appraisal carried even more praise, conclusive evidence that the Bears have settled upon Phipps as starting quarterback as they head into 1980. "He's the guy who took us to the playoffs," explained Armstrong, "and he has to be the quarterback. Even if he's 33, the more he plays the better he'll get. I think he's throwing better than he did at Cleveland" (the club that drafted him No. 1 back in 1970). If Armstrong's decision to designate Phipps as the first-line quarterback needs any support, the record provides it. In the past two years, Phipps's regular season record as a starter is 12-2 (9-1 in '79, 3-1 in '78).

With the quarterback situation settled, for now at least, and a good passing game assured with speedy wide receivers like Brian Baschnagel, James Scott and Rickey Watts on hand to catch Phipps's passes, the Payton-powered running game should be an even greater threat to opposing defenses. With his 1,610 yards in '79, Payton moved into eighth place on the all-time NFL rushing list ahead of John Henry Johnson. The Chicago running back now has career totals of 6,926 yards on 1,884 attempts. While the Chicago passing game was floundering, as it did two seasons ago, Walter Payton was called upon to literally and physically "carry the ball" for the entire offensive attack. Opposing defenses knew exactly what to look for when Chicago had the ball—a ground attempt by either Payton or his running-mate, Roland Harper. Now the rejuvenated aerial game has changed all that, and the Bears have more to offer than merely an overland offensive. This point hasn't evaded Armstrong's thinking either, as he makes clear:

"We became more diversified on offense in 1979's last half, not only in run-pass ratio but also in application. It made us more effective. The trend around the NFL is toward increased scoring, and one of our goals this year is to give our big play people a chance to make those big plays . . . they're Payton, Watts, Scott, Williams, to name just a few. We must provide a diversified offense in which they'll get those chances."

Hardly overlooked in this planning for a more aggressive offense was the first-rate performance of the Chicago defensive unit last season—and the crew returns to action intact. The record speaks for itself. The Bears ranked second in the National Conference in defense against both ground and air attacks (Tampa Bay was first, not only in the NFC but in the NFL as well). They led the NFC in pass interceptions with 29, a total good enough for second place in the entire league. In the matter of opposition scoring, only Tampa Bay and San Diego gave up fewer points than Chicago's 249. All this adds up to one salient fact—the 1980 Bears are marching instead of lumbering, as Bears are wont to do.

Another question is: Will the Bears join the trend to indoor football? Just recently, Chicago Park District President Patrick O'Malley suggested construction of a 14-million-dollar dome over Soldier Field where the Bears play their home games. It was, however, only a suggestion that may, or may not, emerge as a reality. The fact remains, though, that more and more NFL clubs are turning to domed stadiums as the housing arrangement of the future. This raises still another possibility—will the Super Bowl eventually be called the Super Dome?

OFFENSE

Quarterbacks	Ht.	Wt.	Age	Exp.	College
Avellini, Bob	6-2	210	27	6	Maryland
Evans, Vince	6-2	212	25	4	Southern Cal
Phipps, Mike	6-3	209	33	11	Purdue

Phipps apparently is coming into his own as a top NFL quarterback, or at least the Bears think so. Admittedly, he has gained poise in recent seasons and has been through the rough, both in Chicago and in Cleveland where his pro career started. Avellini is still a good man to have around and does have very good days. Evans was hospitalized with a staph infection last season, but is working out with a comeback in mind.

Running Backs	Ht.	Wt.	Age	Exp.	College
Earl, Robin	6-5	240	25	4	Washington
Harper, Roland	5-11	210	27	5	Louisiana Tech
McClendon, Willie	6-1	205	23	2	Georgia
Payton, Walter	5-10	202	26	6	Jackson State
Perrin, Lonnie	6-1	225	29	5	Illinois
Skibinski, John	6-0	222	25	2	Purdue
Williams, Dave	6-2	217	26	4	Colorado
Suhey, Matt	5-11	214	22	R	Penn State

Payton won his fourth consecutive NFC rushing title with 1,610 yards on 369 carries. He has now achieved 20 club records during his five seasons with Chicago. The rest of the Chicago running attack is a supporting cast for Payton, but Williams gets more calls than the others when the top man needs time to catch his breath. Second-round draft choice Matt Suhey will be a good insurance against the possibility that Harper's knee won't be ready after surgery. Earl will be tried at tight end this season, and he says if it doesn't work, "I'll have to change clubs, or professions."

Receivers	Ht.	Wt.	Age	Exp.	College
Baschnagel, Brian (W)	6-0	184	26	5	Ohio State
Cobb, Mike (T)	6-5	243	25	4	Michigan State
Haines, Kris (W)	5-11	180	23	2	Notre Dame
Latta, Greg (T)	6-3	225	28	6	Morgan State
Schubert, Steve (W)	5-10	184	29	7	Massachusetts

	Ht.	Wt.	Age	Exp.	College
Scott, James (W)	6-1	190	28	5	Henderson J.C.
Washington, Harry (W)	6-0	185	24	3	Colorado State
Watts, Rickey	6-1	203	23	2	Tulsa
DeFrance, Chris (W)	6-1	205	23	1	Arizona State

W=wide receiver   T=tight end

Scott's career figures are now 139 receptions with an average of 17.7 yards per catch. Baschnagel's 30 catches led club in '79. Watts replaced Scott in starting lineup and did just fine, averaging 17.5 on 24 receptions, all this action coming in the season's final six weeks. This unit has depth, much to Armstrong's satisfaction.

Interior Linemen	Ht.	Wt.	Age	Exp.	College
Albrecht, Ted (G-T)	6-4	250	26	4	California
Ardizzone, Tony (C)	6-3	240	24	2	Northwestern
Boden, Lynn (G)	6-5	263	27	6	South Dakota State
Jackson, Noah (G)	6-2	265	29	6	Tampa
Jiggetts, Dan (T)	6-4	270	26	5	Harvard
Lick, Dennis (T)	6-3	265	26	5	Wisconsin
Neal, Dan (C)	6-4	255	31	8	Kentucky
Sorey, Revie (G)	6-2	260	27	6	Illinois
Calhoun, Mike (T)	6-4	260	23	1	Notre Dame
Hansen, Rollie (G)	6-3	260	23	1	Eastern Michigan
Moore, Rocco (G)	6-6	276	25	1	Western Michigan
Thompson, Arland (G)	6-3	255	22	R	Baylor
Tabor, Paul (C)	6-4	252	22	R	Oklahoma

T=tackle   G=guard   C=center

This line provided Payton & Co. with good interference since the Chicago rushing offense ranked second in the NFC last season with an average of 155.4 yards per game (even though that was not quite as good as St. Louis's average of 161.4). Albrecht and Lick are powerhouses at the tackles. Neal has started two years at center and hasn't had a single penalty called against him. Jackson and Sorey can lay claim to be among the biggest guards in the business. Top draftees Thompson and Tabor should provide added depth to a crew that's good already.

Kickers	Ht.	Wt.	Age	Exp.	College
Parsons, Bob (P)	6-5	225	30	9	Penn State
Thomas, Bob (Pk)	5-10	175	28	6	Notre Dame
Unruh, Bob (P-Pk)	6-1	190	23	1	Wheaton

Pk=placekicker   P=punter

Parsons' punts didn't travel very far last season, averaging 37.9 per boot, but he did lead the league in punts inside-the-20 with 26. That makes him one of the best at placing the ball where he wants to place it. Thomas has accuracy at placekicking, and is now the seventh leading scorer in Bears' history with 348 points. Thomas has made good 58.1% of his field goals, and that spells out to 72 of 124. Armstrong has few complaints here.

DEFENSE

Front Linemen	Ht.	Wt.	Age	Exp.	College
Hampton, Dan (T-E)	6-5	255	23	2	Arkansas
Harris, Al (E)	6-5	240	24	2	Arizona State
Hartenstine, Mike (E)	6-3	243	27	6	Penn State
Meyers, Jerry (E-T)	6-4	253	26	5	Northern Illinois
Osborne, Jim (T)	6-3	245	31	9	Southern U.
Page, Alan (T)	6-4	225	35	14	Notre Dame
Rydalch, Ron (T)	6-4	260	28	6	Utah
Shearer, Brad (T)	6-3	247	25	2	Texas

E=end   T=tackle

Hampton, Osborne, Page (entering his 14th NFL year) and Hartenstine were the starters at season's end. The defense ranked high among its NFC counterparts in '79, second only to Tampa Bay in total defense in allowing just 281.6 yards per game running and passing. The Bears were equally strong against both ground and air attacks. Moreover, 47 quarterback sacks ranked among the highest totals in the league, strong evidence that the Chicago pass rush is more than merely good.

Linebackers	Ht.	Wt.	Age	Exp.	College
Campbell, Gary (O)	6-1	220	28	4	Colorado
Herron, Bruce (O)	6-2	220	26	3	New Mexico
Hicks, Tom (M)	6-4	235	28	5	Illinois
Kunz, Lee (O)	6-2	225	23	2	Nebraska
Merrill, Mark (M)	6-4	240	25	3	Minnesota
Muckensturm, Jerry (O)	6-4	220	27	5	Arkansas State
Fitzpatrick, Greg (M)	6-2	227	23	1	Youngstown State
Wilson, Otis (O)	6-2	226	22	R	Louisville

O=outside   M=middle

Muckensturm started at left lineback as the season opened ('79) and then proceeded to lead the Bears in tackles with 111. Hicks and Campbell will be starters for the third year when the '80 schedule opens. Add to this already depth-strong group the first-round draft choice who also happens to be a linebacker from Louisville. Otis Wilson, who played at both Syracuse and Louisville, built reputation as a highly aggressive player who always "seems to make things happen." That's recommendation enough for an NFL job.

Defensive Backs	Ht.	Wt.	Age	Exp.	College
Ellis, Allan (CB)	5-10	177	29	7	UCLA
Fencik, Gary (S)	6-1	192	26	5	Yale
Gaines, Wentford (CB)	6-0	185	27	3	Cincinnati
Livers, Virgil (CB)	5-8	183	28	6	Western Kentucky
Plank, Doug (S)	5-11	202	27	6	Ohio State
Schmidt, Terry (CB)	6-0	177	28	7	Ball State
Spivey, Mike (CB)	6-0	198	26	4	Colorado
Walterscheid, Lenny (S)	5-11	190	26	4	Southern Utah
Ulmer, Mike (S)	6-0	194	26	1	Doane

CB=cornerback   S=safety

Chicago pilfered 22 passes in the last eight games of 1979—and had a total of 29 for the season, good enough to lead the NFC in interceptions. Schmidt and Fencik led this larceny parade with six interceptions each while several other Bears had as many as three apiece. These defensive backs are also versatile, in that several of them can play corner or safety if called on. Fencik is coming off surgery on his left knee.

Note: A complete listing of Chicago's 1980 college draft selections can be found on page 268.

DEFENSIVE UNIT

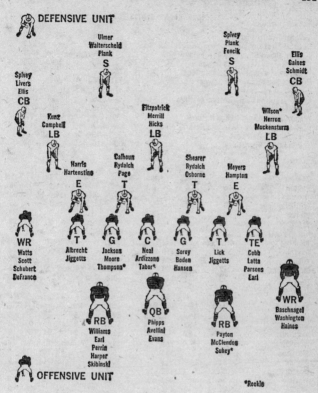

Ulmer
Walterscheid
Plank
S

Spivey
Plank
Fencik
S

Ellis
Gaines
Schmidt
CB

Spivey
Livers
Ellis
CB

Kunz
Campbell
LB

Fitzpatrick
Merrill
Hicks
LB

Wilson*
Herron
Muckensturm
LB

Harris
Hartenstine
E

Calhoun
Rydalch
Page
T

Shearer
Rydalch
Osborne
T

Meyers
Hampton
E

WR
Watts
Scott
Schubert
DeFrance

T
Albrecht
Jiggetts

G
Jackson
Moore
Thompson*

C
Neal
Ardizzone
Tabor*

G
Soray
Boden
Hansen

T
Lick
Jiggetts

TE
Cobb
Latta
Parsons
Earl

RB
Williams
Earl
Perrin
Harper
Skibinski

QB
Phipps
Avellini
Evans

RB
Payton
McClendon
Suhey*

WR
Baschnagel
Washington
Haines

OFFENSIVE UNIT

*Rookie

1979 BEARS STATISTICS

	Bears	Opps.
Total Points Scored	306	249
Total First Downs	262	272
Third Down Efficiency Percentage	36.8	36.0
Yards Rushing—First Downs	2486—140	1978—100
Passes Attempted—Completions	373—195	458—222
Yards Passing—First Downs	2151—98	2528—148
QB Sacked—Yards Lost	31—278	47—380
Interceptions By—Return Average	29—13.9	16—15.0
Punts—Average Yards	93—37.5	90—37.8
Punt Returns—Average Return	39—8.4	54—7.5
Kickoff Returns—Average Return	51—20.7	59—21.2
Fumbles—Ball Lost	21—13	25—14
Penalties—Yards	100—816	103—859

STATISTICAL LEADERS

Scoring	TDs	Rush.	Pass.	Ret.	PATs	FGs	Total
Payton	16	14	2	0	0	0	96
Thomas	0	0	0	0	34—37	16—27	82
Williams	6	1	5	0	0	0	36
Watts	4	0	3	1	0	0	24
Scott	3	0	3	0	0	0	18
Baschnagel	2	0	2	0	0	0	12

Rushing	Atts.	Yds.	Avg.	Longest	TDs
Payton	369	1610	4.4	43 (TD)	14
Williams	127	401	3.2	16	1
McClendon	37	160	4.3	33	1
Earl	35	132	3.8	12	0
Evans	12	72	6.0	17	1
Phipps	27	51	1.9	12	0

Passing	Atts.	Com.	Yds.	Pct.	Int.	Longest	TDs
Phipps	255	134	1535	52.5	8	68 (TD)	9
Evans	63	32	508	50.8	5	65 (TD)	4
Avellini	51	27	310	52.9	3	54 (TD)	2

Receiving	No.	Yds.	Avg.	Longest	TDs
Williams	42	354	8.4	54 (TD)	5
Payton	31	313	10.1	65 (TD)	2
Baschnagel	30	452	15.1	54 (TD)	2
Watts	24	421	17.5	68 (TD)	3
Scott	21	382	18.2	64	3
Latta	15	131	8.7	25	0
Earl	8	56	7.0	19	0

Interceptions	No.	Yds.	Avg.	Longest	TDs
Schmidt	6	44	7.3	20 (TD)	1
Fencik	6	31	5.2	17	0
Hicks	3	85	28.3	66 (TD)	1
Ellis	3	67	22.3	22	0
Plank	3	33	11.0	22	0
Livers	2	41	20.5	30	0
Buffone	2	11	5.5	11	0

Punting	No.	Yds.	Avg.	Longest	Inside 20	Blocked
Parsons	92	3486	37.9	54	26	1

Punt Returns	No.	FCs	Yds.	Avg.	Longest	TDs
Schubert	25	10	238	9.5	77 (TD)	1
Walterscheid	14	5	88	6.3	14	0

Kickoff Returns	No.	Yds.	Avg.	Longest	TDs
Walterscheid	19	427	22.5	44	0
Baschnagel	12	260	21.7	32	0
Watts	14	289	20.6	83 (TD)	1

TAMPA BAY BUCCANEERS

Head Coach: John McKay

5th Year   **Record:** 17–43

1979 RECORD (10-6) (capital letters indicate home games)		
31	DETROIT	16
29	Baltimore	26
21	Green Bay	10
21	LOS ANGELES	6
17	Chicago	13
14	N.Y. Giants	17
14	NEW ORLEANS	42
21	GREEN BAY	3
12	Minnesota	10
14	Atlanta	17
16	Detroit	14
31	N.Y. GIANTS	3
22	MINNESOTA	23
0	CHICAGO	14
7	San Francisco	23
3	KANSAS CITY	0
273		237
	Playoffs	
24	PHILADELPHIA	17
0	LOS ANGELES	9

1980 SCHEDULE (capital letters indicate home games)	
Cincinnati	Sept. 7
LOS ANGELES (night, TV)	Sept. 11
Dallas	Sept. 21
CLEVELAND	Sept. 28
Chicago (night, TV)	Oct. 6
GREEN BAY	Oct. 12
Houston	Oct. 19
San Francisco	Oct. 26
N.Y. GIANTS	Nov. 2
PITTSBURGH	Nov. 9
Minnesota	Nov. 16
DETROIT	Nov. 23
Green Bay at Milwaukee	Nov. 30
MINNESOTA	Dec. 7
Detroit	Dec. 14
CHICAGO (TV)	Dec. 20

As every NFL fan knows, there was a time when the
Tampa Bay Buccaneers were, to be charitable about it,
laughable. It got around that whenever Johnny Carson
ran out of something to talk about on his Tonight Show,
he would use a one-liner about the Buccaneers and
usually get a barrage of guffaws from an appreciative
audience in response. That was during those two agoniz-
ing seasons which found John McKay's newly founded
franchise struggling through a 26-game losing streak
which came to a merciful end in New Orleans on December 11, 1977, when the Bucs swept the Saints off

the Superdome carpet, 33-14. All the joking stopped, too.

Even so, the Buccaneers have continued to play football with a style of their own and, wondrously, that very special style landed them in the 1979 Super Bowl playoffs where they almost won the National Conference championship (losing it to Los Angeles by a narrow 9-0 score). Tampa Bay, thus, has become only the second expansion team to qualify for the playoffs in one of their first four seasons, the Cincinnati Bengals having accomplished the same thing in their third season of 1970.

John McKay was understandably happy over developments, considering what he had been through. "I've never been happier for a group of players," said the former head coach of Southern Cal's national championship teams. "Especially guys like Lee Roy Selmon (DE) and Richard Wood (LB) who have been in Tampa from the beginning, and who had to suffer through it all. As the years go by, they'll look back on what they helped to accomplish and feel proud."

Others on the team can feel proud too, without waiting for the years to go by. Running back Ricky Bell, for instance, was the first player chosen in the 1977 NFL college draft as an All-America from Southern Cal. For two seasons he failed to provide the Bucs with the ball-carrying expertise expected of him, although it wasn't necessarily his fault. His supporting cast, to be sure, was suspect.

Then came 1979 and the Tampa Bay offensive explosion, if it can be called that, with Bell leading the way. He ran for a personal high and club record 1,263 yards behind a Tampa Bay offensive line that also came to life after two years of lethargy. Bell scored nine times to lead the club in TDs, and while the Bucs were rolling up a grand total of 273 points, the defensive unit was piling up a stack of credits of its own. By season's end, the Tampa Bay defense was No. 1 in the NFL, and those 237 points represented the lowest opposition total in the league. Almost suddenly, McKay had achieved that ever elusive offensive-defensive balance for his team, even though he now reluctantly admits, "we can't sneak up on anybody any more."

It has been said that man's best friend is his dog. Still, a good case can be made for terming man's best friend his sense of humor. There's little doubt that John McKay's sense of humor has stood by him valiantly through his days of trial. Now that the front office has renewed his contract for five more years, he can even look back with amusement upon those days when the good citizens of Tampa were crying, "Throw McKay in the Bay." And now that the Buccaneers are winners, and prime-time winners at that with three national TV appearances scheduled for this fall, McKay doesn't have to throw out his famous one-line quips as defense mechanisms. There were moments when he was downright philosophical about the NFL and his coaching situation, such as:

● I promise to have a better team this year, or get myself a new owner.

● I talk rapidly but some people don't listen fast.

● Everybody is unhappy at times, even my wife . . . only she doesn't get interviewed about it.

● I get all my plays from a magazine called *Scholastic Coach,* but the plays don't work unless your offensive line can block people.

● Defensive end Lee Roy Selmon is modest and would get more notoriety if he talked more . . . maybe he should carry a flag and wave it whenever he makes a good play.

● A genius in the NFL is a guy who won last week.

Those observations notwithstanding, if the Buccaneers again come within one game of playing in the Super Bowl, perhaps McKay will have to redefine his concept of an NFL genius, all joking aside.

OFFENSE

Quarterbacks	Ht.	Wt.	Age	Exp.	College
Fusina, Chuck	6-1	195	23	2	Penn State
Rae, Mike	6-0	195	29	5	Southern Cal
Williams, Doug	6-4	215	25	3	Grambling

The statistics on Williams are confusing if not downright contradictory. He completed only 41.8% of his passes last season (166 for 387 throws) but some of those aerials traveled far because his total yardage was 2,448 plus 18 TDs. In fact, his 14.7 yards gained per completion was best in the NFC. Rae played some, enough to throw 36 times for a 47.2% completion book, and was intercepted only once. Williams dropped his football in the wrong hands 18 times. Fusina, the former Penn State All-America, just sits and watches. McKay must be satisfied because the Buccaneers tapped not one quarterback in the '80 college draft.

Running Backs	Ht.	Wt.	Age	Exp.	College
Bell, Ricky	6-2	215	25	4	Southern Cal
Berns, Rick	6-2	205	24	2	Nebraska
Davis, Johnny	6-1	235	24	3	Alabama
Davis, Tony	5-11	210	27	5	Nebraska
DuBose, Jimmy	6-0	220	26	4	Florida
Eckwood, Jerry	6-0	200	26	2	Arkansas
Ragsdale, George	5-11	190	27	4	North Carolina A&T

Bell rushed for 1,263 yards, which made him the sixth best ground gaining ball-carrier in the league last season. Like the Buccaneers themselves, he proved to himself he could do it. Not only that, Bell blossomed out into an excellent blocker and a better-than-average pass catcher with his 25 receptions. Eckwood started out like he was going places. The Arkansas rookie reeled off 528 yards in the first eight games, then managed only 162 in the last eight. Wot happened? Berns was impressive in brief action. DuBose had to nurse a knee injury, but hopes to head back this season. The only running back McKay chose in the recent draft was 10th rounder Brett Davis of Nevada-Las Vegas.

Receivers	Ht.	Wt.	Age	Exp.	College
Foster, Eddie (W)	5-10	185	26	2	Houston
Giles, Jimmie (T)	6-3	245	26	4	Alcorn State

Hagins, Isaac (W)	5-9	180	26	4	Southern U.
Jones, Gordon (W)	6-0	190	23	2	Pittsburgh
Mucker, Larry (W)	5-11	190	26	4	Arizona State
Obradovich, Jim (T)	6-2	230	27	6	Southern Cal
Buggs, Danny (W)	6-2	185	27	6	West Virginia
Seal, Paul (T)	6-4	227	28	7	Michigan
Law, Dennis (W)	6-1	182	25	3	East Tennessee State
Simmrin, Randy (W)	6-1	165	24	1	Southern Cal
House, Kevin (W)	6-0	167	22	R	Southern Illinois

W=wide receiver   T=tight end

Said McKay: "We still don't have a wide receiver who plays like an All-Pro." At any rate, the resulting wide-receiver roster, seen above, resembles the Tampa telephone directory. McKay may have a point for it was a tight end who caught the most passes for the club last season. Giles pulled in 40 while Hagins (who is a wide receiver) was right behind with 39. Beyond those two, running backs Bell and Eckwood were the chief receptionists. Buggs (or "Lightnin' Buggs," as he was known at West Virginia) comes to Tampa in a trade with Washington for cornerback Jeris White.

Interior Linemen	Ht.	Wt.	Age	Exp.	College
Austin, Darrell (G-T-C)	6-4	255	29	6	South Carolina
Hannah, Charley (T)	6-6	260	25	4	Alabama
Horton, Greg (G)	6-4	245	29	5	Colorado
Reavis, Dave (T)	6-5	260	30	6	Arkansas
Roberts, Greg (G)	6-3	260	24	2	Oklahoma
Wilson, Steve (C)	6-3	265	26	5	Georgia
Yarno, George (G)	6-2	255	23	2	Washington State
Snell, Roy (G)	6-3	252	22	R	Wisconsin

T=tackle   G=guard   C=center

The offensive line was the biggest news in Tampa last season. A crew which, in 1978, allowed opposing pass rushers to upend the Buccaneer quarterback 52 times for a league high (or low) turned right around in '79 and permitted the dastardly deed just 12 times, also for a league high (or low). The line also did its job for the running backs and the Tampa passing attack, ranking high among the NFC's final rankings. When the season closed with a 3-0 win over Kansas City, this distinguished front line unit consisted of Reavis and Hannah at tackles, Horton and Roberts at guards (Roberts a rookie who made it big) and Wilson at center. Hannah switched to offense after two seasons at defense and found a happy home. Snell was Tampa Bay's lone first-round draft choice who played tackle in college, but fits best with the pros at guard.

Kickers	Ht.	Wt.	Age	Exp.	College
Blanchard, Tom (P)	6-0	185	31	10	Oregon
Green, Dave (P)	6-0	210	31	7	Ohio
O'Donoghue, Neil (Pk)	6-6	210	27	4	Auburn

Pk=placekicker   P=punter

O'Donoghue kicked well enough to lead the club in scoring with 63 points on 11-of-19 FGs and 30-35 PATs. But McKay wasn't entirely satisfied with the protection the placekicker was given. "We had some problems and had too many kicks blocked," he ventured, "but I don't think the problem was with Neil's kicking. He gets the ball away well." Blanchard, now entering his 10th NFL year, handled the punting after Dave Green was injured. But Blanchard's average fell below 40 yards per punt (39.6) for only the second time in his career. Still, four-tenths of a yard isn't much to quibble about.

DEFENSE

Front Linemen	Ht.	Wt.	Age	Exp.	College
Chambers, Wally (E)	6-6	250	29	7	Eastern Kentucky
Crowder, Randy (T)	6-3	250	28	6	Penn State
Kollar, Bill (E-T)	6-4	250	28	7	Montana State
Lewis, Reggie (E)	6-3	255	24	2	North Texas State
Logan, David (T-E)	6-2	250	24	2	Pittsburgh
Sanders, Gene (E-T)	6-3	260	24	2	Texas A&M
Selmon, Lee Roy (E)	6-3	260	26	5	Oklahoma

E=end   T=tackle

The Buccaneer defense was the absolute best in the NFL last season, topping even that of Pittsburgh, the Super Bowl champion. In every category, the Tampa Bay defenders led the league. They allowed an average total of 246.8 yards per game, rushing and passing. (Pittsburgh yielded 266.9 yards per game.) The Bucs were stingy on the ground, permitting 117.1 yards PG rushing, and were just as unyielding through the air, allowing opposing passers a mere 129.8 yards per contest. It was next to impossible to score a TD passing against Tampa Bay. Only 14 were permitted, an NFL low (with Minnesota's similar 14). It was a three-man defensive front with Lee Roy Selmon at right end (11 sacks and 117 tackles), while Chambers, Crowder and Kollar split the time at nose guard and left end. Nothing to complain about here.

Linebackers	Ht.	Wt.	Age	Exp.	College
Bonness, Rik (M)	6-3	220	26	5	Nebraska
Brown, Aaron (M)	6-2	235	24	3	Ohio State
Johnson, Cecil (O)	6-2	230	25	4	Pittsburgh
Lewis, David (O)	6-4	245	26	4	Southern Cal

Nafziger, Dana (O)	6-1	220	27	4	Cal Poly SLO
Selmon, Dewey (M)	6-1	240	27	5	Oklahoma
Wood, Richard (M)	6-2	230	27	6	Southern Cal
Brantley, Scot (O)	6-0	167	22	R	Florida

O=outside   M=middle

The starting linebacking corps of Wood, Dewey Selmon, Lewis and Johnson enters its fourth year as a unit. Lewis, at 6-4 245, is probably the
biggest outside linebacker in the league. Wood led the club in tackles
for the third time in four years. Selmon is the defensive signal-caller,
and plays with intensity. Johnson gives everybody a hand in the thick
of battle. Nafziger, Aaron Brown and Bonness are backups with a pur-
pose. Brantley, chosen in third round, has been called "a strong and
extremely explosive hitter."

Defensive Backs	Ht.	Wt.	Age	Exp.	College
Brown, Cedric (S)	6-3	205	26	4	Kent State
Cotney, Mark (S)	6-0	205	28	6	Cameron State
Jordan, Curtis (S-CB)	6-2	205	26	5	Texas Tech
Reece, Danny (CB-S)	5-11	195	25	5	Southern Cal
Washington, Mike (CB)	6-3	200	27	5	Alabama
Flowers, Larry (S)	6-1	184	22	R	Texas Tech

CB=cornerback   S=safety

Brown and Washington led the pass interception efforts with three
each, but it was a lackluster achievement. The Buccaneers stole only
14 enemy passes all season long, and tied with Detroit for the league's
most unimpressive showing in this department. Still, Tampa Bay's
pass defense was No. 1 in the NFL, proving that there are more ways
than one to stop the opposition's passing game. With starter Jeris
White and Billy Cesare no longer with the club, some shakeups are
possible here. Flowers was a fourth-round choice.

Note: A complete listing of Tampa Bay's 1980 college draft selections
can be found on page 278.

DEFENSIVE UNIT 3-4 DEFENSE

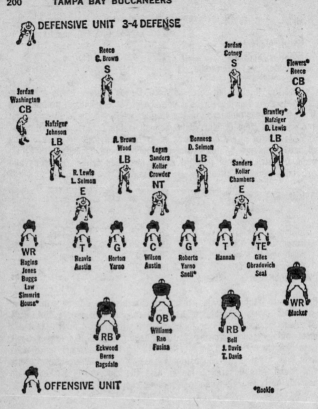

Reece
C. Brown
S

Jordan
Cotney
S

Flowers*
Reece
CB

Jordan
Washington
CB

Nafziger
Johnson
LB

A. Brown
Wood
LB

Logan
Sanders
Kollar
Crowder
NT

Bonness
D. Selmon
LB

Brantley*
Nafziger
D. Lewis
LB

R. Lewis
L. Selmon
E

Sanders
Kollar
Chambers
E

WR
Hagins
Jones
Buggs
Law
Simmrin
House*

Reavis
Austin
T

Horton
Yarno
G

Wilson
Austin
C

Roberts
Yarno
Snell*
G

Hannah
T

Giles
Obradovich
Seal
TE

WR
Mucker

QB
Williams
Rae
Fusina

RB
Eckwood
Berns
Ragsdale

RB
Bell
J. Davis
T. Davis

OFFENSIVE UNIT

*Rookie

1979 BUCCANEERS STATISTICS

	Buccaneers	Opps.
Total Points Scored	273	237
Total First Downs	267	247
Third Down Efficiency Percentage	34.8	32.0
Yards Rushing—First Downs	2437—107	1873—116
Passes Attempted—Completions	434—183	436—250
Yards Passing—First Downs	2612—137	2076—111
QB Sacked—Yards Lost	12—88	40—329
Interceptions By—Return Average	14—17.0	26—12.5
Punts—Average Yards	95—38.7	104—41.1
Punt Returns—Average Return	71—6.2	47—5.7
Kickoff Returns—Average Return	51—18.8	55—22.9
Fumbles—Ball Lost	25—15	44—24
Penalties—Yards	102—905	100—870

STATISTICAL LEADERS

Scoring	TDs	Rush.	Pass.	Ret.	PATs	FGs	Total
O'Donoghue	0	0	0	0	30—35	11—19	63
Bell	9	7	2	0	0	0	54
Giles	7	0	7	0	0	0	42
Mucker	5	0	5	0	0	0	30
Hagins	3	0	3	0	0	0	18
Eckwood	2	2	0	0	0	0	12
Williams	2	2	0	0	0	0	12
J. Davis	2	2	0	0	0	0	12

Rushing	Atts.	Yds.	Avg.	Longest	TDs
Bell	283	1263	4.5	49	7
Eckwood	194	690	3.6	61 (TD)	2
J. Davis	59	221	3.7	16 (TD)	2
Williams	35	119	3.4	16	2
Berns	23	102	4.4	16	0

Passing	Atts.	Com.	Yds.	Pct.	Int.	Longest	TDs
Williams	387	166	2448	41.8	24	66 (TD)	18
Rae	36	17	252	47.2	2	29	1

Receiving	No.	Yds.	Avg.	Longest	TDs
Giles	40	579	14.5	66 (TD)	7
Hagins	39	692	17.7	57	3
Bell	25	248	9.9	26	2
Eckwood	22	268	12.2	31	0
Owens	20	377	18.9	64	0
Mucker	14	268	19.1	42 (TD)	5

Interceptions	No.	Yds.	Avg.	Longest	TDs
C. Brown	3	79	26.3	72	0
Washington	3	64	21.3	49 (TD)	1
White	3	39	13.0	39	0
Wood	2	37	18.5	24	0
D. Lewis	2	19	9.5	11	0

Punting	No.	Yds.	Avg.	Longest	Inside 20	Blocked
Blanchard	93	3679	39.6	58	14	2

Punt Returns	No.	FCs	Yds.	Avg.	Longest	TDs
Reece	70	1	431	6.2	17	0

Kickoff Returns	No.	Yds.	Avg.	Longest	TDs
Ragsdale	34	675	19.9	30	0
Hagins	9	196	21.8	31	0
T. Davis	4	33	8.3	16	0

GREEN BAY PACKERS

Head Coach: Bart Starr

6th Year   Record: 26–47–1

1979 RECORD (5-11) (capital letters indicate home games)			1980 SCHEDULE (capital letters indicate home games)	
3	Chicago	6	CHICAGO	Sept. 7
28	NEW ORLEANS	19	DETROIT at Milwaukee	Sept. 14
10	TAMPA BAY	21	Los Angeles	Sept. 21
21	Minnesota	27	DALLAS at Milwaukee	Sept. 28
27	NEW ENGLAND	14	CINCINNATI	Oct. 5
7	Atlanta	25	Tampa Bay	Oct. 12
24	DETROIT	16	Cleveland	Oct. 19
3	Tampa Bay	21	MINNESOTA	Oct. 26
7	Miami	27	Pittsburgh	Nov. 2
22	N.Y. JETS	27	SAN FRANCISCO at Milwaukee	Nov. 9
19	MINNESOTA	7	N.Y. Giants	Nov. 16
12	Buffalo	19	Minnesota	Nov. 23
10	PHILADELPHIA	21	TAMPA BAY at Milwaukee	Nov. 30
21	Washington	38	Chicago	Dec. 7
14	CHICAGO	15	HOUSTON	Dec. 14
18	Detroit	13	Detroit	Dec. 21
246		316		

The most controversial team in the NFL today is the
Green Bay Packers, and most of the controversy swirls
around the head of Bart Starr who this season begins
his sixth year as head coach of the club he once quarter-
backed in the glory days of Vince Lombardi. Typical
of some comments inevitably engendered by Starr's
26-47-1 head coaching record is this letter received by
the *Football Digest:*

"Do you know who the worst team in football is? It's
the Green Bay Packers. It's not the players' fault, it's
the coaches. They insist on having the secondary play
six to seven yards off the receiver. All any team has
to do is throw 10-yard passes against the Packers on
every play and they'd march down the field each time

they had the ball. Bart Starr might be a nice guy, but he just doesn't know how to coach."

Starr, being one of pro football's most outspokenly honest coaches, admits he has been given plenty of opportunity to succeed with the Packers. He readily agrees that, without a doubt, no other coach except himself would have lasted this long in Green Bay, the club's four-year record being what it is. "I think our people have been very tolerant," says Starr, "and if someone else had that kind of record here, he probably wouldn't be coach."

He still has two years remaining on his current contract and, unless things change drastically, and very quickly, his status appears secure. Unlike other NFL clubs, the Packers are publicly owned by a non-profit corporation which was founded in 1922. There are 4,656½ shares of the club's non-profit stock owned by 1,728 shareholders, many of whom, of course, reside in Green Bay. The corporation is governed by a seven-man executive committee, selected from a 45-member board of directors.

A 1979 corporate statement shows that the Packers, despite their losing record of 5-11, made a net profit of $1,845,265 last year—up 21% over the previous season. TV revenues, of course, comprise a substantial part of this total. Because of their unusual corporate organization, the Packers do not pay dividends to the club's stockholders. All profits must go back into the company, which now has a total of more than $12 million in "retained earnings," drawing interest of about $1 million a year.

Day-to-day decisions are made by the club's general manager (who is also Bart Starr) and he is in total charge of football operations. The executive committee concerns itself mostly with budgetary and construction matters and one committee member, Dominic Olej-

niczak, has served as president of the club for 22 years.
Discussions of a possible replacement for Bart Starr
as head coach haven't reached executive committee
agendas, at least not yet. Olejniczak, however, is aware
of all the talk:

"I feel exactly like the coaches and fans do," he says.
"It was a disappointing season, but the injuries played
an important part and some of the games might easily
have been turned around had we been at full strength.
I think Bart has done everything expected of him in
connection with his contract. It's difficult to say everything is fine, just great. But we must be honest and put
ourselves in his position by understanding the obstacles
and injuries."

In Starr's defense, the 1979 injuries were devastating
to a club which, only the year before, had knocked at
the playoffs' door. The sideline list started early when
linebacker John Anderson broke his arm in training
camp. It was a bad omen. In the very first regular season game, Green Bay's No. 1 draft pick—running back
Eddie Lee Ivery—banged up his knee on his third
NFL carry and he was out for the season. That really
hurt, because in the preseason games Ivery had led the
club in both rushing and receiving.

The list kept growing, and the Green Bay fans (and
stockholders) kept moaning at the club's abysmal luck.
The offensive line lost its top man when tackle Mark
Koncar joined the hospital squad. Defensive end Ezra
Johnson sprained his ankle, badly enough to miss six
games, and another defensive end, Mike Butler,
sported a dislocated elbow that hampered his style on
the field. Running backs Barty Smith, Steve Atkins and
Terdell Middleton all had various injuries and ailments
that kept the offensive unit walking painfully instead of
running all season long. And Lynn Dickey, generally
regarded as the most qualified quarterback on the Green

Bay roster, was still bothered by a broken leg of two years' standing, and didn't play until the 1979 season was nearly over. Add to these two more injured defensive regulars in tackle Carl Barzilauskas and linebacker Mike Hunt, and it's easy to sympathize with Starr and his problems.

The question then remains—if the Packers come back completely healthy, will they be first-rate contenders for the NFC Central title? The answer to that will begin to unfold on Lambeau Field in Green Bay on September 7th when the Packers open their regular season with Chicago's Bears in a game scheduled to begin at high noon.

OFFENSE

Quarterbacks	Ht.	Wt.	Age	Exp.	College
Dickey, Lynn	6-4	220	30	10	Kansas State
Hedberg, Randy	6-3	200	25	2	Minot State
Whitehurst, David	6-2	204	24	4	Furman

Whitehurst continues as the regular starting quarterback and, though his completion percentage of 55.6 is passable (if that's the proper word), there's always something lacking in a quarterback on a losing team. Craig Morton, for instance, set the world on fire for Denver (winning club) but somehow couldn't do it for the New York Giants (who have joined Losers Anonymous). Dickey went into action and threw 119 times, completing half for a 50.4%—and he has again come off the surgical table, this time on his left leg. Now he wants to challenge Whitehurst for the job. In fact, the 1980 projected Green Bay depth chart already lists Dickey as starting quarterback. Hedberg was a spectator his rookie year.

Running Backs	Ht.	Wt.	Age	Exp.	College
Atkins, Steve	6-0	216	23	2	Maryland
Ivery, Eddie Lee	6-0½	210	22	2	Georgia Tech
Johnson, Sammy Lee	6-1	226	27	7	North Carolina
Landers, Walt	6-0	214	26	3	Clark
Middleton, Terdell	6-0	195	24	4	Memphis State
Patton, Ricky	5-11	189	25	3	Jackson State
Simpson, Nate	5-11	190	25	4	Tennessee State
Smith, Barty	6-4	240	27	7	Richmond
Torkelson, Eric	6-2	200	28	7	Connecticut

Four of these running backs are coming off knee surgery, and Starr must be confident of their availability. Not even one running back was among players chosen by Green Bay in the '80 college draft. The four include Ivery (a rookie for whom great things were predicted until his knee interfered), Atkins, Smith and first-string starter Middleton who averaged 3.8 yards on 131 carries last season. The Packer ground game ranked a lowly 11th in the NFC, so there's not much hope for improvement—unless everybody actually gets healthy, knees and all.

Receivers	Ht.	Wt.	Age	Exp.	College
Cassidy, Ron (W)	6-0	175	22	2	Utah State
Coffman, Paul (T)	6-3	218	23	3	Kansas State
Kimball, Bob (W)	6-1	190	23	2	Oklahoma
Lofton, James (W)	6-3	187	23	3	Stanford
Thompson, Audra (W)	6-0	186	27	4	East Texas State
Thompson, John (T)	6-3	228	23	2	Utah State
Tullis, Walter (W)	6-0	170	26	3	Delaware
Nixon, Fred (W)	5-11	194	22	R	Oklahoma

W=wide receiver   T=tight end

Lofton is the chief asset here, if he can get over his feuding with the Green Bay fans and head coach Starr. When he fumbled against the Jets and the fans boo-hoo-ed him, Lofton was anything but lofty in his reaction. Using the sign language, he let the fans know what he thought of them, as much as to say: "Taking this abuse is not part of my contract." Still, Lofton is the main man among Green Bay's receivers, averaging almost 18 yards a catch on 54 receptions last season. Audra Thompson may be slated for the other side to give Lofton a hand. He averaged 15.8 yards on 25 catches. And Coffman performed impressively in his third year, averaging 12.7 yards on 56 catches. Nixon comes up from Oklahoma as a fourth round draftee and may find work, but the company is fast. But there again, Nixon was a 9.6 sprinter in the 100-yards in high school . . . if time hasn't slowed him down.

Interior Linemen	Ht.	Wt.	Age	Exp.	College
Gofourth, Derrel (G)	6-3	260	24	4	Oklahoma State
Harris, Leotis (G)	6-1	267	24	3	Arkansas
Jackson, Mel (G)	6-1	267	25	6	Southern Cal
Koch, Greg (T)	6-4	265	24	4	Arkansas
Koncar, Mark (T)	6-5	268	26	5	Colorado
McCarren, Larry (C)	6-3	238	28	8	Illinois
Nuzum, Rick (C)	6-4	238	27	4	Kentucky
Stokes, Tim (T)	6-5	252	29	7	Oregon
Wellman, Mike (C)	6-3	253	23	2	Kansas
Young, Steve (T)	6-8	264	26	4	Colorado
Kitson, Syd (G)	6-5	253	22	R	Wake Forest

T=tackle   G=guard   C=center

Koncar, probably the team's best offensive lineman, hurt his ankle in preseason and never returned to form, missing several games and limping in and out when he did play. McCarren is a stalwart anchor at center, but he may need better assistance on both right and left if injuries continue to hamper the line. The projected 1980 Green Bay depth chart lists Koncar, Gofourth, McCarren, Harris and Koch as the starters. Young is huge at 6-8 264 and could at least plug some holes, even without moving. Kitson is a third round choice from Wake Forest who could figure in the 1980 offensive blueprint.

Kickers	Ht.	Wt.	Age	Exp.	College
Beverly, David (P)	6-2	180	29	7	Auburn
Birney, Tom (Pk)	6-4	220	23	2	Michigan
Engles, Ricky (P)	5-11	170	25	1	Tulsa
Marcol, Chester (Pk)	6-0	190	30	9	Hillsdale

Pk=placekicker   P=punter

Probably the biggest kicking roster in the NFL. Add to these none other than linebacker John Anderson who kicked one out of two PATs and one field goal in one try from the 30-40-yard range. Marcol missed six of his ten FG attempts, Birney made good seven of his nine kicks. Beverly did all the punting and did it well, averaging 40.4 and ranking fourth among NFC punters.

DEFENSE

Front Linemen	Ht.	Wt.	Age	Exp.	College
Barber, Robert (E)	6-3	240	28	5	Grambling
Barzilauskas, Carl (NT)	6-6	265	28	7	Indiana
Butler, Mike (E)	6-5	265	25	4	Kansas
Johnson, Charles (NT)	6-1	262	22	2	Maryland
Johnson, Ezra (E)	6-4	240	24	4	Morris Brown
Jones, Terry (NT)	6-2	259	23	3	Alabama
Lathrop, Kit (NT)	6-5	253	23	2	Arizona State
Merrill, Casey (E)	6-4	255	22	2	California-Davis

E=end   NT=nose tackle

The Packer defense wasn't exactly impregnable last season. It ranked 13th in NFC total defense, and dead last in the NFL in stopping the opposition's running attack, meaning it didn't stop very often. Opposing running backs gained a total of 2,885 yards against Green Bay, which averages out to 18.03 yards per game. Against the pass, the Packers were a little better but not much so. Still, injuries took their toll here too, with Ezra Johnson out for six weeks and Butler hampered with a dislocated elbow all season. Both, however, are due to start in the three-man line with third-year man Terry Jones in the nose tackle position.

Linebackers	Ht.	Wt.	Age	Exp.	College
Anderson, John (O)	6-3	221	24	3	Michigan
Douglass, Mike (O)	6-0	224	25	3	San Diego State
Gueno, Jim (O)	6-2	220	26	5	Tulane
Hunt, Mike (I)	6-2	240	23	3	Minnesota
McLaughlin, Joe (I)	6-1	235	22	2	Massachusetts
Rudzinski, Paul (I)	6-1	220	23	3	Michigan State
Simmons, Davie (O)	6-4	218	23	2	North Carolina
Weaver, Gary (I)	6-1	225	31	8	Fresno State
Williams, Jack (O)	6-4	225	23	2	Bowling Green
Wingo, Rich (I)	6-1	230	23	2	Alabama
Cumby, George (O)	6-0	214	22	R	Oklahoma

O=outside   I=Inside

As luck would have it, Anderson broke his arm for the second straight year and never really returned to the verve shown his rookie year. Douglass and Weaver didn't play as well as expected, as the dismal showing against the run would indicate. Rookie Rich Wingo made his presence known by setting a club record for unassisted (solo) tackles. Hunt was a starter two years ago, but knee surgery kept him sidelined most of '79. He'll be back.

Defensive Backs	Ht.	Wt.	Age	Exp.	College
Gray, Johnnie (S)	5-11	185	26	6	Fullerton State
Hood, Estus (CB)	5-11	180	24	3	Illinois State
Luke, Steve (S)	6-2	205	26	6	Ohio State
McCoy, Mike (CB)	5-11	183	26	5	Colorado
Sampson, Howard (S)	5-10	185	23	3	Arkansas
Thorson, Mark (S)	5-10	188	24	2	Ottawa (Kansas)
Turner, Wylie (CB)	5-10	182	22	2	Angelo State
Wagner, Steve (S)	6-2	208	25	4	Wisconsin
Lee, Mark (CB)	5-11	181	22	R	Washington

CB=cornerback   S=safety

Gray picked off five enemy aerials to lead the Packer interceptors. McCoy came up with three, as did linebacker Mike Douglass. Hood begins his second season as a starter after inheriting the job left open when Willie Buchanon was traded to the Chargers. Turner gained experience his rookie year and looms as a challenger to the regulars. Starr considers Gray and Luke the equal of any safety tandem in the league. Lee was chosen in the second round at the '80 draft and will get a good look.

Note: A complete listing of Green Bay's 1980 college draft selections can be found on page 270.

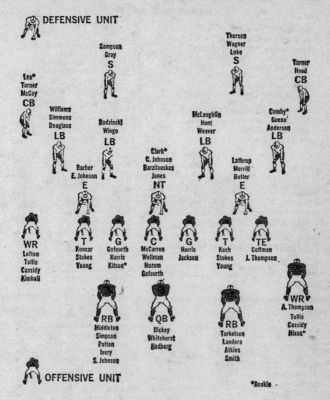

DEFENSIVE UNIT

Thorson
Wagner
Luke
S

Sampson
Gray
S

Turner
Hood
CB

Lee*
Turner
McCoy
CB

Williams
Simmons
Douglass
LB

Rudzinski
Wingo
LB

McLaughlin
Hunt
Weaver
LB

Cumby*
Gueno
Anderson
LB

Barber
E. Johnson
E

Clark*
C. Johnson
Barzilauskas
Jones
NT

Lathrop
Merrill
Butler
E

WR
Lofton
Tullis
Cassidy
Kimball

T
Koncar
Stokes
Young

G
Gofourth
Harris
Kitson*

C
McCarren
Wellman
Nuzum
Gofourth

G
Harris
Jackson

T
Koch
Stokes
Young

TE
Coffman
J. Thompson

WR
A. Thompson
Tullis
Cassidy
Nixon*

RB
Middleton
Simpson
Patton
Ivery
S. Johnson

QB
Dickey
Whitehurst
Hedberg

RB
Torkelson
Landers
Atkins
Smith

OFFENSIVE UNIT

*Rookie

1979 PACKERS STATISTICS

	Packers	Opps.
Total Points Scored	246	316
Total First Downs	279	327
Third Down Efficiency Percentage	39.2	44.0
Yards Rushing—First Downs	1861—121	2882—162
Passes Attempted—Completions	444—240	440—249
Yards Passing—First Downs	2681—133	2762—146
QB Sacked—Yards Lost	47—376	35—279
Interceptions By—Return Average	18—13.5	22—11.2
Punts—Average Yards	69—40.4	64—39.5
Punt Returns—Average Return	28—5.0	43—7.1
Kickoff Returns—Average Return	61—21.2	50—20.0
Fumbles—Ball Lost	34—22	30—14
Penalties—Yards	93—681	106—884

STATISTICAL LEADERS

Scoring	TDs	Rush.	Pass.	Ret.	PATs	FGs	Total
Birney	0	0	0	0	7—10	7—9	28
Marcol	0	0	0	0	16—18	4—10	28
Smith	4	3	1	0	0	0	24
Whitehurst	4	4	0	0	0	0	24
Lofton	4	0	4	0	0	0	24
A. Thompson	4	0	3	1	0	0	24
Coffman	4	0	4	0	0	0	24
Middleton	3	2	1	0	0	0	18

Rushing	Atts.	Yds.	Avg.	Longest	TDs
Middleton	131	495	3.8	28	2
Torkelson	98	401	4.1	15	3
Atkins	42	239	5.7	60	1
Simpson	66	235	3.6	22	1
Smith	57	201	3.5	23	3
Patton	37	134	3.6	14	0
Whitehurst	18	73	4.1	17	4
Landers	17	41	2.4	14	0

Passing	Atts.	Com.	Yds.	Pct.	Int.	Longest	TDs
Whitehurst	322	179	2247	55.6	18	78 (TD)	10

Receiving	No.	Yds.	Avg.	Longest	TDs
Coffman	56	711	12.7	78 (TD)	4
Lofton	54	968	17.9	52	4
A. Thompson	25	395	15.8	50	3
Smith	19	135	8.2	22	1
Torkelson	19	128	6.8	14	0
Middleton	18	155	8.6	29	1
Simpson	11	46	4.2	10	0
Atkins	10	89	8.9	19	0
Tullis	10	173	17.3	52 (TD)	1

Interceptions	No.	Yds.	Avg.	Longest	TDs
Gray	5	66	13.2	35	0
Douglass	3	73	24.3	46	0
McCoy	3	60	20.0	38	0
Hood	2	8	4.0	6	0
Wingo	2	13	6.5	13	0

Punting	No.	Yds.	Avg.	Longest	Inside 20	Blocked
Beverly	69	2785	40.4	65	11	0

Punt Returns	No.	FCs	Yds.	Avg.	Longest	TDs
Odom	15	4	80	5.3	19	0
Gray	13	8	61	4.7	18	0

Kickoff Returns	No.	Yds.	Avg.	Longest	TDs
A. Thompson	15	346	23.1	100 (TD)	1
McCoy	11	248	22.5	41	0
Odom	29	622	21.4	31	0

MINNESOTA VIKINGS

Head Coach: Bud Grant

14th Year   **Record:** 122–59–5

	1979 RECORD (7-9) (capital letters indicate home games)		1980 SCHEDULE (capital letters indicate home games)	
28	SAN FRANCISCO	22	ATLANTA	Sept. 7
7	Chicago	26	PHILADELPHIA	Sept. 14
12	MIAMI	27	Chicago	Sept. 21
27	GREEN BAY	21	Detroit	Sept. 28
13	Detroit	10	PITTSBURGH	Oct. 5
20	DALLAS	36	CHICAGO	Oct. 12
7	N.Y. Jets	14	Cincinnati	Oct. 19
30	CHICAGO	27	Green Bay	Oct. 26
10	TAMPA BAY	12	Washington	Nov. 2
7	St. Louis	37	DETROIT	Nov. 9
7	Green Bay	19	TAMPA BAY	Nov. 16
14	DETROIT	7	GREEN BAY	Nov. 23
23	Tampa Bay	22	New Orleans	Nov. 30
21	Los Angeles	27	Tampa Bay	Dec. 7
10	BUFFALO	3	CLEVELAND	Dec. 14
23	New England	27	Houston	Dec. 21
259		337		

Have the Minnesota Vikings recovered from Fran Tarkenton's decision to retire and, if they have, will Tommy Kramer be the right quarterback to lead them back to the Super Bowl promised land? Those questions await answers as Bud Grant begins his 14th year as Minnesota head coach with one of the NFL's best coaching records—122-59-5—behind him. In fact, 1979 was Grant's first losing season at Minnesota since his debut as head coach in 1967 when the Vikings wound up with a 3-8-3 record. Even more noteworthy was Minnesota's absence from the playoffs for the first time in seven years.

Despite this apparent setback to a long and distinguished record of success, Bud Grant views the situation as something less than disastrous. The 1979 season was a loser, but the Vikings did win three of their last five games. The defeats included a 21-27 overtime loss to Super Bowl-bound Los Angeles and a close 23-27 decision to New England in the season's finale. But it was a midseason slump that really did the Vikings in, that plus the melancholy fact they were out-scored by their opponents—259 to 337. As for fourth quarter scoring, the Vikings were snowed under in that crucial, final period of their 16 games by 124 to 65.

Still, there's little doubt Grant and the Vikings missed some very important people during that downgrading 1979 season. Gone, of course, was Fran Tarkenton but he wasn't the only one. Placekicker Fred Cox, who put many a point on the scoreboard for Minnesota, wasn't around either. He's now a chiropractor in Buffalo, Minnesota. Mike Tinglehoff, who snapped the ball for the Super Bowl teams, has retired to Minneapolis, and punter Neil Clabo is back home in Tennessee. Safety Phil Wise is merely watching the games on TV, too.

As the 1980 season begins, still another member of the famed Purple Gang will be missing, none other than defensive end Jim Marshall who counted 20 NFL years before deciding to retire at age 43. Gone also from the defensive front are Alan Page (now with Chicago) and Carl Eller (who's with Seattle) and all that's left of the Gang is Doug Sutherland and he's a 32-year-old reserve. Chuck Foreman, who used to rush 1,000 yards a season as a routine, faded in recent years and was traded to New England where he may be happier.

With the departure of so many name-players, little wonder Minnesota's six-year reign as NFC Central champion came to an end. Even so, the Vikings finished with a record of 99-43-2 for the 1970s decade, that being second only to the Dallas Cowboys' record of 105-39-0 for the same ten-year period. Will newcomers among the Vikings be able to set the pace for a similar record during the 1980s?

Bud Grant remains calm and cool in the midst of the dire predictions about his club's future. He and offensive coordinator Jerry Burns, for instance, are absolutely satisfied with the showing made by Tommy Kramer as he stepped into the yawning gap left by Tarkenton's retirement. If there's one phase of his passing that must be improved, it's the nagging little matter of throwing interceptions. Kramer's aim was bad 24 times last season, and some of those aerial turnovers were exceedingly costly, especially in games the Vikings lost by a touchdown or less.

Grant also feels some of the younger players are proving themselves with experience, especially center Dennis Swilley and guard Jim Hough who are new starters on the offensive line. Cornerback Dave Roller likewise gave the secondary a boost last season, coming as he did from Green Bay after being released by the Packers. With Marshall no longer the barrier at defensive right end, Grant is hoping Minnesota's No. 1 draftee of 1978, Randy Holloway, will step into the great man's shoes, if that's at all possible.

If the Vikings are to regain lost ground in 1980, they'll have to get off to a fast start against some of the league's toughest teams to beat. These include Philadelphia, Pittsburgh and Chicago (twice) within the span of the first six games. If they can get by those contests all in one piece, they should have a better-than-even chance of being a winner through the remainder of the schedule.

OFFENSE

Quarterbacks	Ht.	Wt.	Age	Exp.	College
Dils, Steve	6-1	190	25	2	Stanford
Kramer, Tommy	6-2	200	25	4	Rice
Reaves, John	6-3	210	30	9	Florida

Kramer was the only Minnesota QB to throw a pass last season and he made a run at several of Fran Tarkenton's club records while completing 55.7%. He became only the second QB in Viking annals to pass for over 3,000 yards, his 3,397 coming close to surpassing Tarkenton's season record of 3,468. Kramer also threw 23 TD passes, just two behind Tark's club record 25. Reaves made no appearances and Dils, the Stanford rookie, went into action only once. He took the snap and handed off to running back Brent McClanahan on a fake punt play against New England. But it was experience, however momentary.

Running Backs	Ht.	Wt.	Age	Exp.	College
Brown, Ted	5-10	198	23	2	North Carolina State
Edwards, Jimmy	5-9	185	28	2	Northeast Louisiana
McClanahan, Brent	5-10	202	30	8	Arizona State
Miller, Robert	5-11	204	27	6	Kansas
Young, Rickey	6-2	195	27	4	Jackson State
Payton, Eddie	5-8	175	29	4	Jackson State
Paschal, Doug	6-2	214	22	R	North Carolina
Jones, Paul	6-2	225	22	9	California

Brown gained 551 yards, averaging 4.2 per carry, in his debut and the former N.C. State All-America has everything it takes to be a thousand-yarder. He has encountered knee problems, however, and is reported a bit miffed over the doctor's original diagnosis on the extent of his injury. Chuck Foreman has gone to New England for a draft choice but Rickey Young is picking up momentum, running for 708 yards and a 3.8 average in '79. Eddie Payton, brother of Walter, could be of help particularly on the special teams. To shore up this unit, two running backs were drafted recently in the fifth round—Doug Paschal and Paul Jones have both the size and speed.

Receivers	Ht.	Wt.	Age	Exp.	College
LeCount, Terry (W)	5-10	172	24	3	Florida
Miller, Kevin (W)	5-10	180	25	3	Louisville
Rashad, Ahmad (W)	6-2	200	31	8	Oregon
Steele, Robert (W)	6-4	195	24	3	North Alabama
Tucker, Bob (T)	6-3	230	35	11	Bloomsburg State
Voigt, Stu (T)	6-1	225	32	11	Wisconsin
White, Sammy (W)	5-11	189	26	5	Grambling
Senser, Joe (T)	6-4	240	24	1	West Chester State

W=wide receiver   T=tight end

Rashad, still the consummate star receiver, set Viking records for a season's reception yards with 1,156. His 243 catches as a Viking is also a club record. He was NFC leader in receptions (80) and yards last season. Running back Rickey Young caught 72 while Sammy White added distance to his 42 receptions, averaging 17 yards per catch. In fact, the Minnesota passing attack didn't do too badly last season, ranking fourth in the NFC. It was defense and the running game that were woefully weak by comparison with the past.

Interior Linemen	Ht.	Wt.	Age	Exp.	College
Goodrum, Charles (G)	6-3	256	30	8	Florida A&M
Hamilton, Wes (G)	6-3	255	27	5	Tulsa
Hough, Jim (G)	6-2	267	24	3	Utah State
Huffman, Dave (C)	6-6	255	23	2	Notre Dame
Myers, Frank (T)	6-5	255	24	3	Texas A&M
Swilley, Dennis (C)	6-3	241	25	4	Texas A&M
Yary, Ron (T)	6-6	255	34	13	Southern Cal
Boyd, Brent (C)	6-3	238	22	R	UCLA

T=tackle   G=guard   C=center

Although Kramer was sacked 37 times last season, the line did a better job for the passing game than it did for the runners. The Viking rushing attack ranked a lowly 13th in the NFC, managing to rack up a mere 110 yards per game. Grant needs to do some patching up here and third round rookie Brent Boyd out of UCLA may be a start (and maybe a starter, too).

Kickers	Ht.	Wt.	Age	Exp.	College
Coleman, Greg (P)	6-0	178	26	4	Florida A&M
Danmeier, Rick (Pk)	6-0	183	28	3	Sioux Falls

Pk=placekicker   P=punter

Danmeier showed consistency in his kicking, making good 28-of-30 PATs and 13 FGs out of 21 attempts, some being bulls-eyes from the 40-yard range. Coleman's punting was just below the 40-yard average at 39.5, but he dropped 23 inside the 20-yard marker in the accurate placement department. Grant must be fairly well satisfied here, for no kickers or punters were chosen in the 1980 draft.

DEFENSE

Front Linemen	Ht.	Wt.	Age	Exp.	College
Holloway, Randy (E)	6-5	245	25	3	Pittsburgh
Mullaney, Mark (E)	6-6	242	27	6	Colorado State
Niehaus, Steve (T)	6-4	255	26	5	Notre Dame
Roller, Dave (T)	6-2	270	31	7	Kentucky

Sutherland, Doug (T)	6-3	250	32	11	Superior State
White, James (T)	6-3	263	27	5	Oklahoma State
Norman, Anthony (E)	6-5	245	25	1	Iowa State
Martin, Doug (T)	6-3	255	22	R	Washington

E=end   T=tackle

This line no longer has the hard-rock quality of the Super Bowl years. Jim Marshall has retired, and the lesser experienced hands have taken over. Doug Martin was only the fourth defensive lineman picked by the Vikings in the first round in the past six years. He has a knee problem but could help shore up that defense. The starters at season's end were Mullaney, Roller, J. White and Marshall (whose backup was Holloway).

Linebackers	Ht.	Wt.	Age	Exp.	College
Blair, Matt (O)	6-5	229	29	7	Iowa State
Hilgenberg, Wally (O)	6-3	229	38	17	Iowa
Luce, Derrel (O)	6-3	227	28	6	Baylor
McNeill, Fred (O)	6-2	229	28	7	UCLA
Siemon, Jeff (M)	6-3	237	30	9	Stanford
Studwell, Scott (M)	6-2	224	26	4	Illinois
Johnson, Dennis (O)	6-3	236	22	R	Southern Cal

O=outside   M=middle

The starters are Blair, Siemon and McNeill, a trio with a combined NFL experience of 20 years (not counting the upcoming season). Blair was the club's leading tackler in '79 with 110 solos. Siemon and McNeill together accounted for 124. Johnson is a fourth round draftee out of Southern Cal. Improvement against the rush is badly needed here.

Defensive Backs	Ht.	Wt.	Age	Exp.	College
Baylor, Tim (S)	6-5	199	26	5	Morgan State
Bryant, Bobby (CB)	6-1	170	36	12	South Carolina State
Hannon, Tom (S)	5-11	193	25	4	Michigan State
Knoff, Kurt (S)	6-2	188	26	5	Kansas
Krause, Paul (S)	6-3	205	38	17	Iowa
Nord, Keith (S)	6-0	197	23	2	St. Cloud State
Turner, John (CB)	6-0	199	24	3	Miami (Fla.)
Wright, Nate (CB)	5-11	180	33	12	San Diego State
Teal, Willie (CB)	5-10	190	22	R	Louisiana State

CB=cornerback   S=safety

Hannon and Wright led the club's pass interceptors with four each, although Wright wound up the season on injured reserve. Krause is thinking about retirement after finishing 1979 with 81 career interceptions, an NFL record. He ranks third in NFL career reception yardage with 1,185 behind Emlen Tunnell (1,282) and Dick (Night Train) Lane (1,207). Among the starters, Hannon appears the best. Second round draftee Willie Teal is expected to mount a strong challenge to Bryant and Wright for a starting cornerback post opposite Turner.

Note: A complete listing of Minnesota's 1980 college draft selections can be found on page 272.

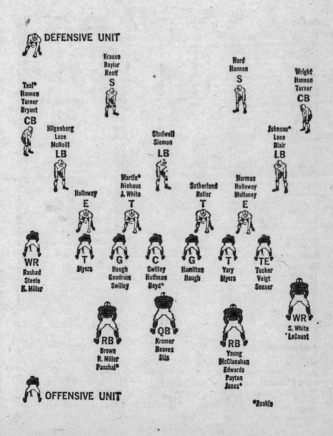

DEFENSIVE UNIT

Krause Baylor Knoff **S**

Nord Hannon **S**

Teal* Hannon Turner Bryant **CB**

Wright Hannon Turner **CB**

Hilgenberg Luce McNeill **LB**

Studwell Siemon **LB**

Johnson* Luce Blair **LB**

Holloway **E**

Martin* Niehaus J. White **T**

Sutherland Roller **T**

Norman Holloway Mullaney **E**

WR Rashad Steele K. Miller

Myers

Hough Goodrum Swilley **G**

Swilley Huffman Boyd* **C**

Hamilton Hough **G**

Yary Myers **T**

Tucker Voigt Senser **TE**

RB Brown R. Miller Paschal*

QB Kramer Reaves Dils

RB Young McClanahan Edwards Payton Jones*

WR S. White LeCount

OFFENSIVE UNIT

*Rookie

1979 VIKINGS STATISTICS

	Vikings	Opps.
Total Points Scored	259	337
Total First Downs	311	297
Third Down Efficiency Percentage	39.7	38.8
Yards Rushing—First Downs	1762—112	2526—148
Passes Attempted—Completions	566—315	424—229
Yards Passing—First Downs	3138—168	2693—132
QB Sacked—Yards Lost	37—258	31—272
Interceptions By—Return Average	22—16.0	24—13.3
Punts—Average Yards	91—39.0	93—39.4
Punt Returns—Average Return	57—4.8	48—6.1
Kickoff Returns—Average Return	61—22.6	59—18.1
Fumbles—Ball Lost	39—17	22—10
Penalties—Yards	96—787	93—677

STATISTICAL LEADERS

Scoring	TDs	Rush.	Pass.	Ret.	PATs	FGs	Total
Danmeier	0	0	0	0	28—30	13—21	66
Rashad	9	0	9	0	0	0	54
Young	7	3	4	0	0	0	42
S. White	4	0	4	0	0	0	24
Foreman	2	2	0	0	0	0	12
Voigt	2	0	2	0	0	0	12
Tucker	2	0	2	0	0	0	12
LeCount	2	0	2	0	0	0	12

Rushing	Atts.	Yds.	Avg.	Longest	TDs
Young	188	708	3.8	26	3
Brown	130	551	4.2	34	1
Foreman	83	215	2.6	16	2
Kramer	31	131	4.2	20	1
R. Miller	35	109	3.1	10	2
McClanahan	14	29	2.1	9	0

Passing	Atts.	Com.	Yds.	Pct.	Int.	Longest	TDs
Kramer	566	315	3397	55.7	24	55 (TD)	23

Receiving	No.	Yds.	Avg.	Longest	TDs
Rashad	80	1156	14.5	52 (TD)	9
Young	72	519	7.2	18	4
S. White	42	715	17.0	55 (TD)	4
Brown	31	197	6.4	35	0
Tucker	24	224	9.3	21	2
Foreman	19	147	7.7	22	0
Voigt	15	139	9.3	18	2

Interceptions	No.	Yds.	Avg.	Longest	TDs
Hannon	4	85	21.3	52	0
N. Wright	4	44	11.0	32	0
Krause	3	49	16.3	18	0
Blair	3	32	10.7	16	0
Bryant	2	50	25.0	29	0
Turner	2	48	24.0	36	0
Knoff	2	25	12.5	15	0

Punting	No.	Yds.	Avg.	Longest	Inside 20	Blocked
Coleman	90	3551	39.5	70	23	1

Punt Returns	No.	FCs	Yds.	Avg.	Longest	TDs
K. Miller	18	2	85	4.7	14	0
Edwards	33	2	186	5.6	42	0
Nord	3	3	11	3.7	7	0

Kickoff Returns	No.	Yds.	Avg.	Longest	TDs
Edwards	44	1103	25.1	83	0
Brown	8	186	23.3	43	0
R. Miller	3	38	12.7	19	0
McClanahan	3	53	17.7	20	0

DETROIT LIONS

Head Coach: Monte Clark

3rd Year   **Record:** 9–23

1979 RECORD (2-14) (capital letters indicate home games)		
16	Tampa Bay	31
24	WASHINGTON	27
10	N.Y. Jets	31
24	ATLANTA	23
10	MINNESOTA	13
17	New England	24
16	Green Bay	24
7	New Orleans	17
17	BUFFALO	20
7	Chicago	35
14	TAMPA BAY	16
7	Minnesota	14
20	CHICAGO	0
7	Philadelphia	44
10	MIAMI	28
13	GREEN BAY	18
219		**365**

1980 SCHEDULE (capital letters indicate home games)	
Los Angeles	Sept. 7
Green Bay at Milwaukee	Sept. 14
ST. LOUIS	Sept. 21
MINNESOTA	Sept. 28
Atlanta	Oct. 5
NEW ORLEANS	Oct. 12
Chicago	Oct. 19
Kansas City	Oct. 26
SAN FRANCISCO	Nov. 2
Minnesota	Nov. 9
BALTIMORE	Nov. 16
Tampa Bay	Nov. 23
CHICAGO (TV)	Nov. 27
St. Louis	Dec. 7
TAMPA BAY	Dec. 14
GREEN BAY	Dec. 21

As expected, the Detroit Lions chose Oklahoma's All-America running back Billy Sims as the No. 1 selection in the 1980 NFL college draft held late last April at New York's Sheraton Hotel. And, as expected, a push-and-pull contest developed over the question of his salary, bonus, and other stipulations he and his agent felt were rightfully theirs in exchange for signing a playing contract. At the outset, Sims was asking for about $4½-million for six years of playing time, and was threatening to ditch the NFL altogether and take his Heisman Trophy with him to play in Canada if the Lions failed to agree to acceptable contract terms. "But we'll get him," said Lions owner William Clay Ford. "There's no way we're going to let Sims go."

Whether he plays in Canada or the U.S.A., Sims appears to be a natural for pro football stardom. Although he's 25 years of age, three years older than the customary NFL rookie, his college record at Oklahoma is impressive to say the least. Speedy, powerful, muscular with his 5-11 height and 212 pounds, Sims runs on huge legs that propel him forward rapidly. Often he runs over a defender rather than around him, and usually gets by the first player to lunge in his direction. At the goal line, he defies gravity and sails over the action for the score. More significantly, Sims is one of those hardy souls who "plays hurt," ignoring an injury which doesn't immobilize him completely.

If all goes "by the book," Sims would undoubtedly supply a lethargic Detroit ground game with a kind of fireworks yet unseen in the Silverdome at Pontiac, Michigan, one of the newer indoor pro football stadiums. (The Super Bowl will be played there in 1982.) During the 1979 season, the Detroit rushing attack was hardly a unit capable of striking fear into opposing defenses. For most of the season, the running game was carried by Dexter Bussey and his eventual replacement, Rick Kane, but the club's total overland efforts could net no better than 1,677 yards—14th best in the NFC. Obviously, whatever Sims has to offer would be an improvement, but it must be borne in mind that the record books are full of Heisman Trophy winners who failed to make it big in the NFL. Pro football is that kind of a game.

And there's the matter of Detroit's offensive line, the people upon whom the ball-carriers depend most when the ball is snapped and running room must be provided. Good blocking is an absolute necessity if backs like Sims, Bussey and Kane are to move at their maximum speed and elusiveness. In 1979, the Detroit ground offense averaged 3.8 yards per carry while NFC team rushing leader St. Louis averaged 4.6. There's a question of how well the present Detroit line can block for a speedy running back, unless new talent is brought in and injuries remain at a minimum.

A 2-14 record is not exactly a morale-builder for the future, but Monte Clark feels that won-lost figures don't tell it all. "I honestly don't believe our players are of the 2-14 type," he insists, "because we have some outstanding players in every position, more at some than at others. But the nucleus is good, and the tough learning experience of '79 will definitely strengthen us." The learning experience was "tough" at that. Of the 14 defeats, eight came by margins of eight points or less. And the Lions held the lead in ten of their games last fall, but could maintain that lead in only two.

The Lions, too, operated under a very unusual personnel situation. The '79 squad totaled 25 players who, at one time or another, had been free agents looking for work. In all, the Lions used 28 new players during the season—players who hadn't been active with the club the previous year. And as many as ten rookies received the call to start at least one regular season game. The addition of such a large number of free agents and rookies to the roster had the inevitable result of making the Lions one of the league's youngest teams, averaging just over three years in NFL experience. A quick glance at the current Detroit roster shows only two players in the double-digit experience category. They're linebacker Charlie Weaver and quarterback Scott Hunter, both of whom are entering their tenth NFL seasons. Only four roster members have as many as nine years' experience and the accent on youth continues (despite Billy Sims' relatively advanced age of 25).

Quarterback Gary Danielson recently signed a one-year contract with Detroit for a reported $195,000 which would make him the highest paid player in Lions' history. By far the most qualified quarterback on the Detroit roster, at this stage at least, Danielson had missed the entire 1979 season after injuring his knee in preseason. This threw the Detroit quarterback situation into a chaos from which the Lions never recovered.

Danielson's backup, Joe Reed, went down with a groin muscle injury in the first regular season game, and rookie Jeff Komlo, the club's ninth round draft choice from the University of Delaware, was the one and only starter. Even though this kind of situation usually develops only in the movies, Komlo came through in great style, showing both poise and ability. By season's end, the Delaware rookie who made it from the NCAA's Division II to the big leagues in one jump had completed 183 passes of 368 attempts for 2,238 yards. The 368 attempts comprise a new Detroit record. Already, Komlo has started 14 games for the Lions, one more than Danielson has in his Detroit career. Looking at it from that angle, when Danielson takes over at quarterback it will be almost as though the backup is replacing the regular.

OFFENSE

Quarterbacks	Ht.	Wt.	Age	Exp.	College
Danielson, Gary	6-2	195	29	4	Purdue
Hunter, Scott	6-2	205	33	10	Alabama
Komlo, Jeff	6-2	205	24	2	Delaware
Reed, Joe	6-1	190	32	8	Mississippi State
Hipple, Eric	6-1½	197	22	R	Utah State

The quarterbacking situation at Detroit last season was, to put it bluntly, a mess. Danielson's loss to injury left the club without a first-line quarterback, and no less than four different passers were sent into the breach, but to no avail. The Lions' passing game wound up with a 12th place NFC rating. Rookie Jeff Komlo played the most but couldn't do it all, but he did complete 49.7% of his throws, not bad at all for a first-year man. There were times, of course, when Monte Clark probably wished he could have had Greg Landry back from Baltimore and sitting on the bench.

Running Backs	Ht.	Wt.	Age	Exp.	College
Bussey, Dexter	6-1	195	28	7	Texas-Arlington
Callicutt, Ken	6-0	190	25	3	Clemson
Gaines, Lawrence	6-1	230	27	4	Wyoming
Kane, Rick	5-11	200	26	4	San Jose State
King, Horace	5-10	205	27	6	Georgia
Robinson, Bo	6-2	225	24	2	West Texas State
Sims, Billy	5-11	212	25	R	Oklahoma

Bussey led this group last season with 625 yards on 144 carries for a 4.3 average but he lost his starting job to Kane in late season. Already unhappy over contract talks, it didn't make Bussey any happier. Kane ran 94 times for 332 yards (3.5 avg.). Maybe Sims will make them all feel like second-raters. King didn't play all that much but averaged 4.1 yards per carry when he did. Anyway, Detroit's rushing offense ranked in the NFC cellar in '79.

Receivers	Ht.	Wt.	Age	Exp.	College
Arnold, John (W)	5-10	175	25	2	Wyoming
Blue, Luther (W)	5-11	180	25	4	Iowa State
Hill, David (T)	6-2	230	26	5	Texas A&I
Norris, Ulysses (T)	6-4	225	23	2	Georgia
Scott, Fred (W)	6-2	180	28	7	Amherst
Thompson, Leonard (W)	5-11	190	28	6	Oklahoma State
Friede, Mike (W)	6-3	192	22	R	Indiana

W=wide receiver   T=tight end

This unit had two starring types last season. Scott had his best season to date with 62 catches for 929 yards, just five receptions short of the club record. Hill was selected for his second straight Pro Bowl appearance but he, too, fell into a dispute with the coach over the lack of passes thrown his way in a loss to Minnesota. He felt, in a word, if they don't throw 'em, you can't catch 'em.

Interior Linemen	Ht.	Wt.	Age	Exp.	College
Baldischwiler, Karl (T)	6-5	265	24	3	Oklahoma
Bolinger, Russ (G)	6-5	250	26	4	Long Beach State
Dorney, Keith (T)	6-5	265	23	2	Penn State
Elias, Homer (G)	6-3	255	25	3	Tennessee State
Fowler, Amos (G)	6-3	250	24	3	Southern Mississippi
Franks, Dennis (C)	6-1	245	27	5	Michigan
Morrison, Don (C-T)	6-5	250	31	9	Texas-Arlington
Pesuit, Wally (G-C)	6-4	250	26	4	Kentucky

Turnure, Tom (C)	6-3	242	22	R	Washington
Ginn, Tom (G)	6-3	244	22	R	Arkansas

T=tackle   G=guard   C=center

What can be said about the line for an offensive unit that ranked in the NFC's cellar? Not very much. Dorney started every game as a rookie, and did well enough to be chosen on several all-rookie teams. Bolinger came off injured reserve and started all games at guard. Injuries along the line were minimal, but that didn't keep the Detroit quarterbacks from being sacked 51 times! Clark must do some rearranging here if the offense is to really get moving.

Kickers	Ht.	Wt.	Age	Exp.	College
Ricardo, Benny (Pk)	5-10	170	26	4	San Diego State
Skladany, Tom (P-Pk)	6-0	195	25	2	Ohio State
Swider, Larry (P)	6-2	195	25	2	Pittsburgh

Pk=placekicker   P=punter

It was a tense moment for the special teams when it was learned that Skladany needed back surgery. As it turned out, he only missed two games, and Swider, a free agent, booted the ball 88 times for a 40.0-yard average. Clark now has the tough problem of choosing between two first-rate punters. Look for either Skladany or Swider to go on the trading block. Ricardo does his job as placekicker and does it well, converting 25-of-27 PATs and making good 10-of-18 FG attempts, including a streak of 24 straight FGs from inside the 40-yard line. From that range, apparently, Ricardo just doesn't miss.

DEFENSE

Front Linemen	Ht.	Wt.	Age	Exp.	College
Baker, Al (E)	6-6	260	24	3	Colorado State
Elam, Cleveland (T)	6-4	250	28	6	Tennessee State
English, Doug (T)	6-5	260	27	6	Texas
Gay, William (E)	6-3	250	25	3	Southern Cal
Pureifory, Dave (E)	6-2	255	31	9	Eastern Michigan
Woodcock, John (T)	6-3	250	26	4	Hawaii

E=end   T=tackle

The front four is known as the "Silver Rush," named after the Lions' home stadium in Pontiac which is called the Silverdome. The "Silver Rush" was well named. Detroit's defense against the pass ranked no less than second among the NFL's 28 clubs—Tampa Bay ranking first. Opposing passers, dumped by the Lions 45 times, could average no more than 152.6 yards per game through the air.

Linebackers	Ht.	Wt.	Age	Exp.	College
Brooks, Jon (O)	6-2	215	23	2	Clemson
Cobb, Garry (O)	6-2	210	23	2	Southern Cal
Cole, Eddie (M)	6-2	235	24	2	Mississippi
Fantetti, Ken (M)	6-2	230	23	2	Wyoming
Harrell, James (O)	6-1	215	23	2	Florida
Mohring, John (O)	6-3	230	24	1	C. W. Post
O'Neil, Ed (M)	6-3	235	28	7	Penn State
Weaver, Charlie (O)	6-2	225	31	10	Southern Cal
White, Stan (O)	6-1	219	31	9	Ohio State

O=outside   M=middle

At times, three rookies manned the linebacking posts with the expected result: inexperienced performances. But the Detroit linebacking corps is undergoing a new life following the retirement of veterans. Weaver is returning to action from knee surgery but faces challenges from rookies such as Fantetti, Harrell and Brooks, all of whom started a number of games in '79. O'Neil also is expected to return to his regular outside spot.

Defensive Backs	Ht.	Wt.	Age	Exp.	College
Allen, Jimmy (S)	6-2	195	28	7	UCLA
Bradley, Luther (CB)	6-2	195	25	3	Notre Dame
Parkin, Dave (S)	6-0	190	24	2	Utah State
Patterson, Don (S)	5-11	175	23	2	Georgia Tech
Stewart, Jim (S)	5-11	190	26	4	Tulsa
Williams, Walt (CB)	6-0	185	26	4	New Mexico State
Worford, Joe (CB)	6-2	205	24	1	Eastern Michigan
Hunter, James (CB)	6-3	195	26	5	Grambling
Leonard, Tony (CB)	5-11	175	27	4	Virginia Union
Lewis, Eddie (CB)	6-0	175	27	5	Kansas
Streeter, Mark (CB)	6-0	182	22	R	Arizona

CB=cornerback   S=safety

Although the Detroit secondary intercepted only 14 passes last season (Allen and Bradley had four each), the pass defense was good. Just 14 TDs were scored by opposing passers, this being one of the lowest totals in the NFC. Injuries hampered Leonard, Williams, Hunter and Allen. The end of '79 found Hunter and Bradley at the corners, Allen and Parkin, a rookie, at the safety posts. If everybody stays healthy, this unit could be one of NFL's best.

Note: A complete listing of Detroit's 1980 college draft selections can be found on page 270.

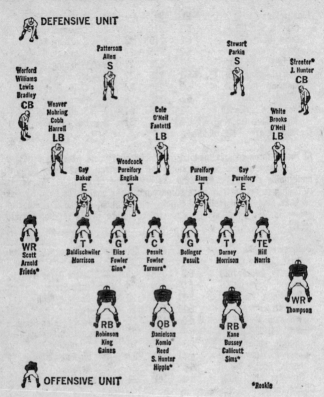

DEFENSIVE UNIT

Patterson
Allen
S

Stewart
Parkin
S

Worford
Williams
Lewis
Bradley
CB

Streeter*
J. Hunter
CB

Weaver
Mohring
Cobb
Harrell
LB

Cole
O'Neil
Fantetti
LB

White
Brooks
O'Neil
LB

Gay
Baker
E

Woodcock
Pureifory
English
T

Pureifory
Elam
T

Gay
Pureifory
E

WR
Scott
Arnold
Friede*

T
Baldischwiler
Morrison

G
Elias
Fowler
Ginn*

C
Pesuit
Fowler
Turnure*

G
Bolinger
Pesuit

T
Dorney
Morrison

TE
Hill
Norris

WR
Thompson

RB
Robinson
King
Gaines

QB
Danielson
Komlo
Reed
S. Hunter
Hipple*

RB
Kane
Bussey
Callicutt
Sims*

OFFENSIVE UNIT

*Rookie

1979 LIONS STATISTICS

	Lions	Opps.
Total Points Scored	219*	365
Total First Downs	227	311
Third Down Efficiency Percentage	32.0	34.0
Yards Rushing—First Downs	1677—85	2515—142
Passes Attempted—Completions	452—218	402—220
Yards Passing—First Downs	2336—131	2442—128
QB Sacked—Yards Lost	51—439	45—345
Interceptions By—Return Average	14—5.2	27—14.7
Punts—Average Yards	98—40.1	83—40.0
Punt Returns—Average Return	45—8.3	57—7.7
Kickoff Returns—Average Return	78—20.1	51—19.4
Fumbles—Ball Lost	37—19	30—12
Penalties—Yards	110—897	118—972
* Includes safety		

STATISTICAL LEADERS

Scoring	TDs	Rush.	Pass.	Ret.	PATs	FGs	Total
Ricardo	0	0	0	0	25—27	10—18	55
Scott	5	0	5	0	0	0	30
Kane	5	4	1	0	0	0	30
Hill	3	0	3	0	0	0	18
Robinson	2	2	0	0	0	0	12
Komlo	2	2	0	0	0	0	12
Thompson	2	0	2	0	0	0	12

Rushing	Atts.	Yds.	Avg.	Longest	TDs
Bussey	144	625	4.3	38	1
Kane	94	332	3.5	26 (TD)	4
Robinson	87	302	3.5	29	2
King	39	160	4.1	23	1
Komlo	31	107	3.6	16	2

Passing	Atts.	Com.	Yds.	Pct.	Int.	Longest	TDs
Komlo	368	183	2238	49.7	23	40	11
S. Hunter	41	18	321	43.9	1	82	1
Reed	32	14	164	43.8	1	50	2
Golsteyn	9	2	16	22.2	2	15	0

Receiving	No.	Yds.	Avg.	Longest	TDs
Scott	62	929	15.0	50	5
Hill	47	569	12.1	40	3
Thompson	24	451	18.8	82	2
King	18	150	8.3	30	0
Bussey	15	102	6.8	22	0
Robinson	14	118	8.4	14	0
Washington	14	192	13.7	29 (TD)	1

Interceptions	No.	Yds.	Avg.	Longest	TDs
Bradley	4	11	2.8	11	0
Allen	4	0	—	—	0
J. Hunter	3	6	2.0	6	0
Williams	2	39	19.5	36 (TD)	1

Punting	No.	Yds.	Avg.	Longest	Inside 20	Blocked
Swider	88	3523	40.0	72	13	0
Skladany	10	406	40.6	52	2	0

Punt Returns	No.	FCs	Yds.	Avg.	Longest	TDs
Arnold	19	4	164	8.6	27	0
Thompson	9	3	117	13.0	31	0
Callicut	4	4	25	6.3	13	0

Kickoff Returns	No.	Yds.	Avg.	Longest	TDs
Arnold	23	539	23.4	69	0
Callicut	24	406	16.9	31	0
Kane	13	281	21.6	37	0
Thompson	6	151	25.2	25	0

LOS ANGELES RAMS

Head Coach: Ray Malavasi

3rd Year

Record: 21—11

1979 RECORD (9-7) (capital letters indicate home games)		
17	OAKLAND	24
13	Denver	9
27	SAN FRANCISCO	24
6	Tampa Bay	21
21	ST. LOUIS	0
35	New Orleans	17
6	Dallas	30
16	SAN DIEGO	40
14	N.Y. GIANTS	20
24	Seattle	0
23	Chicago	27
20	ATLANTA	14
26	San Francisco	20
27	MINNESOTA	21
34	Atlanta	13
14	NEW ORLEANS	29
323		309
	Playoffs	
21	Dallas	19
9	Tampa Bay	0
19	Pittsburgh	31

1980 SCHEDULE (capital letters indicate home games)	
DETROIT	Sept. 7
Tampa Bay (night, TV)	Sept. 11
GREEN BAY	Sept. 21
N.Y. Giants	Sept. 28
SAN FRANCISCO	Oct. 5
St. Louis	Oct. 12
San Francisco	Oct. 19
Atlanta	Oct. 26
NEW ORLEANS	Nov. 2
MIAMI	Nov. 9
New England	Nov. 16
New Orleans (night, TV)	Nov. 24
N.Y. JETS	Nov. 30
Buffalo	Dec. 7
DALLAS (night, TV)	Dec. 15
ATLANTA	Dec. 21

The most significant thing to remember about the Los Angeles Rams as they begin the 1980 campaign in their new home at Anaheim is they began the fourth quarter of Super Bowl XIV at Pasadena by leading the Pittsburgh Steelers, 19-17. Ray Malavasi and his cohorts came that close to bringing off what would have been the most stunning Super Bowl upset since Joe Namath and the Jets whipped Johnny Unitas and the Colts, 16-7, in Super Bowl III. For one brief shining moment, it seemed that the Rams would stage one of those Hollywood happy endings right in their own backyard but, as it turned out, the Steelers got down to business in that fourth quarter and L-A woke up to find it was only a dream.

Still, the Rams no longer have reason to consider themselves merely NFL West Coast Champions as they, almost routinely, regarded themselves during several seasons of playoff miseries. Now they can actually regard themselves as members of the NFL's top echelon and not just the West Coast branch. There should be a new psychology working with the Rams, if the desire to win is strong enough in what George Allen referred to as unaggressive California weather, in which nobody really wants to hit anybody.

There's some favorable psychology working, too, in the move to new headquarters at Anaheim Stadium which, by the way, isn't too far from the previous home at the Coliseum. In fact, a lot of fans who live nearer to Anaheim will travel less to see the games. A glance at a map shows the distances, whether they be to the Coliseum or to Anaheim, are all within the Greater Los Angeles area, one of the nation's biggest urban sprawls. Despite the move, it's becoming increasingly clear that the Rams are not being deserted by their fans. By late spring of this year, season ticket renewals were running at about 90%, which is about normal. In addition, the front office reports some 22,000 new orders for season tickets, all of which indicates a sellout is probable at Anaheim where the stadium's seating capacity is 69,000.

Ray Malavasi is no different from most other coaches who find themselves directing operations from the sidelines at the Super Bowl. Their view is: Don't tamper with a Super Bowl lineup—there's no way to improve upon perfection. But Malavasi has already committed himself to one departure from the Super Bowl XIV cast. Pat Haden will be restored to his starting role at quarterback, even though it reflects in no way on the splendid job Vince Ferragamo did while filling in for the injured Haden after the tenth week of the '79 campaign.

It was in that tenth regular season game, a 24-0 victory over Seattle, that Haden suffered a hand injury upon completing a club record of 13 consecutive passes. Up until that point, Haden had found targets for better than 56% of his passes while playing with an ever-changing group of receivers and offensive linemen in virtually every game. And so, despite Ferragamo's fine performance as the replacement, Malavasi feels understandably justified in returning the starting post to Haden. It must be remembered, too, that some of the quarterbacking credit for putting the Rams into the playoffs belongs to former Minnesota and Atlanta passer Bob Lee who has signed on after Haden was injured. He threw game-winning TDs against San Francisco and also his old colleagues, the Vikings. Lee was used in relief at a time when Ferragamo himself was recovering from a hand injury. The fourth L-A quarterback, former Alabama star Jeff Rutledge, likewise gave a good account of himself when he went into action against Chicago, keeping the Rams out in front until the final seconds when the Bears won, 27-23. One wonders, though, what does Malavasi intend to do with all those quarterbacks?

Perhaps the one big factor that propelled the Rams into the Super Bowl was their rushing attack. Although it wasn't the best in the league, spectacular performances by Wendell Tyler and his running-mate, Cullen Bryant, were pro football at its best. Tyler gained 1,109 yards for the season, much of it along routes cleared by the hard-blocking Bryant who himself contributed 619 yards to the rushing campaign. Malavasi was outspoken in his praise for both:

"Wendell Tyler's statistics speak for themselves," he says. "Some people question his durability, but I have no qualms about that. He is a great back. Cullen Bryant gives us a solid, consistent performance, both as a short-yardage runner and blocker."

The Rams were so blessed with superior running backs that Malavasi decided to trade at least two of the better known ones to other clubs. John Cappelletti, the Heisman Trophy winner from Penn State whose NFL career has been hampered by injuries, went to San Diego and Lawrence McCutcheon, once the main man in L-A's offensive backfield, is now with Denver, hopefully to get a new start on his career.

How does one improve on a Super Bowl lineup? Maybe you don't, but it's a good idea to make sure the depth remains deep. The Rams chose 13 players in the 1980 NFL college draft, including another quarterback, Kevin Scanlon of Arkansas, in the 12th and final round. Nine of those 13 choices were on offense, but the No. 1 selection was All-America safety Johnnie Johnson of Texas, one of the premier college defensive backs in the country. Although he'll challenge two well-entrenched safeties in Dave Elmendorf and Nolan Cromwell, Johnson will probably find plenty of playing time as a punt returner in view of his 8.8-yard average at Texas.

OFFENSE

Quarterbacks	Ht.	Wt.	Age	Exp.	College
Ferragamo, Vince	6-3	212	26	4	Nebraska
Haden, Pat	5-11	185	27	5	Southern Cal
Lee, Bob	6-2	190	34	12	Pacific (Calif.)
Rutledge, Jeff	6-2	202	23	2	Alabama

As everybody knows, Ferragamo took over for the injured Haden and took the Rams all the way to the Super Bowl. But Ray Malavasi has a rule which says no man will lose his job because of an injury. That being the case, look for Haden to resume his starting role when the new season opens. Before a broken little finger on his throwing hand took him out of action, Haden had completed 56.2% of his passes (163 of 290). Malavasi apparently believes in being well prepared with quarterbacks. Lee and Rutledge also get a chance to throw now and then.

Running Backs	Ht.	Wt.	Age	Exp.	College
Bryant, Cullen	6-1	236	29	8	Colorado
Hill, Eddie	6-2	202	23	2	Memphis State
Jodat, Jim	5-11	213	26	4	Carthage
Peacock, Elvis	6-1	208	24	2	Oklahoma
Tyler, Wendell	5-10	195	25	3	UCLA
Thomas, Jewerl	6-0	220	22	R	San Jose State

Tyler's year was his finest as he rolled for 1,109 yards on 218 carries and a 5.1 average. One TD jaunt was for 63 yards. Bryant was his running-mate and the two complemented each other almost to perfection, and they could compliment each other, too, after the season was over. Bryant ran for 619 yards, and provided much of the blocking that kept Tyler on the move. And, in his 177 times of carrying the ball, Bryant fumbled only once. Peacock is still hampered by injuries but will be a quality addition to this corps of brilliant running backs once he's healthy. Thomas is a third round draft choice who wants to join this ground-yardage club.

Receivers	Ht.	Wt.	Age	Exp.	College
Dennard, Preston (W)	6-1	183	25	3	New Mexico
Hill, Drew (W)	5-9	170	24	2	Georgia Tech
Jessie, Ron (W)	6-0	181	32	10	Kansas
Miller, Willie (W)	5-9	172	32	5	Colorado State
Nelson, Terry (T)	6-2	240	29	7	Arkansas-Pine Bluff
Smith, Ron (W)	6-0	185	24	3	San Diego State
Waddy, Billy (W)	5-11	188	26	4	Colorado
White, Walter (T)	6-3	234	29	6	Maryland

W=wide receiver   T=tight end

Pass receiving was all but monopolized by L-A's running backs who came out of the backfield to catch many of the passes thrown by Haden and Ferragamo (Bryant 31, Tyler 32, Peacock 21, McCutcheon 19, etc.). Among the receivers, second-year man Preston Dennard was club leader with 43 for 766 yards and a 17.8-yard average. Jessie and Miller joined the hospital list as the season went along.

Interior Linemen	Ht.	Wt.	Age	Exp.	College
Bain, Bill (G)	6-4	277	28	6	S. Cal
France, Doug (T)	6-5	270	27	6	Ohio State

Gravelle, Gordon (T)	6-5	237	31	9	Brigham Young
Harrah, Dennis (G)	6-5	255	27	6	Miami (Fla.)
Hill, Kent (G)	6-5	260	23	2	Georgia Tech
Ryczek, Dan (C-G)	6-3	242	31	8	Virginia
Saul, Rich (C)	6-3	245	32	11	Michigan State
Slater, Jackie (T)	6-4	271	26	5	Jackson State
Smith, Doug (C-G)	6-3	255	24	3	Bowling Green
Pankey, Irv (T)	6-4	258	22	R	Penn State

T=tackle   G=guard   C=center

Like the defensive line, the offensive forward wall also had its share of injuries. And whenever L-A's starting group played together as a unit, the Rams were usually on the winning side of the score. Early additions to the injured list were France and Harrah, both of whom later returned to action, joining Saul and Slater to present a solid front to opposing defenses. Saul and Harrah received Pro Bowl invitations.

Kickers	Ht.	Wt.	Age	Exp.	College
Clark, Ken (P)	6-2	196	32	2	St. Mary's-Nova Scotia
Corral, Frank (Pk)	6-2	228	25	3	UCLA

Pk=placekicker   P=punter

Neither Corral nor Clark had a blue ribbon season in '79. Corral, consistent as a rookie, was less so as an encore, making good 12 of his 15 FG attempts and 36-39 PATs. An ailing ankle hampered Corral's style somewhat. Clark averaged 40.1 with his 93 punts but has to adjust to the NFL's punting styles after coming south from the Canadian League.

DEFENSE

Front Linemen	Ht.	Wt.	Age	Exp.	College
Brooks, Larry (T)	6-3	253	30	9	Virginia State
Doss, Reggie (E)	6-4	267	24	3	Hampton Institute
Dryer, Fred (E)	6-6	231	34	12	San Diego State
Fanning, Mike (T)	6-6	252	27	6	Notre Dame
Jones, Cody (T)	6-5	244	29	6	San Jose State
Wilkinson, Jerry (E)	6-9	260	24	2	Oregon State
Youngblood, Jack (E)	6-4	244	30	10	Florida
Murphy, Philip (T)	6-5	268	22	R	South Carolina State

E=end   T=tackle

Malavasi faces some problems here due to a rash of injuries. Jack Youngblood's broken leg is on the mend while Brooks has undergone surgery for an injured ankle. Jones had a torn Achilles and must test it out before the season begins. Ready and able are 12-year-man Fred Dryer, Mike Fanning (who replaced Jones at tackle), and two up-and-coming youngsters, Doss and Wilkinson. L-A's defensive line has been awesome in recent years, but recovery from injuries is the key to its future.

Linebackers	Ht.	Wt.	Age	Exp.	College
Andrews, George (O)	6-3	223	25	2	Nebraska
Brudzinski, Bob (O)	6-4	229	25	4	Ohio State
Ekern, Carl (M)	6-3	223	26	4	San Jose State
Harris, Joe (O)	6-1	224	28	5	Georgia Tech
Reynolds, Jack (M)	6-1	227	33	11	Tennessee
Westbrooks, Greg (O)	6-3	220	27	6	Colorado
Youngblood, Jim (O)	6-3	231	30	8	Tennessee Tech

O=outside   M=middle

Jim Youngblood, Reynolds and Brudzinski provide a big plug to the Los Angeles defense unit. Youngblood was hampered by an injured shoulder, but played well enough to get invited to the Pro Bowl. Brudzinski led the club in tackles with 84 in his first full year as a starter. Ekern underwent knee surgery after the first preseason game. Andrews, Harris and Westbrooks played mainly with the special teams.

Defensive Backs	Ht.	Wt.	Age	Exp.	College
Brown, Eddie (S)	5-11	190	28	6	Tennessee
Cromwell, Nolan (S)	6-1	198	25	4	Kansas
Ellis, Ken (CB)	5-11	180	33	11	Southern University
Elmendorf, Dave (S)	6-1	196	31	10	Texas A&M
Justin, Sid (CB)	5-10	170	26	2	Long Beach State
O'Steen, Dwayne (CB)	6-1	193	26	3	San Jose State
Perry, Rod (CB)	5-9	182	27	6	Colorado
Sully, Ivory (S-CB)	6-0	193	23	2	Delaware
Thomas, Pat (CB)	5-9	182	26	5	Texas A&M
Wallace, Jackie (S)	6-3	196	29	7	Arizona
Johnson, Johnnie (S)	6-1	183	22	R	Texas
Irvin, Leroy (S)	5-10	173	22	R	Kansas

CB=cornerback   S=safety

Injuries to Perry and Thomas created problems, and different personnel combinations were used in the secondary last season but with apparent success. Elmendorf and Cromwell are the regular starters at safety. Leading the interceptors last season was Cromwell with five, a total equalled by linebacker Jim Youngblood. Elmendorf played the entire season, garnering three interceptions and making 57 tackles. There's depth a-plenty here, especially with the addition of Texas All-America Johnnie Johnson, L-A's first round draft choice, and Leroy Irvin, a third round choice from Kansas. Johnson, especially, could crack the starting lineup if any of the regulars falter.

Note: A complete listing of Los Angeles's 1980 college draft selections can be found on page 271.

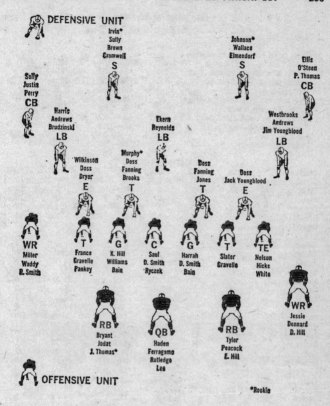

DEFENSIVE UNIT

Irvin*
Sully
Brown
Cromwell
S

Johnson*
Wallace
Elmendorf
S

Ellis
O'Steen
P. Thomas
CB

Sully
Justin
Perry
CB

Harris
Andrews
Brudzinski
LB

Ekern
Reynolds
LB

Westbrooks
Andrews
Jim Youngblood
LB

Wilkinson
Doss
Dryer
E

Murphy*
Doss
Fanning
Brooks
T

Doss
Fanning
Jones
T

Doss
Jack Youngblood
E

WR
Miller
Waddy
R. Smith

France
Gravelle
Pankey
T

K. Hill
Williams
Bain
G

Saul
D. Smith
Ryczek
C

Harrah
D. Smith
Bain
G

Slater
Gravelle
T

Nelson
Hicks
White
TE

WR
Jessie
Dennard
D. Hill

RB
Bryant
Jodat
J. Thomas*

QB
Haden
Ferragamo
Rutledge
Lea

RB
Tyler
Peacock
E. Hill

OFFENSIVE UNIT

*Rookie

1979 RAMS STATISTICS

	Rams	Opps.
Total Points Scored	323	309
Total First Downs	299	266
Third Down Efficiency Percentage	35.5	33.9
Yards Rushing—First Downs	2460—134	1997—115
Passes Attempted—Completions	456—242	454—220
Yards Passing—First Downs	2673—138	2556—133
QB Sacked—Yards Lost	39—359	52—451
Interceptions By—Return Average	25—14.2	29—13.7
Punts—Average Yards	95—39.3	108—40.3
Punt Returns—Average Return	58—5.7	59—6.9
Kickoff Returns—Average Return	66—19.6	58—22.5
Fumbles—Ball Lost	37—21	38—16
Penalties—Yards	98—799	105—993

STATISTICAL LEADERS

Scoring	TDs	Rush.	Pass.	Ret.	PATs	FGs	Total
Corral	0	0	0	0	36—39	13—25	75
Tyler	10	9	1	0	0	0	60
Bryant	5	5	0	0	0	0	30
Dennard	4	0	4	0	0	0	24
Nelson	3	0	3	0	0	0	18
Waddy	3	0	3	0	0	0	18
E. Hill	2	1	1	0	0	0	12
Young	2	0	2	0	0	0	12

Rushing	Atts.	Yds.	Avg.	Longest	TDs
Tyler	218	1109	5.1	63 (TD)	9
Bryant	177	619	3.5	15	5
McCutcheon	73	243	3.3	21	0
Peacock	52	224	4.3	15	0
E. Hill	29	114	3.9	27	1
Haden	16	97	6.1	17	0

Passing	Atts.	Com.	Yds.	Pct.	Int.	Longest	TDs
Haden	290	163	1854	56.2	14	50	11
Ferragamo	110	53	778	48.2	10	71 (TD)	5
Rutledge	32	13	125	40.6	4	22	1
Lee	22	11	243	50.0	1	41 (TD)	2

Receiving	No.	Yds.	Avg.	Longest	TDs
Dennard	43	766	17.8	50	4
Tyler	32	308	9.6	71 (TD)	1
Bryant	31	227	7.3	24	0
Nelson	25	293	11.7	26	3
Peacock	21	261	12.4	49	0
McCutcheon	19	101	5.3	11	0
Smith	16	300	18.8	38	1
Waddy	14	220	15.7	40 (TD)	3
Young	13	144	11.1	23	2
Jessie	11	169	15.4	39	2

Interceptions	No.	Yds.	Avg.	Longest	TDs
Cromwell	5	109	21.8	34	0
Youngblood, Jim	5	89	17.8	34 (TD)	2
O'Steen	4	42	10.5	36	0
Elmendorf	3	39	13.0	32	0

Punting	No.	Yds.	Avg.	Longest	Inside 20	Blocked
Clark	93	3731	40.1	60	17	2

Punt Returns	No.	FCs	Yds.	Avg.	Longest	TDs
Brown	56	19	332	5.9	30	0

Kickoff Returns	No.	Yds.	Avg.	Longest	TDs
D. Hill	40	803	20.1	39	0
E. Hill	15	305	20.3	43	0
Brown	5	103	20.6	28	0

NEW ORLEANS SAINTS

Head Coach: Dick Nolan

3rd Year   **Record:** 15–17

1979 RECORD (8-8) (capital letters indicate home games)			1980 SCHEDULE (capital letters indicate home games)	
34	ATLANTA	40	SAN FRANCISCO	Sept. 7
19	Green Bay	28	Chicago	Sept. 14
14	PHILADELPHIA	26	BUFFALO	Sept. 21
30	San Francisco	21	Miami	Sept. 28
24	N.Y. GIANTS	14	ST. LOUIS	Oct. 5
17	LOS ANGELES	35	Detroit	Oct. 12
42	Tampa Bay	14	ATLANTA	Oct. 19
17	DETROIT	7	Washington	Oct. 26
14	Washington	10	Los Angeles	Nov. 2
3	Denver	10	PHILADELPHIA	Nov. 9
31	SAN FRANCISCO	20	Atlanta	Nov. 16
24	Seattle	38	LOS ANGELES (night, TV)	Nov. 24
37	Atlanta	6	MINNESOTA	Nov. 30
35	OAKLAND	42	San Francisco	Dec. 7
0	SAN DIEGO	35	N.Y. Jets	Dec. 14
29	Los Angeles	14	NEW ENGLAND	Dec. 21
370		360		

Head Coach Dick Nolan has very definitely designated his main area of concern for the Saints as they
enter the new season. It's defense, and he spells that
with a capital D. "We improved last season in several
important areas," Nolan says, "including the running
game, pass protection, rushing the passer and the special
teams, but this year our top priority will be strengthen-
ing the defense."

In some respects, the Saints didn't do all that badly
with their 1979 defensive unit. They set club records for
sacking opposing quarterbacks with 46, and the most
pass interceptions with 26, but they dropped to 22nd
place among NFL clubs in overall defense—20th
against the pass and 23rd against the rush. These rank-

ings obviously must be improved if New Orleans is to become a true contender for the playoffs and beyond.

There's also a strange home-game paradox at work with the Saints. Unlike most other teams which prefer a home field advantage (in almost any sport), they seem to perform better on the road than at home. For the past two seasons, they've won four of seven games (in 1978) and five of eight (in 1979) in other places besides the Louisiana Superdome. This raises an interesting question: Do pro football players find one domed stadium no different from another, or, if you've played in one, have you played in them all?

Much of the hope for a really successful season, a big winning one for the Saints, rests squarely upon the broad shoulders of Archie Manning. Dick Nolan is positive about Manning's ability, saying, "Archie is in the same class with Roger Staubach and Ken Stabler ... He's as good as the best quarterbacks in the league."

That isn't difficult to believe, especially when reviewing Manning's achievements last season when he played virtually every down of all games, and personally called almost every play. After being selected the NFC's Pro Bowl quarterback for the second year in a row, he directed the NFCers to the victory. If the Saints rally around Manning, just a little luck might propel them into the playoffs where anything could happen.

The momentum is already there and needs only to be maintained. As a team, the Saints performed better than ever in several categories while setting new records, especially on offense. Their 370 points were the most ever for New Orleans as were the 46 touchdowns. The total offensive yardage of 5,627 was also a new club mark, along with the 2,476 yards rushing and the first downs total of 315. Likewise, the 5.7 yards gained per play was the highest ever for a Saints' team. On the other side of the ledger, they allowed only 17 quarterback sacks, that too being a new club record down from the 27 of 1969. Another year of similar improvement would almost certainly mean a move to higher ground in the standings.

The Saints have a Cinderella Story for 1979 and it concerns their punter, Rick Partridge who's from Tustin, a suburb of Los Angeles where his family members are season-ticket holders for the Rams games. His teammates call him "Peartree" or "Puntridge," and some people mistake him for Denver's rookie punter Luke Prestridge, but those in the know recognize him as the "come-through" New Orleans rookie who is currently the third best punter in the NFC.

After graduation from the University of Utah, Partridge was drafted No. 8 by Green Bay and thought perhaps he'd won a place on the Packer squad when he out-dueled David Beverly by six yards during the preseason games. But he was released, and during the second regular season week, Partridge was watching the Packers and Saints play a game on television. He also noted that the Saints were playing without a punter since Russell Erxleben, the No. 1 draft choice from Texas, had been injured just three days before. The Saints had even thrown wide receiver Wes Chandler into the breach as a punter, but it was a futile, stop-gap effort.

Partridge joined the Saints as a punter a week later and he made his debut against the San Francisco 49ers. It was both his first and almost his last game for he could do no better than average 31.3 yards on four punts. But Dick Nolan apparently has patience with punters and, despite the shaky start, Partridge went on to become a truly outstanding punter last season, winding it up with a 40.9 average. By Christmas time, the Saints were certain their best gift was—a Partridge.

The Saints made several moves in the 1980 college

draft, aimed at bolstering the sagging defense. Still, the offense came in for consideration, too. Calling him "a premier player you can't pass up," Nolan chose 6-6, 275-pound tackle Stan Brock of Colorado in the first round. The brother of Pete, New England's starting center, Brock will probably compete with newly acquired former Viking Steve Riley for the right tackle spot while Robert Woods moves to guard. To provide even more depth in the secondary, the Saints chose Dave Waymer of Notre Dame in the second round. The 6-1, 188-pounder will try to break into the lineup at safety.

OFFENSE

Quarterbacks	Ht.	Wt.	Age	Exp.	College
Burns, Ed	6-3	210	26	3	Nebraska
Manning, Archie	6-3	200	31	10	Mississippi
Scott, Bobby	6-1	197	31	9	Tennessee

The story of the New Orleans quarterbacks is, of course, the story of Archie Manning. At long last, he seems to have shaken the injury jinx that plagued him for so long. Last season his 3,169 passing yards represented a 60% completion average. He scrambled, or ran, for 186 yards and a 5.3 average—a good pace for a quarterback trying to convert on third down. Maybe, just maybe, some day Manning will be a Super Bowl quarterback.

Running Backs	Ht.	Wt.	Age	Exp.	College
Galbreath, Tony	6-1	230	26	5	Missouri
Holmes, Jack	5-11	210	27	3	Texas Southern
Muncie, Chuck	6-3	233	27	5	California
Strachan, Mike	6-0	200	27	6	Iowa State
Wilson, Wayne	6-3	208	23	2	Shepherd

Muncie and Galbreath provide the Saints with one of the best one-two rushing punches in the NFL. They complement one another much in the same manner as Wendell Tyler and Cullen Bryant of the Rams. Muncie rushed for 1,198 yards last season and Galbreath's 708 wasn't too far behind. Strachan was in there too, averaging 4.5 yards on 6 carries. With this kind of a rushing attack available, Nolan can devote his attention to other problems, with confidence.

Receivers	Ht.	Wt.	Age	Exp.	College
Chandler, Wes (W)	5-11	186	24	3	Florida
Childs, Henry (T)	6-2	220	29	7	Kansas State
Hardy, Larry (T)	6-3	230	24	3	Jackson State
Harris, Ike (W)	6-3	210	28	6	Iowa State
Mauti, Rich (W)	6-0	190	26	4	Penn State
Owens, Tinker (W)	5-11	170	26	4	Oklahoma
Williams, Brooks (T)	6-4	226	26	3	North Carolina

W=wide receiver   T=tight end

Chandler is the big man here. His 1979 season was a triumph, with 65 receptions for 1,069 yards and a 16.4 average. Included were six TDs, all in his second season as a pro. He started all 16 games and went to the Pro Bowl for his 17th. Childs led NFC tight ends with his 51 catches for 846 yards. Harris is an accountant off-season, and therefore accounted for 25 receptions for 395 yards and a 15.8 average on-season of '79. There's depth here as well, with such dependable receivers as Owens and running backs Galbreath and Muncie. Mauti is a special teams expert, returning kickoffs at a 22.2-yard clip.

Interior Linemen	Ht.	Wt.	Age	Exp.	College
Dobler, Conrad (G)	6-3	255	30	9	Wyoming
Hill, John (C)	6-2	246	30	9	Lehigh
Lafary, Dave (G-T)	6-7	280	25	4	Purdue
Pietrzak, Jim (C)	6-5	260	27	6	Eastern Michigan
Riley, Steve (T)	6-6	258	28	7	Southern Cal
Panfil, Doug (T)	6-4	250	23	1	Tulsa
Sturt, Fred (G)	6-4	255	29	6	Bowling Green
Taylor, J. T. (T)	6-4	265	24	3	Missouri
Woods, Robert (T)	6-4	259	30	8	Tennessee State
Zanders, Emanuel (G)	6-1	248	29	7	Jackson State
Brock, Stan (T)	6-6	272	22	R	Colorado

T=tackle   G=guard   C=center

This unit is one of Nolan's best. The opposing pass rush was kept at bay all season long in '79, and managed to filter through to sack the Saints' quarterback (almost always Archie Manning) only 17 times—a total low enough to rank second in the NFL. Compare that figure with the previous three-year totals of 51, 46 and 37 and it's easy to see how far the New Orleans offensive line has come in its improvement. Starters are Taylor and Woods at tackles, Zanders and Dobler at the guards and John Hill at center. This outfit has depth, too. Panfil was on injured reserve his rookie year.

Kickers	Ht.	Wt.	Age	Exp.	College
Partridge, Rick (P)	6-1	175	23	2	Utah
Yepremian, Garo (Pk)	5-8	175	36	13	(None)
Erxleben, Russell (Pk-P)	6-4	219	23	2	Texas

Pk=placekicker   P=punter

Erxleben is scheduled to return to action this season. The No. 1 draft choice was sidelined by injury after the first regular season game. Partridge and Yepremian, however, had first-rate seasons of their own and the Texas rookie, who can both kick and punt, may be hard-pressed to replace either one of them. Partridge averaged 40 yards on his punts and Yepremian showed signs of returning to his old placekicking form at Miami.

DEFENSE

Front Linemen	Ht.	Wt.	Age	Exp.	College
Bennett, Barry (T)	6-4	257	24	3	Concordia (Moorhead)
Campbell, Joe (E)	6-6	254	25	4	Maryland
Fultz, Mike (T)	6-5	278	26	4	Nebraska
Grooms, Elois (E)	6-4	250	27	6	Tennessee Tech
Moore, Derland (T)	6-4	253	29	8	Oklahoma
Price, Elex (T)	6-3	265	30	8	Alcorn State
Reese, Don (E)	6-6	250	29	6	Jackson State
Young, James (E)	6-2	260	30	4	Texas Southern

E=end   T=tackle

The Saints' offensive line managed to sack opposing quarterbacks 46 times last season for a club record, and keen observers see that as an indication of progress of sorts. Grooms and Reese return as the starting ends, both being highly regarded by the coaches. Campbell, the club's No. 1 draft choice in '77, is a good backup who has everything needed to be a starter himself. Bennett started 14 games at tackle in place of injured Elex Price. Moore led the unit in tackles with 58, to go with his five QB sacks. Tackle positions may be the center of a competitive battle before the season begins.

Linebackers	Ht.	Wt.	Age	Exp.	College
Bordelon, Ken (O)	6-4	226	26	4	Louisiana State
Federspiel, Joe (M)	6-2	230	30	9	Kentucky
Harris, Paul (O)	6-2	223	26	3	Alabama
Kovach, Jim (M)	6-2	225	24	2	Kentucky
Mathis, Reggie (O)	6-2	220	24	2	Oklahoma
Sytsma, Stan (M)	6-2	225	23	1	Minnesota
Merlo, Jim (O)	6-1	220	29	7	Stanford

O=outside   M=middle

A lot of questions must be answered here. Kovach is mounting a strong challenge to middle linebacker Joe Federspiel (and it's only a coincidence that both played their college ball at Kentucky). If Kovach does oust Federspiel from a starting role, it'll be quite an achievement, for Federspiel led the Saints with 155 tackles (114 solos) last season, despite playing with a bruised shoulder. Sytsma will also try to crash the middle LB picture, coming off injured reserve. Bordelon, a New Orleans native, became a starter early last season and returned one of his two pass interceptions for a 19-yard TD. Nolan anticipates plenty of competition for jobs with this group.

Defensive Backs	Ht.	Wt.	Age	Exp.	College
Brown, Ray (S)	6-2	202	31	10	West Texas State
Chapman, Clarence (CB)	5-10	185	27	5	Eastern Michigan
Felton, Etic (CB-S)	6-0	200	25	3	Texas Tech
Gray, David (CB)	6-0	190	25	3	E. Los Angeles JC
McGill, Ralph (S)	5-11	178	30	9	Tulsa
Myers, Tom (S)	6-0	180	30	9	Syracuse
Schwartz, Don (S)	6-1	191	24	3	Washington State
Waymer, Dave (CB)	6-1	186	22	R	Notre Dame
Jolly, Mike (S)	6-3½	177	22	R	Michigan

CB=cornerback   S=safety

Best indication of this unit's status is the fact that New Orleans chose two defensive backs in the second and third rounds of the recent college draft. Notre Dame cornerback Dave Waymer and Michigan safety Mike Jolly both stand a good chance of starting as rookies. Even though a club record 26 passes were intercepted in '79, and injuries did play a part in a defensive let-down, rookies saw quite a bit of playing time. Starting cornerbacks are Chapman and Felton but Felton may be shifted to a safety spot. Brown enters his 10th year at strong safety and has 37 career interceptions.

Note: A complete listing of New Orleans's 1980 college draft selections can be found on page 273.

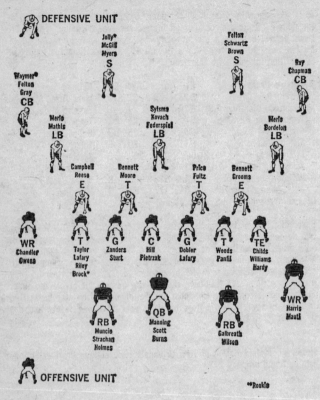

DEFENSIVE UNIT

Jolly
McGill
Myers
S

Felton
Schwartz
Brown
S

Waymer
Felton
Gray
CB

Ray
Chapman
CB

Merlo
Mathis
LB

Sytsma
Kovach
Federspiel
LB

Merlo
Bordelon
LB

Campbell
Reese
E

Bennett
Moore
T

Price
Fultz
T

Bennett
Grooms
E

WR
Chandler
Owens

T
Taylor
Lafary
Riley
Brock*

G
Zanders
Sturt

C
Hill
Pietrzak

G
Dobler
Lafary

T
Woods
Panfil

TE
Childs
Williams
Hardy

WR
Harris
Mauti

RB
Muncie
Strachan
Holmes

QB
Manning
Scott
Burns

RB
Galbreath
Wilson

OFFENSIVE UNIT

**Rookie

1979 SAINTS STATISTICS

	Saints	Opps.
Total Points Scored	370*	360
Total First Downs	315	334
Third Down Efficiency Percentage	40.0	43.9
Yards Rushing—First Downs	2476—160	2469—147
Passes Attempted—Completions	428—257	488—265
Yards Passing—First Downs	3151—135	3066—168
QB Sacked—Yards Lost	17—140	46—391
Interceptions By—Return Average	26—13.5	22—9.0
Punts—Average Yards	69—39.5	71—39.0
Punt Returns—Average Return	30—7.7	32—7.0
Kickoff Returns—Average Return	66—20.0	76—20.0
Fumbles—Ball Lost	24—14	33—16
Penalties—Yards	93—822	98—871

* Includes safety

STATISTICAL LEADERS

Scoring	TDs	Rush.	Pass.	Ret.	PATs	FGs	Total
Yepremian	0	0	0	0	39—40	12—16	75
Galbreath	10	9	1	0	1—2	2—3	67
Muncie	11	11	0	0	0	0	66
Chandler	6	0	6	0	0	0	36
Strachan	6	6	0	0	0	0	36
Childs	5	0	5	0	0	0	30
Harris	2	0	2	0	0	0	12
Manning	2	2	0	0	0	0	12
Erxleben	0	0	0	0	4—4	2—2	10

Rushing	Atts.	Yds.	Avg.	Longest	TDs
Muncie	238	1198	5.0	69 (TD)	11
Galbreath	189	708	3.7	27	9
Strachan	62	276	4.5	23	6
Manning	35	186	5.3	20	2
Holmes	17	68	4.0	14	0

Passing	Atts.	Com.	Yds.	Pct.	Int.	Longest	TDs
Manning	420	252	3169	60.0	20	85	15
Galbreath	3	2	70	66.7	1	48	0

Receiving	No.	Yds.	Avg.	Longest	TDs
Chandler	65	1069	16.4	85	6
Galbreath	58	484	8.3	38	1
Childs	51	846	16.6	51	5
Muncie	40	308	7.7	28	0
Harris	25	395	15.8	42	2

Interceptions	No.	Yds.	Avg.	Longest	TDs
Myers	7	127	18.1	52 (TD)	1
Hughes	4	62	15.5	40	0
Felton	4	53	13.3	53	0
Schwartz	2	31	15.5	22	0
Bordelon	2	24	12.0	19 (TD)	1
Chapman	2	12	6.0	12	0

Punting	No.	Yds.	Avg.	Longest	Inside 20	Blocked
Partridge	57	2330	40.9	61	16	0
Erxleben	4	148	37.0	40	1	0

Punt Returns	No.	FCs	Yds.	Avg.	Longest	TDs
Mauti	27	13	218	8.1	33	0
Chandler	3	3	13	4.3	8	0

Kickoff Returns	No.	Yds.	Avg.	Longest	TDs
Mauti	36	801	22.2	39	0
Wilson	11	230	20.9	31	0
Holmes	8	120	15.0	20	0
Chandler	7	136	19.4	37	0

ATLANTA FALCONS

Head Coach: Leeman Bennett
4th Year   **Record:** 22–24

1979 RECORD (6-10) (capital letters indicate home games)		1980 SCHEDULE (capital letters indicate home games)	
40	New Orleans	34	Minnesota	Sept. 7
14	Philadelphia	10	New England	Sept. 14
17	DENVER	20	MIAMI	Sept. 21
23	Detroit	24	San Francisco	Sept. 28
7	WASHINGTON	16	DETROIT	Oct. 5
25	GREEN BAY	7	N.Y. JETS	Oct. 12
19	Oakland	50	New Orleans	Oct. 19
15	San Francisco	20	LOS ANGELES	Oct. 26
28	SEATTLE	31	Buffalo	Nov. 2
17	TAMPA BAY	14	St. Louis	Nov. 9
3	N.Y. Giants	24	NEW ORLEANS	Nov. 19
14	Los Angeles	20	CHICAGO	Nov. 23
6	NEW ORLEANS	37	WASHINGTON	Nov. 30
28	San Diego	26	Philadelphia	Dec. 7
13	LOS ANGELES	34	SAN FRANCISCO	Dec. 14
31	SAN FRANCISCO	21	Los Angeles	Dec. 21
300		388		

In view of their 6-10 record of last season, it was no secret that the Atlanta Falcons intended to go on a shopping spree at the annual NFL college draft in New York. The list of sought-after items included tight end, the linebacker corps and in the defensive secondary. How did the shopping spree go? Only time and perhaps a full NFL schedule of games hold the answer, but the Falcons themselves feel their choices will strengthen the team at the crucial positions.

In all, fourteen players were selected and ten of those were for the three positions cited above. Among them was the No. 1 Atlanta choice, tight end Junior Miller of Nebraska, who the Falcon coaches believe might be the needed spark to provide Atlanta with an explosive offense. The 6-4, 235-pound Miller runs the forty yards in 4.6 seconds and seven of his 21 catches last season were good for touchdowns. "We were very fortunate to get Miller (No. 7 in first round)," says head coach Leeman Bennett, "because we feel he's the best pure tight end to come along since Russ Francis and Riley Odoms. He's got great hands, size and quickness with the speed to be a deep threat."

The Falcons made only four other offensive selections. I. M. Hipp, who set new rushing records at Nebraska while playing on the same team with Miller, was picked up in the fourth round. Down the line, wide receiver Mike Smith of Grambling was chosen in the seventh round, center Glenn Keller of Texas in the ninth, and fullback Quinn Jones of Tulsa in the twelfth. "Hipp could be a sleeper," says Bennett, meaning the Nebraska running back could do better than wide-awake people expect. "He had an injury-plagued senior year, but we liked his ability."

Nine defensive players were chosen, and the Falcons hope there is a safety in that number (which is almost the same as safety in numbers). Among defensive backs chosen who might become either safeties or cornerbacks in the Falcon secondary were Earl Jones of Norfolk State in the third round; Kenny Johnson of Mississippi State (fifth round); Mike Davis of Colorado (sixth); Walt Bellamy of Virginia Military (tenth); and Mike Babb of Oklahoma (eleventh).

The recent retirement of 12-year Falcon veteran Greg Brezina made the choice of linebacker especially important for the defensive unit's future. With Brezina's departure in mind, the Falcons chose Buddy Curry of North Carolina in the second round. "He reminds us very much of Fulton Kuykendall," says Bennett, referring to still another Atlanta linebacker, but Curry will have plenty of competition for a job even with Brezina's position wide open. No less than three other rookie linebackers will be on hand, including Jim Laughlin of Ohio State, Brad Vasser of Pacific University (Calif.) and Al Richardson of Georgia Tech.

Picking immediate starters from the draft crop is not an unusual occurrence with the Falcons. The past three drafts have given Atlanta such immediate starters as tackle Warren Bryant, guard R. C. Thieleman, defensive tackle Wilson Faumuina, safety Mike Kenn, tackle Tom Pridemore, defensive end Don Smith, and running back William Andrews. "I believe we'll have at least three potential starters among the rookies this year," predicts Bennett. "After all, no one was projecting William Andrews as a starter a year ago."

From a purely statistical point, the Falcons were a much better team last year than in 1978. For one thing, there was a 60-point difference in offensive scoring. Several reasons have been advanced for this improvement, including the continued progress of quarterback Steve Bartkowski and the coming of age of a young offensive line.

Perhaps the biggest difference was noted in the rushing attack. Here, a trio of rookies crashed their way into immediate stardom. One was Andrews, the Auburn fullback who surprised most observers by not only becoming a starter in his rookie season, but by also setting a new club rushing record with his 1,043 yards.

The offensive line is strong with the accent on youth, and experience may be all that's needed to make tackles such as Mike Kenn and Warren Bryant among the league's best. Defensively, the club still has problems after allowing the opposition to score nearly 400 points in '79. And if the defensive unit has an extremely weak area it has to be pass defense which was unimpressive all season long.

The schedule opens on the road with games at Minnesota and New England before the Miami Dolphins come to Ayalnat Stadium for the inaugural home contest. Then the Falcons fly off to San Francisco for another on-the-road contest, their fourth in three weeks. How they fare in those opening road games should provide a key to their 1980 future—and also make or break the immediate careers of some of those handpicked rookies.

OFFENSE

Quarterbacks	Ht.	Wt.	Age	Exp.	College
Bartkowski, Steve	6-4	213	28	6	California
Fortner, Larry	6-4	212	25	1	Miami (O.)
Jones, June	6-4	200	27	4	Portland State
Moroski, Mike	6-4	200	23	2	California-Davis

Bartkowski who like Archie Manning at New Orleans, had his trials and tribulations as a rookie trying to get on with his job, seems to be gaining lost ground as he enters his sixth NFL year. Last season he set new club records for attempts, completions, yards and TD passes. Jones continues as his principal backup, although Moroski got a chance to throw 15 times his rookie season and completed eight for a very respectable 53.3 average with no interceptions.

Running Backs	Ht.	Wt.	Age	Exp.	College
Andrews, William	6-0	200	25	2	Auburn
Bean, Bubba	5-11	195	26	4	Texas A&M
Cain, Lynn	6-1	205	25	2	Southern Cal
Mayberry, James	5-11	210	23	2	Colorado
Stanback, Haskel	6-0	210	28	7	Tennessee
Strong, Ray	5-9	184	24	3	Nevada-Las Vegas
Hipp, I. M.	5-10	190	22	R	Nebraska

Three rookie running backs gave the Falcons something to be proud of last season. Third round choice Andrews rushed for 1,023 yards, including three 100-yard games. Cain, a fourth round choice from Southern California, gained 295 yards for a noteworthy 4.7-yard average, before going out with a knee injury. Mayberry didn't play as much, but when he did his yard-per-rush average was a healthy 4.3 (193 yards on 45 carries). With regulars like Bean and Stanback still around and in good shape, and the addition of Nebraska ground-gainer I. M. Hipp, the Atlanta rushing game is headed outward again.

Receivers	Ht.	Wt.	Age	Exp.	College
Francis, Wallace (W)	5-11	190	29	8	Arkansas AM&N
Gilbert, Lewis (T)	6-4	225	24	2	Florida
Jackson, Alfred (W)	5-11	176	25	3	Texas
Jenkins, Alfred (W)	5-10	172	28	6	Morris Brown
Mikeska, Russ (T)	6-3	225	25	2	Texas A&M
Pearson, Dennis (W)	5-11	177	25	3	San Diego State
Ryckman, Billy (W)	5-11	172	25	4	Louisiana Tech
Wright, James (T)	6-3	240	24	2	Texas Christian
Miller, Junior (T)	6-4	236	22	R	Nebraska

W=wide receiver   T=tight end

Francis and Jenkins return from banner years as pass catchers. With Bartkowski tossing the ball his way, Francis set club records for most receptions 74, yards 1,014, and TD passes with eight. Jenkins came back after missing all of '78 with injury and caught 50 for 858 yards and a 17.2 average. Running back Williams Andrews received 39 passes on patterns out of the backfield. Bennett has good depth here, and first round draft choice Junior Miller adds to it.

Interior Linemen	Ht.	Wt.	Age	Exp.	College
Bryant, Warren (T)	6-6	270	25	4	Kentucky
Correal, Chuck (C)	6-3	247	24	2	Penn State
Howell, Pat (G)	6-5	253	23	2	Southern Cal
Kenn, Mike (T)	6-6	257	24	3	Michigan
McKinnely, Phil (T)	6-4	248	26	5	UCLA
Ryczek, Paul (C)	6-2	230	28	7	Virginia
Scott, Dave (G)	6-4	285	27	5	Kansas
Thielemann, R. C. (G)	6-4	247	25	4	Arkansas
Van Note, Jeff (C)	6-2	247	34	12	Kentucky

T=tackle   G=guard   C=center

Bennett says the main need in the offensive line is "more speed." Beyond that, the unit performed with the best last season, ranking fourth in the entire NFL with total yardage gained averaging 351.7 per game. The offense ranked third in both NFC rushing and passing, with the line permitting the opposing pass rush to upend the quarterback only 17 times. The starters are tackles Bryant and Kenn, guards Thielemann and Scott, and center Van Note. They're likely to remain that way.

Kickers	Ht.	Wt.	Age	Exp.	College
James, John (P)	6-3	200	31	9	Florida
Mazzetti, Tim (Pk)	6-1	175	24	3	Pennsylvania

Pk=placekicker   P=punter

James continues to satisfy the Atlanta coaches with his punting ability. He averaged 39.7 per boot last season, but his net average of 36.2 yards ranked him among the NFL's best in that category. Mazzetti, who became a hero in the 1978 playoffs, struggled through a hard season in '79, missing six extra point attempts and converting only 13 of his 25 field goal efforts.

DEFENSE

Front Linemen	Ht.	Wt.	Age	Exp.	College
Faumuina, Wilson (T)	6-5	275	26	4	San Jose State
Fields, Edgar (T)	6-2	255	26	4	Texas A&M
Lewis, Mike (T)	6-4	261	31	10	Arkansas AM&N
Merrow, Jeff (E)	6-4	230	27	6	West Virginia
Smith, Don (E)	6-5	248	23	2	Miami (Fla.)
Yeates, Jeff (E)	6-3	248	29	9	Boston College
Zele, Mike (T)	6-3	236	24	2	Kent State

E=end   T=tackle

The starters here are Yeates, Smith and Merrow at ends (Merrow was on injured reserve at season's end), Faumuina and Fields at tackles. Like other Falcon units, improvement is regarded as a necessity along the defensive line if Atlanta is to accomplish its long awaited turn-around. Only a few seasons ago, the rugged Falcon defense was the talk of the NFL. The pass rush wasn't up to its former strength and the opposing QB was sacked just 29 times, eight of those coming against Green Bay. Bennett has his work cut out for him here.

Linebackers	Ht.	Wt.	Age	Exp.	College
Cabral, Brian (O)	6-0	209	24	2	Colorado
Daykin, Tony (O)	6-1	215	25	4	Georgia Tech
Kuykendall, Fulton (O)	6-5	225	27	6	UCLA
McCartney, Ron (O)	6-1	220	26	4	Tennessee
McClain, Dewey (O)	6-3	236	26	5	East Central
Pennywell, Robert (M)	6-1	222	26	5	Grambling
Williams, Joel (M)	6-0	215	24	2	Wisconsin-La Crosse
Curry, Buddy (O)	6-2	224	22	R	North Carolina
Laughlin, Jim (O)	6-1½	218	22	R	Ohio State
Vasser, Brad (O)	6-2	220	22	R	Pacific (Calif.)

O=outside   M=middle

The linebackers didn't perform up to Bennett's expectations in '79. Main cogs like Kuykendall and Brezina were hampered by injuries, and Pennywell couldn't adjust to their inability to perform up to standard. Williams showed good form his rookie year and could make a contribution to solving the depth problem at linebacker where, Bennett says, improvement is a must.

Defensive Backs	Ht.	Wt.	Age	Exp.	College
Byas, Rick (CB)	5-9	180	30	7	Wayne State (Mich.)
Easterling, Ray (S)	6-0	192	31	9	Richmond
Glazebrook, Bob (S)	6-1	200	24	3	Fresno State
King, Jerome (CB)	5-10	173	25	1	Purdue
Lawrence, Rolland (CB)	5-10	179	29	8	Tabor
Moriarty, Tom (S)	6-0	185	27	4	Bowling Green
Pridemore, Tom (S-CB)	5-10	186	24	3	West Virginia
Reed, Frank (S)	5-11	193	26	5	Washington
Jones, Earl (CB)	6-0½	180	22	R	Norfolk State
Johnson, Kenny (S)	5-11	170	22	R	Mississippi State

CB=cornerback   S=safety

Pass defense was one reason the Falcons floundered in '79. After all, finishing 26th in the NFL's aerial defense statistics isn't much of a recommendation. Injuries, of course, took their toll. Reed, considered the best of these, went out with a knee injury in midseason. Lawrence, who does show consistency, led the secondary pass interceptors for the fifth consecutive year. What does the Atlanta secondary need most? Bennett says "speed and depth." Rookies Jones and Johnson will try to oblige.

Note: A complete listing of Atlanta's 1980 college draft selections can be found on page 267.

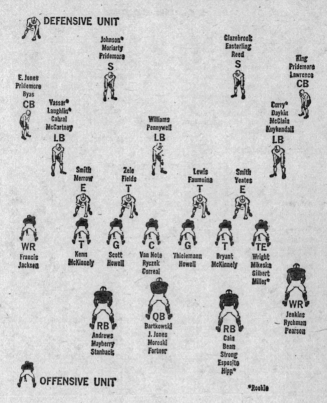

🏈 DEFENSIVE UNIT

Johnson*
Moriarty
Pridemore
S

Glazebrook
Easterling
Reed
S

King
Pridemore
Lawrence
CB

E. Jones
Pridemore
Byas
CB

Vassar*
Laughlin*
Cabral
McCartney
LB

Williams
Pennywell
LB

Curry*
Daykin
McClain
Kuykendall
LB

Smith
Merrow
E

Zele
Fields
T

Lewis
Faumuina
T

Smith
Yeates
E

WR
Francis
Jackson

Kenn
McKinnely
T

Scott
Howell
G

Van Note
Ryczek
Correal
C

Thielemann
Howell
G

Bryant
McKinnely
T

Wright
Mikeska
Gilbert
Miller*
TE

RB
Andrews
Mayberry
Stanback

QB
Bartkowski
J. Jones
Moroski
Fortner

RB
Cain
Bean
Strong
Esposito
Hipp*

WR
Jenkins
Rychman
Pearson

🏈 OFFENSIVE UNIT

*Rookie

1979 FALCONS STATISTICS

	Falcons	Opps.
Total Points Scored	300*	388
Total First Downs	303	311
Third Down Efficiency Percentage	37.1	43.1
Yards Rushing—First Downs	2200—125	2159—109
Passes Attempted—Completions	478—250	484—268
Yards Passing—First Downs	2726—151	3596—177
QB Sacked—Yards Lost	54—398	29—203
Interceptions By—Return Average	15—14.9	23—15.7
Punts—Average Yards	84—39.2	73—35.9
Punt Returns—Average Return	26—7.2	41—6.3
Kickoff Returns—Average Return	73—18.8	62—21.5
Fumbles—Ball Lost	32—20	33—21
Penalties—Yards	102—943	98—823

* Includes safety

STATISTICAL LEADERS

Scoring	TDs	Rush.	Pass.	Ret.	PATs	FGs	Total
Mazzetti	0	0	0	0	31—37	13—25	70
Francis	8	0	8	0	0	0	48
Andrews	5	3	2	0	0	0	30
Stanback	5	5	0	0	0	0	30
Cain	4	2	2	0	0	0	24
Jenkins	3	0	3	0	0	0	18
Bartkowski	2	2	0	0	0	0	12
Mayberry	2	1	0	1	0	0	12
Ryckman	2	0	2	0	0	0	12

Rushing	Atts.	Yds.	Avg.	Longest	TDs
Andrews	239	1023	4.3	23	3
Bean	88	393	4.5	60 (TD)	1
Cain	63	295	4.7	35 (TD)	2
Stanback	36	202	5.6	55 (TD)	5
Mayberry	45	193	4.3	21	1

Passing	Atts.	Com.	Yds.	Pct.	Int.	Longest	TDs
Bartkowski	379	203	2502	53.6	20	57	17
Jones	83	38	505	45.8	3	49	2
Moroski	15	8	97	53.3	0	23	0

Receiving	No.	Yds.	Avg.	Longest	TDs
Francis	74	1013	13.7	42	8
Jenkins	50	858	17.2	57	3
Andrews	39	309	7.9	34	2
Mitchell	16	118	7.4	14	2
Cain	15	181	12.1	28	2
Stanback	13	89	6.8	22	0
Bean	12	137	11.4	49	0

Interceptions	No.	Yds.	Avg.	Longest	TDs
Lawrence	6	120	20.0	38	0
Easterling	2	0	—	—	0
Reed	2	0	—	—	0
Pridemore	2	20	10.0	20	0

Punting	No.	Yds.	Avg.	Longest	Inside 20	Blocked
James	83	3296	39.7	62	12	1

Punt Returns	No.	FCs	Yds.	Avg.	Longest	TDs
Pearson	12	10	115	9.6	60	0
Ryckman	12	5	72	6.0	15	0

Kickoff Returns	No.	Yds.	Avg.	Longest	TDs
Pearson	30	577	19.2	29	0
Strong	15	343	22.9	33	0
Pridemore	9	111	12.3	21	0
Cain	7	149	21.3	33	0
Stanback	6	106	17.7	24	0

SAN FRANCISCO 49ers

Head Coach: Bill Walsh

2nd Year   **Record:** 2–14

1979 RECORD (2-14) (capital letters indicate home games)			1980 SCHEDULE (capital letters indicate home games)	
22	Minnesota	28	New Orleans	Sept. 7
13	DALLAS	21	ST. LOUIS	Sept. 14
24	Los Angeles	27	N.Y. Jets	Sept. 21
21	NEW ORLEANS	30	ATLANTA	Sept. 28
9	San Diego	31	Los Angeles	Oct. 5
24	SEATTLE	35	Dallas	Oct. 12
16	N.Y. Giants	32	LOS ANGELES	Oct. 19
20	ATLANTA	15	TAMPA BAY	Oct. 26
27	CHICAGO	28	Detroit	Nov. 2
10	Oakland	23	Green Bay at Milwaukee	Nov. 9
20	New Orleans	31	Miami	Nov. 16
28	DENVER	38	N.Y. GIANTS	Nov. 23
20	LOS ANGELES	26	NEW ENGLAND	Nov. 30
10	St. Louis	13	NEW ORLEANS	Dec. 7
23	TAMPA BAY	7	Atlanta	Dec. 14
21	Atlanta	31	BUFFALO	Dec. 21
308		**416**		

At first glance, the San Francisco two-year record
was like one of those movies in which the action runs
backwards—interesting, but running backwards in a
pattern seemingly all its own. The 49ers became the
first NFL team to lose 14 games in a single season not
once, but twice, and in consecutive seasons too. The
record book shows 14-game losers on three other occasions, one of which was also last season—the Detroit
Lions who went 2-14. The others were Tampa Bay
0-14 in 1976, and the Frankford Yellowjackets of
1930 who came in with a 4-14 record.

Still, identifications of this kind don't bother 49ers
coach Bill Walsh who begins his second year at the

helm in San Francisco. He joined the 49ers after a highly successful college coaching career at Stanford and as an assistant specializing in the passing game with the San Diego Chargers and Cincinnati Bengals. In fact, his work with Dan Fouts at San Diego is often listed as one of Walsh's prime achievements.

The losing record aside, the 49ers did rise from the 13th ranked NFC offensive team in 1978 to third in 1979, Walsh's first year at the controls as both head coach and general manager. The 1979 ranking includes first in NFC passing and sixth in total offense among all 28 NFL clubs.

Walsh's specialty of training quarterbacks found fertile ground in San Francisco. Within the time span of his first season as coach, he took Steve DeBerg, a virtually unheard of quarterback from San Jose State, and developed him into an effective passer and signal caller. In his second pro season of 1978, after not playing for even one down in his first, DeBerg connected for 45% of his passes. In his first year under Walsh, DeBerg not only completed 60% of his passes, he also broke Fran Tarkenton's NFL records for passes attempted and completed in one season. DeBerg was 347 for 578 attempts, Tarkenton's marks were 345 for 572. That should convince anyone who doubts Walsh's ability to develop a good passer.

The 49ers caught more than 50 passes while ten other receivers achieved double digits in receptions as Walsh opened up a wide variety of passing plays. Also used in the aerial attack were tight ends, running backs and any other legally eligible pass receivers a team can field. As such, the 49ers fell into step with an NFL trend that resulted in a veritable explosion of passing plays last season.

They also exhibited potential strengths in other areas. They achieved 200 first downs passing, the most by any NFL team, and the offensive line was kind to quarterbacks Steve DeBerg and Joe Montana, allowing opposing sackers to seep through just 17 times. But defensively it was thumbs down, San Francisco being ranked 20th among the NFL's 28 clubs after allowing a total game average of 337.1 yards rushing and passing.

The 49ers entered the 1980 draft with eight choices, but when all the smoke cleared away at the New York Sheraton Hotel last April, Walsh had picked up eleven players with the help of some strategic trades. First, San Francisco's second pick in the first round was traded to the New York Jets in exchange for that club's two first round picks, Nos. 13 and 20. The Jets chose wide receiver Johnny (Lam) Jones of Texas with their newly acquired high choice. Then, the 49ers proceeded to choose running back Earl Cooper of Rice and defensive tackle Jim Stuckey of Clemson with the choices received from the Jets.

Cooper, who stands 6-2 and weighs 227, will be a running-mate for Paul Hofer in the 49ers' offensive backfield. Hofer rushed for 615 yards last season and caught passes for 662 more. "Cooper will be one of the fastest runners in pro football when he's at full stride," says Walsh, who seems to usually know what he's talking about.

The other first round selection, defensive tackle Jim Stuckey, is 6-4, weighs 250 and started every game with Clemson's good teams since the eighth contest of his freshman year. Linebacker Keena Turner, chosen in the second round, played his college football at the same high school in Chicago that Hall of Famer Dick Butkus attended. And, of course, the 49ers coaches hope that some of that high school rubs off on Turner who will get a try at weakside linebacker. In the third round, San Francisco discovered Jim Miller, a barefooted punter from Mississippi who made All-America with a 43.4-yard average.

But the most important acquisition of all may have come to San Francisco not from the draft, but through a trade with the Dallas Cowboys. Linebacker Thomas (Hollywood) Henderson, dismissed by coach Tom Landry, was exchanged for a 1981 draft choice. The five-year veteran was himself a No. 1 draft pick. Walsh is happy about it: "We feel we're getting a top player—a man we expect to add experience and leadership. He comes to us from an organization that taught him how to play the game right, and that's sure to benefit us."

How does Walsh view the NFC West in the coming campaign. For openers, he picks the Rams to again win the division title with "their talent and depth," as he put it. He also feels the New Orleans Saints have offensive talent unrivaled by any other NFC team, but he adds: "I think they may be inconsistent and lose some games they shouldn't." As for the Falcons, he believes "they could move ahead of somebody, but I don't think they're ready to win it." And what about the 49ers? "We could be a factor," he says, "but it all depends on how quickly the new people from the draft come through and help us."

OFFENSE

Quarterbacks	Ht.	Wt.	Age	Exp.	College
DeBerg, Steve	6-2	205	26	4	San Jose State
Huff, Gary	6-1	200	29	7	Florida State
Montana, Joe	6-2	200	24	2	Notre Dame

As Walsh puts it: "Steve DeBerg is probably the most improved quarterback in the NFL." Impressive, too, is the fact that San Francisco led the NFC in passing achievement, averaging 227.6 yards per game. DeBerg was also hardworking, and even broke Fran Tarkenton's NFL record for most passes attempted in one season. DeBerg threw 578 times to Tarkenton's 572 (in 1978). His backup, Joe Montana of Notre Dame fame, can't be dismissed, however, and could challenge. Montana threw 23 times last season and completed 13 for a fine 56.5 completion percentage.

Running Backs	Ht.	Wt.	Age	Exp.	College
Elliott, Lenvil	6-0	210	29	8	Northeast Missouri
Ferrell, Bobby	6-0	213	28	5	UCLA
Francis, Phil	6-1	215	23	2	Stanford
Hofer, Paul	6-0	195	28	5	Mississippi
Jackson, Wilbur	6-2	219	29	6	Alabama
Aldridge, Jerry	6-2	220	24	1	Angelo State
Cooper, Earl	6-2	227	22	R	Rice

The most obvious name on the roster is the one that isn't there—O. J. Simpson, now retired and whose next step in the NFL will undoubtedly be the Pro Football Hall of Fame. In his final season, Orange Juice was the club's second leading ground gainer with 460 yards. Hofer led the overland attack with 615 yards on 123 carries for an impressive 5.0-yard average. Minor injuries kept Hofer from full-time on the field last season, and he might well be a thousand-yarder when healthy. Aldridge is strong and speedy but remains an unknown after undergoing knee surgery. Walsh regards Jackson as one of the best blocking and receiving backs in football. Cooper was one of San Francisco's two first round draft choices, but will he literally fumble his chances?

Receivers	Ht.	Wt.	Age	Exp.	College
Young, Charlie (T)	6-4	240	29	8	Southern Cal
Anderson, Terry (W)	5-9	182	25	3	Bethune-Cookman
Bruer, Bob (T)	6-5	235	27	2	Mankato State
Clark, Dwight (W)	6-3	205	23	2	Clemson
Harrison, Ken (W)	6-0	170	27	4	Southern Methodist
MacAfee, Ken (T)	6-4	245	24	3	Notre Dame
Owens, James (W)	5-11	188	25	2	UCLA
Ramson, Eason (T)	6-2	234	24	3	Washington State
Robinson, Jimmy (W)	5-9	170	27	5	Georgia Tech
Shumann, Mike (W)	6-0	175	25	3	Florida State
Solomon, Freddie (W)	5-11	188	27	6	Tampa

W=wide receiver   T=tight end

The personnel is obviously very deep here. Among the regulars, Solomon had his best NFL season with 57 receptions even though injury prevented him from continuing after 11 weeks of play. Owens will play at wide receiver, but may also see action as a defensive back. Charlie Young, formerly of Philadelphia and the Super Bowl Rams, comes up the coast from L-A in a draft choice trade and could become the starting tight end. But MacAfee, who started at TE last season, will have to be dislodged. The former Notre Dame All-America blocks well, and catches key passes, which should help him in the competition.

Interior Linemen	Ht.	Wt.	Age	Exp.	College
Ayers, John (G)	6-5	247	27	4	West Texas State
Barrett, Jean (T)	6-6	250	29	8	Tulsa
Cross, Randy (G)	6-3	255	26	5	UCLA
Downing, Walt (C-G)	6-3	254	24	3	Michigan
Fahnhorst, Keith (T)	6-6	263	28	7	Minnesota
Hughes, Ernie (G)	6-3	250	25	2	Notre Dame
Knutson, Steve (G-T)	6-3	254	29	5	Southern Cal
Quillan, Fred (C)	6-5	254	24	3	Oregon
Singleton, Ron (T)	6-7	267	28	4	Grambling

T=tackle   G=guard   C=center

Singleton and Ayers, both now entering their fourth NFL years, gave DeBerg excellent pass protection, with opposing pass rushers getting through for only 17 sacks. Quillan performed well in his first year as starting center, while Cross and Fahnhorst are developing Pro Bowl-type abilities. Best recommendation for the 49er offensive line is the high rating the San Francisco offense enjoyed at the close of 1979. The offensive unit stood third in total NFC yardage, and at the very top of the NFC's passing performances. The rushing offense wasn't all that good, reflecting the mere 460 yards on 120 carries gained by O. J. Simpson in his swan song with the NFL.

Kickers	Ht.	Wt.	Age	Exp.	College
Wersching, Ray (Pk)	5-11	210	30	8	California
Miller, Jim (P)	5-11	180	22	R	Mississippi

Pk=placekicker   P=punter

Rookie Miller is a third round choice from Mississippi who consistently (in college) punted for 40 yards and has the distinction of never having one of his punts blocked. Wersching made everybody happy, on the 49er bench that is, with his 32-for-35 PATs and 20 field goals out of 24 attempts. He was especially accurate at the medium distances.

DEFENSE

Front Linemen	Ht.	Wt.	Age	Exp.	College
Board, Dwaine (E)	6-5	245	24	2	North Carolina A&T
Hardman, Cedrick (E)	6-4	244	32	11	North Texas State
Reese, Archie (E)	6-3	262	24	3	Clemson

2

Vaughan, Ruben (T)	6-2	264	24	2	Colorado
Vincent, Ted (T)	6-4	265	24	3	Wichita State
Webb, Jimmy (T)	6-5	245	28	6	Mississippi State
Fry, Willie (T)	6-3½	245	25	2	Notre Dame
Stuckey, Jim (T)	6-4	244	22	R	Clemson
Dion, Terry (E)	6-4½	250	22	R	Oregon
Times, Kenneth (T)	6-3	245	22	R	Southern University

E=end   T=tackle

There are plans afoot to switch Reese from end to tackle, and Webb from tackle to end. Reese's size may render him more effective on the inside. Webb can play either tackle or end and may finally be designated a backup. Vincent, a former Bengal, is slated for the other tackle post and there's hope that 11-year-man Cedrick Hardman will return to his great form of other seasons. Injuries kept him at a disadvantage last season, and finally landed him on the reserve list. Three draft choices of defensive linemen in the first five rounds testify to the importance Walsh gives the rebuilding program. Stuckey was one of two 49er first round picks.

Linebackers	Ht.	Wt.	Age	Exp.	College
Bunz, Dan (M)	6-4	230	25	3	Long Beach State
Ceresino, Gordy (M)	6-0	224	23	2	Stanford
Bradley, Ed (O)	6-1	225	30	8	Wake Forest
Harper, Willie (O)	6-2	215	30	7	Nebraska
Henderson, Thomas (O)	6-2	220	27	6	Langston
Hilton, Scott (O)	6-4	230	26	2	(None)
Martin, Bob (O)	6-1	214	27	5	Nebraska
McIntyre, Jeff (O)	6-3	232	25	2	Arizona State
Morton, Dave (M)	6-2	224	25	2	UCLA
Nelson, Bob (O)	6-4	230	27	4	Nebraska
Seaborn, Thomas (O)	6-3	215	23	2	Michigan
Stewart, Steve (O)	6-3	215	24	3	Minnesota
Turner, Keena (O)	6-1	215	22	R	Purdue
Puki, Craig (O)	6-1	219	22	R	Tennessee
Hodge, David (O)	6-3	216	22	R	Houston

O=outside   M=middle

There's a lot of weeding out to be done here. Three rookies have joined 11 linebackers who were already on the roster. How many linebackers will Walsh need? A lot depends on whether he uses the 3-4 or the 4-3 defensive lineup. At the end of '79, it was the conventional 4-3 alignment with Harper, Bunz and Hilton the starters. Turner, Puki and Hodge all have good college records behind them, playing for such nationally ranked teams as Purdue, Tennessee and Houston. If there's strength in numbers, Walsh has it at linebacker. And if there's strength in self-assurance, Walsh as a wealth of that, too, with the arrival of Thomas (Hollywood) Henderson by trade with Dallas.

Defensive Backs	Ht.	Wt.	Age	Exp.	College
Cornelius, Charles (CB)	5-9	178	28	4	Bethune-Cookman
Gray, Tim (S)	6-1	200	28	6	Texas A&M
Hicks, Dwight (S)	6-1	189	24	2	Michigan
Johnson, Charles (CB)	5-10	180	24	2	Grambling
Johnson, Eric (S)	6-1	192	28	4	Washington State
Morgan, Melvin (CB)	6-0	186	27	5	Mississippi Valley
Perry, Scott (S)	6-0	185	26	4	Williams
Rhodes, Ray (CB)	5-11	185	30	7	Tulsa
Williams, Gerard (CB)	6-1	184	28	4	Langston
Churchman, Ricky (S)	6-0	204	22	R	Texas

CB=cornerback   S=safety

Morgan can play any position in the secondary, and will return to left cornerback. He is coming off surgery for an injured shoulder. Cornelius played 14 games as starting cornerback and performed well enough to rate a first-line backup post for 1980, at the very least. Hardworking Gerard Williams is the starter at right corner. Hicks and Gray are the safeties, with Hicks being the club interception leader last season (5). Fourth round choice Ricky Churchman comes up from Texas with good credentials at safety.

Note: A complete listing of San Francisco's 1980 college draft selections can be found on page 277.

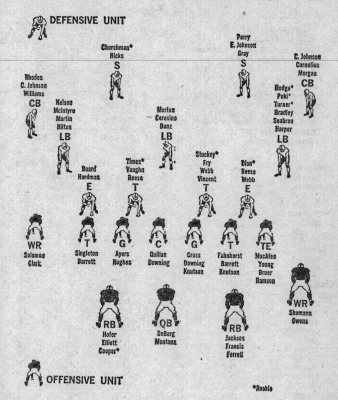

DEFENSIVE UNIT

Perry
E. Johnson
Gray
S

Churchman*
Hicks
S

C. Johnson
Cornelius
Morgan
CB

Rhodes
C. Johnson
Williams
CB

Nelson
McIntyre
Martin
Hilton
LB

Morton
Ceresino
Bunz
LB

Hodge*
Puki*
Turner*
Bradley
Seabron
Harper
LB

Board
Hardman
E

Times*
Vaughn
Reese
T

Stuckey*
Fry
Webb
Vincent
T

Dion*
Reese
Webb
E

WR
Solomon
Clark

T
Singleton
Barrett

G
Ayers
Hughes

C
Quillan
Downing

G
Cross
Downing
Knutson

T
Fahnhorst
Barrett
Knutson

TE
MacAfee
Young
Bruer
Ramson

WR
Shumann
Owens

RB
Hofer
Elliott
Cooper*

QB
DeBerg
Montana

RB
Jackson
Francis
Ferrell

OFFENSIVE UNIT

*Rookie

1979 49ers STATISTICS

	49ers	Opps.
Total Points Scored	308	416
Total First Downs	336	326
Third Down Efficiency Percentage	45.3	47.7
Yards Rushing—First Downs	1932—120	2213—136
Passes Attempted—Completions	602—361	441—262
Yards Passing—First Downs	3641—200	3180—160
QB Sacked—Yards Lost	17—119	29—227
Interceptions By—Return Average	15—11.4	21—16.9
Punts—Average Yards	72—36.5	73—38.6
Punt Returns—Average Return	44—7.1	37—7.1
Kickoff Returns—Average Return	75—20.5	68—20.1
Fumbles—Ball Lost	37—18	33—19
Penalties—Yards	95—853	119—858

STATISTICAL LEADERS

Scoring	TDs	Rush.	Pass.	Ret.	PATs	FGs	Total
Wersching	0	0	0	0	32—35	20—24	92
Hofer	9	7	2	0	0	0	54
Solomon	8	1	7	0	0	0	48
MacAfee	4	0	4	0	0	0	24
Shumann	4	0	4	0	0	0	24
Elliott	3	3	0	0	0	0	18
Simpson	3	3	0	0	0	0	18

Rushing	Atts.	Yds.	Avg.	Longest	TDs
Hofer	123	615	5.0	47	7
Simpson	120	460	3.8	22	3
Jackson	114	375	3.3	16	2
Elliott	33	135	4.1	12	3
Francis	31	118	3.8	16	1
DeBerg	17	10	0.6	8	0

Passing	Atts.	Com.	Yds.	Pct.	Int.	Longest	TDs
DeBerg	578	347	3652	60.0	21	50	17
Montana	23	13	96	56.5	0	18	1

Receiving	No.	Yds.	Avg.	Longest	TDs
Hofer	58	662	11.4	44	2
Solomon	57	807	14.2	44 (TD)	7
Jackson	53	422	8.0	34	0
Shumann	39	452	11.6	39	4
Francis	32	198	6.2	19	0
Bruer	26	254	9.8	19	1
MacAfee	24	266	11.1	50	4
Elliott	23	197	8.6	30	0
Clark	18	232	12.9	30	0
Owens	10	121	12.1	17	0

Interceptions	No.	Yds.	Avg.	Longest	TDs
Hicks	5	57	11.4	29	0
Williams	4	38	9.5	22	0
Cornelius	3	54	18.0	54	0

Punting	No.	Yds.	Avg.	Longest	Inside 20	Blocked
Melville	71	2626	37.0	53	15	0

Punt Returns	No.	FCs	Yds.	Avg.	Longest	TDs
Solomon	23	2	142	6.2	14	0
Hicks	13	3	120	9.2	33	0
Dungy	8	3	52	6.5	11	0

Kickoff Returns	No.	Yds.	Avg.	Longest	TDs
Owens	41	1002	24.4	85 (TD)	1
Elliott	9	170	18.9	33	0
Hofer	8	124	15.5	23	0
Francis	7	102	14.6	23	0
Ferrell	6	78	13.0	18	0

THE 1980 NFL COLLEGE DRAFT

Team-by-team, round-by-round
lists of each NFL club's 1980
college draft choices

NATIONAL FOOTBALL LEAGUE
45th ANNUAL SELECTION MEETING

New York Sheraton Hotel, New York City, April 29-30, 1980

NOTE: The number to the left of each player's name designates round in which he was chosen; number in the fourth column designates the order of selection among 333 players drafted. It will also be noted that some clubs made no choices in certain rounds, and that some had two or more choices in certain rounds. This is because draft choices are often traded before selection begins—usually in exchange for experienced NFL players of some merit in their positions.

ATLANTA FALCONS

1	MILLER, Junior	TE	7	Nebraska
2	CURRY, Buddy	LB	36	North Carolina
3	JONES, Earl	DB	63	Norfolk State
4	LAUGHLIN, Jim	LB	91	Ohio State
4	HIPP, I. M.	RB	104	Nebraska
5	VASSAR, Brad	LB	117	Pacific
5	JOHNSON, Kenny	DB	137	Mississippi State
6	DAVIS, Mike	DB	146	Colorado
7	SMITH, Mike	WR	172	Grambling
8	RICHARDSON, Al	LB	201	Georgia Tech
9	KELLER, Glen	C	228	West Texas State
10	BELLAMY, Walt	DB	257	Virginia Military
11	BABB, Mike	DB	284	Oklahoma
12	JONES, Quinn	RB	313	Tulsa

BALTIMORE COLTS

1	DICKEY, Curtis	RB	5	Texas A&M
1	HATCHETT, Derrick	DB	24	Texas
2	DONALDSON, Ray	C	32	Georgia
2	FOLEY, Tim	T	51	Notre Dame
4	BUTLER, Raymond	WR	88	Southern California
6	FOOTE, Chris	C	144	Southern California
7	ROBERTS, Wesley	DE	170	Texas Christian
8	WALTER, Ken	T	195	Texas Tech
9	BRIGHT, Mark	RB	227	Temple
10	STEWART, Larry	T	254	Maryland
11	WHITLEY, Eddy	TE	280	Kansas State
12	BIELSKI, Randy	K	311	Towson State
12	SIMS, Marvin	RB	324	Clemson

BUFFALO BILLS

1	RITCHER, Jim	C	16	North Carolina State
2	CRIBBS, Joe	RB	29	Auburn
2	BRADLEY, Gene	RB	37	Arkansas State
3	BRAMMER, Mark	TE	67	Michigan State
3	SCHMEDING, John	G	71	Boston College
4	PARKER, Ervin	LB	93	South Carolina State
5	PYBURN, Jeff	DB	119	Georgia
5	LEE, Keith	DB	129	Colorado State
8	KRUEGER, Todd	QB	202	Northern Michigan
9	DAVIS, Kent	DB	231	S.E. Missouri
10	CATER, Greg	P	259	Tenn.-Chattanooga
11	GORDON, Joe	DT	286	Grambling
12	LAPHAM, Roger	TE	316	Maine

CHICAGO BEARS

1	WILSON, Otis	LB	19	Louisville
2	SUHEY, Matt	RB	46	Penn State
4	THOMPSON, Arland	G	103	Baylor
5	TABOR, Paul	C	130	Oklahoma
6	GUESS, Mike	DB	156	Ohio State
7	TOLBERT, Emanuel	WR	183	Southern Methodist
8	CLARK, Randy	G	215	Northern Illinois
9	SCHONERT, Turk	QB	242	Stanford
10	STEPHENS, Willie	DB	269	Texas Tech
11	JUDGE, Chris	DB	296	Texas Christian
12	FISHER, Robert	TE	323	Southern Methodist

CINCINNATI BENGALS

1	MUNOZ, Anthony	T	3	Southern California
2	CRISWELL, Kirby	LB	31	Kansas
3	HORN, Rod	DT	59	Nebraska
4	GLASS, Bill	G	86	Baylor
5	HICKS, Bryan	DB	113	McNeese State
6	HEATH, Jo Jo	DB	141	Pittsburgh
6	MELONTREE, Andrew	LB	159	Baylor
7	SIMPKINS, Ron	LB	167	Michigan
7	JOHNSON, Gary Don	DT	168	Baylor
8	LYLES, Mark	RB	196	Florida State
9	BRIGHT, Greg	DB	224	Morehead State
10	VITIELLO, Sandro	K	252	Massachusetts
11	ALEXIS, Alton	WR	281	Tulane
12	WRIGHT, Mike	QB	308	Vanderbilt

CLEVELAND BROWNS

1	WHITE, Charles	RB	27	Southern California
2	CROSBY, Cleveland	DE	54	Arizona
3	ODOM, Cliff	LB	72	Texas Arlington
4	CREWS, Ron	DE	99	Nevada-Las Vegas
4	McDONALD, Paul	QB	109	Southern California
5	FRANKS, Elvis	DE	116	Morgan State
8	COPELAND, Jeff	LB	209	Texas Tech
9	DEWALT, Roy	RB	236	Texas Arlington
10	FIDEL, Kevin	C	263	San Diego State
11	SALES, Roland	RB	294	Arkansas
12	JACKSON, Marcus	DT	321	Purdue

DALLAS COWBOYS

3	ROE, Bill	LB	78	Colorado
3	JONES, James	RB	80	Mississippi State
4	PETERSEN, Kurt	DE	105	Missouri
5	HOGEBOOM, Gary	QB	133	Central Michigan
6	NEWSOME, Tim	RB	162	Winston-Salem
7	BROWN, Lester	RB	189	Clemson
8	SAVAGE, Larry	LB	216	Michigan State
9	FLOWERS, Jackie	WR	246	Florida State
10	TEAGUE, Matthew	DE	273	Prairie View
11	PADJEN, Gary	LB	300	Arizona State
12	WELLS, Norm	DE	330	Northwestern

DENVER BRONCOS

2	JONES, Rulon	DE	42	Utah State
3	CARTER, Larry	DB	74	Kentucky
4	PARROS, Rick	RB	107	Utah State
5	HARDEN, Mike	DB	131	Michigan
5	SHORT, Laval	DT	136	Colorado
6	BISHOP, Keith	G	157	Baylor
7	HAVEKOST, John	G	184	Nebraska
8	COLEMAN, Don	WR	197	Oregon
9	BRACELIN, Greg	LB	243	California
10	SEAY, Virgil	WR	270	Troy State
11	FARRIS, Phil	WR	297	North Carolina

DETROIT LIONS

1	SIMS, Billy	RB	1	Oklahoma
3	TURNURE, Tom	C	57	Washington
3	FRIEDE, Mike	WR	62	Indiana
4	HIPPLE, Eric	QB	85	Utah State
5	STREETER, Mark	DB	111	Arizona
5	GINN, Tom	G	120	Arkansas
6	DIETERICH, Chris	T	140	North Carolina State
7	MURRAY, Ed	K	166	Tulane
9	JETT, DeWayne	WR	222	Hawaii
9	TUINEI, Tom	DT	223	Hawaii
10	HENDERSON, Henry (Donnie)	DB	251	Utah State
11	SMITH, Wayne	DB	278	Purdue
12	WILLIAMS, Ray	KR	307	Washington State

GREEN BAY PACKERS

1	CLARK, Bruce	DE	4	Penn State
1	CUMBY, George	LB	26	Oklahoma
2	LEE, Mark	DB	34	Washington
3	KITSON, Syd	G	61	Wake Forest
4	NIXON, Fred	WR	87	Oklahoma
6	SWANKE, Karl	G	143	Boston College
7	AYDELETTE, Buddy	T	169	Alabama
8	SMITH, Tim	DB	199	Oregon State
9	SAALFELD, Kelly	C	226	Nebraska
10	WHITE, Jafus	DB	253	Texas A&I
11	SKILES, Ricky	LB	283	Louisville
12	STEWART, James	DB	310	Memphis State

HOUSTON OILERS

2	FIELDS, Angelo	T	38	Michigan State
2	SKAUGSTAD, Daryle	DT	52	California
3	SMITH, Tim	WR-P	79	Nebraska
4	COMBS, Chris	TE	106	New Mexico
5	CORKER, John	LB	134	Oklahoma State
7	BRADSHAW, Craig	QB	182	Utah State
8	BAILEY, Harold	RB	217	Oklahoma State
9	HARRIS, Ed	RB	244	Bishop
11	PRESTON, Eddie	WR	301	Western Kentucky
12	PITTS, Wiley	WR	328	Temple

KANSAS CITY CHIEFS

1	BUDDE, Brad	G	11	Southern California
3	HADNOT, James	RB	66	Texas Tech
4	KLUG, Dave	LB	94	Concordia, Minn.
5	CARSON, Carlos	WR	114	Louisiana State
5	PENSICK, Dan	DT	115	Nebraska
6	GARCIA, Bubba	WR	147	Texas-El Paso
6	HEATER, Larry	RB	164	Arizona
8	STEPNEY, Sam	LB	203	Boston University
9	DONOVAN, Tom	WR	230	Penn State
10	MARTINOVICH, Rob	T	261	Notre Dame
11	MARKHAM, Dale	DT	287	North Dakota
12	BREWINGTON, Mike	LB	314	East Carolina

LOS ANGELES RAMS

1	JOHNSON, Johnnie	DB	17	Texas
2	PANKEY, Irv	T	50	Penn State
3	THOMAS, Jewerl	RB	58	San Jose State
3	IRVIN, Leroy	DB	70	Kansas
3	MURPHY, Phillip	DT	82	South Carolina State
6	GUMAN, Mike	RB	154	Penn State
7	COLLINS, Kirk	DB	176	Baylor
7	ELLIS, Gerry	RB	192	Missouri
8	PETTIGREW, Tom	T	220	Eastern Illinois
9	FARMER, George	WR	248	Southern
10	GRUBER, Bob	T	276	Pittsburg
11	GREER, Terry	WR	304	Alabama State
12	SCANLON, Kevin	QB	332	Arkansas

MIAMI DOLPHINS

1	McNEAL, Don	DB	21	Alabama
2	STEPHENSON, Dwight	C	48	Alabama
3	BARNETT, Bill	DE	75	Nebraska
4	BAILEY, Elmer	WR	100	Minnesota
6	BYRD, Eugene	WR	158	Michigan State
7	ROSE, Joe	TE	185	California
8	ALLEN, Jeff	DB	212	Cal-Davis
8	WOODLEY, David	QB	214	Louisiana State
9	GOODSPEED, Mark	T	239	Nebraska
10	LANTZ, Doug	C	271	Miami, Ohio
10	LONG, Ben	LB	272	South Dakota
11	DRISCOLL, Phil	DE	279	Mankato State
12	STONE, Chuck	G	325	North Carolina State

MINNESOTA VIKINGS

1	MARTIN, Doug	DT	9	Washington
2	TEAL, Willie	DB	30	Louisiana State
3	BOYD, Brent	C	68	UCLA
4	JOHNSON, Dennis	LB	92	Southern California
5	PASCHAL, Doug	RB	121	North Carolina
5	JONES, Paul	RB	122	California
6	YAKAVONIS, Ray	DE	148	East Stroudsburg, Pa.
7	JOHNSON, Henry	LB	174	Georgia Tech
9	MOSLEY, Dennis	RB	232	Iowa
10	BROWN, Kenny	WR	258	Nebraska
11	HARRELL, Sam	RB	288	East Carolina
12	LANE, Thomas	DB	315	Florida A&M

NEW ENGLAND PATRIOTS

1	JAMES, Roland	DB	14	Tennessee
1	FERGUSON, Vagas	RB	25	Notre Dame
2	McGREW, Larry	LB	45	Southern California
3	McMICHAEL, Steve	DT	73	Texas
5	McDOUGALD, Doug	DE-DT	124	Virginia Tech
6	BROWN, Preston	WR	160	Vanderbilt
7	KEARNS, Tom	G	180	Kentucky
8	HOUSE, Mike	TE	208	Pacific
9	BURGET, Barry	LB	235	Oklahoma
10	DANIEL, Tom	C	266	Georgia Tech
11	HUBACH, Mike	P	293	Kansas
12	JORDAN, Jimmy	QB	320	Florida State

NEW ORLEANS SAINTS

1	BROCK, Stan	T	12	Colorado
2	WAYMER, Dave	DB	41	Notre Dame
4	JOLLY, Mike	DB	96	Michigan
6	BOYD, Lester	LB	150	Kentucky
7	MORUCCI, Mike	RB	177	Bloomsburg, Pa.
8	EVANS, Chuck	LB	206	Stanford
9	MORDICA, Frank	RB	233	Vanderbilt
10	WEBB, Tanya	DE	262	Michigan State
11	WOODARD, George	RB	289	Texas A&M
12	LEWIS, Kiser	LB	318	Florida A&M

NEW YORK GIANTS

1	HAYNES, Mark	DB	8	Colorado
3	LAPKA, Myron	DT	64	Southern California
4	PITTMAN, Dan	WR	90	Wyoming
5	BLOUNT, Tony	DB	118	Virginia
6	BRUNNER, Scott	QB	145	Delaware
7	HEBERT, Darryl	DB	179	Oklahoma
7	LINNIN, Chris	DE	181	Washington
8	HARRIS, Ken	RB	200	Alabama
9	WONSLEY, Otis	RB	229	Alcorn State
10	SANFORD, Joe	T	256	Washington
11	BERNISH, Steve	DE	285	South Carolina
12	LANSFORD, Mike	K	312	Washington

NEW YORK JETS

1	JONES, Johnny (Lam)	WR	2	Texas
2	RAY, Darrol	DB	40	Oklahoma
2	CLAYTON, Ralph	WR-RB	47	Michigan
3	MEHL, Lance	LB	69	Penn State
4	JOHNSON, Jesse	DB	95	Colorado
5	ZIDD, Jim	LB	123	Kansas
6	VISGER, George	DE-DT	149	Colorado
6	SCHREMP, Tom	DE-DT	152	Wisconsin
7	BATTON, Bob	RB	178	Nevada-Las Vegas
7	LEVERETT, Bennie	RB	190	Bethune-Cookman
8	DZIAMA, Jeff	LB	205	Boston College
9	PETERS, Joe	DT	234	Arizona State
10	BINGHAM, Guy	C	260	Montana
11	ZACHERY, James	LB	290	Texas A&M
12	DUMARS, David	DB	317	N.E. Louisiana

OAKLAND RAIDERS

1	WILSON, Marv	QB	15	Brigham Young
2	MILLEN, Matt	LB	43	Penn State
5	LEWIS, Kenny	LB	125	Virginia Tech
5	ADAMS, John	LB	126	Louisiana State
5	BOWENS, William	LB	128	North Alabama
7	BARNWELL, Malcolm	WR	173	Virginia Union
8	HILL, Ken	DB	194	Yale
10	CARTER, Walter	DT	264	Florida State
11	MASSEY, Mike	LB	291	Arkansas
12	MUHAMMAD, Calvin	WR	322	Texas Southern

PHILADELPHIA EAGLES

1	YOUNG, Roynell	DB	23	Alcorn State
2	HARRINGTON, Perry	RB	53	Jackson State
5	RIVERS, Nate	WR	135	South Carolina State
6	MURTHA, Greg	T	161	Minnesota
7	WARD, Terrell	DB	188	San Diego State
8	CURCIO, Mike	LB	218	Temple
9	HARRIS, Bob	T	245	Bowling Green
11	JUKES, Lee	WR	298	North Carolina State
11	BROWN, Thomas	DE	302	Baylor
12	FIELDS, Howard	DB	329	Baylor

PITTSBURGH STEELERS

1	MALONE, Mark	QB	28	Arizona State
2	KOHRS, Bob	LB	35	Arizona State
2	GOODMAN, John	DE	56	Oklahoma
3	SYDNOR, Ray	TE	83	Wisconsin
4	HURLEY, Bill	QB	110	Syracuse
5	WOLFLEY, Craig	G	138	Syracuse
6	ILKIN, Tunch	C	165	Indiana State
7	JOHNSON, Nate	WR	193	Hillsdale
8	WALTON, Ted	DB	221	Connecticut
9	McCALL, Ron	WR	249	Arkansas-Pine Bluff
10	WILSON, Woodrow	DB	250	North Carolina State
10	FRITZ, Ken	G	277	Ohio State
11	POLLARD, Frank	RB	305	Baylor
12	VACLAVIK, Charles	DB	306	Texas
12	McGRIFF, Tyrone	G	333	Florida A&M

ST. LOUIS CARDINALS

1	GREER, Curtis	DE	6	Michigan
2	MARSH, Doug	TE	33	Michigan
3	SINNOTT, John	T	60	Brown
3	BAKER, Charles	LB	81	New Mexico
4	LISCH, Rusty	QB	89	Notre Dame
6	ACKER, Bill	DT	142	Texas
7	APUNA, Ben	LB	171	Arizona State
8	BRANCH, Dupree	DB	198	Colorado State
8	HUDSON, Grant	DT	211	Virginia
9	MAYS, Stafford	DE	225	Washington
10	BROWN, Rush	DT	255	Ball State
11	BROWN, Delrick	DB	282	Houston
12	GRAY, Tyrone	WR	309	Washington State

SAN DIEGO CHARGERS

4	LUTHER, Ed	QB	101	San Jose State
4	GREGOR, Bob	DB	108	Washington State
6	HARRINGTON, LaRue	RB	151	Norfolk State
6	HAMILTON, Wayne	LB	163	Alabama
7	LOEWEN, Chuck	G	175	South Dakota State
7	DODDS, Stuart	P	191	Montana State
8	SIRMONES, Curtis	RB	219	North Alabama
9	WHITMAN, Steve	RB	247	Alabama
11	SINGLETON, John	DE	303	Texas-El Paso
12	PRICE, Harry	WR	331	McNeese State

SAN FRANCISCO 49ers

1	COOPER, Earle	RB	13	Rice
1	STUCKEY, Jim	DT	20	Clemson
2	TURNER, Keena	LB	39	Purdue
3	MILLER, Jim	P	65	Mississippi
3	PUKI, Craig	LB	77	Tennessee
4	CHURCHMAN, Ricky	DB	84	Texas
4	DION, Terry	DE	97	Oregon
4	HODGE, David	LB	98	Houston
5	TIMES, Kenneth	DT	112	Southern
6	WILLIAMS, Herb	DB	139	Southern
8	LEOPOLD, Bobby	LB	210	Notre Dame
9	HARTWIG, Dan	QB	237	California Lutheran

SEATTLE SEAHAWKS

1	GREEN, Jacob	DE	10	Texas A&M
2	HINES, Andre	T	44	Stanford
4	DION, Terry	DE	97	Oregon
5	STEELE, Joe	RB	127	Washington
5	JACOBS, Daniel	DE	132	Winston-Salem
6	McNEAL, Mark	DE	153	Idaho
8	MINOR, Vic	DB	204	N.E. Louisiana
8	COSGROVE, Jack	C	207	Pacific
9	SWIFT, Jim	T	238	Iowa
10	ESSINK, Ron	T	265	Grand Valley
10	REAVES, Billy	WR	274	Morris Brown
11	ENA, Tali	RB	292	Washington State
12	GILBERT, Presnell	DB	319	U.S. International

TAMPA BAY BUCCANEERS

1	SNELL, Ray	G	22	Wisconsin
2	HOUSE, Kevin	WR	49	Southern Illinois
3	BRANTLEY, Scot	LB	76	Florida
4	FLOWERS, Larry	DB	102	Texas Tech
7	LEONARD, Jim	C	186	Santa Clara
8	GODDARD, Derrick	DB	213	Drake
9	CARTER, Gerald	WR	240	Texas A&M
10	HAWKINS, Andy	LB	267	Texas A&I
10	DAVIS, Brett	RB	275	Nevada-Las Vegas
11	JONES, Terry	DE	299	Central State, Okla.
12	COLEMAN, Gene	DB	326	Miami

WASHINGTON REDSKINS

1	MONK, Art	WR	18	Syracuse
2	MENDENHALL, Mat	DE	55	Brigham Young
6	BELL, Farley	LB	155	Cincinnati
7	JONES, Melvin	G	187	Houston
9	McCULLOUGH, Lawrence	WR	241	Illinois
10	WALKER, Lewis	RB	268	Utah
11	MATOCHA, Mike	DE	295	Texas-Arlington
12	EMMETT, Marcene	DB	327	North Alabama

CHUCK NOLL: THE QUIET
DYNASTY-MAKER

Duquesne University in the City of Pittsburgh wasn't about to overlook one of its most eligible local candidates for an honorary degree. Who else deserved scholarly recognition any more than the head coach of the four-time Super Bowl champion Pittsburgh Steelers? After all, if special achievement goes unrewarded by academic acclaim, then certainly higher education lacks an appreciation for its own mission in society.

It was Chuck Noll's first honorary degree, an honorary "doctorate of humanitarian services," for his contributions to Pittsburgh's civic pride. The citation, presented in the midst of the traditional black flowing robes and mortarboard caps, reads this way:

"Although this city has been a Gateway to the West and a forge to a great nation, it took men in black and gold to finally knock the chip off Pittsburgh's shoulder. The Pittsburgh Steelers, by your design, were the focus of a decade of sports revolution which has given this city a new reflection in the Mirror of America."

Those are mighty fancy words for a man like Chuck Noll who believes in simple, straight-forward language, whether he's talking to his players or to news media representatives who often throw up their hands in frustration when trying to get an unusual quote or one-liner from the Steeler coach. Just before Super Bowl XIV in Los Angeles, Noll was holding a news conference near the Steelers' practice facility which was located several miles from the city itself. Members of the press and television networks had arrived by special bus from the NFL headquarters hotel, the Los Angeles Marriott. While notebooks were unlimbered and pencils made ready at tables placed around the large room, Chuck Noll strode to the platform to make his comments over a microphone that worked perfectly. Everyone could hear his every word as he related the manner in which the Steelers had overcome early defense problems brought on by injuries, and he particularly singled out defensive tackles Tom Beasley and Gary Dunn for their contributions in overcoming those problems. With those two helping to alleviate matters, he went on, the injury situation gradually improved and the rest was Steeler history, Noll's comments concluded. They survived the playoffs and there they were, in the Super Bowl again. What's more, they were favored to win by almost everyone who wanted to express an opinion.

Noll's remarks were typical of his approach to a news conference, dwelling as he did upon the mundane, often boring subjects like defensive tackles, injuries, and so on instead of something exciting that could make a headline, such as a possible change in game strategy, or a switch in the lineup to provide a better counter to the Los Angeles defense. None of that. Only just plain Noll. And when he had completed his remarks, the Pittsburgh coach asked:

"Any questions?"

There were none. The media representatives were convinced.

As every fan knows by now, Chuck Noll is one of the most successful coaches in NFL history which goes back to 1920. Only four head coaches have won four league championships, and Noll is one of them. For the record, Vince Lombardi won five. Noll's overall eleven-year record with the Steelers is 100-57-1. Going into this, his twelfth season as head coach, Noll has won four Super Bowls, twice as many as any other coach. And should the Steelers reach the Super Bowl again this season and win, they will match Green Bay's incredible string of five championships in seven years, an accomplishment considered the most outstanding team feat in pro football history.

This season marks the 48-year-old Noll's 28th straight in professional football, a career that began in 1953 when the Cleveland Browns, right there in his hometown, chose him in the 21st round of the annual NFL college draft. He played guard and then linebacker for the Browns for seven years and then, at age 27, retired as a player to go into coaching which, all along, had been his ultimate goal.

The opportunity came quickly. When a coaching position at his alma mater, the University of Dayton, failed to materialize, he joined the staff of the newly organized Los Angeles Chargers whose head coach was Sid Gillman. It was 1960, first year of the newly organized American Football League, and the L-A Chargers were charter members—later to become the San Diego Chargers. Noll spent six years as a defensive assistant with the club which won five division titles and two AFL championships during that period.

In 1966, while the NFL and AFL were still two separate leagues, Noll returned to the NFL at Baltimore as a defensive coach with the Colts, whose head coach at that time was Don Shula, later of Miami fame. Noll remained in Baltimore three years while the club enjoyed three of its best seasons, losing just seven regular season games and winning the NFL title in 1968 before bowing to the New York Jets in Super Bowl III, one of the truly historic pro football games of all time.

Then, in 1969, Noll arrived in Pittsburgh to become

the 14th head coach of the Steelers who, at that precise moment, had experienced only four winning seasons in 19 years. Almost immediately, he instituted a policy of building a new team through the college draft, or by the signing of free agents immediately following the draft—among them college players of merit who, somehow, had been overlooked in the choosing. No trades, and the result was that, during the championship season of 1979, every Steeler on the squad was a "home-grown" product—either a draftee or a free agent. This made the Pittsburgh club unique in modern NFL history.

Even though Noll's style is low key and he practices, above all, an economy of words, one of his greatest attributes is the desire to talk in a special way—the very special way of a teacher. Unlike many other NFL coaches, and individuals in other professions as well, Noll enjoys the teaching phase of his work more than any other. This, obviously, is another reason for his team's success. The tedious process of working on a man-to-man basis with players at every position, and encouraging them to improve upon this or that weakness, appeals to Noll's teaching instincts and he excels at it.

Away from football, he has a wide variety of interests, being well-read and conversant on a myriad of subjects outside the realm of pro football. He flies his own plane which he uses often when scouting college players. For hobbies, he has golf, tennis, scuba driving, photography, gardening and, yes, Noll enjoys classical music along with the pleasures of being a wine connoisseur and a food gourmet. Married, he and his wife Marianne have a 22-year-old son, Chris, a student at the University of Rhode Island.

Still, as some observers insist, Chuck Noll is the coach nobody knows and always seems more comfortable when left in the background, away from the hoopla and fanfare that go with being a Super Bowl coach. Why, then, doesn't Noll like publicity?

"Publicity," he says in revealing a strategic secret, "doesn't help you win . . . if it did, I'd be more interested in it."

THE MEDIA AND THE NFL:
A LOVE/HATE RELATIONSHIP?

By Herbert M. Furlow

Every year on the Friday evening preceding Super
Bowl Sunday, wherever the game is played, Commissioner Pete Rozelle throws his annual Super Bowl party
for the NFL's official family, their friends, relatives,
honored guests and members of the press, radio and
television who have credentials to cover the big game.
Over the years, the party has become *the* social event
of Super Bowl week, an extravaganza exceeded in
grandeur and panoramic sweep only by the nationally
televised half-time show presented at the game itself.
As for the food, whoever thought up the idea of cornu-
copia, the horn of plenty, surely must have had the
Super Bowl party in mind.

The Super Bowl XIV bash was attended by 3,000
guests at the Pasadena Civic Center, a building large
and spacious enough to accommodate even the length-
iest of guest lists. There was dancing to music from the
Big Band Era, there was food, and there were bars
around the floor for those who cared to imbibe. And
there was ice, plenty of ice, and all of it came from
Alaska. If the big party was to have any problems, re-
frigeration or a shortage of ice wouldn't be among
them.

It was the Alaskan city of Seward that decided to
donate the ice, taken from a glacier in the Harding

Ice Field and estimated to be about 6,000 years old. Glacial ice, it seems, stays frozen for a long time and 200 pounds of it was air shipped to Los Angeles for delivery to the Pasadena Civic Center after a 150-mile motor trip over icy mountain roads. The idea to donate something to the Super Bowl festivities came when it was learned that Seward's mayor, Ray Hugli, would be attending the game.

It was a media event, carried out against the background of the biggest media event of all—Super Bowl XIV. Now ice from Alaska is no different from any other ice—it eventually thaws. But something that apparently didn't thaw last January during and after Super Bowl week, and perhaps still remains frozen, are relation between some members of the media and a growing number of NFL players, officials, and others who from time to time take a dim view of the way football stories are handled.

As late as last March, United Press International reported from Rancho Mirage, Calif., that Commissioner Pete Rozelle had issued a scathing attack against "some elements of the Los Angeles media." Rozelle was particularly angered by news reports that he was trying to block the Oakland Raiders in their proposed move to Los Angeles because he himself wanted to operate an expansion franchise in L-A after the Rams left for Anaheim. Rozelle branded the report as "a total fabrication" and added: "I don't like it when total misrepresentations are made . . . things just made up without any evidence and printed as ritual fact."

Rozelle, of course, didn't direct his remarks at *all* media. His complaint was against those which adhere to the old line of "never let the facts stand in the way of a good story." As every journalist knows, that approach to the facts is still employed by some, not only in reporting pro football but in other types of news as well. It would seem that, unfortunately, one preroga-tive of a free press is the freedom to make up things.

By and large, however, most complaints NFL players have with the news media concern personalities, or the way some writers and broadcasters handle their stories. Conflicts between athletic personalities and reporters are constantly finding space in the sports pages and broadcasts. Within the past year, these tiffs between players and writers seem to have grown in numbers— and violence. One of these involved a pushing and shoving match between Houston quarterback Dan Pas-torini (now of Oakland) and sportswriter Dale Robert-son of the *Houston Post*.

And Ken Stabler, now with the Houston Oilers, ap-parently has little use for some reporters, especially the ones who had reported incidents involving drugs in Gulf Shores, Alabama. One of these reporters was Bob Padecky of the *Sacramento Bee*. Padecky walked up to Stabler at Oakland's California training camp and said:

"Ken, I'd like to ask you some questions."

Padecky, reportedly, never got the chance. Stabler gave him a colloquial two-word reply that even the editors of modern English usage dictionaries haven't heard of yet.

One of the NFL's newest stars, running back Ottis (O. J.) Anderson of the Cardinals, isn't sure whether he likes mixing it up in conversation with reporters.

"I don't really enjoy talking to the press," says the St. Louis O. J., "because all you're doing is setting me up. Put my name in the paper and they'll come shooting for me. I ought to make you talk to Jim Hart or Mel Gray or Pat Tilley. Make them somebody's mark . . ."

During the two weeks' training period prior to Super Bowl XIV, the Los Angeles Rams, almost to a man, became pretty much soured on the media because of

the constant portrayal of Ray Malavasi as a coach
doomed to lose. One writer, in referring to the NFC
championship game between the Rams and Buccaneers,
called it the Runner-up Bowl, "a game for losers played
by losers." That didn't set well at all with the Rams,
some of whom talked of boycotting the press during
Super Bowl week. Such a move was never officially
adopted, but some Rams did clam up and became downright uncooperative when approached by reporters looking for a quote or two to justify their trip to Pasadena.

Last September, when it was announced that New
England cornerback Raymond Clayborn was being fined
$2,000 for his confrontation with sportswriter Will Mc-
Donough of the *Boston Globe,* Commissioner Rozelle
stated the NFL's position on relations with those who
cover pro football for the media. "They are a critical
link between professional football and the fans on
whose continuing interest in the game the livelihood
of all its participants ultimately depends. Sportswriters
are entitled to player cooperation by the terms of
every NFL player's contract. And far more funda-
mentally, members of the news media are at least entitled to freedom from physical interference, from
threats of bodily harm and from openly challenging
verbal abuse at the hands of players while they are
simply doing their jobs."

Not all players, to be sure, find dealing with the
media difficult at all times. Los Angeles defensive end
Jack Youngblood was going through his practice rou-
tines just before Super Bowl XIV when he was approached by a young lady journalist who asked him
what it sounded like when everybody ran into each
other out on the football field.

"It sounds like guys running into each other, grunting
and groaning," Youngblood answered, without the trace
of a smile.

An hour or so later the same lady journalist turned up at the Steelers' practice field and sought out linebacker Jack Lambert for a question.

"What did she ask me?" reported Lambert a little later on. "She asked me what it felt like when I hit somebody," Lambert said, with a look of disbelief on his face.

Maybe player-media relations will thaw out after all.

NATIONAL FOOTBALL LEAGUE 1979 STATISTICS

- Final 1979 NFL Standings & Results of Championship Playoff Games

- Regular Season AFC & NFC Individual Statistical Leaders

- Regular Season AFC & NFC Team Statistics

AMERICAN FOOTBALL CONFERENCE

Final 1979 Standings

	W	L	T	Pct.	Pts.	Opps.
Eastern Division						
Miami*	10	6	0	.625	341	257
New England	9	7	0	.563	411	326
N.Y. Jets	8	8	0	.500	337	383
Buffalo	7	9	0	.438	268	279
Baltimore	5	11	0	.313	271	351
Central Division						
Pittsburgh*	12	4	0	.750	416	262
Houston†	11	5	0	.688	362	331
Cleveland	9	7	0	.563	359	352
Cincinnati	4	12	0	.250	337	421
Western Division						
San Diego*	12	4	0	.750	411	246
Denver†	10	6	0	.625	289	262
Seattle	9	7	0	.563	378	372
Oakland	9	7	0	.563	365	337
Kansas City	7	9	0	.438	238	262

* Division champion
† Wild card for playoffs

1979 CHAMPIONSHIP PLAYOFF RESULTS

AFC First Round: Houston 13, Denver 7 (at Houston)
AFC Divisional Playoff: Houston 17, San Diego 14 (at San Diego)
AFC Divisional Playoff: Pittsburgh 34, Miami 14 (at Pittsburgh)
AFC Championship Game: Pittsburgh 27, Houston 13 (at Pittsburgh)
Super Bowl XIV: Pittsburgh 31, Los Angeles 19 (at Pasadena Rose Bowl)

LEADING SCORERS

	TDs	Rush.	Pass.	Ret.	Pts.
Touchdown Leaders					
Campbell, Hou.	19	19	0	0	114
P. Johnson, Cin.	15	14	1	0	90
Smith, Sea.	15	11	4	0	90

	TDs	Rush.	Pass.	Ret.	Pts.
Csonka, Mia.	13	12	1	0	78
Morgan, N.E.	13	0	12	1	78
Harris, Pitt.	12	11	1	0	72
C. Williams, S.D.	12	12	0	0	72
M. Pruitt, Clev.	11	9	2	0	66
Jefferson, S.D.	10	0	10	0	60
Thornton, Pitt.	10	6	4	0	60

Best Performance: 4 TDs for 24 points by Roland Hooks of Buffalo vs. Cincinnati, Sept. 9, 1979; by Clarence Williams of San Diego vs. Buffalo, Sept. 16, 1979; by Jerry Butler of Buffalo vs. The N.Y. Jets, Sept. 23, 1979.

	PATs	FGs	Longest	Pts.
Leading Kick Scorers				
Smith, N.E.	46-49	23-33	47	115
Bahr, Pitt.	50-52	18-30	47	104
Fritsch, Hou.	41-43	21-25	51	104
Herrera, Sea.	43-46	19-23	49	100
von Schamann, Mia.	36-40	21-29	53	99
Breech, Oak.	41-45	18-27	47	95
Cockroft, Clev.	38-43	17-29	51	89
Bahr, Cin.	40-42	13-23	55	79
Mike-Mayer, Buff.	17-18	20-29	42	77
Wood, S.D.	34-38	13-21	42	73

LEADING PASSERS
(192 Attempts)

	Atts.	Com.	Pct. Com.	Yds.	Avg. Yds.	Had Int.	TDs	Rat- ing*
Fouts, S.D.	530	332	62.6	4082	7.70	24	24	82.6
Stabler, Oak.	498	304	61.0	3615	7.26	22	26	82.2
Anderson, Cin.	339	189	55.8	2340	6.90	10	16	80.9
Zorn, Sea.	505	285	56.4	3661	7.25	18	20	77.6
Grogan, N.E.	423	206	48.7	3286	7.77	20	28	77.5
Bradshaw, Pitt.	472	259	54.9	3724	7.89	25	26	77.0
Landry, Balt.	457	270	59.1	2932	6.42	15	15	75.3
Ferguson, Buff.	458	238	52.0	3572	7.80	15	14	74.5
Sipe, Clev.	535	286	53.5	3793	7.09	26	28	73.1
Griese, Mia.	310	176	56.8	2160	6.97	16	14	71.8

	Atts.	Com.	Pct. Com.	Yds.	Avg. Yds.	Had Int.	TDs	Rat- ing*
Morton, Den.	370	204	55.1	2626	7.10	19	16	70.7
Todd, N.Y.	334	171	51.2	2660	7.96	22	16	66.4
Pastorini, Hou.	324	163	50.3	2090	6.45	18	14	61.9
Fuller, K.C.	270	146	54.1	1484	5.50	14	6	55.8

Longest: 84 yards by Joe Ferguson to Curtis Brown of Buffalo vs. San Diego, Sept. 16, 1979 (TD)

* Official NFL passing ratings are based on percentage of completions, average yards gained, TD passing percentage, interception percentage

LEADING PASS RECEIVERS

	No.	Yds.	Avg.	Longest	TDs
Washington, Balt. (rb)	82	750	9.1	43	3
Joiner, S.D.	72	1008	14.0	39	4
Stallworth, Pitt.	70	1183	16.9	65	8
Largent, Sea.	66	1237	18.7	55	9
Upchurch, Den.	64	937	14.6	47	7
Jefferson, S.D.	61	1090	17.9	65	10
Logan, Clev.	59	982	16.6	46	7
Branch, Oak.	59	844	14.3	66	6
Bass, Cin.	58	724	12.5	50	3
Chester, Oak.	58	712	12.3	39	8
Casper, Oak.	57	771	13.5	42	3
Newsome, Clev.	55	781	14.2	74	9
McCauley, Balt. (rb)	55	575	10.5	35	3
Lewis, Buff.	54	1082	20.0	55	2
Moses, Den.	54	943	17.5	64	6
Doornink, Sea. (rb)	54	432	8.0	42	1
van Eeghen, Oak. (rb)	51	474	9.3	36	2
C. Williams, S.D. (rb)	51	352	6.9	14	0
Moore, Mia.	48	840	17.5	53	6
Butler, Buff.	48	834	17.4	75	4
Smith, Sea. (rb)	48	499	10.4	35	4

(rb)—denotes running back

Best Performance: 13 receptions for 130 yards by Joe Washington of Baltimore vs. Kansas City, Sept. 2, 1979

INTERCEPTION LEADERS

	No.	Yds.	Longest	TDs
Reinfeldt, Hou.	12	205	39	0
Barbaro, K.C.	7	142	70	1
Hayes, Oak.	7	100	52	2
J. Wilson, Hou.	6	135	66	1
Nixon, Buff.	6	81	43	0
Jauron, Cin.	6	41	12	0
Owens, N.Y.	6	41	15	0
Lambert, Pitt.	6	29	23	0
Foley, Den.	6	14	7	0

Longest: 96 yards by Ray Griffin of Cincinnati vs. San Diego, Nov. 11, 1979 (TD)

LEADING RUSHERS

	Atts.	Yds.	Avg.	Longest	TDs
Campbell, Hou.	368	1697	4.6	61	19
M. Pruitt, Clev.	264	1294	4.9	77	9
Harris, Pitt.	267	1186	4.4	71	11
Gaines, N.Y.	186	905	4.9	52	0
Washington, Balt.	242	884	3.7	26	4
P. Johnson, Cin.	243	865	3.6	35	14
Csonka, Mia.	220	837	3.8	22	12
van Eeghen, Oak.	223	818	3.7	19	7
Smith, Sea.	194	775	4.0	31	11
Dierking, N.Y.	186	767	4.1	40	3
McKnight, K.C.	153	755	4.9	84	8
C. Williams, S.D.	200	752	3.8	55	12
Williams, Mia.	184	703	3.8	39	3
A. Griffin, Cin.	140	688	4.9	63	0
Thornton, Pitt.	118	585	5.0	75	6
Brown, Buff.	172	574	3.3	25	1
Cunningham, N.E.	159	563	3.5	27	5
Ivory, N.E.	143	522	3.7	52	1
Doornink, Sea.	152	500	3.3	26	8
Miller, Buff.	139	484	3.5	75	1

Best Performance: 195 yards in 33 attempts by Earl Campbell of Houston vs. Dallas, Nov. 22, 1979 (2 TDs)
Longest: 84 yards by Ted McKnight of Kansas City vs. Seattle, Sept. 30, 1979

LEADING PUNTERS

	No.	Yds.	Avg.	Longest	Blocked
Grupp, K.C.	89	3883	43.6	74	1
Guy, Oak.	69	2939	42.6	71	1
McInally, Cin.	89	3678	41.3	61	2
Evans, Clev.	69	2844	41.2	59	2
Ramsey, N.Y.	73	2979	40.8	64	0
Parsley, Hou.	93	3777	40.6	59	0
Colquitt, Pitt.	68	2733	40.2	61	0
Roberts, Mia.	69	2772	40.2	68	1
Weaver, Sea.	66	2651	40.2	60	3
Prestridge, Den.	89	3555	39.9	63	0
Jackson, Buff.	96	3671	38.2	60	0
Dilts, Balt.	99	3657	36.9	53	2
Hare, N.E.	83	3038	36.6	58	1
West, S.D.	75	2736	36.5	62	0

Longest: 74 yards by Bob Grupp of Kansas City vs. San Diego, Nov. 4, 1979

PUNT RETURN LEADERS

	No.	Yds.	Avg.	Longest	TDs
Nathan, Mia.	28	306	10.9	86	1
Smith, K.C.	58	612	10.6	88	2
D. Hall, Clev.	29	295	10.2	47	0
Upchurch, Den.	30	304	10.1	44	0
Morgan, N.E.	29	289	10.0	80	1
Fuller, S.D.	46	448	9.7	27	0
Smith, Pitt.	16	146	9.1	38	0
Harper, N.Y.	33	290	8.8	51	0
Bell, Pitt.	45	378	8.4	27	0
Moody, Buff.	38	318	8.4	32	0
Lusby, Cin.	32	260	8.1	40	0
Glasgow, Balt.	44	352	8.0	75	1
T. Green, Sea.	19	138	7.3	30	0
Ellender, Hou.	31	203	6.5	36	0

Longest: 88 yards by J. T. Smith of Kansas City vs. Oakland, Sept. 23, 1979

KICKOFF RETURN LEADERS

	No.	Yds.	Avg.	Longest	TDs
Brunson, Oak.	17	441	25.9	89	0
Matthews, Oak.	35	873	24.9	104	1
Owens, S.D.	35	791	22.6	40	0
Nathan, Mia.	45	1016	22.6	43	0
Glasgow, Balt.	50	1126	22.5	58	0
Clark, N.E.	37	816	22.1	38	0
L. Anderson, Pitt.	34	732	21.5	44	0
Ellender, Hou.	24	514	21.4	35	0
Harper, N.Y.	55	1158	21.1	52	0
Belton, K.C.	22	463	21.0	52	0
Turner, Cin.	55	1149	20.9	36	0
Moore, Sea.	31	641	20.7	39	0
Moody, Buff.	27	556	20.6	35	0
T. Green, Sea.	32	651	20.3	31	0
D. Hall, Clev.	50	1014	20.3	33	0

Longest: 104 yards by Ira Matthews of Oakland vs. San Diego, Oct. 25, 1979 (TD)

AMERICAN FOOTBALL CONFERENCE
1979 Team Statistics

	Yds.	Rush.	Pass.	Avg. PG
Total Offense				
Pittsburgh	6258*	2603	3655	391.1*
Cleveland	5772	2281	3491	360.8
San Diego	5583	1668	3915*	348.9
Seattle	5557	1967	3590	347.3
New England	5470	2252	3218	341.9
New York Jets	5244	2646*	2598	327.8
Oakland	5174	1763	3411	323.4
Denver	5142	2036	3106	321.4
Miami	4950	2187	2763	309.4
Baltimore	4846	1674	3172	302.9
Buffalo	4837	1621	3216	302.3
Houston	4827	2571	2256	301.7
Cincinnati	4639	2329	2310	289.9
Kansas City	3976	2316	1660	248.5

* Conference leader

	Atts.	Yds.	Avg.	Avg. PG
Rushing Offense				
New York Jets	634*	2646*	4.2	165.4*
Pittsburgh	561	2603	4.6*	162.7
Houston	616	2571	4.2	160.7
Cincinnati	560	2329	4.2	145.6
Kansas City	569	2316	4.1	144.8
Cleveland	504	2281	4.5	142.6
New England	604	2252	3.7	140.8
Miami	561	2187	3.9	136.7
Denver	525	2036	3.9	127.3
Seattle	500	1967	3.9	122.9
Oakland	491	1763	3.6	110.2
Baltimore	515	1674	3.3	104.6
San Diego	481	1668	3.5	104.3
Buffalo	474	1621	3.4	101.3

	Atts.	Com.	Pct.	Int.	Avg. PG	QB Sacks
Passing Offense						
San Diego	541	338*	62.5*	25	244.7*	31
Pittsburgh	492	272	55.3	26	228.4	27
Seattle	523	292	55.8	18	224.4	23*
Cleveland	545	289	53.0	27	218.2	43
Oakland	513	311	60.6	23	213.2	36
New England	475	237	49.9	23	201.1	49
Buffalo	465	241	51.8	15*	201.0	43
Baltimore	550*	313	56.9	19	198.3	52
Denver	476	260	54.6	23	194.1	43
Miami	416	235	56.5	22	172.7	29
New York Jets	369	190	51.5	25	162.4	32
Cincinnati	426	228	53.5	15*	144.4	63
Houston	386	195	50.5	21	141.0	32
Kansas City	361	190	52.6	18	103.8	42

	Yds.	Rush.	Pass.	Avg. PG
Total Defense				
Pittsburgh	4270*	1709	2561	266.9*
New England	4323	1770	2553	270.2
Miami	4439	1702	2737	277.4
San Diego	4456	1907	2549	278.5
Denver	4852	1693*	3159	303.3
Kansas City	4971	1847	3124	310.7
Houston	4990	2225	2765	311.9

* Conference leader

	Yds.	Rush.	Pass.	Avg. PG
Buffalo	5011	2481	2530*	313.2
Baltimore	5074	2306	2768	317.1
Oakland	5486	2374	3112	342.9
Cleveland	5650	2604	3046	353.1
New York Jets	5821	1706	4115	363.8
Seattle	5834	2375	3459	364.6
Cincinnati	5911	2219	3692	369.4

	Atts.	Yds.	Avg.	Avg. PG
Rushing Defense				
Denver	502	1693*	3.4*	105.8*
Miami	484	1702	3.5	106.4
New York Jets	502	1706	3.4	106.6
Pittsburgh	506	1709	3.4	106.8
New England	495	1770	3.6	110.6
Kansas City	522	1847	3.5	115.4
San Diego	475*	1907	4.0	119.2
Cincinnati	528	2219	4.2	138.7
Houston	522	2225	4.3	139.1
Baltimore	559	2306	4.1	144.1
Oakland	534	2374	4.4	148.4
Seattle	533	2375	4.5	148.4
Buffalo	617	2481	4.0	155.1
Cleveland	577	2604	4.5	162.8

	Atts.	Com.	Pct.	Int.	Avg. PG	QB Sacks
Passing Defense						
Buffalo	382*	193*	50.5	24	158.1*	23
San Diego	472	261	55.3	28	159.3	42
New England	467	246	52.7	20	159.6	57*
Pittsburgh	480	226	47.1*	27	160.1	49
Miami	418	230	55.0	23	171.1	36
Houston	465	242	52.0	34*	172.8	51
Baltimore	411	203	49.4	23	173.0	39
Cleveland	468	271	57.9	16	190.4	31
Oakland	471	247	52.4	24	194.5	33
Kansas City	528	296	56.1	23	195.3	38
Denver	512	296	57.8	19	197.4	19
Seattle	508	317	62.4	17	216.2	37
Cincinnati	492	275	55.9	20	230.8	32
New York Jets	570	339	59.5	21	257.2	22

* Conference leader

NATIONAL FOOTBALL CONFERENCE

Final 1979 Standings

	W	L	T	Pct.	Pts.	Opps.
Eastern Division						
Dallas*	11	5	0	.688	371	313
Philadelphia†	11	5	0	.688	339	282
Washington	10	6	0	.625	348	295
N.Y. Giants	6	10	0	.375	237	323
St. Louis	5	11	0	.313	307	358
Central Division						
Tampa Bay*	10	6	0	.625	273	237
Chicago†	10	6	0	.625	306	249
Minnesota	7	9	0	.438	259	337
Green Bay	5	11	0	.313	246	316
Detroit	2	14	0	.125	219	365
Western Division						
Los Angeles*	9	7	0	.563	323	309
New Orleans	8	8	0	.500	370	360
Atlanta	6	10	0	.375	300	388
San Francisco	2	14	0	.125	308	416

* Division champion
† Wild card for playoffs

1979 CHAMPIONSHIP PLAYOFF RESULTS

NFC First Round: Philadelphia 27, Chicago 17 (at Philadelphia)
NFC Divisional Playoff: Tampa Bay 24, Philadelphia 17 (at Tampa Bay)
NFC Divisional Playoff: Los Angeles 21, Dallas 19 (at Dallas)
NFC Championship Game: Los Angeles 9, Tampa Bay 0 (at Tampa Bay)
Super Bowl XIV: Pittsburgh 31, Los Angeles 19 (at Pasadena Rose Bowl)

LEADING SCORERS

	TDs	Rush.	Pass.	Ret.	Pts.
Touchdown Leaders					
Payton, Chi.	16	14	2	0	96
Montgomery, Phil.	14	9	5	0	84
Riggins, Wash.	12	9	3	0	72
Carmichael, Phil.	11	0	11	0	66

	TDs	Rush.	Pass.	Ret.	Pts.
Muncie, N.O.	11	11	0	0	66
Taylor, N.Y.	11	7	4	0	66
Anderson, St.L.	10	8	2	0	60
Galbreath, N.O.	10	9	1	0	60
Hill, Dall.	10	0	10	0	60
Tyler, L.A.	10	9	1	0	60

Best Performance: 4 TDs for 24 points by Ahmad Rashad of Minnesota vs. San Francisco, Sept. 2, 1979; by Wilbert Montgomery of Philadelphia vs. Washington, Oct. 7, 1979

	PATs	FGs	Longest	Pts.
Leading Kick Scorers				
Moseley, Wash.	39-39	25-33	53	114
Franklin, Phil.	36-39	23-31	59	105
Septien, Dall.	40-44	19-29	51	97
Wersching, S.F.	32-35	20-24	47	92
Thomas, Chi.	34-37	16-27	44	82
Corral, L.A.	36-39	13-25	49	75
Yepremian, N.O.	39-40	12-16	44	75
Mazzetti, Atl.	31-37	13-25	48	70
Danmeier, Minn.	28-30	13-22	44	67
O'Donoghue, T.B.	30-35	11-19	44	63

LEADING PASSERS
(192 Attempts)

	Atts.	Com.	Pct. Com.	Yds.	Avg. Yds.	Had Int.	TDs	Rat- ing*
Staubach, Dall.	461	267	57.9	3586	7.78	11	27	92.4
Theismann, Wash.	395	233	59.0	2797	7.08	13	20	84.0
Jaworski, Phil.	374	190	50.8	2669	7.14	12	18	76.8
Manning, N.O.	420	252	60.0	3169	7.55	20	15	75.6
DeBerg, S.F.	578	347	60.0	3652	6.32	21	17	73.1
Kramer, Minn.	566	315	55.7	3397	6.00	24	23	69.7
Phipps, Chi.	255	134	52.5	1535	6.02	8	9	69.7
Haden, L.A.	290	163	56.2	1854	6.39	14	11	68.2
Bartkowski, Atl.	380	204	53.7	2505	6.59	20	17	67.2
Simms, N.Y.	265	134	50.6	1743	6.58	14	13	65.9
Whitehurst, G.B.	322	179	55.6	2247	6.98	18	10	64.5

	Atts.	Com.	Pct. Com.	Yds.	Avg. Yds.	Had Int.	TDs	Rating*
Hart, St.L.	378	194	51.3	2218	5.87	20	9	55.2
Williams, T.B.	397	166	41.8	2448	6.17	24	18	52.6
Komlo, Det.	368	183	49.7	2238	6.08	23	11	52.6

Longest: 85 yards by Archie Manning to Wes Chandler of New Orleans vs. San Francisco, Sept. 23, 1979.

* Official NFL passing ratings are based on percentage of completions, average yards gained, TD passing percentage, interception percentage

LEADING PASS RECEIVERS

	No.	Yds.	Avg.	Longest	TDs
Rashad, Minn.	80	1156	14.5	52	9
Francis, Atl.	74	1013	13.7	42	8
Young, Minn. (rb)	72	519	7.2	18	4
Chandler, N.O.	65	1069	16.4	85	6
Scott, Det.	62	929	15.0	50	5
Hill, Dall.	60	1062	17.7	75	10
Hofer, S.F. (rb)	58	662	11.4	44	2
Galbreath, N.O. (rb)	58	484	8.3	38	1
Tilley, St.L.	57	938	16.5	37	6
Solomon, S.F.	57	807	14.2	44	7
Coffman, G.B.	56	711	12.7	78	4
D. Pearson, Dall.	55	1026	18.7	56	8
Lofton, G.B.	54	968	17.9	52	4
Jackson, S.F. (rb)	53	422	8.0	34	0
Carmichael, Phil.	52	872	16.8	50	11
Childs, N.O.	51	846	16.6	51	5
Jenkins, Atl.	50	858	17.2	57	3
Hill, Det.	47	569	12.1	34	3
Buggs, Wash.	46	631	13.7	45	1
Dorsett, Dall. (rb)	45	375	8.3	32	1

Best Performance: 15 receptions for 116 yards by Rickey Young of Minnesota vs. New England, Dec. 16, 1979 (1 TD)

INTERCEPTION LEADERS

	No.	Yds.	Longest	TDs
Parrish, Wash.	9	65	23	0
Myers, N.O.	7	127	52	1
Lawrence, Atl.	6	120	38	0
Lavender, Wash.	6	77	27	0
Stone, St.L.	6	70	30	0
Schmidt, Chi.	6	44	20	1
Fencik, Chi.	6	31	17	0

Longest: 78 yards by Carl Allen of St. Louis vs. Chicago, Dec. 16, 1979

LEADING RUSHERS

	Atts.	Yds.	Avg.	Longest	TDs
Payton, Chi.	369	1610	4.4	43	14
Anderson, St.L.	331	1605	4.8	76	8
Montgomery, Phil.	338	1512	4.5	62	9
Bell, T.B.	283	1263	4.5	49	7
Muncie, N.O.	238	1198	5.0	69	11
Riggins, Wash.	260	1153	4.4	66	9
Tyler, L.A.	218	1109	5.1	63	9
Dorsett, Dall.	250	1107	4.4	41	6
Andrews, Atl.	239	1023	4.3	23	3
Galbreath, N.O.	189	708	3.7	27	9
Young, Minn.	188	708	3.8	26	3
Taylor, N.Y.	198	700	3.5	31	7
Eckwood, T.B.	194	690	3.6	61	2
Bussey, Det.	144	625	4.3	38	1
Bryant, L.A.	177	619	3.5	15	5
Kotar, N.Y.	160	616	3.9	32	3
Hofer, S.F.	123	615	5.0	47	7
Brown, Minn.	130	551	4.2	34	1
Harris, Phil.	107	504	4.7	80	2
Middleton, G.B.	131	495	3.8	28	2

Best Performance: 197 yards in 30 attempts by Wilbert Montgomery of Philadelphia vs. Cleveland, Nov. 4, 1979 (1 TD)
Longest: 80 yards by Leroy Harris of Philadelphia vs. Green Bay, Nov. 25, 1979

LEADING PUNTERS

	No.	Yds.	Avg.	Longest	Blocked
Jennings, N.Y.	104	4445	42.7	72	0
D. White, Dall.	76	3168	41.7	73	0
Partridge, N.O.	57	2330	40.9	61	0
Beverly, G.B.	69	2785	40.4	65	0
Clark, L.A.	93	3731	40.1	60	2
Swider, Det.	88	3523	40.0	72	0
James, Atl.	83	3296	39.7	62	1
Blanchard, T.B.	93	3679	39.6	58	2
Runager, Phil.	74	2927	39.6	57	1
Coleman, Minn.	90	3551	39.5	70	1
Little, St.L.	79	3060	38.7	63	2
Bragg, Wash.	78	2998	38.4	74	0
Parsons, Chi.	92	3486	37.9	54	1
Melville, S.F.	71	2626	37.0	53	1

Longest: 74 yards by Mike Bragg of Washington vs. N.Y. Giants, Nov. 25, 1979

PUNT RETURN LEADERS

	No.	Yds.	Avg.	Longest	TDs
Sciarra, Phil.	16	182	11.4	38	0
Schubert, Chi.	25	238	9.5	77	1
Henry, Phil.	35	320	9.1	34	0
Arnold, Det.	19	164	8.6	27	0
Hardeman, Wash.	24	207	8.6	52	0
Mauti, N.O.	27	218	8.1	33	0
Wilson, Dall.	35	236	6.7	13	0
Harrell, St.L.	32	205	6.4	68	0
Solomon, S.F.	23	142	6.2	14	0
Reece, T.B.	70	431	6.2	17	0
Brown, L.A.	56	332	5.9	30	0
Edwards, Minn.	33	186	5.6	42	0
K. Miller, Minn.	18	85	4.7	14	0
Odom, N.Y.	24	106	4.4	19	0

Longest: 77 yards by Steve Schubert of Chicago vs. Detroit, Nov. 4, 1979 (TD); by Lee Nelson of St. Louis vs. Chicago, Dec. 16, 1979

KICKOFF RETURN LEADERS

	No.	Yds.	Avg.	Longest	TDs
Edwards, Minn.	44	1103	25.1	83	0
Green, St.L.	41	1005	24.5	106	1
Owens, S.F.	41	1002	24.4	85	1
Henry, Phil.	28	668	23.9	53	0
Arnold, Det.	23	539	23.4	69	0
Harrell, St.L.	22	497	22.6	53	0
Walterscheid, Chi.	19	427	22.5	44	0
Mauti, N.O.	36	801	22.3	39	0
Hammond, Wash.	25	544	21.8	39	0
Odom, N.Y.	44	949	21.6	75	0
Hardeman, Wash.	19	404	21.3	33	0
Springs, Dall.	38	780	20.5	70	0
D. Hill, L.A.	40	803	20.1	39	0
Ragsdale, T.B.	34	675	19.9	30	0

Longest: 106 yards by Roy Green of St. Louis vs. Dallas, Oct. 21, 1979 (TD)

NATIONAL FOOTBALL CONFERENCE
1979 Team Statistics

	Yds.	Rush.	Pass.	Avg. PG
Total Offense				
Dallas	5968*	2375	3593	373.0*
New Orleans	5627	2476	3151	351.7
San Francisco	5573	1932	3641*	348.3
St. Louis	5184	2582*	2602	324.0
Los Angeles	5133	2460	2673	320.8
Tampa Bay	5049	2437	2612	315.6
Philadelphia	5031	2421	2610	314.4
Atlanta	4929	2200	2729	308.1
Washington	4904	2328	2576	306.5
Minnesota	4903	1764	3139	306.4
Chicago	4637	2486	2151	289.8
Green Bay	4542	1861	2681	283.9
Detroit	4013	1677	2336	250.8
New York Giants	3774	1820	1954	235.9

* Conference leader

	Atts.	Yds.	Avg.	Avg. PG
Rushing Offense				
St. Louis	566	2582*	4.6*	161.4*
Chicago	627*	2486	4.0	155.4
New Orleans	551	2476	4.5	154.8
Los Angeles	592	2460	4.2	153.8
Tampa Bay	609	2437	4.0	152.3
Philadelphia	567	2421	4.3	151.3
Dallas	578	2375	4.1	148.4
Washington	609	2328	3.8	145.5
Atlanta	500	2200	4.4	137.5
San Francisco	480	1932	4.0	120.8
Green Bay	483	1861	3.9	116.3
New York Giants	498	1820	3.7	113.8
Minnesota	487	1764	3.6	110.3
Detroit	441	1677	3.8	104.8

	Atts.	Com.	Pct.	Int.	Avg. PG	QB Sacks
Passing Offense						
San Francisco	602*	361*	60.0*	21	227.6*	17
Dallas	503	287	57.1	13*	224.6	41
New Orleans	428	257	60.0*	22	196.9	17
Minnesota	566	315	55.7	24	196.2	37
Atlanta	479	251	52.4	23	170.6	54
Green Bay	444	240	54.1	22	167.6	47
Los Angeles	456	242	53.1	29	167.1	39
Tampa Bay	434	183	42.2	26	163.3	12*
Philadelphia	410	209	51.0	13*	163.1	34
St. Louis	492	248	50.4	24	162.6	39
Washington	401	235	58.6	15	161.0	34
Detroit	452	218	48.2	27	146.0	51
Chicago	373	195	52.3	16	134.4	31
New York Giants	401	190	47.4	22	122.1	59

	Yds.	Rush.	Pass.	Avg. PG
Total Defense				
Tampa Bay	3949*	1873*	2076*	246.8*
Chicago	4506	1978	2528	281.6
Los Angeles	4553	1997	2556	284.6
Dallas	4586	2115	2471	286.6
Philadelphia	4745	2271	2474	296.6
Detroit	4957	2515	2442	309.8
St. Louis	5077	2204	2873	317.3

* Conference leader

	Yds.	Rush.	Pass.	Avg. PG
Washington	5146	2154	2992	321.6
Minnesota	5223	2526	2697	326.4
New York Giants	5378	2452	2926	336.1
San Francisco	5393	2213	3180	337.1
New Orleans	5535	2469	3066	345.9
Green Bay	5647	2885	2762	352.9
Atlanta	5759	2163	3596	359.9

	Atts.	Yds.	Avg.	Avg. PG
Rushing Defense				
Tampa Bay	539	1873*	3.5*	117.1*
Chicago	519	1978	3.8	123.6
Los Angeles	548	1997	3.6	124.8
Dallas	500*	2115	4.2	132.2
Washington	541	2154	4.0	134.6
Atlanta	555	2163	3.9	135.2
St. Louis	567	2204	3.9	137.8
San Francisco	544	2213	4.1	138.3
Philadelphia	515	2271	4.4	141.9
New York Giants	618	2452	4.0	153.3
New Orleans	521	2469	4.7	154.3
Detroit	638	2515	3.9	157.2
Minnesota	583	2526	4.3	157.9
Green Bay	639	2885	4.5	180.3

	Atts.	Com.	Pct.	Int.	Avg. PG	QB Sacks
Passing Defense						
Tampa Bay	436	250	57.3	14	129.8*	40
Detroit	402*	220	54.7	14	152.6	45
Dallas	435	207*	47.6*	13	154.4	43
Philadelphia	459	243	52.9	22	154.6	45
Chicago	458	222	48.5	29*	158.0	47
Los Angeles	454	220	48.5	25	159.8	52*
Minnesota	424	229	54.0	22	168.6	30
Green Bay	440	249	56.6	18	172.6	35
St. Louis	478	258	54.0	18	179.6	28
New York Giants	463	253	54.6	21	182.9	32
Washington	470	234	49.8	26	187.0	47
New Orleans	488	265	54.3	26	191.6	46
San Francisco	441	262	59.4	15	198.8	29
Atlanta	487	268	55.0	15	224.8	29

* Conference leader

LET'S LOOK AT THE RECORDS

- A selection of all-time NFL individual records

- NFL 1000-yard rushers

- NFL all-time individual champions

- NFC divisional winners and championship playoff results, 1921–79

- AFC divisional winners and championship playoff results, 1960–79

- All-time Super Bowl results and a selection of records, 1967–80

- AFC–NFC Pro Bowl results, 1971–80

- Professional Football Hall of Fame

FOOTNOTING THE FOOTNOTES

The **Chicago Cardinals,** sometimes listed as "Chi Cards" in the records, existed from 1920 through 1959 and moved to St. Louis beginning with the 1960 season.

The **Cleveland Rams** were in that Ohio city from 1937 through the 1946 season, moving to Los Angeles in 1947.

The **Boston Redskins** played in the Massachusetts capital from 1932 through 1936; they elected to begin the 1937 season in Washington.

Before they traveled to Kansas City to begin the 1963 season, the **Chiefs** were in Dallas for three years where they were known as the **Texans.**

The **New England Patriots** were the **Boston Patriots** from 1960 through 1970. For those years, they are listed as "Boston" in the records that follow.

The **New York Jets** were called the **Titans** when they first took the field in 1960. They became the Jets beginning with the 1963 season.

The **San Diego Chargers** had the same name in Los Angeles for one season, 1960, the first year of the modern American Football League, which eventually became the basis for the American Conference of the NFL.

The **Detroit Lions** began their history as the **Portsmouth** (O.) **Spartans** from 1930 through 1933. They changed their name and moved to Motor City in 1934.

National Football League
A SELECTION OF
ALL-TIME INDIVIDUAL RECORDS

Most total points in lifetime
George Blanda, 2002; Chicago Bears 1949–58, Baltimore 1959, Houston
1960–66, Oakland 1967–75; 9 TDs, 943 PATs, 335 FGs
Jim Bakken, 1380; St. Louis 1962–78; 534 PATs, 282 FGs
Jim Turner, 1439; N.Y. Jets 1964–70, Denver 1971–79; 1 TD, 521 PATs,
304 FGs

Most points in one season
Paul Hornung, 176 (Green Bay 1960); 15 TDs, 41 PATs, 15 FGs
Gino Cappelletti, 155 (Boston 1964); 7 TDs, 38 PATs, 25 FGs
Gino Cappelletti, 147 (Boston 1961); 8 TDs, 49 PATs, 17 FGs

Most points in rookie season
Gale Sayers, 132 (Chicago 1965); 22 TDs
Doak Walker, 128 (Detroit 1950); 11 TDs, 38 PATs, 8 FGs
Cookie Gilchrist, 128 (Buffalo 1962); 15 TDs, 14 PATs, 8 FGs
Chester Marcol, 128 (Green Bay 1972); 29 PATs, 33 FGs
Gene Mingo, 123 (Denver 1960); 6 TDs, 33 PATs, 18 FGs

Most points in one game
Ernie Nevers, 40—Chicago Cardinals vs. Chicago Bears, Nov. 28, 1929
(6 TDs, 4 PATs)
William (Dub) Jones, 36—Cleveland vs. Chicago Bears, Nov. 25, 1951
(6 TDs)
Gale Sayers, 36—Chicago vs. San Francisco, Dec. 12, 1965 (6 TDs)
Paul Hornung, 33—Green Bay vs. Baltimore, Oct. 8, 1961 (4 TDs,
6 PATs, 1 FG)

Most touchdowns in one season
O. J. Simpson, 23 (Buffalo 1975); 16 run, 7 pass
Chuck Foreman, 22 (Minnesota 1975); 13 run, 9 pass
Gale Sayers, 22 (Chicago 1965); 14 run, 6 pass, 1 punt ret., 1 KO ret.
Jim Brown, 21 (Cleveland 1965); 17 run, 4 pass

Most touchdowns in rookie season
Gale Sayers, 22 (Chicago 1965); 14 run, 6 pass, 1 punt ret., 1 KO ret.
Cookie Gilchrist, 15 (Buffalo 1962); 13 run, 2 pass
Billy Howton, 13 (Green Bay 1952); 13 pass
Bob Hayes, 13 (Dallas 1965); 1 run, 12 pass
Tony Dorsett, 13 (Dallas 1977); 12 run, 1 pass
Earl Campbell, 13 (Houston 1978); 13 run
John Jefferson, 13 (San Diego 1978); 13 pass

Most PATs in one season
George Blanda, 64 (Houston 1961)
Danny Villanueva, 56 (Dallas 1966)
George Blanda, 56 (Oakland 1967)

Most FGs in one season
Jim Turner, 34 (N.Y. Jets 1968)
Chester Marcol, 33 (Green Bay 1972)
Jim Turner, 32 (N.Y. Jets 1969)

Most rushing attempts in one season
Walter Payton, 369 (Chicago 1979)
Earl Campbell, 368 (Houston 1979)
Walter Payton, 339 (Chicago 1977)
Wilbert Montgomery, 338 (Philadelphia 1979)

Most yards rushing in one season
O. J. Simpson, 2003 (Buffalo 1973)
Jim Brown, 1863 (Cleveland 1963)
Walter Payton, 1852 (Chicago 1977)

Best average rushing gain for one season
Beattie Feathers, 9.94 (Chicago Bears 1934); 101 atts., 1004 yds.
Bobby Douglass, 6.87 (Chicago 1972); 141 atts., 968 yds.
Dan Towler, 6.78 (Los Angeles 1951); 126 atts., 854 yds.

Most touchdowns rushing in one season
Earl Campbell, 19 (Houston 1979)
Jim Taylor, 19 (Green Bay 1962)
Jim Brown, 17 (Cleveland 1958 and 1965)

Most passes attempted in one season
Steve DeBerg, 578 (San Francisco 1979)
Fran Tarkenton, 572 (Minnesota 1978)
Tommy Kramer, 556 (Minnesota 1979)
Brian Sipe, 535 (Cleveland 1979)
Dan Fouts, 530 (San Diego 1979)

Most passes completed in one season
Steve DeBerg, 347 (San Francisco 1979)
Fran Tarkenton, 345 (Minnesota 1978)
Dan Fouts, 332 (San Diego 1979)
Tommy Kramer, 315 (Minnesota 1979)
Ken Stabler, 304 (Oakland 1979)
Archie Manning, 291 (New Orleans 1978)

Most passing yards in one season
Dan Fouts, 4082 (San Diego 1979)
Joe Namath, 4007 (N.Y. Jets 1967)
Brian Sipe, 3793 (Cleveland 1979)
Sonny Jurgensen, 3747 (Washington 1967)
Terry Bradshaw, 3724 (Pittsburgh 1979)

Most touchdown passes in one season
George Blanda, 36 (Houston 1961)
Y. A. Tittle, 36 (N.Y. Giants 1963)
Daryle Lamonica, 34 (Oakland 1969)

Fewest passes intercepted in one season (Qualifiers)
1—Joe Ferguson (Buffalo 1976)
3—Gary Wood (N.Y. Giants 1964); Bart Starr (Green Bay 1966)
4—Sammy Baugh (Washington 1945); Harry Gilmer (Detroit 1955);
Charlie Conerly (N.Y. Giants 1959); Bart Starr (Green Bay 1964);
Roger Staubach (Dallas 1971); Len Dawson (Kansas City 1975)

Most pass receptions in one season
Charlie Hennigan, 101 (Houston 1964)
Lionel Taylor, 100 (Denver 1961)
Johnny Morris, 93 (Chicago 1964)

Most yards gained receiving in one season
Charlie Hennigan, 1746 (Houston 1961)
Lance Alworth, 1602 (San Diego 1965)
Charlie Hennigan, 1546 (Houston 1964)

Most touchdowns receiving in one season
Don Hutson, 17 (Green Bay 1942)
Elroy Hirsch, 17 (Los Angeles 1951)
Bill Groman, 17 (Houston 1961)
Art Powell, 16 (Oakland 1963)
Cloyce Box, 15 (Detroit 1952)
Ulmo (Sonny) Randle, 15 (St. Louis 1960)

Most interceptions in one season
Richard (Night Train) Lane, 14 (Los Angeles 1952)
Dan Sandifer, 13 (Washington 1948)
Orban (Spec) Sanders, 13 (N.Y. Yanks 1950)

Most interception yards in one season
Charley McNeil, 349 (San Diego 1961)
Don Doll, 301 (Detroit 1949)
Richard (Night Train) Lane, 298 (Los Angeles 1952)

Best punting average for one season
(At least 35 punts to qualify)
Sammy Baugh, 51.4 (Washington 1940)
R. Yale Lary, 48.9 (Detroit 1963)
Sammy Baugh, 48.7 (Washington 1941)

Longest punt
Steve O'Neal, 98 yds.—N.Y. Jets vs. Denver, Sept. 21, 1969
Don Chandler, 90 yds.—Green Bay vs. San Francisco, Oct. 10, 1965
Bob Waterfield, 88 yds.—Los Angeles vs. Green Bay, Oct. 17, 1948

NFL's Exclusive
1000-YARD RUSHERS CLUB

Year	Player	Team	Yards
1934	Beattie Feathers	Chicago	1,004
1947	Steve Van Buren	Philadelphia	1,008
1949	Steve Van Buren	Philadelphia	1,146
	Tony Canadeo	Green Bay	1,052
1953	Joe Perry	San Francisco	1,018
1954	Joe Perry	San Francisco	1,049
1956	Rick Casares	Chicago	1,126
1958	Jim Brown	Cleveland	1,527
1959	Jim Brown	Cleveland	1,329
	J.D. Smith	San Francisco	1,036
1960	Jim Brown	Cleveland	1,257
	Jim Taylor	Green Bay	1,101
	John David Crow	St. Louis	1,071
1961	Jim Brown	Cleveland	1,408
	Jim Taylor	Green Bay	1,307
1962	Jim Taylor	Green Bay	1,474
	John Henry Johnson	Pittsburgh	1,141
	Cookie Gilchrist	Buffalo	1,096
	Abner Haynes	Dallas Texans	1,049
	Dick Bass	Los Angeles	1,033
	Charlie Tolar	Houston	1,012
1963	Jim Brown	Cleveland	1,863
	Clem Daniels	Oakland	1,099
	Jim Taylor	Green Bay	1,018
	Paul Lowe	San Diego	1,010
1964	Jim Brown	Cleveland	1,446
	Jim Taylor	Green Bay	1,169
	John Henry Johnson	Pittsburgh	1,048
1965	Jim Brown	Cleveland	1,544
	Paul Lowe	San Diego	1,121
1966	Jim Nance	Boston	1,458
	Gale Sayers	Chicago	1,231
	Leroy Kelly	Cleveland	1,141
	Dick Bass	Los Angeles	1,090

Year	Player	Team	Yards
1967	Jim Nance	Boston	1,216
	Leroy Kelly	Cleveland	1,205
	Hoyle Granger	Houston	1,194
	Mike Garrett	Kansas City	1,087
1968	Leroy Kelly	Cleveland	1,239
	Paul Robinson	Cincinnati	1,023
1969	Gale Sayers	Chicago	1,032
1970	Larry Brown	Washington	1,125
	Ron Johnson	N.Y. Giants	1,027
1971	Floyd Little	Denver	1,133
	John Brockington	Green Bay	1,105
	Larry Csonka	Miami	1,051
	Steve Owens	Detroit	1,035
	Willie Ellison	Los Angeles	1,000
1972	O.J. Simpson	Buffalo	1,251
	Larry Brown	Washington	1,216
	Ron Johnson	N.Y. Giants	1,182
	Larry Csonka	Miami	1,117
	Marv Hubbard	Oakland	1,100
	Franco Harris	Pittsburgh	1,055
	Calvin Hill	Dallas	1,036
	Mike Garrett	San Diego	1,031
	John Brockington	Green Bay	1,027
	Eugene Morris	Miami	1,000
1973	O.J. Simpson	Buffalo	2,003
	John Brockington	Green Bay	1,144
	Calvin Hill	Dallas	1,142
	Lawrence McCutcheon	Los Angeles	1,097
	Larry Csonka	Miami	1,003
1974	Otis Armstrong	Denver	1,407
	Don Woods	San Diego	1,162
	O.J. Simpson	Buffalo	1,125
	Lawrence McCutcheon	Los Angeles	1,109
	Franco Harris	Pittsburgh	1,006
1975	O.J. Simpson	Buffalo	1,817
	Franco Harris	Pittsburgh	1,246
	Lydell Mitchell	Baltimore	1,193
	Jim Otis	St. Louis	1,076
	Chuck Foreman	Minnesota	1,070
	Greg Pruitt	Cleveland	1,067
	John Riggins	N.Y. Jets	1,005
	Dave Hampton	Atlanta	1,002
1976	O.J. Simpson	Buffalo	1,503
	Walter Payton	Chicago	1,390
	Delvin Williams	San Francisco	1,203
	Lydell Mitchell	Baltimore	1,200

Year	Player	Team	Yards
1976	Lawrence McCutcheon	Los Angeles	1,168
	Chuck Foreman	Minnesota	1,155
	Franco Harris	Pittsburgh	1,128
	Mike Thomas	Washington	1,101
	Rocky Bleier	Pittsburgh	1,036
	Mark van Eeghen	Oakland	1,012
	Otis Armstrong	Denver	1,008
	Greg Pruitt	Cleveland	1,000
1977	Walter Payton	Chicago	1,852
	Mark van Eeghen	Oakland	1,273
	Lawrence McCutcheon	Los Angeles	1,238
	Franco Harris	Pittsburgh	1,162
	Lydell Mitchell	Baltimore	1,159
	Chuck Foreman	Minnesota	1,112
	Greg Pruitt	Cleveland	1,086
	Sam Cunningham	New England	1,015
	Tony Dorsett	Dallas	1,007
1978	Earl Campbell	Houston	1,450
	Walter Payton	Chicago	1,395
	Tony Dorsett	Dallas	1,325
	Delvin Williams	Miami	1,258
	Wilbert Montgomery	Philadelphia	1,220
	Terdell Middleton	Green Bay	1,116
	Franco Harris	Pittsburgh	1,082
	Mark van Eeghen	Oakland	1,080
	Terry Miller	Buffalo	1,060
	Tony Reed	Kansas City	1,053
	John Riggins	Washington	1,014
1979	Earl Campbell	Houston	1,697
	Walter Payton	Chicago	1,610
	Ottis Anderson	St. Louis	1,605
	Wilbert Montgomery	Philadelphia	1,512
	Mike Pruitt	Cleveland	1,294
	Ricky Bell	Tampa Bay	1,263
	Chuck Muncie	New Orleans	1,198
	Franco Harris	Pittsburgh	1,186
	John Riggins	Washington	1,153
	Wendell Tyler	Los Angeles	1,109
	Tony Dorsett	Dallas	1,107
	William Andrews	Atlanta	1,023

The National Football League's
ALL-TIME TOP TEN SCORERS

Player	Seasons	TDs	PATs	FGs	Pts.
George Blanda	26	9	943	335	2,002
Jim Turner*	16	1	521	305	1,439
Jim Bakken	17	0	534	282	1,380
Fred Cox	15	0	519	282	1,365
Lou Groza	17	1	641	234	1,349
Jan Stenerud*	13	0	394	279	1,231
Gino Cappelletti†	11	42	350	176	1,130
Bruce Gossett	11	0	374	219	1,031
Don Cockroft*	12	0	393	200	993
Garo Yepremian*	12	0	407	192	983

The National Football League's
ALL-TIME TOP TEN RUSHERS

Player	Seasons	Yds.	Atts.
Jim Brown	9	12,312	2,359
O. J. Simpson*	11	11,236	2,404
Jim Taylor	10	8,597	1,941
Franco Harris*	8	8,563	2,012
Joe Perry	14	8,378	1,737
Larry Csonka*	11	8,081	1,891
Leroy Kelly	10	7,274	1,727
John Riggins*	9	6,822	1,666
John Henry Johnson	13	6,803	1,571
Lydell Mitchell*	8	6,518	1,668

* Active at end of 1979 season
† Includes four 2-point conversions

The National Football League's
ALL-TIME TOP TEN PASS RECEIVERS

Player	Seasons	Caught	Yds.
Charley Taylor	13	649	9,117
Don Maynard	15	633	11,834
Raymond Berry	13	631	9,275
Fred Biletnikoff	14	589	8,974
Lionel Taylor	10	567	7,195
Lance Alworth	11	542	10,266
Bobby Mitchell	11	521	7,954
Billy Howton	12	503	8,459
Harold Jackson*	12	497	8,846
Tommy McDonald	12	495	8,410

The National Football League's
ALL-TIME TOP TEN PASS INTERCEPTORS

Player	Seasons	No.	Yds.
Paul Krause*	16	81	1,185
Emlen Tunnell	14	79	1,282
Dick (Night Train) Lane	14	68	1,207
Dick LeBeau	13	62	762
Emmitt Thomas	13	58	937
Bob Boyd	9	57	994
Johnny Robinson	12	57	741
Pat Fischer	16	56	941
Lem Barney	12	56	1,051
Willie Brown	16	54	472

* Active at end of 1979 season

The National Football League's
ALL-TIME TOP TEN PUNTERS
(300 or More Punts)

Player	Seasons	No.	Avg.
Sammy Baugh	16	338	45.1
Tommy Davis	11	511	44.7
Yale Lary	11	503	44.3
Horace Gillom	7	385	43.8
Jerry Norton	11	358	43.8
Don Chandler	12	660	43.5
Jerrel Wilson	16	1,068	43.2
Ray Guy*	7	487	43.0
Norm Van Brocklin	12	523	42.9
Danny Villanueva	8	488	42.8

The National Football League's
ALL-TIME TOP TEN PUNT RETURNERS

Player	Seasons	No.	Yds.	Avg.
Billy Johnson*	6	151	2,023	13.4
George McAfee	8	112	1,431	12.8
Jack Christiansen	8	85	1,084	12.8
Claude Gibson	5	110	1,381	12.6
Rick Upchurch*	5	183	2,298	12.5
Bill Dudley	9	124	1,515	12.2
Mike Haynes	3	83	991	11.9
Mack Herron	3	84	982	11.7
Bill Thompson*	11	157	1,814	11.6
Mike Fuller*	5	182	2,090	11.4

* Active at end of 1979 season

The National Football League's
ALL-TIME TOP TEN KICKOFF RETURNERS
(75 or More Returns)

Player	Seasons	No.	Yds.	Avg.
Gale Sayers	7	91	2781	30.6
Lynn Chandnois	7	92	2720	29.6
Abe Woodson	9	193	5538	28.7
Claude (Buddy) Young	6	90	2514	27.9
Travis Williams	5	102	2801	27.5
Joe Arenas	7	139	3798	27.3
Clarence Davis	7	79	2140	27.0
Steve Van Buren	8	76	2030	26.7
Lenny Lyles	12	81	2161	26.7
Eugene (Mercury) Morris	8	111	2947	26.5

PRO FOOTBALL HALL OF FAME TOP 20
LEADING LIFETIME PASSERS
(1,500 or more career attempts)

Player	Yrs.	Att.	Comp.	Yds.	TD	Int.	Rating
Otto Graham†	10	2626	1464	23,584	174	135	86.8
Roger Staubach*	11	2958	1685	22,700	153	109	83.5
Sonny Jurgensen	18	4262	2433	32,224	255	189	82.8
Len Dawson	19	3741	2136	28,711	239	183	82.6
Fran Tarkenton	18	6467	3686	47,003	342	266	80.5
Bert Jones*	7	1592	890	11,435	78	56	80.3
Bart Starr†	16	3149	1808	24,718	152	138	80.3
Ken Stabler*	10	2481	1486	19,078	150	143	79.9
Ken Anderson*	9	2785	1570	20,030	125	101	79.1
Johnny Unitas†	18	5186	2830	40,239	290	253	78.2
Frank Ryan	13	2133	1090	16,042	149	111	77.7
Bob Griese	13	3329	1865	24,302	186	168	77.0
Norm Van Brocklin†	12	2895	1553	23,611	173	178	75.3
Sid Luckman†	12	1744	904	14,686	137	132	75.0
Don Meredith	9	2308	1170	17,199	135	111	74.7
Roman Gabriel	16	4498	2366	29,444	201	149	74.5
Y. A.Tittle†	17	4395	2427	33,070	242	248	74.4
Earl Morrall	21	2689	1379	20,809	161	148	74.2
Greg Landry*	11	2204	1227	15,383	95	96	73.6
Frank Albert	7	1564	831	10,795	115	98	73.5

* Active at end of 1979 season   † Pro Football Hall of Fame members

National Football Conference
DIVISIONAL WINNERS AND
PLAYOFF CHAMPIONSHIP RESULTS, 1921–79

NOTE: Wild card qualifiers (WC) are teams that have the best fourth and fifth place records in each conference at close of regular season's schedule, or teams that qualify otherwise in case of ties.

The National Football League was organized on Sept. 17, 1920, and was at first called the American Professional Football Association. The name was changed in 1922. During that first season of 1920, there was no organized schedule of games and the number of clubs varied from week to week; at one point there was a total of 13.

During the period 1967–69, the National Football League consisted of two conferences, the Eastern and the Western; each had two divisions. In the Eastern Conference they were the Capitol (Ca) and the Century (Cy); in the Western Conference they were the Coastal (Co) and the Central (Ce). Playoffs were between the divisional champions in each conference, and these were followed by the NFL championship game between the conference winners.

During the period 1953–66, the NFL consisted of two conferences, the Eastern and the Western, with no divisions. The NFL championship game was played between the two conference winners.

During the period 1950–52, the NFL consisted of two conferences, the American and the National, with no divisions. The NFL championship game was played between the two conference winners.

During the period 1933–49, the NFL consisted of two divisions, the Eastern and the Western. The NFL championship game was played between the two division winners.

During the period 1921–32, the NFL operated as a single division, with the membership over the years ranging from eight clubs to as many as 22. Therefore, there were no divisional playoffs or championship games. Title winners for those years were the clubs that finished with the best won-lost records.

Year	Winners	Record	Pct.	Coach
1979	Dallas Cowboys (E)	11–5–0	.688	Tom Landry
	Tampa Bay Buccaneers (C)	10–6–0	.625	John McKay
	Los Angeles Rams (W)	9–7–0	.563	Ray Malavasi
	Philadelphia Eagles (WC)	11–5–0	.688	Dick Vermeil
	Chicago Bears (WC)	10–6–0	.625	Neill Armstrong

First-round playoff: Eagles 27, Bears 17
Divisional playoffs: Buccaneers 24, Eagles 17; Rams 21, Cowboys 19
NFC championship game: Rams 9, Buccaneers 0
Super Bowl XIV: Steelers (AFC) 31, Rams (NFC) 19

Year	Winners	Record	Pct.	Coach
1978	Dallas Cowboys (E)	12–4–0	.750	Tom Landry
	Minnesota Vikings (C)	8–7–1	.531	Bud Grant
	Los Angeles Rams (W)	12–4–0	.750	Ray Malavasi
	Philadelphia Eagles (WC)	9–7–0	.563	Dick Vermeil
	Atlanta Falcons (WC)	9–7–0	.563	Leeman Bennett

First-round playoff: Falcons 14, Eagles 13
Divisional playoffs: Cowboys 27, Falcons 20; Rams 34, Vikings 10
NFC championship game: Cowboys 28, Rams 0
Super Bowl XIII: Steelers (AFC) 35, Cowboys (NFC) 31

1977	Dallas Cowboys (E)	12–2–0	.857	Tom Landry
	Minnesota Vikings (C)	9–5–0	.643	Bud Grant
	Los Angeles Rams (W)	10–4–0	.714	Chuck Knox
	Chicago Bears (WC)	9–5–0	.643	Jack Pardee

Divisional playoffs: Cowboys 37, Bears 7; Vikings 14, Rams 7
NFC championship game: Cowboys 23, Vikings 6
Super Bowl XII: Cowboys (NFC) 27, Broncos (AFC) 10

1976	Dallas Cowboys (E)	11–3–0	.786	Tom Landry
	Minnesota Vikings (C)	11–2–1	.821	Bud Grant
	Los Angeles Rams (W)	10–3–1	.750	Chuck Knox
	Washington Redskins (WC)	10–4–0	.714	George Allen

Divisional playoffs: Vikings 35, Redskins 20; Rams 14, Cowboys 12
NFC championship game: Vikings 24, Rams 13
Super Bowl XI: Raiders (AFC) 32, Vikings (NFC) 14

1975	St. Louis Cardinals (E)	11–3–0	.786	Don Coryell
	Minnesota Vikings (C)	12–2–0	.857	Bud Grant
	Los Angeles Rams (W)	12–2–0	.857	Chuck Knox
	Dallas Cowboys (WC)	10–4–0	.714	Tom Landry

Divisional playoffs: Rams 35, Cardinals 23; Cowboys 17, Vikings 14
NFC championship game: Cowboys 37, Rams 7
Super Bowl X: Steelers (AFC) 21, Cowboys (NFC) 17

1974	St. Louis Cardinals (E)	10–4–0	.714	Don Coryell
	Minnesota Vikings (C)	10–4–0	.714	Bud Grant
	Los Angeles Rams (W)	10–4–0	.714	Chuck Knox
	Washington Redskins (WC)	10–4–0	.714	George Allen

Divisional playoffs: Vikings 30, Cardinals 14; Rams 19, Redskins 10
NFC championship game: Vikings 14, Rams 10
Super Bowl IX: Steelers (AFC) 16, Vikings (NFC) 6

1973	Dallas Cowboys (E)	10–4–0	.714	Tom Landry
	Minnesota Vikings (C)	12–2–0	.857	Bud Grant
	Los Angeles Rams (W)	12–2–0	.857	Chuck Knox
	Washington Redskins (WC)	10–4–0	.714	George Allen

Year	Winners	Record	Pct.	Coach
	Divisional playoffs: Vikings 27, Redskins 20; Cowboys 27, Rams 16			
	NFC championship game: Vikings 27, Cowboys 10			
	Super Bowl VIII: Dolphins (AFC) 24, Vikings (NFC) 7			
1972	Washington Redskins (E)	11–3–0	.786	George Allen
	Green Bay Packers (C)	10–4–0	.714	Dan Devine
	San Francisco 49ers (W)	8–5–1	.607	Dick Nolan
	Dallas Cowboys (WC)	10–4–0	.714	Tom Landry
	Divisional playoffs: Cowboys 30, 49ers 28; Redskins 16, Packers 3			
	NFC championship game: Redskins 26, Cowboys 3			
	Super Bowl VII: Dolphins (AFC) 14, Redskins (NFC) 7			
1971	Dallas Cowboys (E)	11–3–0	.786	Tom Landry
	Minnesota Vikings (C)	11–3–0	.786	Bud Grant
	San Francisco 49ers (W)	9–5–0	.643	Dick Nolan
	Washington Redskins (WC)	9–4–1	.786	George Allen
	Divisional playoffs: Cowboys 20, Vikings 12; 49ers 24, Redskins 20			
	NFC championship game: Cowboys 14, 49ers 3			
	Super Bowl VI: Cowboys (NFC) 24, Dolphins (AFC) 3			
1970	Dallas Cowboys (E)	10–4–0	.714	Tom Landry
	Minnesota Vikings (C)	12–2–0	.857	Bud Grant
	San Francisco 49ers (W)	10–3–1	.769	Dick Nolan
	Detroit Lions (WC)	10–4–0	.714	Joe Schmidt
	Divisional playoffs: Cowboys 5, Lions 0; 49ers 17, Vikings 14			
	NFC championship game: Cowboys 17, 49ers 10			
	Super Bowl V: Colts (AFC) 16, Cowboys (NFC) 13			
1969	Dallas Cowboys (Ca)	11–2–1	.846	Tom Landry
	Cleveland Browns (Cy)	10–3–1	.769	Blanton Collier
	Los Angeles Rams (Co)	11–3–0	.786	George Allen
	Minnesota Vikings (Ce)	12–2–0	.857	Bud Grant
	Conference championship games: Browns 38, Cowboys 14; Vikings 23, Rams 20			
	NFL championship game: Vikings 27, Browns 7			
	Super Bowl IV: Chiefs (AFL) 23, Vikings (NFL) 7			
1968	Dallas Cowboys (Ca)	12–2–0	.857	Tom Landry
	Cleveland Browns (Cy)	10–4–0	.714	Blanton Collier
	Baltimore Colts (Co)	13–1–0	.929	Don Shula
	Minnesota Vikings (Ce)	8–6–0	.571	Bud Grant
	Conference championship games: Browns 31, Cowboys 20; Colts 24, Vikings 14			
	NFL championship game: Colts 34, Browns 0			
	Super Bowl III: Jets (AFL) 16, Colts (NFL) 7			
1967	Dallas Cowboys (Ca)	9–5–0	.643	Tom Landry
	Cleveland Browns (Cy)	9–5–0	.643	Blanton Collier
	Los Angeles Rams (Co)	11–1–0	.917	George Allen

Year	Winners	Record	Pct.	Coach
	Green Bay Packers (Ce)	9–4–1	.692	Vince Lombardi
	Conference championship games: Cowboys 52, Browns 14; Packers 28, Rams 7			
	NFL championship game: Packers 21, Dallas 17.			
	Super Bowl II: Packers (NFL) 33, Raiders (AFL) 14			
1966	Dallas Cowboys (E)	10–3–1	.769	Tom Landry
	Green Bay Packers (W)	12–2–0	.857	Vince Lombardi
	NFL championship game: Packers 34, Cowboys 27			
	Super Bowl I: Packers (NFL) 35, Chiefs (AFL) 10			
1965	Cleveland Browns (E)	11–3–0	.786	Blanton Collier
	{ Green Bay Packers (W)	10–3–1	.769	Vince Lombardi
	{ Baltimore Colts (W)	10–3–1	.769	Don Shula
	Western Conference tie playoff: Packers 13, Colts 10 (14:39 overtime)			
	NFL championship game: Packers 23, Browns 12			
1964	Cleveland Browns (E)	10–3–1	.769	Blanton Collier
	Baltimore Colts (W)	12–2–0	.857	Don Shula
	NFL championship game: Browns 27, Colts 0			
1963	New York Giants (E)	11–3–0	.786	Allie Sherman
	Chicago Bears (W)	11–1–2	.917	George Halas
	NFL championship game: Bears 14, Giants 10			
1962	New York Giants (E)	12–2–0	.857	Allie Sherman
	Green Bay Packers (W)	13–1–0	.929	Vince Lombardi
	NFL championship game: Packers 16, Giants 7			
1961	New York Giants (E)	10–3–1	.769	Allie Sherman
	Green Bay Packers (W)	11–3–0	.786	Vince Lombardi
	NFL championship game: Packers 37, Giants 0			
1960	Philadelphia Eagles (E)	10–2–0	.833	Buck Shaw
	Green Bay Packers (W)	8–4–0	.667	Vince Lombardi
	NFL championship game: Eagles 17, Packers 13			
1959	New York Giants (E)	10–2–0	.833	Jim Howell
	Baltimore Colts (W)	9–3–0	.750	Weeb Ewbank
	NFL championship game: Colts 31, Giants 16			
1958	{ New York Giants (E)	9–3–0	.750	Jim Howell
	{ Cleveland Browns (E)	9–3–0	.750	Paul Brown
	Baltimore Colts (W)	9–3–0	.750	Weeb Ewbank
	Eastern Conference tie playoff: Giants 10, Browns 0			
	NFL championship game: Colts 23, Giants 17 (8:15 overtime)			
1957	Cleveland Browns (E)	9–2–1	.818	Paul Brown
	{ Detroit Lions (W)	8–4–0	.667	George Wilson
	{ San Francisco 49ers (W)	8–4–0	.667	Frankie Albert
	Western Conference tie playoff: Lions 31, 49ers 27			
	NFL championship game: Lions 59, Browns 14			
1956	New York Giants (E)	8–3–1	.727	Jim Howell
	Chicago Bears (W)	9–2–1	.818	Paddy Driscoll
	NFL championship game: Giants 57, Bears 7			

Year	Winners	Record	Pct.	Coach
1955	Cleveland Browns (E)	9–2–1	.818	Paul Brown
	Los Angeles Rams (W)	8–3–1	.727	Sid Gillman
	NFL championship game: Browns 38, Rams 14			
1954	Cleveland Browns (E)	9–3–0	.750	Paul Brown
	Detroit Lions (W)	9–2–1	.818	Buddy Parker
	NFL championship game: Browns 56, Lions 10			
1953	Cleveland Browns (E)	11–1–0	.917	Paul Brown
	Detroit Lions (W)	10–2–0	.833	Buddy Parker
	NFL championship game: Lions 17, Browns 16			
1952	Cleveland Browns (A)	11–1–0	.917	Paul Brown
	{Detroit Lions (N)	9–3–0	.750	Buddy Parker
	{Los Angeles Rams (N)	9–3–0	.750	Hamp Pool*
	National Conference tie playoff: Lions 31, Rams 21			
	NFL-championship game: Lions 17, Browns 7			
1951	Cleveland Browns (A)	11–1–0	.917	Paul Brown
	Los Angeles Rams (N)	8–4–0	.667	Joe Stydahar
	NFL championship game: Rams 24, Browns 17			
1950	{Cleveland Browns (A)	10–2–0	.833	Paul Brown
	{New York Giants (A)	10–2–0	.833	Steve Owen
	{Los Angeles Rams (N)	9–3–0	.750	Joe Stydahar
	{Chicago Bears (N)	9–3–0	.750	George Halas
	American Conference tie playoff: Browns 8, Giants 3			
	National Conference tie playoff: Rams 24, Bears 14			
	NFL championship game: Browns 30, Rams 28			
1949	Philadelphia Eagles (E)	11–1–0	.917	Greasy Neale
	Los Angeles Rams (W)	8–2–2	.800	Clark Shaughnessy
	NFL championship game: Eagles 14, Rams 0			
1948	Philadelphia Eagles (E)	9–2–1	.818	Greasy Neale
	Chicago Cardinals (W)	11–1–0	.917	Jimmy Conzelman
	NFL championship game: Eagles 7, Cardinals 0			
1947	{Philadelphia Eagles (E)	8–4–0	.667	Greasy Neale
	{Pittsburgh Steelers (E)	8–4–0	.667	Jock Sutherland
	Chicago Cardinals (W)	9–3–0	.750	Jimmy Conzelman
	Eastern Division tie playoff: Eagles 21, Steelers 0			
	NFL championship game: Cardinals 28, Eagles 21			
1946	New York Giants (E)	7–3–1	.700	Steve Owen
	Chicago Bears (W)	8–2–1	.800	George Halas
	NFL championship game: Bears 24, Giants 14			
1945	Washington Redskins (E)	8–2–0	.800	Dudley De Groot
	Cleveland Rams (W)	9–1–0	.900	Adam Walsh
	NFL championship game: Rams 15, Redskins 14			
1944	New York Giants (E)	8–1–1	.889	Steve Owen
	Green Bay Packers (W)	8–2–0	.800	Curly Lambeau
	NFL championship game: Packers 14, Giants 14			

* Joe Stydahar resigned as Rams coach after the first game of 1952.

Year	Winners	Record	Pct.	Coach
1943	⎰ Washington Redskins (E)	6–3–1	.667	Arthur Bergman
	⎱ New York Giants (E)	6–3–1	.667	Steve Owen
	Chicago Bears (W)	8–1–1	.889	George Halas
	Eastern Division tie playoff: Redskins 28, Giants 0			
	NFL championship game: Bears 41, Redskins 21			
1942	Washington Redskins (E)	10–1–0	.909	Ray Flaherty
	Chicago Bears (W)	11–0–0	1.000	George Halas
	NFL championship game: Redskins 14, Bears 6			
1941	New York Giants (E)	8–3–0	.727	Steve Owen
	⎰ Chicago Bears (W)	10–1–0	.909	George Halas
	⎱ Green Bay Packers (W)	10–1–0	.909	Curly Lambeau
	Western Division tie playoff: Bears 33, Packers 14			
	NFL championship game: Bears 37, Giants 9			
1940	Washington Redskins (E)	9–2–0	.818	Ray Flaherty
	Chicago Bears (W)	8–3–0	.727	George Halas
	NFL championship game: Bears 73, Redskins 0			
1939	New York Giants (E)	9–1–1	.900	Steve Owen
	Green Bay Packers (W)	9–2–0	.818	Curly Lambeau
	NFL championship game: Packers 27, Giants 0			
1938	New York Giants (E)	8–2–1	.800	Steve Owen
	Green Bay Packers (W)	8–3–0	.727	Curly Lambeau
	NFL championship game: Giants 23, Packers 17			
1937	Washington Redskins (E)	8–3–0	.727	Ray Flaherty
	Chicago Bears (W)	9–1–1	.900	George Halas
	NFL championship game: Redskins 28, Bears 21			
1936	Boston Redskins (E)	7–5–0	.583	Ray Flaherty
	Green Bay Packers (W)	10–1–1	.909	Curly Lambeau
	NFL championship game: Packers 21, Redskins 6			
1935	New York Giants (E)	9–3–0	.750	Steve Owen
	Detroit Lions (W)	7–3–2	.700	Milo Creighton
	NFL championship game: Lions 26, Giants 7			
1934	New York Giants (E)	8–5–0	.615	Steve Owen
	Chicago Bears (W)	13–0–0	1.000	George Halas
	NFL championship game: Giants 30, Bears 13			
1933	New York Giants (E)	11–3–0	.786	Steve Owen
	Chicago Bears (W)	10–2–1	.833	George Halas
	NFL championship game: Bears 23, Giants 21			
1932	Chicago Bears	7–1–6	.875	Ralph Jones
1931	Green Bay Packers	12–2–0	.857	Curly Lambeau
1930	Green Bay Packers	10–3–1	.769	Curly Lambeau
1929	Green Bay Packers	12–0–1	1.000	Curly Lambeau
1928	Providence Steam-Rollers	8–1–2	.889	Jim Conzelman
1927	New York Giants	11–1–1	.917	Earl Potteiger
1926	Frankford (Pa.) Yellowjackets	14–1–1	.933	Guy Chamberlain
1925	Chicago Cardinals	11–2–1	.846	Norman Barry

1924	Cleveland Bull Dogs	7–1–1	.875	Guy Chamberlain
1923	Canton Bulldogs	11–0–1	1.000	Guy Chamberlain
1922	Canton Bulldogs	10–0–2	1.000	Guy Chamberlain
1921	Chicago Bears	10–1–1	.909	George Halas

DIVISION WINNERS AND
PLAYOFF CHAMPIONSHIP RESULTS, 1960–79

NOTE: Wild card qualifiers (WC) are teams that have the best fourth and fifth place records in each conference at close of regular season's schedule, or teams that qualify otherwise in case of ties.

During the period 1960–69, the American Football League consisted of two divisions, the Eastern and Western. The AFL championship games were between winners of the two divisions. (In 1969, divisional playoffs were between the first- and second-place teams in each of the two AFL divisions; the two winners met for the league championship.) The American Football League merged with the National Football League beginning with the 1970 season.

Year	Winners	Record	Pct.	Coach
1979	Miami Dolphins (E)	10–6–0	.625	Don Shula
	Pittsburgh Steelers (C)	12–4–0	.750	Chuck Noll
	San Diego Chargers	12–4–0	.750	Don Coryell
	Houston Oilers (WC)	11–5–0	.688	Bum Phillips
	Denver Broncos (WC)	10–6–0	.625	Red Miller

First-round playoff: Oilers 13, Broncos 7
Divisional playoffs: Oilers 17, Chargers 14; Steelers 34, Dolphins 14
AFC championship game: Steelers 27, Oilers 13
Super Bowl XIV: Steelers (AFC) 31, Rams (NFC) 19

Year	Winners	Record	Pct.	Coach
1978	New England Patriots (E)	11–5–0	.688	Chuck Fairbanks
	Pittsburgh Steelers (C)	14–2–0	.875	Chuck Noll
	Denver Broncos (W)	10–6–0	.625	Red Miller
	Miami Dolphins (WC)	11–5–0	.688	Don Shula
	Houston Oilers (WC)	10–6–0	.625	Bum Phillips

First-round playoff: Oilers 17, Dolphins 9
Divisional playoffs: Steelers 33, Broncos 10; Oilers 31, Patriots 14
AFC championship game: Steelers 34, Oilers 5
Super Bowl XIII: Steelers (AFC) 35, Cowboys (NFC) 31

Year	Winners	Record	Pct.	Coach
1977	Baltimore Colts (E)	10–4–0	.714	Ted Marchibroda
	Pittsburgh Steelers	9–5–0	.643	Chuck Noll
	Denver Broncos (W)	12–2–0	.857	Red Miller
	Oakland Raiders (WC)	11–3–0	.786	John Madden

Divisional playoffs: Broncos 34, Steelers 21; Raiders 37, Colts 31 (15:43 overtime)
AFC championship game: Broncos 20, Raiders 17
Super Bowl XII: Cowboys (NFC) 27, Broncos (AFC) 10

Year	Winners	Record	Pct.	Coach
1976	Baltimore Colts (E)	11–3–0	.786	Ted Marchibroda
	Pittsburgh Steelers (C)	10–4–0	.714	Chuck Noll
	Oakland Raiders (W)	13–1–0	.929	John Madden
	New England Patriots (WC)	11–3–0	.786	Chuck Fairbanks

Year	Winners	Record	Pct.	Coach
	Divisional playoffs: Raiders 24, Patriots 21; Steelers 40, Colts 14			
	AFC championship game: Raiders 24, Steelers 7			
	Super Bowl XI: Raiders (AFC) 32, Vikings (NFC) 14			
1975	Baltimore Colts (E)	10–4–0	.714	Ted Marchibroda
	Pittsburgh Steelers (C)	12–2–0	.857	Chuck Noll
	Oakland Raiders (W)	11–3–0	.786	John Madden
	Cincinnati Bengals (WC)	11–3–0	.786	Paul Brown
	Divisional playoffs: Steelers 28, Colts 10; Raiders 31, Bengals 28			
	AFC championship game: Steelers 16, Raiders 10			
	Super Bowl X: Steelers (AFC) 21, Cowboys (NFC) 17			
1974	Miami Dolphins (E)	11–3–0	.786	Don Shula
	Pittsburgh Steelers (C)	10–3–1	.750	Chuck Noll
	Oakland Raiders (W)	12–2–0	.857	John Madden
	Buffalo Bills (WC)	9–5–0	.643	Lou Saban
	Divisional playoffs: Raiders 28, Dolphins 26; Steelers 32, Bills 14			
	AFC championship game: Steelers 24, Raiders 13			
	Super Bowl IX: Steelers (AFC) 16, Vikings (NFC) 6			
1973	Miami Dolphins (E)	12–2–0	.857	Don Shula
	Cincinnati Bengals (C)	10–4–0	.714	Paul Brown
	Oakland Raiders (W)	9–4–1	.679	John Madden
	Pittsburgh Steelers (WC)	10–4–0	.714	Chuck Noll
	Divisional playoffs: Raiders 33, Steelers 14; Dolphins 34, Bengals 16			
	AFC championship game: Dolphins 27, Raiders 10			
	Super Bowl VIII: Dolphins (AFC) 24, Vikings (NFC) 7			
1972	Miami Dolphins (E)	14–0–0	1.000	Don Shula
	Pittsburgh Steelers (C)	11–3–0	.786	Chuck Noll
	Oakland Raiders (W)	10–3–1	.750	John Madden
	Cleveland Browns (WC)	10–4–0	.714	Nick Skorich
	Divisional playoffs: Steelers 13, Raiders 7; Dolphins 20, Browns 14			
	AFC championship game: Dolphins 21, Steelers 17			
	Super Bowl VII: Dolphins (AFC) 14, Redskins (NFC) 7			
1971	Miami Dolphins (E)	10–3–1	.769	Don Shula
	Cleveland Browns (C)	9–5–0	.643	Nick Skorich
	Kansas City Chiefs (W)	10–3–1	.769	Hank Stram
	Baltimore Colts (WC)	10–4–0	.714	Don McCafferty
	Divisional playoffs: Dolphins 27, Chiefs 24 (22:40 overtime); Colts 20, Browns 3			
	AFC championship game: Dolphins 21, Colts 0			
	Super Bowl VI: Cowboys (NFC) 24, Dolphins (AFC) 3			
1970	Baltimore Colts (E)	11–2–1	.846	Don McCafferty
	Cincinnati Bengals (C)	8–6–0	.571	Paul Brown

Year	Winners	Record	Pct.	Coach
	Oakland Raiders (W)	8–4–2	.667	John Madden
	Miami Dolphins (WC)	10–4–0	.714	Don Shula
	Divisional playoffs: Colts 17, Bengals 0; Raiders 21, Dolphins 14			
	AFC championship game: Colts 27, Raiders 17			
	Super Bowl V: Colts (AFC) 16, Cowboys (NFC) 13			
1969	New York Jets (E)	10–4–0	.714	Weeb Ewbank
	Oakland Raiders (W)	12–1–1	.923	John Madden
	Houston Oilers (E-2d)	6–6–2	.500	Wally Lemm
	Kansas City Chiefs (W-2d)	11–3–0	.786	Hank Stram
	Divisional playoffs: Chiefs 13, Jets 6; Raiders 56, Oilers 7			
	AFL championship game: Chiefs 17, Raiders 7			
	Super Bowl IV: Chiefs (AFL) 23, Vikings (NFL) 7			
1968	New York Jets (E)	11–3–0	.786	Weeb Ewbank
	Oakland Raiders (W)	12–2–0	.857	Johnny Rauch
	Kansas City Chiefs (W)	12–2–0	.857	Hank Stram
	Western Division tie playoff: Raiders 41, Chiefs 6			
	AFL championship game: Jets 27, Raiders 23			
	Super Bowl III: Jets (AFL) 16, Colts (NFL) 7			
1967	Houston Oilers (E)	9–4–1	.692	Wally Lemm
	Oakland Raiders (W)	13–1–0	.929	Johnny Rauch
	AFL championship game: Raiders 40, Oilers 7			
	Super Bowl II: Packers (NFL) 33, Raiders (AFL) 14			
1966	Buffalo Bills (E)	9–4–1	.692	Joel Collier
	Kansas City Chiefs (W)	11–2–1	.846	Hank Stram
	AFL championship game: Chiefs 31, Bills 7			
	Super Bowl I: Packers (NFL) 35, Chiefs (AFL) 10			
1965	Buffalo Bills (E)	10–3–1	.769	Lou Saban
	San Diego Chargers (W)	9–2–3	.818	Sid Gillman
	AFL championship game: Bills 23, Chargers 0			
1964	Buffalo Bills (E)	12–2–0	.857	Lou Saban
	San Diego Chargers (W)	8–5–1	.615	Sid Gillman
	AFL championship game: Bills 20, Chargers 7			
1963	Boston Patriots (E)	7–6–1	.538	Mike Holovak
	Buffalo Bills (E)	7–6–1	.538	Lou Saban
	San Diego Chargers (W)	11–3–1	.786	Sid Gillman
	Eastern Division tie playoff: Patriots 26, Bills 8			
	AFL championship game: Chargers 51, Patriots 10			
1962	Houston Oilers (E)	11–3–0	.786	Pop Ivy
	Dallas Texans (W)	11–3–0	.786	Hank Stram
	AFL championship game: Texans 20, Oilers 17 (17:54 overtime)			
1961	Houston Oilers (E)	10–3–1	.769	Wally Lemm
	San Diego Chargers (W)	12–2–0	.857	Sid Gillman
	AFL championship game: Oilers 10, Chargers 3			
1960	Houston Oilers (E)	10–4–0	.714	Lou Rykmus
	Los Angeles Chargers (W)	10–4–0	.714	Sid Gillman
	AFL championship game: Oilers 24, Chargers 16			

A Selection of
SUPER BOWL RESULTS AND RECORDS, 1967–80

Results

Super Bowl XIV at Pasadena, Jan. 20, 1980
Pittsburgh Steelers (AFC) 31, Los Angeles Rams (NFC) 19
Attendance: 103,985

Super Bowl XIII at Miami, Jan. 21, 1979
Pittsburgh Steelers (AFC) 35, Dallas Cowboys (NFC) 31
Attendance: 78,656

Super Bowl XII at New Orleans, Jan. 15, 1978
Dallas Cowboys (NFC) 27, Denver Broncos (AFC) 10
Attendance: 76,400

Super Bowl XI at Pasadena, Jan. 9, 1977
Oakland Raiders (AFC) 32, Minnesota Vikings (NFC) 14
Attendance: 100,421

Super Bowl X at Miami, Jan. 18, 1976
Pittsburgh Steelers (AFC) 21, Dallas Cowboys (NFC) 17
Attendance: 80,187

Super Bowl IX at New Orleans, Jan. 12, 1975
Pittsburgh Steelers (AFC) 16, Minnesota Vikings (NFC) 6
Attendance: 80,997

Super Bowl VIII at Houston, Jan. 13, 1974
Miami Dolphins (AFC) 24, Minnesota Vikings (NFC) 7
Attendance: 71,882

Super Bowl VII at Los Angeles, Jan. 14, 1973
Miami Dolphins (AFC) 14, Washington Redskins (NFC) 7
Attendance: 90,182

Super Bowl VI at New Orleans, Jan. 16, 1972
Dallas Cowboys (NFC) 24, Miami Dolphins (AFC) 3
Attendance: 81,023

Super Bowl V at Miami, Jan. 17, 1971
Baltimore Colts (AFC) 16, Dallas Cowboys (NFC) 13
Attendance: 79,204

Super Bowl IV at New Orleans, Jan. 11, 1970
Kansas City Chiefs (AFL) 23, Minnesota Vikings (NFL) 7
Attendance: 80,562

Super Bowl III at Miami, Jan. 12, 1969
New York Jets (AFL) 16, Baltimore Colts (NFL) 7
Attendance: 75,389

Super Bowl II at Miami, Jan. 14, 1968
Green Bay Packers (NFL) 33, Oakland Raiders (AFL) 14
Attendance: 75,546

Super Bowl I at Los Angeles, Jan. 15, 1967
Green Bay Packers (NFL) 35, Kansas City Chiefs (AFL) 10
Attendance: 61,946

Summary: AFL–AFC teams have won ten Super Bowls and lost four.

Super Bowl
INDIVIDUAL RECORDS

Scoring

Most points scored in one game
Don Chandler, 15—Green Bay vs. Oakland, Jan. 14, 1968 (3 PATs, 4 FGs)

Most touchdowns scored in one game
2—Max McGee, Green Bay vs. Kansas City, Jan. 15, 1967 (2 passes); Elijah Pitts, Green Bay vs. Kansas City, Jan. 15, 1967 (2 runs); Bill Miller, Oakland vs. Green Bay, Jan. 14, 1968 (2 passes); Larry Csonka, Miami vs. Minnesota, Jan. 13, 1974 (2 runs); Pete Banaszak, Oakland vs. Minnesota, Jan. 9, 1977 (2 runs); John Stallworth, Pittsburgh vs. Dallas, Jan. 21, 1979 (2 passes); Franco Harris, Pittsburgh vs. Los Angeles, Jan. 20, 1980 (2 runs)

Most PATs in one game
Don Chandler, 5—Green Bay vs. Kansas City, Jan. 15, 1967 (5 attempts); Roy Gerela, 5—Pittsburgh vs. Dallas, Jan. 21, 1979

Most FGs in one game
Don Chandler, 4—Green Bay vs. Oakland, Jan. 14, 1968

Longest field goal
Jan Stenerud, 48 yards—Kansas City vs. Minnesota, Jan. 11, 1970

Most safeties in one game
1—Dwight White, Pittsburgh vs. Minnesota, Jan. 12, 1975; Reggie Harrison, Pittsburgh vs. Dallas, Jan. 18, 1976

Rushing

Most attempts in one game
Franco Harris, 34—Pittsburgh vs. Minnesota, Jan. 12, 1975 (158 yards)

Most yards gained in one game
Franco Harris, 158—Pittsburgh vs. Minnesota, Jan. 12, 1968 (34 attempts)

Most touchdowns rushing in one game
2—Elijah Pitts, Green Bay vs. Kansas City, Jan. 15, 1967; Larry Csonka, Miami vs. Minnesota, Jan. 13, 1974; Pete Banaszak, Oakland vs. Minnesota, Jan. 9, 1977; Franco Harris, Pittsburgh vs. Los Angeles, Jan. 20, 1980

Passing

Most attempts in one game
Fran Tarkenton, 35—Minnesota vs. Oakland, Jan. 9, 1977 (17 completions)

Most completions in one game
Fran Tarkenton, 18—Minnesota vs. Miami, Jan. 13, 1974 (28 attempts)

Highest completion percentage in one game
(At least 10 attempts to qualify)
Bob Griese, 72.7—Miami vs. Washington, Jan. 14, 1973 (8 out of 11)

Most yards passing in one game
Terry Bradshaw, 318—Pittsburgh vs. Dallas, Jan. 21, 1979

Most touchdowns passing in one game
Terry Bradshaw, 4—Pittsburgh vs. Dallas, Jan. 21, 1979

Pass Receptions

Most receptions in one game
George Sauer, 8—New York Jets vs. Baltimore, Jan. 12, 1969

Most yards gained in one game
Lynn Swann, 161—Pittsburgh vs. Dallas, Jan. 18, 1976 (4 receptions, 1 TD)
Max McGee, 138—Green Bay vs. Kansas City, Jan. 15, 1967 (7 receptions, 2 TDs)

Punting

Most punts in one game
Ron Widby, 9—Dallas vs. Baltimore, Jan. 17, 1971

Highest punting average for one game
(At least 3 punts to qualify)
Jerrel Wilson, 48.5—Kansas City vs. Minnesota, Jan. 11, 1970 (4 punts)

Longest punt
Jerrel Wilson, 61 yards—Kansas City vs. Green Bay, Jan. 15, 1967

Fumbles

Most fumbles in one game
Roger Staubach, 3—Dallas vs. Pittsburgh, Jan. 18, 1976

Super Bowl
TEAM RECORDS

Scoring

Most points scored in one game
Green Bay, 35—vs. Kansas City, Jan. 15, 1967
Pittsburgh, 35—vs. Dallas, Jan. 21, 1979

Most points scored by both teams in one game
66—Pittsburgh (35) vs. Dallas (31), Jan. 21, 1979

Fewest points scored by both teams in one game
21—Washington (7) vs. Miami (14), Jan. 14, 1973

Most touchdowns in one game
Green Bay, 5—vs. Kansas City, Jan. 15, 1967
Pittsburgh, 5—vs. Dallas, Jan. 21, 1979

Most PATs in one game
Green Bay, 5—vs. Kansas City, Jan. 15, 1967
Pittsburgh, 5—vs. Dallas, Jan. 21, 1979

Most FGs in one game
Green Bay, 4—vs. Oakland, Jan. 14, 1968

First Downs

Most first downs in one game
Dallas, 23—vs. Miami, Jan. 16, 1972

Fewest first downs in one game
Minnesota, 9—vs. Pittsburgh, Jan. 12, 1975

Most first downs by both teams in one game
41—Oakland (21) vs. Minnesota (20), Jan. 9, 1977

Fewest first downs by both teams in one game
24—Dallas (10) vs. Baltimore (14), Jan. 17, 1971

Total Net Yards Gained

Most yards gained in one game
Oakland, 429—vs. Minnesota, Jan. 9, 1977

Fewest yards gained in one game
Minnesota, 119—vs. Pittsburgh, Jan. 12, 1975

Most yards gained by both teams in one game
782—Oakland (429) vs. Minnesota (353), Jan. 9, 1977

Fewest yards gained by both teams in one game
452—Minnesota (119) vs. Pittsburgh (333), Jan. 12, 1975

Rushing

Most attempts in one game
Pittsburgh, 57—vs. Minnesota, Jan. 12, 1975

Fewest attempts in one game
Kansas City, 19—vs. Green Bay, Jan. 15, 1967
Minnesota, 19—vs. Kansas City, Jan. 11, 1970

Most yards gained in one game
Oakland, 266—vs. Minnesota, Jan. 9, 1977

Fewest yards gained in one game
Minnesota, 17—vs. Pittsburgh, Jan. 12, 1975

Most touchdowns rushing in one game
Green Bay, 3—vs. Kansas City, Jan. 15, 1967
Miami, 3—vs. Minnesota, Jan. 13, 1974

Passing

Most passes attempted in one game
Minnesota, 44—vs. Oakland, Jan. 9, 1977

Fewest passes attempted in one game
Miami, 7—vs. Minnesota, Jan. 13, 1974

Most passes completed in one game
Minnesota, 24—vs. Oakland, Jan. 9, 1977

Fewest passes completed in one game
Miami, 6—vs. Minnesota, Jan. 13, 1974

Most passes attempted by both teams in one game
70—Baltimore (41) vs. New York Jets (29), Jan. 12, 1969

Fewest passes attempted by both teams in one game
35—Miami (7) vs. Minnesota (28), Jan. 13, 1974

Most passes completed by both teams in one game
36—Minnesota (24) vs. Oakland (12), Jan. 9, 1977

Fewest passes completed by both teams in one game
20—Pittsburgh (9) vs. Minnesota (11), Jan. 12, 1975

Most yards gained passing in one game
Pittsburgh, 309—vs. Los Angeles, Jan. 20, 1980

Fewest yards gained in one game
Denver, 35—vs. Dallas, Jan. 15, 1978

Most yards gained passing by both teams in one game
503—Pittsburgh (309) vs. Los Angeles (194), Jan. 20, 1980

Fewest yards gained by both teams in one game
156—Miami (69) vs. Washington (87), Jan. 14, 1973

Most times tackled attempting passes (QB sacks) in one game
Dallas, 7—vs. Pittsburgh, Jan. 18, 1976

Most touchdown passes in one game
Pittsburgh, 4—vs. Dallas, Jan. 21, 1979

Punting

Most punts in one game
Dallas, 9—vs. Baltimore, Jan. 17, 1971

Fewest punts in one game
Pittsburgh, 2—vs. Los Angeles, Jan. 20, 1980

Most punts by both teams in one game
13—Dallas (9) vs. Baltimore (4), Jan. 17, 1971; Pittsburgh (7) vs. Minnesota (6), Jan. 12, 1975

Fewest punts by both teams in one game
7—Baltimore (3) vs. New York Jets (4), Jan. 12, 1969; Minnesota (3) vs. Kansas City (4), Jan. 11, 1970; Los Angeles (5) vs. Pittsburgh (2), Jan. 20, 1980

Highest punting average for one game
Kansas City, 48.5—vs. Minnesota, Jan. 11, 1970 (4 punts)

Lowest punting average for one game
Washington, 31.2—vs. Miami, Jan. 14, 1973 (5 punts)

Penalties

Most penalties in one game
Dallas, 12—vs. Denver, Jan. 15, 1978 (94 yards)

Fewest penalties in one game
Miami, 0—vs. Dallas, Jan. 16, 1972
Pittsburgh, 0—vs. Dallas, Jan. 18, 1976

Most penalties, both teams, in one game
20—Dallas (12) vs. Denver (8), Jan. 15, 1978

Fewest penalties, both teams, in one game
2—Pittsburgh (0) vs. Dallas (2), Jan. 18, 1976

Most yards penalized in one game
Dallas, 133—vs. Baltimore, Jan. 17, 1971 (10 penalties)

Most yards penalized, both teams, in one game
164—Dallas (133) vs. Baltimore (31), Jan. 17, 1971

Fewest yards penalized, both teams, in one game
15—Miami (0) vs. Dallas (15), Jan. 16, 1972

Fumbles

Most fumbles in one game*
Dallas, 6—vs. Denver, Jan. 15, 1978

Most fumbles, both teams, in one game*
10—Dallas (6) vs. Denver (4), Jan. 15, 1978

Fewest fumbles, both teams, in one game
0—Pittsburgh (0) vs. Los Angeles (0), Jan. 20, 1980

---

* Includes fumbles both lost and recovered

AFC–NFC PRO BOWL
RESULTS, 1971–80

Jan. 27, 1980, at Honolulu
NFC 37, AFC 27
Attendance: 48,060

Jan. 29, 1979, at Los Angeles
NFC 13, AFC 7
Attendance: 38,333

Jan. 23, 1978, at Tampa
NFC 14, AFC 13
Attendance: 50,716

Jan. 17, 1977, at Seattle
AFC 24, NFC 14
Attendance: 65,000

Jan. 26, 1976, at New Orleans
NFC 23, AFC 20
Attendance: 32,108

Jan. 20, 1975, at Miami
NFC 17, AFC 10
Attendance: 26,484

Jan. 20, 1974, at Kansas City
AFC 15, NFC 13
Attendance: 51,482

Jan. 21, 1973, at Dallas
AFC 33, NFC 28
Attendance: 47,879

Jan. 23, 1972, at Los Angeles
AFC 26, NFC 13
Attendance: 53,647

Jan. 24, 1971, at Los Angeles
NFC 27, AFC 6
Attendance: 48,222

PROFESSIONAL FOOTBALL
HALL OF FAME
Canton, Ohio

Four additional all-time pro football greats were named to the Professional Football Hall of Fame as members of the Class of 1980, bringing the total number of former players so honored to 106. The newest members of this very select group are:

● Herb Adderley, a ball-hawking cornerback who starred for both the Green Bay Packers and Dallas Cowboys.

● Deacon Jones, a defensive end whose 14-year career included service with the Los Angeles Rams, San Diego Chargers and Washington Redskins.

● Bob Lilly, a defensive tackle who stayed with the same club throughout his 14-year career—the Dallas Cowboys.

● Jim Otto, who for 15 years was the only starting center the Oakland Raiders ever had.

The Professional Football Hall of Fame was dedicated on September 7, 1963, at Canton, Ohio, site of the original meeting in 1920 that led to the formation of the National Football League. Each year, new members are chosen by the Hall of Fame National Board of Selectors which is made up of media representatives from the various professional football cities.

A brief reference to pro football's historical background will aid the understanding of biographical sketches which follow. The *first* American Football League (AFL) was organized in 1926 and consisted of nine clubs, but it was disbanded after that one season. This was followed by the second AFL which survived two seasons, 1936-37, and the third which operated in 1940 and 1941. The fourth, and eminently more successful AFL, was organized in 1960 and eventually merged with the National Football League in 1970.

The All-American Football Conference (AAFC) was organized in 1946 with eight clubs taking the field. The AAFC was active for four seasons before it, too, merged with the National Football League in 1950.

Roster of Members

Adderley, Herb—Michigan State; cornerback, 6′ 0″, 200 lbs.; Green Bay Packers 1961–69, Dallas Cowboys 1970–72 . . . Took immediate command in Packers' defensive backfield immediately after being drafted as Green Bay's No. 1 pick in 1960 . . . Going on to win all-NFL honors five times . . . Played in four of first six Super Bowls, returning an interception 60 yards for a clinching TD for the Packers in Super Bowl II. He also played in seven NFL championship games over the 11-year period 1961–71 and his teams won all seven titles—the Packers five times and the Cowboys twice . . . To be identified with champions that often, he had to be doing something right, and he was . . . During his 12-year career, Adderley pulled in 48 interceptions, returning them 1,046 yards for a 21.8-yard average . . . Possessed with great speed, he doubled as a kickoff returner with Green Bay, averaging a career 25.7 yards on 120 returns . . . Born June 8, 1939, in Philadelphia, Pa.

Alworth, Lance—Arkansas; wide receiver, 6′ 0″, 184 lbs.; San Diego Chargers 1962–70, Dallas Cowboys 1970–71 . . . Nicknamed "Bambi," as the graceful speedster was popularly known . . . All-America choice at Arkansas . . . Second round choice of Oakland Raiders in 1962 AFL college draft . . . Eventually became one of only two players ever to gain 10,000 yards on pass receptions (the other was Don Maynard) . . . Filled the AFL record book with his exploits . . . Caught at least one pass in string of 96 consecutive games . . . Career mark of 542 receptions for 10,266 yards and 85 touchdowns . . . Great pass catcher in heavy traffic . . . When traded to Dallas Cowboys in 1971, Tom Landry taught him in the arts of blocking, a task he performed superbly as well . . . Born Aug. 3, 1940, in Houston, Tex.

Battles, Cliff—West Virginia Wesleyan; halfback, 6′ 1″, 201 lbs.; Boston Braves 1932, Boston Redskins 1933–36, Washington Redskins 1937 . . Phi Beta Kappa scholar, triple-threat grid star at West Virginia Wesleyan . . . NFL rushing champ, 1933, 1937 . . . All-NFL choice, 1933,

1936, 1937 . . . Six-year career rushing, 3,542 yards . . . First to
gain over 200 yards in one game, 1933 . . . Scored three spectacular
touchdowns in division-clinching win over Giants, 1937 . . . Retired
after 1937 season when salary was frozen at $3,000 . . . Born May 1,
1910, in Akron, Ohio.

Baugh, Sammy—Texas Christian; quarterback, 6′ 2″, 180 lbs.; Washington Redskins 1937–52 . . . Two-time TCU All-America . . . No. 1 draft
choice, 1937 . . . Split career between tailback, T-quarterback . . .
Premier passer who influenced great offensive revolution . . . All-NFL
six years . . . NFL passing, punting, interception champ, 1943 . . .
Six-time NFL passing leader . . . History's top punter . . . Career
record: 21,886 yards and 186 touchdowns passing, intercepted only
28 times, punting average 45.1 . . . Born March 17, 1914, in Temple,
Texas.

Bednarik, Chuck—Pennsylvania; center-linebacker, 6′ 3″, 230 lbs.; Philadelphia Eagles 1949–62 . . . Two-time Pennsylvania All-America . . .
Eagles' bonus draft choice, 1949 . . . NFL's last "iron man" star . . .
Rugged, durable, bulldozing blocker, bone-jarring tackler . . . Missed
only three games in 14 years . . . Eight times All-NFL . . . Played in
eight Pro Bowls, Most Valuable Player in 1954 game . . . Named
NFL's all-time center, 1969 . . . Played 58 minutes, made game-
saving tackle in 1960 NFL title game . . . Born May 1, 1925, in
Bethlehem, Pa.

Bell, Bert—Pennsylvania; league administrator, owner Philadelphia
Eagles 1933–40, owner Pittsburgh Steelers 1941–46 . . . Weathered
heavy financial losses as Eagles' owner, 1933–40, Steelers co-owner,
1941–46 . . . Built NFL image to unprecedented heights as commissioner, 1946–1959 . . . Generaled NFL's war with All-American Football Conference . . . Set up farsighted television policies . . . Established strong anti-gambling controls . . . Recognized NFL Players'
Association . . . Born Feb. 25, 1895, in Philadelphia, Pa. . . . Died
Oct. 11, 1959, at the age of 64.

Berry, Raymond—Southern Methodist; end, 6′ 2″, 187 lbs.; Baltimore
Colts 1955–67 . . . Formed exceptional pass-catch team with Johnny
Unitas . . . Caught then-record 631 passes for 9,275 yards, 68 touch-
downs . . . All-NFL in 1958, 1959 1960 . . . Played in five Pro Bowl
games . . . Fumbled only once in 13-season career . . . Set NFL title
game mark with 12 catches for 178 yards in 1958 overtime game . . .
Colts' 20th-round future choice in 1954 . . . Born Feb. 27, 1933, in
Corpus Christi, Texas.

Bidwell, Charles W.—Loyola of Chicago; owner-administrator, Chicago
Cardinals 1933–37 . . . Purchased Cardinals' franchise in 1933 . . .
Staunch faith in NFL stood as guiding light during dark Depression
years . . . Dealt All-American Football Conference its most stunning
blow with $100,000 signing of Charley Trippi in 1947 . . . Built
famous "Dream Backfield" but died before it could bring him an
NFL championship . . . Financial help saved Bears' ownership for
George Halas in 1932 . . . Born Sept. 16, 1895, in Chicago, Ill. . . .

Died at the age of 51 on April 19, 1947, only months before his Chicago Cardinals won their first NFL championship in a 28–21 victory over Philadelphia.

Brown, Jim—Syracuse; fullback, 6′ 2″, 228 lbs.; Cleveland Browns 1957–65 . . . Syracuse All-America, 1956 . . . Browns' No. 1 draft pick, 1957 . . . Most awesome runner in history . . . Led NFL rushers eight years . . . All-NFL eight of nine years . . . NFL's Most Valuable Player, 1958, 1965 . . . Rookie of the Year, 1957 . . . Played in nine straight Pro Bowls . . . Career marks: 12,312 yards rushing, 262 receptions, 15,459 combined net yards, 756 points scored . . . Born Feb. 17, 1936, in St. Simons, Ga.

Brown, Paul—Miami (Ohio); coach, Cleveland Browns of AAFC 1946–49, Cleveland Browns of NFL 1950–62, Cincinnati Bengals 1968–75 . . . Exceptionally successful coach at all levels of football . . . Organized Browns in All-American Football Conference in 1946 . . . Built great Cleveland dynasty with 158–48–8 record, four AAFC titles, three NFL crowns, only one losing season in 17 years . . . A revolutionary innovator with many coaching "firsts" to his credit . . . Born Sept. 7, 1908, in Norwalk, Ohio.

Brown, Roosevelt—Morgan State; offensive tackle, 6′ 3″, 255 lbs.; New York Giants 1953–65 . . . Black All-America at Morgan State, 1951–1952 . . . Giants' 27th pick in 1953 draft . . . Joined Giants as a green 20-year-old . . . Quickly won starting role, held it for 13 seasons . . . Excellent downfield blocker, classic pass protector, fast, mobile . . . All-NFL eight straight years, 1956–63 . . . Played in nine Pro Bowl games . . . Named NFL's Lineman of the Year, 1956 . . . Born Oct. 20, 1932, in Charlottesville, Va.

Butkus, Dick—Illinois; linebacker, 6′ 3″, 245 lbs.; Chicago Bears 1965–73 . . . All-America at Illinois, joined the Bears as first round draftee in 1965 . . . As middle linebacker, devastated opposition offensive platoons . . . Joined Gale Sayers, also a rookie of 1965, to become the most famous offensive-defensive duo in the contemporary NFL . . . Butkus won all-NFL acclaim eight times and played in as many Pro Bowls . . . His career totals show 22 interceptions and 25 opposing fumbles recovered . . . Born Dec. 9, 1942, in Chicago, Ill.

Canadeo, Tony—Gonzaga; halfback, 5′ 11″ 195 lbs.; Green Bay Packers 1941–44, 1946–52 . . . Gonzaga Little All-America, 1939 . . . Multi-talented two-way performer . . . Averaged 75 yards all categories in 116 NFL games . . . Led Packers' air game, 1943 . . . Used as heavy-duty runner on return from service, 1946 . . . Became third back to pass 1,000-yard mark in one season, 1949 . . . All-NFL 1943, 1949 . . . Career record: 4,197 yards rushing, 1,642 yards passing, 186 points, 69 pass receptions . . . Born May 5, 1919, in Chicago, Ill.

Carr, Joe—no college; league administrator, National Football League 1921–39 . . . Sportswriter, promoter who founded Columbus Pan-handles team, 1904 . . . NFL co-organizer, 1920 . . . NFL president, 1921–1939 . . . Gave NFL stability, integrity with rigid enforcement of rules . . . Introduced standard player's contract . . . Barred use of collegians in NFL play . . . Worked tirelessly to interest financially capable new owners . . . Born Oct. 22, 1880, in Columbus, Ohio . . Died May 20, 1939, at the age of 58.

Chamberlin, Guy—Nebraska; end, 6' 2", 220 lbs.; coach, Canton Bulldogs (pre-NFL) 1919, Decatur Staleys 1920, Chicago Staleys 1921, Canton Bulldogs 1922–23, Cleveland Bulldogs 1924, Frankford Yellowjackets 1925–26, Chicago Cardinals 1927–28 . . . Legendary grid hero at Nebraska . . . Became premier end of the NFL in the 1920s . . . Extremely durable two-way performer . . . Player-coach of four NFL championship teams: 1922–1923 Canton Bulldogs, 1924 Cleveland Bulldogs, 1926 Frankford Yellowjackets . . . Six-year coaching record 56–14–5 for a remarkable .780 percentage . . . Born Jan. 16, 1894, at Blue Springs, Neb. . . . Died April 4, 1967, at the age of 73.

Christiansen, Jack—Colorado State University; defensive back, 6' 1", 185 lbs.; Detroit Lions 1951–58 . . . Left safety stalwart on three title teams . . . All-NFL six straight years, 1952–57 . . . Played in five Pro Bowls . . . Formidable defender, return specialist . . . Opposition's standard rule: "Don't pass in his area, don't punt to him" . . . NFL interception leader, 1953, 1957 . . . Career marks: 46 steals for 717 yards, three touchdowns; 85 punt returns for 1,084 yards, record eight touchdowns . . . Born Dec. 20, 1928, in Sublette, Kan.

Clark, Earl (Dutch)—Colorado College; quarterback, 6' 0", 185 lbs.; Portsmouth Spartans 1931–32, Detroit Lions 1934–38 . . . Colorado College All-America, 1928 . . . Called signals, played tailback, did everything superbly well . . . Quiet, quick-thinking, exceptional team leader . . . NFL's last drop-kicking specialist . . . All-NFL six of seven years . . . NFL scoring champ three years . . . Generaled Lions to 1935 NFL title . . . Scored 368 points on 42 touchdowns, 71 PATs, 15 field goals . . . Player-coach final two seasons . . . Born Oct. 11, 1906, in Fowler, Colo.

Connor, George—Notre Dame; tackle-linebacker, 6' 3", 240 lbs.; Chicago Bears 1948–55 . . . All-America at both Holy Cross and Notre Dame . . . Boston Yanks' No. 1 draft pick, 1948 . . . Quickly traded to Bears . . . All-NFL at three positions—offensive tackle, defensive tackle, linebacker . . . All-NFL five years . . . Two-way performer throughout career . . . First of big, fast, agile linebackers . . . Exceptional at diagnosing enemy plays . . . Played in first four Pro Bowl games . . . Born Jan. 21, 1925, in Chicago, Ill.

Conzelman, Jimmy—Washington (Missouri); quarterback, 6' 0", 180 lbs.; coach-owner, Decatur Staleys 1920, Rock Island Independents 1921–22, Milwaukee Badgers 1923–24, Detroit Panthers 1925–26, Providence Steamrollers 1927–30, Chicago Cardinals 1940–42, 1946–48 . . . Multi-talented athlete, editor, executive, song-writer, orator . . . Began NFL career with Staleys, 1920 . . . Player-coach of four NFL teams in the 1920s, including 1928 champion Providence . . . Player-coach-owner of Detroit team, 1925–1926 . . . Knee injury ended ten-year playing career, 1929 . . . Coached Cardinals to 1947 NFL, 1948

division crowns . . . Born March 6, 1898, in St. Louis, Mo. . .
Died July 31, 1970, at the age of 72.

Donovan, Art—Boston College; defensive tackle, 6' 3", 265 lbs.; Baltimore Colts 1950, New York Yanks 1951, Dallas Texans 1952, Baltimore Colts 1953–61 . . . First Colt to enter Pro Football Hall of Fame . . . Began NFL play as 26-year-old rookie in 1950 . . . Vital part of Baltimore's climb to powerhouse status in the 1950s . . . All-NFL 1954–57 . . . Played in five Pro Bowls . . . Great morale builder on Colts teams . . . Son of famous boxing referee of same name . . . Played at Boston College after World War II Marines service . . Born June 5, 1925, in the Bronx, N.Y.

Driscoll, John (Paddy)—Northwestern; quarterback, 5' 11", 160 lbs.; Hammond Pros (pre-NFL) 1919, Decatur Staleys 1920, Chicago Cardinals 1920–25, Chicago Bears 1926–29 . . . Triple-threat on attack, flawless on defense . . . Drop-kicked record four field goals one game, 1925 . . . Drop-kicked 50-yard field goal, 1924 . . . Scored 27 points one game, 1923 . . . 23 precision punts stymied Red Grange's NFL debut, 1925 . . . Sold by Cards to Bears, 1926, to thwart signing with rival 1926 AFL, which operated for one season . . . Sparked Bears four years . . . All-NFL six times . . . Born Jan. 11, 1896, in Evanston, Ill.

Dudley, Bill—Virginia; halfback, 5' 10", 176 lbs.; Pittsburgh Steelers 1942, 1945–46, Detroit Lions 1947–49, Washington Redskins 1950–51, 1953 . . . Virginia's first All-America, 1941 . . . Steelers No. 1 draft choice, 1942 . . . Small, slow with unorthodox style, but exceptionally versatile, awesomely efficient . . . Won rare triple crown (NFL rushing, interception, punt return titles), 1946 . . . All-NFL 1942, 1946 . . . Most Valuable Player, 1946 . . . Gained 8,147 combined net yards, scored 484 points, had 23 interceptions in career . . . Born Dec. 24, 1921, in Bluefield, Va.

Edwards, Albert Glen (Turk)—Washington State; tackle, 6' 2½", 260 lbs.; Boston Braves 1932, Boston Redskins 1933–36, Washington Redskins 1937–40 . . . Rose Bowl star, Washington State All-America, 1930 . . . Joined new Boston team for $150 a game, 1932 . . . Giant of his era . . . Immovable, impregnable 60-minute workhorse . . . Steamrolling blocker, smothering tackler . . . Official All-NFL 1932, 1933, 1936, 1937 . . . Bizarre knee injury suffered at pre-game coin toss ended career in 1940 . . . Just before a game that year between the Washington Redskins and the New York Giants, Edwards, as captain of the Redskins, met his long-time friend Mel Hein, captain of the Giants, in mid-field for the customary coin toss to choose goals. The coin was tossed, they shook hands, then Edwards turned toward the Washington sidelines and promptly twisted his knee as his foot became caught in the turf. The injury was such that Edwards never played again . . . Born Sept. 28, 1907, in Mold, Wash.

Ewbank, Weeb—Miami (O.); Became the only man to coach championship teams in both the AFL and NFL, leading the Baltimore Colts to NFL titles in 1958 and 1959, and the New York Jets to the AFL title in 1968 . . . Stunned the sporting world by leading the Jets to upset victory over Colts in Super Bowl III . . . Developed two of game's greatest quarterbacks, Johnny Unitas and Joe Namath . . . Stood at the threshold of pro football's doorway to greatness in 1958 when he led Colts to NFL championship in a 23-17 overtime victory over the New York Giants . . . This game, often termed "the greatest ever played," was first NFL title contest to be viewed on national TV and did much to launch pro football toward its present popularity . . . Retired from coaching after 1973 season with the Jets . . . Born May 6, 1907, in Richmond, Ind.

Fears, Tom—Santa Clara and UCLA; end, 6' 2", 215 lbs.; Los Angeles Rams 1948–56 . . . Led NFL receivers first three seasons, 1948–50 . . . Top season mark: 84 catches, 1950 . . . Had three touchdown receptions in 1950 division title game . . . Caught 73-yard pass to win 1951 NFL title . . . Caught record 18 passes one game, 1950 . . . All-NFL 1949, 1950 . . . Career mark: 400 catches for 5,397 yards, 38 touchdowns . . . Precise pattern-runner, specialized in the so-called "button-hook route" in which a receiver runs forward a certain distance, then reverses himself and turns back a few steps to meet the oncoming pass . . . Born Dec. 3, 1923, in Los Angeles, Calif.

Flaherty, Ray—Gonzaga; coach, Boston Redskins 1936, Washington Redskins 1937–42, New York Yanks (AAFC) 1946–48, Chicago Hornets (AAFC) 1949 . . . Compiled 80–37–5 coaching record . . . Won four Eastern division titles, two NFL titles with Redskins, two AAFC divisional crowns with Yankees . . . Introduced behind-the-line screen pass in 1937 NFL title game . . . Two-platoon system with one rushing, one passing unit also a Flaherty first . . . Played end with Los Angeles Wildcats (1926 AFL), New York Yankees, New York Giants . . . All-NFL 1928, 1932 . . . Born Sept. 1, 1904, in Spokane, Wash.

Ford, Len—Michigan; defensive end, 6' 6", 260 lbs.; Los Angeles Dons (AAFC) 1948–49, Cleveland Browns 1950–57, Green Bay Packers 1958 . . . Caught 67 passes as two-way end with Dons, 1948–1949 . . . After AAFC folded, Browns converted him to full-time defensive end, altered defenses to take advantage of his exceptional pass-rushing skills . . . Overcame serious injuries in 1950 to earn All-NFL honors five times, 1951–55 . . . Played in four Pro Bowls . . . Recovered 20 opposition fumbles in career . . . Born Feb. 18, 1926, in Washington, D.C.

Fortmann, Dan, M.D.—Colgate; guard, 6' 0", 210 lbs.; Chicago Bears 1936–43 . . . Bears' No. 9 pick in first NFL draft, 1936 . . . At 19, became youngest starter in NFL . . . 60-minute line leader, battering-ram blocker . . . Deadly tackler, genius at diagnosing enemy plays . . . All-NFL six straight years, 1938–43 . . . Phi Beta Kappa scholar at Colgate . . . Earned medical degree while playing in NFL . . . Born April 11, 1916, in Pearl River, N.Y.

George, Bill—Wake Forest; linebacker, 6' 2", 230 lbs.; Chicago Bears 1952–65, Los Angeles Rams 1966 . . . Bears' No. 2 future draft choice, 1951 . . . One of first great middle linebackers . . . Called Bears' defensive signals eight years . . . Exceptionally astute strategist, on-the-field innovator . . . All-NFL eight years . . . Played in eight straight Pro Bowls, 1955-62 . . . Career record: 18 interceptions, 16 opposition fumbles recovered . . . 14 years service longest of any Bear . . . Born Oct. 27, 1930, in Waynesburg, Pa.

Gifford, Frank—Southern California; halfback-flanker, 6′ 1″, 195 lbs.; New York Giants 1952–60, 1962–64 . . . Hailed as a genuine triple-threat in his rookie season with the Giants . . . Likened to an old-time "iron man" . . . Played single tailback and also T-quarterback . . . Punter, defensive back, kickoff returner, you name it, Gifford could do them all . . . All-NFL in 1955, 1956, 1957, 1959 . . . NFL Most Valuable Player, 1956 . . . Born Aug. 16, 1930, in Santa Monica, Calif.

Graham, Otto—Northwestern; quarterback, 6′ 1″, 195 lbs.; Cleveland Browns (AAFC) 1946–49, Cleveland Browns (NFL) 1950–55 . . . College tailback, switched to T-quarterback in pros . . . Guided Browns to ten division or league crowns in ten years . . . Topped AAFC passers four years, NFL two years . . . All-League nine of ten years . . . Four touchdown passes in 1950 NFL title win . . . Had three touchdowns running, three touchdowns passing in 1954 NFL title game . . . Career passes for 23,584 yards, 174 touchdowns . . . Scored 276 points on 46 touchdowns . . . Born Dec. 6, 1921, in Waukegan, Ill.

Grange, Harold (Red)—Illinois; halfback, 6′ 0″, 185 lbs.; Chicago Bears 1925, New York Yankees (AFL) 1926, New York Yankees (NFL) 1927, Chicago Bears 1929–34 . . . Three-time All-America, 1923–25 . . . Earned "Galloping Ghost" fame as whirling dervish runner at Illinois . . . Joined Bears on Thanksgiving Day, 1925 . . . Magic name produced first huge pro football crowds on 17-game barn-storming tour . . . With manager, founded rival American Football League, 1926 . . . Missed entire 1928 season with injury . . . Excelled on defense in latter years . . . Born June 13, 1903, in Forksville, Pa.

Gregg, Forrest—Southern Methodist; tackle-guard, coach, 6′ 4″, 250 lbs.; Green Bay Packers 1956, 1958–70, Dallas Cowboys 1971, coach Cleveland Browns 1975 to present . . . Member of All-NFL teams eight times . . . Member of three Super Bowl squads—Green Bay 1967 and 1968, Dallas Cowboys 1972 . . . Played in eight Pro Bowls . . . Career 15 seasons, 192 games . . . Born Oct. 18, 1933, in Birthright, Texas.

Groza, Lou—Ohio State; offensive tackle-placekicker, 6′ 3″, 250 lbs.; Cleveland Browns (AAFC) 1946–49, Cleveland Browns (NFL) 1950–59, 1961–67 . . . Last of "original" Browns to retire . . . Regular offensive tackle, 1947–59 . . . Back injury forced layoff, 1960 . . . Kicking specialist only, 1961–67 . . . All-NFL tackle six years . . . NFL Player of the Year, 1954 . . . In nine Pro Bowls . . . Last-second field goal won 1950 NFL title game . . . Scored 1,608 points in 21 years . . . Played in four AAFC, nine NFL title games . . . Born Jan. 25, 1924, in Martin's Ferry, Ohio.

Guyon, Joe—Carlisle and Georgia Tech; halfback, 6′ 1″, 180 lbs.; Canton Bulldogs (pre-NFL) 1919, Canton Bulldogs 1920, Cleveland Indians

1921, Oorang Indians 1922–23, Rock Island Independents 1924, Kansas City Cowboys 1924–25, New York Giants 1927 . . . Thorpe's teammate at Carlisle . . . All-America tackle at Georgia Tech, 1918 . . . Triple-threat halfback in pros . . . Extremely fierce competitor . . . Played with Thorpe on four NFL teams . . . Touchdown pass gave Giants win over Bears for 1927 NFL title . . . Professional baseball injury ended gridiron career, 1928 . . . Born Nov. 26, 1892, on White Earth Indian Reservation in Minnesota.

Halas, George—Illinois; founder, owner, coach, Chicago Bears starting in 1920 . . . Truly "Mr. Everything" of pro football . . . Founded Decatur Staleys, attended league organizational meeting in 1920 . . . Only person associated with NFL throughout first 50 years . . . Coached Bears for 40 seasons, won seven NFL titles . . . 325 coaching wins most by far in pro history . . . Recorded many firsts in pro coaching, administration . . . Also played end for 11 seasons . . . Born Feb. 2, 1895, in Chicago, Ill.

Healey, Ed—Dartmouth; tackle, 6' 3", 220 lbs.; Rock Island Independents 1920–22, Chicago Bears 1922–27 . . . Three-year end at Dartmouth . . . Left coaching job to seek tryout with Rock Island in new league, 1920 . . . Converted to tackle as pro . . . Sold to Bears for $100 in 1922—first player sale in NFL . . . Became perennial All-Pro with Bears . . . Rugged, two-way star . . . Called "most versatile tackle ever" by Halas . . . Starred in Bears' long barn-storming tour after 1925 season . . . Born Dec. 28, 1894, in Indian Orchard, Mass.

Hein, Mel—Washington State; center, 6' 2", 225 lbs.; New York Giants 1931–45 . . . Played 25 years in school, college, pros . . . 1930 All-America . . . Wrote to three NFL clubs offering his services . . . Giants bid high at $150 per game . . . 60-minute regular for 15 years . . . Injured only once, never missed a game . . . All-NFL eight straight years, 1933–40 . . . NFL's Most Valuable Player, 1938 . . . Flawless ball-snapper, powerful blocker, superior pass defender . . . Born Aug. 22, 1909, in Reading, Calif.

Henry, Wilbur Pete (Fats)—Washington & Jefferson; tackle, 6' 0", 250 lbs.; Canton Bulldogs 1920–23, 1925–26, New York Giants 1927, Pottsville Maroons 1927–28 . . . Three-year Washington and Jefferson All-America . . . Signed with Bulldogs same day NFL was organized, 1920 . . . Largest player of his time, bulwark of Canton's championship lines, 1922–23 . . . 60-minute performer, also punted, kicked field goals . . . Set NFL marks for longest punt (94 yards), longest drop-kick field goal (50 yards) . . . Born Oct. 31, 1897, at Mansfield, Ohio.

Herber, Arnie—Wisconsin and Regis College; quarterback, 6' 0", 200 lbs.; Green Bay Packers 1930–40, New York Giants 1944–45 . . . Joined Packers as 19-year-old rookie . . . Threw touchdown pass first pro game . . . Exceptional long passer . . . Teamed with Don Hutson for first great pass-catch combo . . . NFL passing leader, 1932, 1934, 1936 . . . Triggered four Packers' title teams . . . Left retirement to lead 1944 Giants to NFL Eastern crown . . . Lifetime passes gained

8,033 yards, 66 touchdowns . . . Born April 2, 1910, in Green Bay, Wis.

Hewitt, Bill—Michigan; end, 5′ 11″, 191 lbs.; Chicago Bears 1932–36, Philadelphia Eagles 1937–39, Phil–Pitt 1943 (that year Philadelphia and Pittsburgh played as a unit) . . . First to be named All-NFL with two teams—1933, 1934, 1936 Bears; 1937 Eagles . . . Famous for super-quick defensive charge . . . Fast, elusive, innovative on offense . . . Invented many trick plays to fool opposition . . . Middle man on forward-lateral that gave Bears 1933 NFL title . . . Played without helmet until rules change forced use . . . Born Oct. 8, 1909, in Bay City, Mich.

Hinkle, Clarke—Bucknell; fullback, 5′ 11″, 201 lbs.; Green Bay Packers 1932–41 . . . One of the most versatile stars in NFL annals . . . Fullback on offense, linebacker on defense . . . Famous for head-on duels with Nagurski . . . Did everything well—ran, passed, punted, place-kicked, caught passes . . . Savage blocker, vicious tackler, adept pass defender . . . All-NFL four years . . . Rushed 3,860 yards, scored 373 points, averaged 43.4 yards on punts . . . Top NFL scorer, 1938 . . . Born April 10, 1912, in Toronto, Ohio.

Hirsch, Elroy (Crazylegs)—Wisconsin and Michigan; halfback, end, 6′ 2″ 190 lbs.; Chicago Rockets (AAFC) 1946–48, Los Angeles Rams 1949–57 . . . Led College All-Stars upset of Rams, 1946 . . . Became key part of Rams' revolutionary "three-end" offense, 1949 . . . Led NFL in receiving, scoring, 1951 . . . Ten of 17 touchdown catches, 1951, were long-distance bombs . . . Mixed sprinter speed with halfback elusiveness . . . Named all-time NFL flanker, 1969 . . . Career record: 387 catches for 7,209 yards, 60 touchdowns; 405 points scored . . . Born June 17, 1923, in Wausau, Wis.

Hubbard, Robert (Cal)—Centenary and Geneva; tackle, 6′ 5″, 250 lbs.; New York Giants 1927–28, Green Bay Packers 1929–33, 1935, New York Giants 1936, Pittsburgh Pirates 1936 . . . Most feared lineman of his time . . . Rookie star with Giants' great defensive team, 1927 . . . Played end with Giants, switched to tackle with Packers . . . Anchored line for Packers' title teams, 1929–31 . . . Excelled as a blocker, backed up line on defense . . . Extremely fast, strong . . . All-NFL six years, 1928–33 . . . Named NFL's all-time offensive tackle, 1969 . . . Born Oct. 11, 1900, in Keytesville, Mo.

Hunt, Lamar—Southern Methodist; league founder, owner, Dallas Texans 1960–62, Kansas City Chiefs 1963 to present . . . Continually frustrated in attempts to gain NFL franchise . . . Developed idea, became driving force behind organization of rival American Football League, 1959 . . . Founded Dallas Texans, 1960 . . . Moved team to Kansas City in 1963; there solid club, organization provided AFL with stability, strength during AFL-NFL war . . . Spearheaded merger negotiations with NFL . . . Born Aug. 2, 1932, in El Dorado, Ark.

Hutson, Don—Alabama; end, 6′ 1″, 180 lbs.; Green Bay Packers 1935–45 . . . Alabama All-America, 1934 . . . NFL's first "super end" . . . Also place-kicked, played safety . . . NFL receiving champ eight years . . . Topped scorers five times . . . All-NFL nine years . . Most Valuable Player, 1941, 1942 . . . Had 488 catches for 7,991 yards, 99 touchdowns . . Scored 823 points . . . Caught passes in 95 straight games, 1937–45 . . . Named NFL's all-time end, 1969 . . . Born Jan. 31, 1913, in Pine Bluff, Ark.

Jones, Deacon—South Carolina State and Mississippi Vocational; defensive end, 6′ 4″, 272 lbs.; Los Angeles Rams, 1961–71; San Diego Chargers 1972–73; Washington Redskins 1974 . . . After election by the Rams in the 1961 college draft's 14th round, by the late 1960s Jones had become the most honored defensive lineman in pro football . . . His speed, agility and quickness helped make him one of the finest pass rushers in the business . . . Only by chance did two Rams scouts, taking notes on running backs in a college football game, notice that Jones was outrunning everybody on the field, including the backs they were scouting . . . Won unanimous all-NFL honors for six straight years, 1965–70 . . . Played in seven consecutive Pro Bowls . . . Extremely durable, he missed only three of 196 regular season games in 14 NFL campaigns . . . Born Dec. 9, 1938, in Eatonville, Fla.

Kiesling, Walt—St. Thomas (Minnesota); guard, 6′ 2″, 245 lbs.; coach, Duluth Eskimos 1926–27, Pottsville Maroons 1928, Chicago Cardinals 1929–33, Chicago Bears 1934, Green Bay Packers 1935–36, Pittsburgh Pirates 1937–38, Pittsburgh Steelers 1939–42, 1954–56 . . . 34-year career as pro player, assistant coach, head coach . . . Rugged two-way lineman with six NFL teams . . . All-NFL, 1932 . . . Starred on Bears' unbeaten juggernaut, 1934 . . . Also co-head coach of 1943 Phil–Pitt, 1944 Card–Pitt teams . . . Assistant with Packers, Steelers 14 seasons . . . Led Steelers to first winning season, 1942 . . . Born May 27, 1903, in St. Paul, Minn. . . . Died March 2, 1962, at the age of 58.

Kinard, Frank (Bruiser)—Mississippi; tackle, 6′ 1″, 210 lbs.; Brooklyn Dodgers 1938–44, New York Yankees (AAFC) 1946–47 . . . Two-time Mississippi All-America . . . Dodgers' second-round draft pick, 1938 . . . Small for tackle position, but tough, aggressive, fast, durable . . . . Out with injuries only once . . . 60-minute performer . . . Outstanding blocker, smothering tackler . . . First man to earn both All-NFL and All-AAFC honors . . . All-NFL 1940, 1941, 1943, 1944 . . . All-AAFC, 1946 . . . Born Oct. 23, 1914, in Pelahatchie, Miss.

Lambeau, Earl (Curly)—Notre Dame; founder, coach, Green Bay Packers 1919–49, Chicago Cardinals 1950–51, Washington Redskins 1952–53 . . . Founded pre-NFL Packers in 1919 . . . Coach-general manager for Packers until 1949 . . . Credited with keeping pro football alive in Green Bay . . . First coach to make forward pass an integral part of the offense . . . 33-year NFL coaching record: 231–133–23 with six championships in Green Bay . . . Played halfback for 11 years until 1929 . . . Born April 9, 1898, in Green Bay, Wis. . . . Died June 1, 1965, at the age of 67.

Lane, Dick (Night Train)—Scottsbluff Junior College; defensive back, 6′2″

210 lbs.; Los Angeles Rams 1952–53, Chicago Cardinals 1954–59, Detroit Lions 1960–65 . . . Joined Rams as free agent after four years in Army . . . Set NFL interception record (14) as rookie, 1952 . . . All-NFL five years . . . Named to six Pro Bowls . . . Selected all-time NFL cornerback, 1969 . . . Career interception record: 68 for 1,207 yards, five touchdowns . . . Gambler on field who made spectacular plays . . . Deadly open-field tackler . . . Very fast, agile, aggressive . . . His colorful nickname, "Night Train," derives from playing days when he would often spin his favorite recording of the song by the same name. Later he married singer Dinah Washington, whose theme song, coincidentally, was "Night Train" . . . Born April 16, 1928, in Austin, Texas.

Lary, Yale—Texas A&M; punter and defensive back, 5' 11", 189 lbs.; Detroit Lions 1952–64 (minus 2-year stint in U.S. Army) . . . Joined Lions in 1952 as a No. 3 draft choice . . . Played in Pro Bowl after his second NFL year . . . Career totals include 50 interceptions . . . Returned three punts for TDs during first five NFL seasons . . . As punter, averaged 44.28 yards on 503 career punts, which ranks him less than a yard behind all-time leader Sammy Baugh . . . Born Nov. 24, 1930, in Fort Worth, Texas.

Lavelli, Dante—Ohio State; end, 6' 0", 199 lbs.; Cleveland Browns (AAFC) 1946–49, Cleveland Browns (NFL) 1950–56 . . . Played only three college games, served in U.S. infantry before turning pro . . . Top AAFC receiver as rookie, scored winning touchdown in title game, 1946 . . . Caught 11 passes in 1950 NFL championship . . . All-AAFC, 1946–1947 . . . All-NFL 1951, 1953 . . . In three Pro Bowls . . . Caught 386 passes for 6,488 yards, 62 touchdowns . . . Had record 24 catches in six NFL title games . . . Nicknamed "Glue Fingers" . . . Born Feb. 23, 1923, in Hudson, Ohio.

Layne, Bobby—Texas; quarterback, 6' 2", 190 lbs.; Chicago Bears 1948, New York Bulldogs 1949, Detroit Lions 1950–58, Pittsburgh Steelers 1958–62 . . . Texas All-America, 1947 . . . Led Lions to four divisional, three NFL titles in 1950s . . . Exceptional field leader, at best in clutch . . . Last-second touchdown pass won 1953 NFL title game . . . Also kicked field goals . . . All-NFL 1952, 1956 . . . NFL scoring champ, 1956 . . . Career record: 1,814 completions for 26,768 yards, 196 touchdowns; 2,451 yards rushing; 372 points scored . . . Born Dec. 19, 1926, in Santa Anna, Texas.

Leemans, Alfonse (Tuffy)—George Washington U.; running back, 6' 0", 200 lbs.; New York Giants 1936–43 . . . Starred in college with GW Colonials . . . Then became No. 2 choice of the New York Giants in the NFL's first college draft in 1936 . . . Named outstanding player in 1936 College All-Star game in which the collegians tied Detroit, 7–7 . . . As a rookie fullback, he led NFL in rushing with 830 yards . . . His career statistics range from rushing and passing to punt returns, pass receiving and interceptions . . . Retired in 1943 with 3,142 yards rushing and 2,324 yards passing to his credit . . . Scored 20 touchdowns on foot and passed for 16 more . . . Born Nov. 12, 1912, in Superior, Wis.

Lilly, Bob—Texas Christian; defensive tackle, 6′ 5″, 260 lbs.; Dallas Cowboys 1961–74 . . . A consensus All-American at Texas Christian, Lilly became the Cowboys' first-ever draft choice in 1961 . . . He remained with Dallas throughout his 14-year career, becoming also the first-ever full-time Cowboy chosen to the Hall of Fame . . . Even though in his first year he won NFL Rookie of the Year acclaim as a defensive end, Lilly was shifted to defensive tackle in his third season, with spectacular results . . . Continually battling double-team and even triple-team opposition, he was rarely delayed in his relentless pursuit of a ball carrier . . . Played in 196 consecutive regular season games, seven championship contests, two Super Bowls and ten Pro Bowls . . . Associates say: "Lilly had grace. His style was clean and pure, a monument to the spirit of athletic competition" . . . Says Dallas defensive line coach Ernie Stautner: "Being mean just wasn't Bob's style. He even tried it, but being roughhouse didn't work for him. He just couldn't do it. Still, Bob was the finest tackle I've ever seen" . . . Born July 26, 1939, in Throckmorton, Texas.

Lombardi, Vince—Fordham; coach, Green Bay Packers 1959–67, Washington Redskins 1969 . . . Began head coaching career at age 45 . . . Transformed Green Bay into winner in two seasons . . . Acclaimed NFL Man of the Decade in the 1960s . . . Gave Packers 89–29–4 record, five NFL titles, first two Super Bowl crowns in nine years . . . Led 1969 Redskins to first winning record in 14 years . . . Noted taskmaster, never had a losing season . . . Born June 11, 1913, in Brooklyn, N.Y. . . . Died Sept. 3, 1970, at the age of 57.

Luckman, Sid—Columbia; quarterback, 6′ 0″, 195 lbs.; Chicago Bears 1939–50 . . . No. 1 draft pick, 1939 . . . Columbia tailback who became first great T-quarterback as a pro . . . Performance in 73–0 title win, 1940, started mass rush to T-formation . . . Superb signal-caller, ball-handler . . . All-NFL five times, Most Valuable Player, 1943 . . . Threw seven touchdown passes one game, 1943 . . . Had five touchdown passes, 1943 title game . . . Career passing: 14,683 yards, 139 touchdowns . . . Born Nov. 21, 1916, in Brooklyn, N.Y.

Lyman, William Roy (Link)—Nebraska; tackle, 6′ 2″, 252 lbs.; Canton Bulldogs 1922–23, Cleveland Bulldogs 1924, Canton Bulldogs 1925, Frankford Yellowjackets 1925, Chicago Bears 1926–28, 1930–31, 1933–34 . . . Very agile, large for his day . . . Pioneered more sophisticated defensive play with shifting, sliding style . . . Starred on four title teams: 1922–23 Canton, 1924 Cleveland, 1933 Bears . . . Joined Bears for barn-storming tour after 1925 season . . . Played on only one losing team in 16 seasons of college, pro ball . . . Born November 30, 1898, in Table Rock, Neb.

Mara, Tim—no college; founder-administrator, New York Giants 1925–59 . . . Paid $2,500 for Giants' franchise in 1925, thus giving NFL vital showcase in nation's largest city . . . Withstood heavy financial losses

until Red Grange's debut in Polo Grounds turned tide . . . Bore brunt
of fight against rival AFL in 1926, and against AAFC, 1946–49 . . .
Built Giants into perennial powerhouse with three NFL and eight
divisional titles . . . Born July 29, 1887, in New York, N.Y. . . . Died
Feb. 17, 1959, at the age of 71.

Marchetti, Gino—San Francisco; defensive end, 6′ 4″, 245 lbs.; Dallas
Texans 1952, Baltimore Colts 1953–64, 1966 . . . Named top defensive
end of NFL's first 50 years . . . New York Yanks' No. 2 draftee, 1952;
team moved to Dallas for Gino's rookie season . . . Selected for
record 11 straight Pro Bowls but missed one game because of injury
suffered in 1958 NFL overtime title game . . . All-NFL seven years,
1957 to 1962, 1964 . . . All-around great defender, best known for
vicious pass rushing . . . Born Jan. 2, 1927, in Smithers, W. Va.

Marshall, George Preston—Randolph-Macon; founder-administrator, Boston
Braves 1932, Boston Redskins 1933–36, Washington Redskins 1937–69
. . . Acquired Boston franchise, 1932 . . . Moved team to Washington,
1937 . . . Flamboyant, controversial, innovative master showman . . .
Pioneered gala halftime pageants, organized first team band . . .
Sponsored progressive rules changes, splitting NFL into two divisions
with title playoff, 1933 . . . Produced six divisional, two NFL titles
in 1936–45 period . . . Born Oct. 11, 1897, in Grafton, W. Va. . . .
Died Aug 9, 1969, at the age of 71.

Matson, Ollie—San Francisco; halfback; 6′ 2″, 220 lbs.; Chicago Cardinals
1952, 1954–58, Los Angeles Rams 1959–62, Detroit Lions 1963. Philadelphia Eagles 1964–66 . . . San Francisco U. defensive All-America
. . . U.S. Olympic medal winner in track, 1952 . . . No. 1 draft pick,
1952 . . . All-NFL four years, 1954–57 . . . Traded to Rams for nine
players, 1959 . . . Career ledger: 12,844 combined net yards, 5,173
yards rushing, 222 receptions, 438 points, record nine touchdowns
on punt, kickoff returns . . . Played in five Pro Bowl games . . .
Most Valuable Player in 1956 Pro Bowl . . . Born May 1, 1930, in
Trinity, Texas.

McAfee, George—Duke; halfback, 6′ 0″, 177 lbs.; Chicago Bears 1940–
41, 1945–50 . . . Phenomenal two-way star, a long-distance scoring
threat on any play . . . Scored 234 points, gained 5,022 combined net
yards, intercepted 21 passes in eight seasons . . . NFL punt-return
champ, 1948 . . . Holds career punt-return average record—12.78
yards . . . Left-handed passer, kicker . . . Pioneered use of low-cut
shoes . . . All-NFL 1941 . . . Navy service came at peak of career
. . . Born March 13, 1918, in Ironton, Ohio.

McElhenny, Hugh—Washington; halfback, 6′ 1″, 198 lbs.; San Francisco
49ers 1952–60, Minnesota Vikings 1961–62. New York Giants 1963,
Detroit Lions 1964 . . . Washington U. All-America . . . 49ers' No. 1
draft pick, 1952 . . . Scored 40-yard touchdown on first pro play
. . . Had phenomenal first season, winning All-NFL, Rookie-of-Year
honors . . . Played in six Pro Bowls . . . Most Valuable Player of 1958
Pro Bowl . . . Gained 11,375 combined net yards in 13 years . . .
Record includes 5,281 yards rushing, 264 pass receptions, 360 points

. . . Nicknamed "The King" . . . Born Dec. 31, 1928, in Los Angeles, Calif.

McNally, John (Blood)—St. John's (Minnesota); halfback, 6′ 0″, 185 lbs.; Milwaukee Badgers 1925–26, Duluth Eskimos 1926–27, Pottsville Maroons 1928, Green Bay Packers 1929–33, Pittsburgh Pirates 1934, Green Bay Packers 1935–36, Pittsburgh Pirates 1937–38, Pittsburgh Steelers 1939 . . . Famed "vagabond halfback," totally unpredictable fun-maker on and off the field . . . Assumed "Johnny Blood" alias from Valentino movie title, **Blood and Sand** . . . Superb runner with breakaway speed, exceptional pass receiver . . . Scored 37 touchdowns, 224 points in 15 seasons with five NFL teams . . . Official All-NFL 1931 . . . Pittsburgh player-coach, 1937–39 . . . Born Nov. 27, 1904, in New Richmond, Wis.

Michalske, August (Mike)—Penn State; guard, 6′ 0″, 209 lbs.; New York Yankees (AFL) 1926, New York Yankees (NFL) 1927–28, Green Bay Packers 1929–35, 1937 . . . All-America at Penn State . . . Rookie year with 1926 American Football League Yankees . . . Anchored Packers' championship lines, 1929, 1930, 1931 . . . 60-minute workhorse who specialized in blitzing on defense . . . Pioneered idea of using fullbacks at guard to capitalize on size, speed . . . All-NFL 1929, 1930, 1931, 1935 . . . First guard elected to Pro Football Hall of Fame . . . Born April 24, 1903, in Cleveland, Ohio.

Millner, Wayne—Notre Dame; end, 6′ 0″, 191 lbs.; Boston Redskins 1936, Washington Redskins 1937–41, 1945 . . . Two-time Notre Dame All-America . . . Hero of famous Ohio State upset in 1935 . . . Fierce competitor in crucial games . . . Caught 55-yard, 77-yard touchdown passes in 1937 NFL championship . . . Starred on four Redskins' divisional title teams . . . Top Redskin receiver at retirement with 124 catches . . . Career interrupted by Navy service . . . Player-coach in final 1945 season . . . Born Jan. 31, 1913, in Roxbury, Mass.

Mix, Ron—Southern Cal; tackle, 6′ 4″, 250 lbs.; San Diego Chargers (AFL) 1960–69, Oakland Raiders 1971 . . . Played a role in San Diego's high-powered attack for entire AFL decade (before merger with NFL in 1970) . . . Won all-league honors first nine seasons in AFL . . . Played in seven AFL All-Star Games (equivalent of the NFL Pro Bowl) . . . Once described as a "disciplined technician and a perfectionist," he had rare distinction of being called on only two holding penalties in his first nine seasons . . . Born March 10, 1938, in Los Angeles.

Moore, Lenny—Penn State; flanker-running back, 6′ 1″, 198 lbs.; Baltimore Colts 1956–67 . . . No. 1 draft choice, 1956 . . . Rookie of Year, 1956 . . . Started as a flanker, moved to running back in 1961 . . . Amassed 11,213 combined net yards, 5,174 yards rushing, 363 receptions for 6,039 yards . . . Scored 113 touchdowns, 678 points . . . All-NFL five years . . . Played in seven Pro Bowls . . . Comeback Player of the Year, 1964 . . . Scored touchdowns in record 18 straight games, 1963–65 . . . Born Nov. 25, 1933, in Reading, Pa.

Motley, Marion—South Carolina State and Nevada; fullback, 6′ 1″, 238

lbs.; Cleveland Browns (AAFC) 1946–49, Cleveland Browns (NFL) 1950–
53, Pittsburgh Steelers 1955 . . . Deadly pass blocker, peerless
runner on Browns' famed trap play . . . Also played linebacker early
in career . . . All-time AAFC rushing champ . . . Top NFL rusher,
1950 . . . All-AAFC three years, All-NFL in 1950 . . . Lifetime rushing:
828 carries, 4,720 yards . . . 5.7-yard career average all-time record
. . . Caught 85 passes, scored 234 points in nine years . . . Played
in 1951 Pro Bowl . . . Born June 5, 1920, in Leesburg, Ga.

Nagurski, Bronko—Minnesota; fullback, 6' 2", 225 lbs.; Chicago Bears
1930–37, 1943 . . . Joined Bears after legendary college career at
Minnesota . . . Became pro football's symbol of power, ruggedness
. . . A bulldozing runner on offense, a bone-crushing linebacker on
defense . . . Gained 4,031 yards in nine seasons . . . All-NFL 1932,
1933, 1934 . . . His two touchdown passes clinched Bears' 1933 title
win . . . Helped 1943 Bears to NFL crown after six-year retirement
. . . Born Nov. 3, 1908, in Rainy River, Ontario, Canada.

Neale, Earle (Greasy)—West Virginia Wesleyan; coach, Philadelphia Eagles
1941–50 . . . Extensive college coaching career preceded entry into
NFL in 1941 . . . Quickly built second-division Eagles into a contender . . . Produced three straight Eastern division crowns and
NFL championships in 1948 and 1949 . . . Both NFL titles came by
shutout scores . . . Using an assumed name, played end with the
pre-NFL Canton Bulldogs . . . Born Nov. 5, 1891, in Parkersburg,
W. Va. . . . Died Nov. 2, 1973, at the age of 81.

Nevers, Ernie—Stanford; fullback, 6' 1", 205 lbs.; Duluth Eskimos 1926–
27, Chicago Cardinals 1929–31 . . . Stanford All-America, 1925 Rose
Bowl hero . . . Lured from pro baseball career by Eskimos . . . Truly
a do-everything "iron man," playing 1,714 of 1,740 minutes in 29-
game season . . . Missed 1928 with injuries, returned with Cardinals,
1929 . . . Scored record 40 points in one game against Bears, 1929
. . . All-League all five NFL seasons . . . Player-coach two years each
in Duluth and Chicago . . . Born June 11, 1903, in Willow River, Minn.

Nitschke, Ray—Illinois; linebacker, 6' 3", 235 lbs.; Terrorized NFL
offenses for 15 seasons, nine of them under the late Vince Lombardi . . . Known as "quarterback" of the Green Bay defenses
during dynasty years of the 1960's . . . No. 3 draft pick of the
Packers in 1958 after leading Illinois in scoring as a college fullback . . . Despite 6.5–yard rushing average at Illinois, he was
assigned to defense with Packers and quickly became Mr. Linebacker himself . . . In 1969, he was named the top linebacker of
the NFL's first 50 years, a designation fully approved by many of
his fellow players on both sides of the field . . . Pass defense
was a Nitschke specialty, netting him 21 career interceptions for
385 yards and two touchdowns . . . Born Dec. 29, 1936, in
Elmwood Park, Ill.

Nomellini, Leo—Minnesota; defensive tackle, 6' 3", 284 lbs.; San Francisco 49ers 1950–63 . . . Two-time Minnesota All-America . . . 49ers'
first-ever NFL draft choice, 1950 . . . Played every 49ers game for

14 seasons, 174 regular-season and 266 pro games in all . . . Excellent defensive pass rusher, bulldozing offensive blocker . . . All-NFL six times—two years on offense, four years on defense . . . Named NFL's all-time defensive tackle . . . Played in ten Pro Bowl games . . . Born June 19, 1924, in Lucca, Italy.

Otto, Jim—Miami (Fla.); center, 6' 2", 255 lbs.; Oakland Raiders, 1960–74 . . . Joined the newly founded Oakland Raiders in 1960 and for the next 15 seasons held an absolute monopoly on the starting center position . . . For ten straight seasons was chosen all-AFL, then went on to become all-AFC after the AFL-NFL merger of 1970 . . . Played in nine AFL All-Star Games and three Pro Bowls . . . Started in 10 regular season games in addition to 73 preseason, 13 post-season and 12 all-star contests—a total of 308 football games as a Raider. During his sojourn with Oakland, the Raiders won seven divisional championships and met the Green Bay Packers in Super Bowl II . . . Born Jan. 5, 1938, in Wausau, Wis.

Owen, Steve—Phillips University; coach, tackle, 6' 2", 235 lbs.; Kansas City Cowboys 1924–25, New York Giants 1926–53 . . . Great defensive star of the 1920s . . . Captained Giants' 1927 title team, which held foe to record low 20 points . . . Coached Giants 23 years from 1931 to 1953 . . . Coaching record: 150–100–17, eight divisional, two NFL title teams . . . A-formation offense, umbrella defense, two-platoon system among his many coaching innovations . . . Born April 21, 1898, at Cleo Springs, Okla. . . . Died May 17, 1964, at the age of 66.

Parker, Clarence (Ace)—Duke; quarterback, 5' 11", 168 lbs.; Brooklyn Dodgers 1937–41, Boston Yanks 1945, New York Yankees (AAFC) 1946 . . . All-America tailback at Duke . . . Dodgers' No. 1 draftee in 1937, but signed Philadelphia Athletics baseball contract, expecting to play pro football briefly . . . All-NFL 1938, 1940 . . . NFL's Most Valuable Player, 1940 . . . Triple-threat, two-way back who paced Dodgers to their greatest seasons in 1940, 1941 . . . Spearheaded Yankees to AAFC Eastern title in 1946 . . . Born May 17, 1912, in Portsmouth, Va.

Parker, Jim—Ohio State; guard, tackle, 6' 3", 273 lbs.; Baltimore Colts 1957–67 . . . First full-time offensive lineman named to Pro Football Hall of Fame . . . Exceptional blocker, specialized in protecting quarterback . . . All-NFL eight straight years, 1958–65 . . . Played half of 11-year career at tackle, half at guard . . . Played in eight Pro Bowl games . . . No. 1 draft choice in 1957 . . . Two-time All-America, Outland Trophy winner at Ohio State . . . Born April 3, 1934, in Macon, Ga.

Perry, Joe—Compton Junior College; fullback, 6' 0", 200 lbs.; San Francisco 49ers (AAFC) 1948–49, San Francisco 49ers (NFL) 1950–60, Baltimore Colts 1961–62, San Francisco 49ers 1963 . . . Didn't play college football . . . Spotted playing service football by pro scouts . . . Signed as free agent by 49ers . . . Extremely quick runner who earned nickname "The Jet" . . . First to gain over 1,000 yards two straight years, 1953–54 . . . Career record: 12,505 combined net yards, 9,723 yards rushing, 260 receptions, 513 points . . . Played in three Pro Bowls . . . Born Jan. 27, 1927, in Stevens, Ark.

Pihos, Pete—Indiana; end, 6′ 1″, 210 lbs.; Philadelphia Eagles 1947–55 . . . Indiana All-America, 1943 . . . No. 3 draft pick in 1945 even though he couldn't play until 1947 . . . 60-minute star on Eagles' title teams, 1948–49 . . . Caught winning touchdown pass in 1949 NFL championship . . . All-NFL six times in nine seasons . . . Played in first six Pro Bowls . . . Three-time NFL receiving champ, 1953–55 . . . Career record: 373 catches for 5,619 yards, 378 points . . . Born Oct. 22, 1923, in Orlando, Fla.

Ray, Hugh (Shorty)—Illinois; technical advisor on rules and supervisor of officials . . . Only 5′ 6″ and 136 lbs., but a giant of pro football . . . NFL Supervisor of Officials, 1938–52 . . . Worked tirelessly to improve officiating techniques . . . Streamlined rules to improve tempo of play, increase safety . . . Visited each team annually to educate players, coaches . . . Said to have made 300,000 notations as technical observer . . . Born Sept. 21, 1884, in Highland Park, Ill. . . . Died Sept. 16, 1956, at the age of 71.

Reeves, Dan—Georgetown; owner-administrator, Cleveland Rams 1941–45, Los Angeles Rams 1946–71 . . . One of game's greatest innovators . . . Opened up West Coast to major sports by moving Rams to Los Angeles, 1946 . . . Experiments in game TV paved way for modern NFL policies . . . First postwar NFL owner to sign a black (Kenny Washington), 1946 . . . First to employ full-time scouting staff . . . Born June 30, 1912, in New York, N.Y. . . . Died April 15, 1971, at the age of 58.

Robustelli, Andy—Arnold College; defensive end, 6′ 0″, 230 lbs.; Los Angeles Rams 1951–55, New York Giants 1956–64 . . . Rams' 19th round draft pick, 1951 . . . On winning team 13 of 14 years . . . In eight NFL title games, seven Pro Bowls . . . All-NFL seven years—two with Rams, five with Giants . . . Named NFL's top player by Maxwell Club, 1962 . . . Exceptionally smart, quick, strong . . . Superb pass rusher . . . Recovered 22 opponents' fumbles in career . . . Missed only one game in 14 years . . . Born Dec. 6, 1925, in Stamford, Conn.

Rooney, Arthur J. (Art)—Georgetown; founder-administrator, Pittsburgh Steelers (Pirates), starting in 1933 . . . One of most revered of all sports personalities . . . Bought new Pittsburgh Pirates' franchise for $2,500 in 1933 . . . Renamed team Steelers in 1938 . . . His faith in pro football a guiding light during the dark Depression years . . . Startled NFL with $15,000 signing of fabled Whizzer White in 1938 . . . Organized, operated Western Pennsylvania semipro grid teams before 1933 . . . Born Jan. 27, 1901, in Coulterville, Pa.

Sayers, Gale—Kansas; halfback, 6′ 0″, 200 lbs.; Chicago Bears 1965–71 . . . All-America at Kansas U., where he rushed for 6.5 average yards over three years . . . Brilliant rookie season in 1965 when named All-NFL running back and Rookie of the Year . . . Electrified fans with

spectacular runbacks of kickoffs and punts . . . Suffered left knee
injury in 1968, then came back in 1969 to rush 1,032 yards for the
season, first time on record any NFL running back hit 1,000-plus
yards coming off knee surgery . . . Subsequent injury to right knee,
and also to one foot, forced his retirement at age 28 . . . He had
become an NFL legend in his own time . . . Born May 30, 1943, in
Wichita, Kan.

Schmidt, Joe—Pittsburgh; linebacker, 6′ 0″, 222 lbs.; Detroit Lions
1953–65; coach, Detroit Lions 1967–72 . . . Pittsburgh All-America,
1952 . . . Lions' No. 7 draft pick, 1953 . . . Mastered new middle
linebacking position which evolved in the 1950s . . . A superb field
leader . . . Exceptional at diagnosing foe's plays . . . All-NFL eight
years . . . Played in Pro Bowl nine straight years, 1955–63 . .
Team captain nine years . . . Lions' Most Valuable Player four times
. . . Had 24 career interceptions . . . Born Jan. 18, 1932, in Pittsburgh, Pa.

Starr, Bart—Alabama; quarterback, 6′ 1″, 195 lbs.; Green Bay Packers
1956–71; coach, Green Bay Packers 1975 to present . . . Finished pro
playing career in 1971 with 57.4 pass-completion average, one of NFL's
highest career marks . . . Considered prototype of ideal field general
. . . Cool, unflappable, calculating in reading enemy defenses . . .
Threw 294 consecutive passes at one point in his career without an
interception . . . NFL's leading passer, 1962, 1964, 1966 . . . Born
Jan. 9, 1934, in Montgomery, Ala.

Stautner, Ernie—Boston College; defensive tackle, 6′ 2″, 235 lbs.; Pittsburgh Steelers 1950–63 . . . No. 2 draft pick, 1950 . . . Bulwarked
strong Pittsburgh defense for 14 years . . . Saw spot service at
offensive guard . . . Known for excellent mobility, burning desire, extreme ruggedness, unusual durability . . . All-NFL 1956, 1958 . . .
Played in nine Pro Bowls, winning Best Lineman Award, 1957 . . .
Recovered 21 opponents' fumbles, scored three safeties in career . . .
Born April 20, 1925, in Calm, Bavaria.

Strong, Ken—New York University; halfback, 5′ 11″, 210 lbs.; Staten
Island Stapletons 1929–32, New York Giants 1933–35, New York
Yanks (AFL) 1936–37, New York Giants 1939, 1944–47 . . . N.Y.U.
All-America, 1928 . . . Excelled in every phase of game—blocking,
running, passing, punting, place-kicking, defense . . . Scored 17 points
to pace Giants to 1934 title . . . All-NFL 1934 . . . Scored 64 points
to top NFL, 1933 . . . Served as place-kicking specialist only, 1944–47
. . . Led NFL in field goals, 1944 . . . Scored 479 points in 14 NFL
years . : . Born Aug. 6, 1906, in New Haven, Conn.

Stydahar, Joe—West Virginia; tackle, 6′ 4″, 230 lbs.; Chicago Bears
1936–42, 1945–46 . . . Bears' No. 1 choice in first-ever NFL draft,
1936 . . . 60-minute performer who bulwarked Bears' line in famous
"Monsters of the Midway" era . . . Played on five divisional and
three NFL championship teams . . . Named to official All-NFL team
four years, 1937–40 . . . Often played without helmet early in career

. . . Later coached 1950–52 Rams, 1953–54 Cardinals . . . Born March 3, 1912, in Kaylor, Pa.

Taylor, Jim—Louisiana State; fullback, 6′ 0″, 216 lbs.; Green Bay Packers 1958–66, New Orleans Saints 1967 . . . L.S.U. All-America, 1957 . . . Packers' No. 2 draft pick, 1958 . . . 1,000-yard rusher five straight years, 1960–64 . . . Rushed for 8,597 yards, caught 225 passes, amassed 10,538 combined net yards, scored 558 points . . . Led NFL rushers, scorers, had record 19 touchdowns rushing in 1962 . . . Excelled in 1962 NFL title game . . . Ferocious runner, rugged blocker, prime disciple of "run to daylight" doctrine . . . Born Sept. 20, 1935, in Baton Rouge, La.

Thorpe, Jim—Carlisle; halfback, 6′ 1″, 190 lbs.; Canton Bulldogs (pre-NFL) 1915–17, 1919, Canton Bulldogs 1920, Cleveland Indians 1921, Oorang Indians 1922–23, Toledo Maroons 1923, Rock Island Independents 1924, New York Giants 1925, Canton Bulldogs 1926, Chicago Cardinals 1928 . . . All-America halfback at Carlisle, 1912 Olympic decathlon champion . . . First big-name athlete to play pro football, signing with pre-NFL Canton Bulldogs in 1915 . . . Named "The Legend" on the all-time NFL team . . . Voted top American athlete of first half of 20th century . . . First president of American Professional Football Association, 1920 . . . Born May 28, 1888, in Prague, Okla.

Tittle, Y. A.—Louisiana State; quarterback, 6′ 0″, 200 lbs.; Baltimore Colts (AAFC) 1948–49, Baltimore Colts (NFL) 1950, San Francisco 49ers 1951–60, New York Giants 1961–64 . . . AAFC Rookie of the Year, 1948 . . . Joined 49ers in 1951 after Colts disbanded . . . Career record: 2,427 completions, 33,070 yards, 242 touchdowns, 13 games over 300 yards passing . . . Paced 1961, 1962, 1963 Giants to division titles . . . Threw 33 touchdown passes in 1962, 36 in 1963 . . . NFL's Most Valuable Player in 1961, 1963 . . . All-NFL 1957, 1962, 1963 . . . Played in six Pro Bowls . . . Born Oct. 24, 1926, in Marshall, Texas.

Trafton, George—Notre Dame; center, 6′ 2″, 235 lbs.; Decatur Staleys 1920, Chicago Staleys 1921, Chicago Bears 1922–32 . . . Turned pro after one year at Notre Dame . . . First center to play for Staleys . . . 60-minute star, excelled on defense . . . First center to rove on defense . . . First to snap ball with one hand . . . Colorful, aggressive, smart . . . Defiantly wore No. 13 . . . Nicknamed "The Brute" . . . Named top NFL center of the 1920s . . . Born Dec. 6, 1896, in Chicago, Ill.

Trippi, Charley—Georgia; halfback, quarterback, 6′ 0″, 185 lbs.; Chicago Cardinals 1944–55 . . . Cards' No. 1 future draft pick, 1945 . . . Georgia All-America, 1946 . . . Played in four Chicago All-Star games as collegian . . . $100,000 signee during AAFC-NFL war, 1947 . . . Final link in Cards' famed "Dream Backfield" . . . Scored two touchdowns in 1947 NFL title win . . . All-NFL 1948 . . . Extremely versatile —played halfback five years, quarterback two years, defense two years . . . Born Dec. 14, 1922, in Pittston, Pa.

Tunnell, Emlen—Toledo University, Iowa; defensive back, 6′ 1″, 200

lbs.; New York Giants 1948–58, Green Bay Packers 1959–61 . . .
Signed as free agent, 1948 . . . Known as Giants' "offense on defense," keyed famous "umbrella defense" of 1950s . . . Gained more
yards (923) on interceptions, kick returns than NFL rushing leader,
1952 . . . Set career marks in interceptions (79 for 1,282 yards), punt
returns (258 for 2,209 yards) . . . All-NFL four years . . . Played in
nine Pro Bowls . . . Named NFL's all-time safety, 1969 . . . Born
March 29, 1925, in Bryn Mawr, Pa.

Turner, Clyde (Bulldog)—Hardin-Simmons; center, 6' 2", 235 lbs.; Chicago Bears 1940–52 . . . Hardin-Simmons Little All-America . . . Bears'
No. 1 draft pick, 1940 . . . Rookie starter at age of 20 . . . Terrific
blocker, superb pass defender, flawless ball-snapper . . . Had halfback speed . . . Led NFL with eight interceptions in 1942 . . . Stole
16 passes in career . . . All-NFL six times . . . Anchored four NFL
championship teams . . . Intercepted four passes in five NFL title
games . . . Born Nov. 10, 1919, in Sweetwater, Texas.

Unitas, Johnny—Louisville; quarterback, 6' 1", 195 lbs.; Baltimore Colts
1956–72, San Diego Chargers 1973 . . . Joined Colts in 1956 after
being drafted and cut by Pittsburgh the year before . . . Became
synonymous with the winning tradition of the 1958–59 Colts then
continued through the 1960s . . . Played in four NFL championship
games and one AFC title contest . . . Named all-NFL five times and
played in 10 Pro Bowls . . . Has staggering career figures, 2830
completions in 5186 attempts, good for 40,239 yards and 290 TDs
. . . Even had career rushing total of 1777 yards . . . His most
remarkable achievement may never be surpassed in the records:
a string of 47 consecutive games starting in 1956 and ending in
1960 in which he threw at least one touchdown pass . . . Born
May 7, 1933, in Louisville, Ky.

Van Brocklin, Norm—Oregon; quarterback, 6' 1", 190 lbs.; Los Angeles
Rams 1949–57, Philadelphia Eagles 1958–60, coach, Minnesota
Vikings 1961–66, coach, Atlanta Falcons 1968–74 . . . Oregon All-
America, 1948 . . . Rams' No. 4 draftee, 1949 . . . Led NFL in pass-
ing three years, punting twice . . . Career mark: 1,553 completions
for 23,611 yards, 173 touchdowns . . . 73-yard pass gave Rams 1951
title . . . Passed for 554 yards in one game, 1951 . . . Led Eagles
to 1960 NFL crown . . . NFL's Most Valuable Player, 1960 . . .
Threw eight touchdown passes in eight Pro Bowl games . . . Born
March 15, 1926, in Eagle Butte, S.D.

Van Buren, Steve—Louisiana State; halfback, 6' 1", 200 lbs.; Philadelphia Eagles 1944–51 . . . No. 1 draft pick, 1944 . . . All-NFL four
of first five years . . . Provided Eagles a battering-ram punch . .
Won NFL rushing title four times . . . 1944 punt-return, 1945 kickoff-
return champ . . . Scored only touchdown in 7–0 title win, 1948 . . .
Rushed for record 196 yards in 1949 finale . . . Career marks: 5,860
yards rushing, 464 points scored . . . Surpassed 1,000 yards in rushing twice . . . Born Dec. 28, 1920, in La Ceiba, Honduras.

Waterfield, Bob—UCLA; quarterback, 6' 2", 200 lbs.; Cleveland Rams

1945, Los Angeles Rams 1946–52 . . . Cleveland Rams' No. 3 future
draft pick, 1944 . . . NFL's Most Valuable Player as rookie, 1945 . . .
Two touchdown passes keyed Rams' 1945 title win . . . All-NFL three
years, NFL passing champ twice . . . Career marks include 11,849
yards, 98 touchdowns passing; 573 points on 13 touchdowns, 315
PATs, 60 field goals, 42.4-yard punting average . . . Also played defense first four years, intercepted 20 passes . . . Born July 26, 1920,
in Elmira, N.Y.

Willis, Bill (Deacon)—Ohio State; offensive and defensive guard, 6′ 2½″
215 lbs.; Cleveland Browns (AAFC) 1946–49, Cleveland Browns (NFL)
1950–53 . . . All-America at tackle for Ohio State . . . Coached at
Kentucky State College for three years . . . Joined the Cleveland
Browns (AAFC) in 1946, remained with them for four years, and was
named All-AAFC three times . . . All-NFL middle guard 1951, 1952,
1953 . . . In defensive line play, he uncoiled out of a crouch, moving
at 70 miles per hour and specializing in dumping opposing centers in
the quarterback's lap . . . Born Oct. 5, 1921, in Columbus, Ohio.

Wilson, Larry—Utah; defensive back, 6′ 0″, 190 lbs.; St. Louis Cardinals,
1960–72; Although a star running back in college, he was quickly
shifted to the defensive backfield on joining the Cardinals who had
just moved from Chicago to St. Louis . . . Eventually became one of
the premier free safeties in all of pro football . . . Specialized in
the "safety blitz," a technique he used to stymie many an enemy
offensive march . . . Played in eight Pro Bowls . . . During 1966
season, stole at least one pass in seven straight games, leading the
NFL that year with 10 interceptions . . . Career marks were 52
interceptions returned for 800 yards and five touchdowns . . .
Born March 24, 1938, in Rigby, Idaho.

Wojciechowicz, Alex—Fordham; center-linebacker, 6′ 0″, 235 lbs.;
Detroit Lions 1938–46, Philadelphia Eagles 1949–50 . . . Two-time
Fordham All-America, center of famed "Seven Blocks of Granite" line
. . . Lions' No. 1 draft pick, 1938 . . . Played four games first week
as pro . . . Authentic "iron man" for eight and a half years with
Lions . . . Joined Eagles as defensive specialist strictly . . . Known
for exceptionally wide center stance . . . Outstanding pass defender
with 16 lifetime interceptions . . . Born Aug. 12, 1915, in South
River, N.J.

OFFICIATING
IN THE NFL

- In the NFL, Full Possession
  Is Six Points of the Law

- Names and civilian occupations
  of 1980 NFL Officials

IN THE NFL, FULL POSSESSION IS
SIX POINTS OF THE LAW

A season or so ago, the big outcry at playoff time was over fumbles, with the outcome of several crucial games revolving around the inability of running backs to hold onto the ball. Caught in the midst of these miscues were the officials, who often had to decide whether a player had fumbled before or after he was tackled, usually without really getting a chance to see what had happened. And they are under no mandate from the league to call what they can't see.

If fumbles were rampant two seasons ago, the "in" word during the 1979 campaign was "possession." There were several controversial calls by officials during the regular season and in the playoffs (with no beefs by either side in Super Bowl XIV) and the biggest rhubarb of all erupted after the Pittsburgh Steelers won the AFC championship game with Houston, 27-13, on their way to the Super Bowl. What happened was this:

With Pittsburgh leading late in the third quarter, 17-10, Dan Pastorini tossed a six-yard pass to Mike Renfro who apparently scored a touchdown, making the score 17-16. But no, official Donald Orr, who was nearest the play, ruled that Renfro did not have full possession of the ball before he stepped out of bounds beyond the end zone, Or putting it another way, Orr ruled that Renfro bobbled the ball as he crossed the end line. Therefore the TD was null and void.

Renfro, of course, stormed over to Orr and vehemently protested the decision. And Houston Coach Bum Phillips lost a good bit of his usually calm composure over this one. But the decision stood and Houston had to settle for a field goal, making the score 17-13 with Pittsburgh still in front and victory bound.

Then came the after-game movies and videotape replays of the instant, slow-motion and long-drawn-out variety. Post-mortems were held in Houston and New York, showing the disputed play from several different angles with the NFL standing by Orr's original decision that Renfro didn't have *full* possession of the ball as he was going out of the end zone. But it was, admittedly, a tough one to call, with supervisor of officials Art McNally agreeing that Renfro might have acquired full possession (as the rules require) just before he dragged his foot across the end line. As such, the call takes its place among those decisions so well known in football and other sports as "judgment calls."

NFL teams, in the balance of things, win some and lose some of these controversial calls. For the past three years, Commissioner Pete Rozelle and Art McNally have held special film showings of controversial calls for members of the media to view during Super Bowl week. The most recent film session in Los Angeles dealt not only with the "full possession" call, it also reviewed several other notable hassles as well, including another decision in a regular season Houston-Pittsburgh game that this time went against the Steelers. It was a Monday night contest in Houston which the Oilers won, 20-17. With two minutes left in the game, Pittsburgh's Matt Bahr completed a successful onside kick that would have given the Steelers the ball and a good chance to score. But the official ruling was that the ball had not traveled the mandatory 10 yards so

Houston took possession and ran out the clock. Said Commissioner Rozelle at the Los Angeles film session:

"About the onsides kick in the Pittsburgh-Houston game, our films showed that the ball did go the required 10 yards and that the official made a mistake. It happened very quickly and the official was in error. Pittsburgh should have had the ball with 1:10 to go."

The Steelers were victims of another mistaken call in their playoff game with Miami, even though they won this one, 34-14. Again, Rozelle reviewed the controversial play:

"Miami punted the ball and, on the play, the head linesman was screened from the ball," he explained. "When the official saw the ball take a strange bounce, he thought it had hit Steeler Dwayne Woodruff on the foot. No one had a better view so we blew the call. Our films showed that the ball never hit Woodruff."

The officials, however, were found to be correct on at least two calls questioned during the season. One came in the Dallas-Los Angeles NFC title game won by the Rams, 21-19. The films showed that Cowboy receiver Tony Hill was indeed out of bounds when he took what appeared to be a touchdown pass from Ron Springs. The official call was correct although verbal steam flew at the time it was made.

Still another official decision, in a final season game between Dallas and Washington which clinched a playoff berth for the Cowboys, hinged on just who is eligible to call a time out in the last second of play. After squandering two big leads in the game, 17-0 and 34-21, the Redskins were losing 35-34 and had just 33 seconds in which to position a potential winning field goal from the accurate foot of Mark Moseley. After they moved the ball to their own 49-yard line, only five seconds were left as quarterback Joe Theismann threw a 9-yard pass to tight end Don Warren. Then, one second remained as Warren was tackled, but time apparently expired while Theismann vainly tried to call a time out and leave the way open for a one-second field goal try. The officials, however, ruled the game was over. Rozelle's comments came after films showed the action with the clock ticking away:

"Only a designated captain can call time out. The captains were Joe Theismann and George Starke. Theismann did not advise the referee before the pass play that he wanted a time out. In any event, the referee must wait for the ball to be whistled dead before he can call time out. We clocked the play, and time ran out before Theismann could call one."

Despite a continued interest in videotape instant replays as a possible method of resolving controversial decisions in pro football, the NFL owners have again turned thumbs down on the idea as unfeasible and much too expensive. The NFL Competition Committee has taken this position for the third straight year.

But with an eye to those "full possession" calls on the sidelines and in the end zones, a study was authorized to check the feasibility of assigning two additional officials to all post-season (playoff) games. Under preliminary thinking, these two officials would have no authority to call fouls, but would assist the regular seven-man officiating crew in plays involving the sidelines and end lines, plus ball possession calls when spotting the out-of-bounds movements of receivers and running backs.

ROSTER OF
1980
NATIONAL FOOTBALL LEAGUE
OFFICIALS

REFEREES

Barth, Gene—No. 14, St. Louis University, president, oil company, Florissant, Mo., 10th year.

Cashion, Red—No. 8, Texas A&M, chairman of board, insurance co., Bryan, Texas, 9th year.

Dreith, Ben—No. 12, Colorado State University, teacher-counselor, Denver Public Schools, 21st year.

Frederic, Bob—No. 16, Colorado, president, printing and lithographing co., Denver, 13th year.

Haggerty, Pat—No. 4, Colorado State College, teacher and coach Denver Public Schools, 16th year.

Heberling, Chuck—No. 18, Washington & Jefferson, executive administrator state high school athletic program, Pittsburgh, 16th year.

Jorgensen, Dick—No. 6, Wisconsin, president, commercial bank, Champaign, Illinois, 13th year.

LePore, Cal—No. 5, recreation unit director, Chicago, 15th year.

Markbreit, Jerry—No. 9, University of Illinois, sales manager, Skokie, Illinois, 5th year.

McCarter, Gordon—No. 20, Western Reserve, industrial sales, Cleveland, 14th year.

McElwee, Bob—No. 10, U.S. Naval Academy, construction engineer, Haddonfield, N.J., 5th year.

Seeman, Jerry—No. 17, Winona State, central office school administrator, Fridley, Minnesota, 6th year.

Silva, Fred—No. 17, San Jose State, sales manager, consumer sales co., San Francisco, Calif., 14th year.

Tunney, Jim—No. 3, Occidental, president of motivation company and professional speaker, Lakewood, Ca., 21st year.

Wyant, Fred—No. 11, West Virginia, regional insurance sales director, Star City, W. Va., 15th year.

UMPIRES

Boylston, Bob—No. 5, U. of Alabama, manufacturers representative, Tucker, Ga., 3rd year.

Conway, Al—No. 7, Army, polyester product manager, Kansas City, Mo., 12th year.

Demmas, Art—No. 14, Vanderbilt, investments and financial planning, insurance co., Nashville, 13th year.

Fiffick, Ed—No. 17, Marquette University, podiatric physician, Youngstown, Ohio, 2nd year.

Hamilton, Dave—No. 12, Utah University, assistant to medical director, Atascadero, Calif., 6th year.

Harder, Pat—No. 8, Wisconsin, executive vice-president, automobile leasing co., Hartland, Wisconsin, former NFL player, 15th year.

Hensley, Tommy—No. 19, Tennessee, transportation sales representative, Knoxville, 14th year.

Keck, John—No. 4, Cornell College, petroleum and automobile parts distributor, Des Moines, 9th year.

Kramer, Tony—No. 16, Dayton, transportation area sales manager, Centerville, Ohio, 6th year.

Morcroft, Ralph—No. 15, Ohio State, baseball operations director, Hollywood, Fla., 20th year.

Moss, Dave—No. 18, Dartmouth, insurance, Birmingham, Mich., 1st year.

Myers, Tom—No. 10, San Jose State, owner auto leasing company, San Jose, Calif., 2nd year.

Palazzi, Lou—No. 3, Penn State, landscape architect, Scranton, Pa., former NFL player, 29th year.

Sinkovitz, Frank—No. 20, Duke, president, marketing company, Harrisburg, Pa., former NFL player, 23rd year.

Wells, Gordon—No. 11, Occidental, college professor physical education, Huntington Beach, Calif., 9th year.

HEAD LINESMEN

Bergman, Jerry—No. 17, DuQuesne, transportation manager, Pittsburgh, 15th year.

Dodez, Ray—No. 15, Wooster, telephone company executive, Akron, Ohio, 13th year.

Glover, Frank—No. 20, Morris Brown, assistant area superintendent, Atlanta Public Schools, 9th year.

Hagerty, Ligouri—No. 9, Syracuse, manager sporting goods co., Glen Burnie, Maryland, 5th year.

Hamer, Dale—No. 12, California State, accountant and analyst, Pittsburgh, 3rd year.

Kragseth, Norm—No. 16, Northwestern, physical education department chairman, Minneapolis, 7th year.

Marion, Ed—No. 12, Pennsylvania, vice president, pension marketing, insurance co., Portland, Maine, 21st year.

Miles, Leo—No. 3, Virginia State, university athletic director, Washington, D.C., former NFL player, 12th year.

Peters, Walt—No. 14, Indiana State, insurance broker, King of Prussia, Pa., 13th year.

Ross, Bill—No. 4, U. of Missouri, collegiate professor, Kansas City, Mo., 8th year.

Semon, Sid—No. 5, U. of Southern California, chairman of physical education department, Torrance, Calif., 3rd year.

Toler, Burl—No. 18, San Francisco, director of adult and community education, S.F. Community College District, 16th year.

Veteri, Tony—No. 7, sales manager, consumer product, Mt. Vernon, N.Y., 20th year.

Williams, Dale—No. 8, Cal. State-Northridge, coordinator of athletic officials, Highland Park, Calif., 1st year.

LINE JUDGES

Beeks, Bob—No. 16, Lincoln, police community relations officer, St. Louis, 13th year.

Botchan, Ron—No. 12, Occidental, college professor, Los Angeles, 1st year.

Carrabine, Gene—No. 5, Notre Dame, commercial supervisor, Merrillville, Indiana, 3rd year.

Dooley, Tom—No. 7, Virginia Military Institute, general contractor, Charlotte, N.C., 3rd year.

Everett, John—No. 14, U. of Illinois, assistant principal, Chicago Board of Education, Chicago, 2nd year.

Fette, Jack—No. 9, district sales manager, sporting goods company, Kansas City, Mo., 16th year.

Glass, Bama—No. 15, U. of Colorado, owner consumer products, Arvada, Colorado, 2nd year.

Gosier, Wilson—No. 4, Fort Valley State, teacher coordinator, Decatur, Ga., 1st year.

Hantak, Richard—No. 18, S.E. Missouri, guidance counselor, St. Louis, Mo., 3rd year.

Hawk, Dave—No. 19, SMU, vice president, manufacturing co., Corsicana, Texas, 9th year.

Johnson, Jack—No. 6, Pacific Lutheran Univ., college coordinator, student programs, Tacoma, Washington, 5th year.

Marshall, Vern—No. 10, Linfield College, counseling coordinator, Portland, Oregon, 5th year.

McKenzie, Dick—No. 8, Ashland, office manager, Wellington, Ohio, 3rd year.

McLaughlin, Bob—No. 3, Xavier Univ., regional sales manager, Cincinnati, Ohio, 3rd year.

Orem, Dale—No. 17, Louisville, owner sporting goods company, Jeffersonville, Ind., 1st year.

Reynolds, Bill—No. 11, West Chester State, junior high teacher and coach, Springfield, Pa., 6th year.

BACK JUDGES

Baetz, Paul—No. 3, Heidelberg, vice president/marketing, Barrington, Ill., 3rd year.

Clymer, Roy—No. 17, New Mexico State, area manager gas company, El Reno, Okla., 1st year.

Douglas, Ray—No. 5, University of Baltimore, traffic manager, Ellicott City, Md., 13th year.

Javie, Stan—No. 6, Georgetown, vice president, paint company, Philadelphia, Pa., 30th year.

Jury, Al—No. 14, San Bernardino Valley, state traffic officer, Rialto, Calif., 3rd year.

Kearney, Jim—No. 12, Pennsylvania, account manager, Springfield, Pa., 3rd year.

Kelleher, Tom—No. 7, Holy Cross, president, marketing company, Miami, 21st year.

Knight, Pat—No. 11, Southern Methodist U., general manager, lumber co., San Antonio, Texas, former NFL player, 8th year.

Poole, Jim—No. 16, San Diego State, college physical education professor, Westminster, Calif., 6th year.

Rosser, Jimmy—No. 10, Auburn, personnel director, Martinsville, Va., 4th year.

Sanders, J. W.—No. 15, Southern Illinois, physical education professor, Highland Park, Ill., 1st year.

Swanson, Bill—No. 20, Lake Forest, manufacturers representative, Libertyville, Ill., 17th year.

Tompkins, Ben—No. 4, Texas, attorney, Fort Worth, 10th year.

Wedge, Don—No. 8, Ohio Wesleyan, national sales manager, Troy, Ohio, 9th year.

Williams, Banks—No. 9, Houston, sales manager, Houston, 3rd year.

SIDE JUDGES

Cathcart, Royal—No. 16, U. of California-Santa Barbara, commercial real estate sales, Irvine, Calif., former NFL player, 10th year.

Creed, Richard—No. 15, Louisville, real estate management, Poland, Ohio, 3rd year.

DeSouza, Ron—No. 18, Morgan State, vice-president student affairs, Annapolis, Md., 1st year.

Ferguson, Dick—No. 10, West Virginia, commissioner of officials, San Jose, Calif., 7th year.

Jacob, Vince—No. 11, wireman special apparatus, Verona, Pa., 6th year.
Jones, Nathan—No. 3, Lewis and Clark College, high school principal, Portland, Oregon, 4th year.
Klemmer, Grover—No. 8, California, dept. chairman and athletic director, San Francisco Board of Education, 18th year.
Look, Dean—No. 9, Michigan State, vice president, insurance company, E. Lansing, Michigan, 9th year.
Mace, Gil—No. 5, Westminster, sales representative, Library, Pa., 7th year.
Murphy, Ron—No. 14, Michigan State, manufacturers representative, Dallas, Tex., 1st year.
Osborne, Jim—No. 20, Villanova University, sales/marketing executive, Erdenheim, Pa., 3rd year.
Parry, Dave—No. 12, Wabash, high school athletic director, Michigan City, Indiana, 6th year.
Quinby, William—No. 7, Iowa State, industrial relations director, Cedar Rapids, Iowa, 3rd year.
Spencer, Willie—No. 6, Prairie View, central office administrator, Houston, 3rd year.
Rice, Bob—No. 19, Denison, teacher and coach, Cleveland, 12th year.
Ward, Ed—No. 4, Southern Methodist, executive director, motor freight association, Austin, Texas, 3rd year.

FIELD JUDGES

Cole, Jimmy—No. 10, Memphis State, land development, Germantown, Tenn., 9th year.
Dolack, Dick—No. 3, Ferris State, pharmacist, Muskegon, Michigan, 15th year.
Graf, Fritz—No. 7, Western Reserve, area manager, medical and hospital equipment co., Akron, Ohio, 21st year.
Hakes, Don—No. 6, Bradley University, high school dean of students, South Holland, Ill., 4th year.
Kingzett, Bill—No. 4, Hiram, athletic coordinator, Lyndhurst, Ohio, 6th year.
Lewis, Bob—No. 18, operations, air force base, San Antonio, Texas, 5th year.
Mallette, Pat—No. 16, Nebraska, high school administration, Blair, Neb., 12th year.
Merrifield, Ed—No. 20, Missouri, sales manager, Leawood, Kansas, 6th year.
Musser, Charley—No. 19, North Carolina State, sales manager, oil company, Naperville, Ill., 16th year.
O'Brien, Bill—No. 9, Indiana, university department chairman-professor, Carbondale, Ill., 14th year.

Orr, Don—No. 10, Vanderbilt, executive vice-president, machine co., Nashville, Tenn., 10th year.

Stanley, Bill—No. 5, Univ. of Redlands, college athletic director, Whittier, Calif., 7th year.

Swearingen, Fred—No. 8, Ohio U., real estate broker, Carlsbad, Calif., 21st year.

Terzian, Armen—No. 11, Southern California, director of physical education, San Francisco School District, 20th year.

Vaughan, Jack—No. 14, Mississippi State, real estate broker, Ponchatoula, La., 5th year.

Wortman, Bob—No. 12, Findlay, insurance agent, Findlay, Ohio, 15th year.